Praise for
Kristine Kathryn Rusch

"Rusch is a great storyteller—easily the equal of Patterson or Koontz."

—Analog

"Whether [Rusch] writes high fantasy, horror, sf, or contemporary fantasy, I've always been fascinated by her ability to tell a story with that enviable gift of invisible prose. She's one of those very few writers whose style takes me right into the story—the words and pages disappear as the characters and their story swallows me whole....Rusch has style."

—Charles de Lint

"Kristine Kathryn Rusch's crime stories are exceptional, both in plot and in style."

—Ed Gorman, *Mystery Scene Magazine*

"Rusch's greatest strength…is her ability to close down a story and leave the reader feeling that the author could not possibly have wrung any more satisfaction out of the piece."

—The Kansas City Star

"Kristine Kathryn Rusch is one of the best writers in the field."

"[Rusch's] writing style is simple but elegant, and her characterization excellent."

"Rusch knows how to construct a science fiction thriller that'll keep you turning pages right up until the end."

Praise for the Retrieval Artist series

"Rusch defines emotional and intellectual cores in her stories and then plots the most fruitful and gorgeously panoramic orbits around them."

"What links [Miles Flint] to his most memorable literary ancestors is his hard-won ability to perceive the complex nature of morality and live with the burden of his own inevitable failure."

Praise for the Smokey Dalton series
(writing as Kris Nelscott)

"Nelscott's series setting, in the turbulent late '60s, gives her books layers of issues of racism, class, and war, all of which still seem to remain sadly timely today."

—Oregonian

"Nelscott has her own, very distinct voice, and her series creates its own deeply satisfying pleasures and cogent points."

—Seattle Times

"(A) crime writer deliberately taking chances."

—Chicago Tribune

"It's not hard to draw parallels between Nelscott's PI Smokey Dalton and Walter Mosley's Easy Rawlins, another secretive, canny black man trying to solve mysteries while circumspectly navigating the white world. But Dalton's no knock-off. (Would you label the hundreds of hard-boiled detectives who've appeared in Raymond Chandler's wake mere Marlow Xeroxes because they're white?)"

—Entertainment Weekly

Also by
Kristine Kathryn Rusch

The Retrieval Artist Series:

The Smokey Dalton Series (as Kris Nelscott):

Secrets & Lies

Kristine Kathryn Rusch

wmg PUBLISHING

Secrets & Lies

Copyright © 2013 by Kristine Kathryn Rusch
Published 2013 by WMG Publishing
www.wmgpublishing.com
Cover art copyright © Darrenw/Dreamstime
Book and cover design copyright © 2013 by WMG Publishing
Cover design by Allyson Longueira/WMG Publishing
ISBN-13: 978-0-615-91913-3
ISBN-10: 0-615-91913-8

"Cowboy Grace" by Kristine Kathryn Rusch was first published in *The Silver Gryphon,* edited by Gary Turner and Marty Halpern, Golden Gryphon, 2003

"Spinning" by Kristine Kathryn Rusch was first published in *Ellery Queen Mystery Magazine,* July, 2000

"Jury Duty" by Kristine Kathryn Rusch was first published in *Crimewave 8,* 2005

"The Perfect Man" by Kristine Kathryn Rusch was first published in *Murder Most Romantic,* edited by Martin H. Greenberg and Denise Little, Cumberland House Press, 2001

"The Secret Lives of Cats" by Kristine Kathryn Rusch was first published in *Ellery Queen Mystery Magazine,* July, 2008

"Discovery" by Kristine Kathryn Rusch was first published in *Alfred Hitchcock's Mystery Magazine,* November, 2008

"Patriotic Gestures" by Kristine Kathryn Rusch was first published in *Scene of The Crime,* edited by Dana Stabenow, Running Press, 2008

"Details" by Kristine Kathryn Rusch was first published in *Ellery Queen Mystery Magazine,* December, 1998

"G-Men" by Kristine Kathryn Rusch was first published in *Sideways in Crime,* edited by Lou Anders, Solaris Books, 2008

"The Retrieval Artist" by Kristine Kathryn Rusch was first published in *Analog SF,* June, 2000

Contents

Secrets & Lies

INTRODUCTION

I LOVE SHORT STORIES. I read a lot of them. I have also edited short fiction at times throughout my career, first for Pulphouse Publishing, then for *The Magazine of Fantasy & Science Fiction*, and now for *Fiction River*. They are my very favorite fictional form.

Because I read a lot of short fiction, I write a lot of short fiction. I write in all the genres that I read, which is to say, in all genres. I have eclectic tastes, which shows up in my own fiction.

Even though I published my first mystery story in 1989, I never thought of myself as a mystery writer. I thought mysteries too hard to write. Still, I dabbled. *Ellery Queen Mystery Magazine* and *Alfred Hitchcock Mystery Magazine* published some of my dabbles, but mostly my fiction appeared in anthologies.

People noticed. To my surprise, I got nominated for mystery awards. My stories were selected for best-of-the-year anthologies. Still, I felt like a dabbler. It wasn't until I published my Smokey Dalton mystery series (which I write under the name Kris Nelscott) that I felt like a real mystery writer.

And it wasn't until I published my first mystery collection, *Little Miracles and Other Tales of Murder* (Five Star, 2001), that I realized just how much acclaim my mystery short stories had received. People notice my mystery stories, much to my surprise. And people *like* those stories, which pleases me to no end.

So I decided to put together another collection, this one of the mystery stories that have received the most acclaim.

Short fiction doesn't have sales records like novels do. The only way to know if readers like your short stories is if those readers nominate the stories for awards or pick them for recommended reading lists. The stories in this volume have made it into six best-of-the-year collections and have been nominated for or have won eight awards.

Even though these stories bear the label "mystery," they're very diverse. You'll find hardboiled stories, cozies, and more than a few private detectives. Two stories—"G-Men" and "Details"—have historical settings. One—"The Retrieval Artist"—is set in the future. The rest are set here and now, mostly in the American West. Many have female protagonists, and many originated from incidents in my own life.

At the end of this book, I discuss what inspired the story. Please don't skip ahead and read that section until you've read the stories. I put some spoilers in there because I can't talk about the stories without revealing too much.

I write a lot of mystery short stories. These ten are just the crème de la crème, as chosen by the readers. I hope you agree with them.

Enjoy!

—*Kristine Kathryn Rusch*
Lincoln City, Oregon
November 4, 2013

COWBOY GRACE

*E*VERY WOMAN tolerates misogyny," Alex said. She slid her empty beer glass across the bar, and tucked a strand of her auburn hair behind her ear. "How much depends on how old she is. The older she is the less she notices it. The more she expects it."

"Bullshit." Carole took a drag on her Virginia Slim, crossed her legs, and adjusted her skirt. "I don't tolerate misogyny."

"Maybe we should define the word," Grace said, moving to the other side of Carole. She wished her friend would realize how much the smoking irritated her. In fact, the entire night was beginning to irritate her. They were all avoiding the topic du jour: the tiny wound on Grace's left breast, stitches gone now, but the skin still raw and sore.

"Mis-ah-jenny." Carole said, as if Grace were stupid. "Hatred of women."

"From the Greek," Alex said. "Misos or hatred and gyne or women."

"Not," Carole said, waving her cigarette as if it were a baton, "misogamy, which is also from the Greek. Hatred of marriage. Hmm. Two male misos wrapped in one."

The bartender, a diminutive woman dressed wearing a red and white cowgirl outfit, complete with fringe and gold buttons, snickered. She set down a napkin in front of Alex and gave her another beer.

"Compliments," she said, "of the men at the booth near the phone."

Alex looked. She always looked. She was tall, busty, and leggy, with a crooked nose thanks to an errant pitch Grace had thrown in the 9th grade, a long chin and eyes the color of wine. Men couldn't get enough of her. When Alex rebuffed them, they slept with Carole and then talked to Grace.

The men in the booth near the phone looked like corporate types on a junket. Matching gray suits, different ties—all in a complimentary shade of pink, red, or cranberry—matching haircuts (long on top, styled on the sides), and differing goofy grins.

"This is a girl bar," Alex said, shoving the glass back at the bartender. "We come here to diss men, not to meet them."

"Good call," Carole said, exhaling smoke into Grace's face. Grace agreed, not with the smoke or the rejection, but because she wanted time with her friends. Without male intervention of any kind.

"Maybe we should take a table," Grace said.

"Maybe." Carole crossed her legs again. Her mini was leather, which meant that night she felt like being on display. "Or maybe we should send drinks to the cutest men we see."

They scanned the bar. Happy Hour at the Oh Kaye Corral didn't change much from Friday to Friday. A jukebox in the corner, playing Patty Loveless. Cocktail waitresses in short skirts and ankle boots with big heels. Tin stars and Wild West art on the walls, unstained wood and checkered tablecloths adding to the effect. One day, when Grace had Alex's courage and Carole's gravely voice, she wanted to walk in, belly up to the bar, slap her hand on its polished surface, and order whiskey straight up. She wanted someone to challenge her. She wanted to pull her six-gun and have a stare-down, then and there. Cowboy Grace, fastest gun in the West. Or at least in Racine on a rainy Friday night.

"I don't see cute," Alex said. "I see married, married, divorced, desperate, single, single, never-been-laid, and married."

Grace watched her make her assessment. Alex's expression never changed. Carole was looking at the men, apparently seeing whether or not she agreed.

Typically, she didn't.

"I dunno," she said, pulling on her cigarette. "Never-Been-Laid's kinda cute."

"So try him," Alex said. "But you'll have your own faithful puppy dog by this time next week, and a proposal of marriage within the month."

Carole grinned and slid off the stool. "Proposal of marriage in two weeks," she said. "I'm that good."

She stubbed out her cigarette, grabbed the tiny leather purse that matched the skirt, adjusted her silk blouse and sashayed her way toward a table in the middle.

Grace finally saw Never-Been-Laid. He had soft brown eyes, and hair that needed trimming. He wore a shirt that accented his narrow shoulders, and he had a laptop open on the round table. He was alone. He had his feet tucked under the chair, crossed at the ankles. He wore dirty tennis shoes with his Gap khakis.

"Cute?" Grace said.

"Shhh," Alex said. "It's a door into the mind of Carole."

"One that should remain closed." Grace moved to Carole's stool. It was still warm. Grace shoved Carole's drink out of her way, grabbed her glass of wine, and coughed. The air still smelled of cigarette smoke.

Carole was leaning over the extra chair, giving Never-Been-Laid a view of her cleavage, and the guys at the booth by the phone a nice look at her ass, which they seemed to appreciate.

"Where the hell did that misogyny comment come from?" Grace asked.

Alex looked at her. "You want to get a booth?"

"Sure. Think Carole can find us?"

"I think Carole's going to be deflowering a computer geek and not caring what we're doing." Alex grabbed her drink, stood, and walked to a booth on the other side of the Corral. Dirty glasses from the last occupants were piled in the center, and the red-and-white checked vinyl tablecloth was sticky.

They moved the glasses on the edge of the table and didn't touch the dollar tip, which had been pressed into a puddle of beer.

Grace set her wine down and slid onto her side. Alex did the same on the other side. Somehow they managed not to touch the tabletop at all.

"You remember my boss?" Alex asked as she adjusted the tiny fake gas lamp that hung on the wall beside the booth.

"Beanie Boy?"

She grinned. "Yeah."

"Never met him."

"Aren't you lucky."

Grace already knew that. She'd heard stories about Beanie Boy for the last year. They had started shortly after he was hired. Alex went to the company Halloween party and was startled to find her boss dressed as one of the Lollipop Kids from the Wizard of Oz, complete with striped shirt, oversized lollipop and propeller beanie.

"Now what did he do?" Grace asked.

"Called me honey."

"Yeah?" Grace asked.

"And sweetie, and doll-face, and sugar."

"Hasn't he been doing that for the last year?"

Alex glared at Grace. "It's getting worse."

"What's he doing, patting you on the butt?"

"If he did, I'd get him for harassment, and he knows it."

She had lowered her voice. Grace could barely hear her over Shania Twain.

"This morning one of our clients came in praising the last report. I wrote it."

"Didn't Beanie Boy give you credit?"

"Of course he did. He said, 'Our little Miss Rogers wrote it. Isn't she a doll?'"

Grace clutched her drink tighter. This didn't matter to her. Her biopsy was benign. She had called Alex and Carole and told them. They'd suggested coming here. So why weren't they offering a toast to her life? Why weren't they celebrating, really celebrating, instead of rerunning the same old conversation in the same old bar in the same old way? "What did the client do?"

"He agreed, of course."

"And?"

"And what?"

"Is that it? Didn't you speak up?"

"How could I? He was praising me, for godssake."

Grace sighed and sipped her beer. Shania Twain's comment was that didn't impress her much. It didn't impress Grace much either, but she knew better than to say anything to Alex.

Grace looked toward the middle of the restaurant. Carole was standing behind Never-Been-Laid, her breasts pressed against his back, her ass on view to the world, her head over his shoulder peering at his computer screen.

Alex didn't follow her gaze like Grace had hoped. "If I were ten years younger, I'd tell Beanie Boy to shove it."

"If you were ten years younger, you wouldn't have a mortgage and a Mazda."

"Dignity shouldn't be cheaper than a paycheck," she said.

"So confront him."

"He doesn't think he's doing anything wrong. He treats all the women like that."

Grace sighed. They'd walked this road before. Job after job, boyfriend after boyfriend. Alex, for all her looks, was like Joe McCarthy protecting the world from the Red Menace: she saw anti-female everywhere, and most of it, she was convinced, was directed at her.

"You don't seem very sympathetic," Alex said.

She wasn't. She never had been. And with all she had been through in the last month, *alone* because her two best friends couldn't bear to talk about the Big C, the lock that was usually on Grace's mouth wasn't working.

"I'm not sympathetic," Grace said. "I'm beginning to think you're a victim in search of a victimizer."

"That's not fair, Grace," Alex said. "We tolerate this stuff because we were raised in an anti-woman society. It's gotten better, but it's not perfect. You tell those Xers stuff like this and they shake their heads. Or the new ones. What're they calling themselves now? Generation Y? They were raised on Title IX. Hell, they pull off their shirts after winning soccer games. Imagine us doing that."

"My cousin got arrested in 1977 in Milwaukee on the day Elvis Presley died for playing volleyball," Grace said. Carole was actually rubbing herself on Never-Been-Laid. His face was the color of the red checks in the tablecloth.

"What?"

Grace turned to Alex. "My cousin. You know, Barbie? She got arrested playing volleyball."

"They didn't let girls play volleyball in Milwaukee?"

"It was 90 degrees, and she was playing with a group of guys. They pulled off their shirts because they were hot and sweating, so she did the same. She got arrested for indecent exposure."

"God," Alex said. "Did she go to jail?"

"Didn't even get her day in court."

"Everyone gets a day in court."

Grace shook her head. "The judge took one look at Barbie, who was really butch in those days, and said, 'I'm sick of you girls coming in here and arguing that you should have equal treatment for things that are clearly unequal. I do not establish Public Decency laws. You may show a bit of breast if you're feeding a child, otherwise you are in violation of—some damn code.' Barbie used to quote the thing chapter and verse."

"Then what?" Alex asked.

"Then she got married, had a kid, and started wearing nail polish. She said it wasn't as much fun to show her breasts legally."

"See?" Alex said. "Misogyny."

Grace shrugged. "Society, Alex. Get used to it."

"That's the point of your story? We've been oppressed for a thousand years and you say, 'Get used to it'?"

"I say Brandi Chastain pulls off her shirt in front of millions—"

"Showing a sports bra."

"—and she doesn't get arrested. I say women head companies all the time. I say things are better now than they were when I was growing up, and I say the only ones who oppress us are ourselves."

"I say you're drunk."

Grace pointed at Carole, who was wet-kissing Never-Been-Laid, her arms wrapped around his neck and her legs wrapped around his waist. "She's drunk. I'm just speaking out."

"You never speak out."

Grace sighed. No one had picked up the glasses and she was tired of looking at that poor drowning dollar bill. There wasn't going to be any celebration. Everything was the same as it always was—at least to Alex and Carole. But Grace wanted something different.

She got up, threw a five next to the dollar, and picked up her purse.

"Tell me if Carole gets laid," Grace said, and left.

Outside Grace stopped and took a deep breath of the humid, exhaust-filled air. She could hear the clang of glasses even in the parking lot and the rhythm of Mary Chapin Carpenter praising passionate kisses. Grace had had only one glass of wine and a lousy time, and she wondered why people said old friends were the best friends. They were supposed to raise toasts to her future, now restored. She'd even said the "b" word and Alex hadn't noticed. It was as if the cancer scare had happened to someone they didn't even know.

Grace was going to be forty years old in three weeks. Her two best friends were probably planning a version of the same party they had held for her when she turned thirty. A male stripper whose sweaty body repulsed her more than aroused her, too many black balloons, and aging jokes that hadn't been original the first time around.

Forty years old, an accountant with her own firm, no close family, no boyfriend, and a resident of the same town her whole life. The only time she left was to visit cousins out east, and for what? Obligation?

There was no joy left, if there'd ever been any joy at all.

She got into her sensible Ford Taurus, bought at a used car lot for well under Blue Book, and drove west.

***

It wasn't until she reached Janesville that she started to call herself crazy, and it wasn't until she drove into Dubuque that she realized how little tied her to her hometown.

An apartment without even a cat to cozy up to, a business no more successful than a dozen others, and people who still saw her as a teenager wearing granny glasses, braces and hair too long for her face. Grace, who was always there. Grace the steady, Grace the smart. Grace, who helped her friends out of their financial binds, who gave them a shoulder to cry on, and a degree of comfort because their lives weren't as empty as her own.

When she had told Alex and Carole that her mammogram had come back suspicious, they had looked away. When she told them that she had found a lump, they had looked frightened.

I can't imagine life without you, Gracie, Carole had whispered.

Imagine it now, Grace thought.

The dawn was breaking when she reached Cedar Rapids, and she wasn't really tired. But she was practical, had always been practical, and habits of a lifetime didn't change just because she had run away from home at the age of 39.

She got a hotel room and slept for eight hours, got up, had dinner in a nice steak place, went back to the room and slept some more. When she woke up Sunday morning to bells from the Presbyterian Church across the street, she lay on her back and listened for a good minute before she realized they were playing "What a Friend We Have in Jesus." And she smiled then, because Jesus had been a better friend to her in recent years than Alex and Carole ever had.

At least Jesus didn't tell her his problems when she was praying about hers. If Jesus was self-absorbed he wasn't obvious about it. And he didn't seem to care that she hadn't been inside a church since August of 1978.

The room was chintz, the wallpaper and the bedspread matched, and the painting on the wall was chosen for its color not for its technique. Grace sat up and wondered what she was doing here, and thought about going home.

To nothing.

So she got in her car and followed the Interstate, through Des Moines, and Lincoln and Cheyenne, places she had only read about, places she had never seen. How could a woman live for forty years and not see the country of her birth? How could a woman do nothing except what she was supposed to from the day she was born until the day she died?

In Salt Lake City, she stared at the Mormon Taber-nacle, all white against an azure sky. She sat in her car and watched a groundskeeper maintain the flowers, and re-membered how it felt to take her doctor's call.

A lot of women have irregular mammograms, particularly at your age. The breast tissue is thicker, and often we get clouds.

Clouds.

There were fluffy clouds in the dry desert sky, but they were white and benign. Just like her lump had turned out to be. But for a hellish month, she had thought about that lump, feeling it when she woke out of a sound sleep, won-dering if it presaged the beginning of the end. She had never felt her mortality like this before, not even when her mother, the only parent she had known, had died. Not even when she realized there was no one remaining of the generation that had once stood between her and death.

No one talked about these things. No one let her talk about them either. Not just Alex and Carole, but Michael, her second-in-command at work, or even her doctor, who kept assuring her that she was young and the odds were in her favor.

Young didn't matter if the cancer had spread through the lymph nodes. When she went in for the lumpectomy almost two weeks ago now, she had felt a curious kind of relief, as if the doctor had removed a tick that had burrowed under her skin. When he had called with the news that the lump was benign, she had thanked him calmly and continued with her day, filing corporate tax returns for a consulting firm.

No one had known the way she felt. Not relieved. No. It was more like she had received a reprieve.

The clouds above the Tabernacle helped calm her. She plugged in her cell phone for the first time in days and listened to the voice mail messages, most of them from Michael, growing increasingly worried about where she was.

Have you forgotten the meeting with Boyd's? he'd asked on Monday.

Do you want me to file Charlie's extension? he'd demanded on Tuesday.

Where the hell are you? he cried on Wednesday and she knew, then, that it was okay to call him, that not even the business could bring her home.

Amazing how her training had prepared her for moments like these and she hadn't even known it. She had savings, lots of them, because she hadn't bought a house even though it had been prudent to do so. She had been waiting, apparently, for Mr. Right, or the family her mother had always wanted for her, the family that would never come. Her money was invested properly, and she could live off the interest if she so chose. She had just never chosen to before.

And if she didn't want to be found, she didn't have to be. She knew how to have the interest paid through offshore accounts so that no one could track it. She even knew a quick and almost legal way to change her name. Traceable, but she hadn't committed a crime. She didn't need to hide well, just well enough that a casual search wouldn't produce her.

Not that anyone would start a casual search. Once she sold the business, Michael would forget her and Alex and Carole, even though they would gossip about her at Oh Kaye's every Friday night for the rest of their lives, wouldn't summon the energy to search.

She could almost hear them now: *She met some guy,* Carole would say. *And he killed her,* Alex would add, and then they would argue until last call, unless Carole found some man to entertain her, and Alex someone else to complain to. They would miss Grace only when they screwed up, when they needed a shoulder, when they couldn't stand being on their own. And even then, they probably wouldn't realize what it was they had lost.

***

Because it amused her, she had driven north to Boise, land of the white collar, to make her cell call to Michael. Her offer to him was simple: cash her out of the business and call it his own. She named a price, he dickered half-heartedly, she refused to negotiate. Within two days, he had wired the money to a blind money market account that she had often stored cash in for the firm.

She let the money sit there while she decided what to do with it. Then she went to Reno to change her name.

Reno had been a surprise. A beautiful city set between mountains like none she had ever seen. The air was dry, the downtown tacky, the people friendly. There were bookstores and slot machines and good restaurants. There were cheap houses and all-night casinos and lots of strange places. There was even history, of the Wild West kind.

For the first time in her life, Grace fell in love.

And to celebrate the occasion, she snuck into a quickie wedding chapel, found the marriage licenses, took one, copied down the name of the chapel, its permit number, and all the other pertinent information, and then returned to her car. There she checked the boxes, saying she had seen the driver's licenses and birth certificates of the people involved, including a fictitious man named Nathan Reinhart, and *viola!* she was married. She had a new name, a document the credit card companies would accept, and a new beginning all at the same time.

***

Using some of her personal savings, she bought a house with lots of windows and a view of the Sierras. In the mornings, light bathed her kitchen, and in the evenings, it caressed her living room. She had never seen light like this—clean and pure and crisp. She was beginning to understand why artists moved west to paint, why people used to exclaim about the way light changed everything.

The lack of humidity, of dense air pollution, made the air clearer. The elevation brought her closer to the sun.

She felt as if she were seeing everything for the very first time.

And hearing it, too. The house was silent, much more silent than an apartment, and the silence soothed her. She could listen to her television without worrying about the people in the apartment below, or play her stereo full blast without concern about a visit from the super.

There was a freedom to having her own space that she hadn't realized before, a freedom to living the way she wanted to live, without the rules of the past or the expectations she had grown up with.

And among those expectations was the idea that she had to be the strong one, the good one, the one on whose shoulder everyone else cried. She had no friends here, no one who needed her shoulder, and she had no one who expected her to be good.

Only herself.

Of course, in some things she was good. Habits of a lifetime died hard. She began researching the best way to invest Michael's lump sum payment—and while she researched, she left the money alone. She kept her house clean and her lawn, such as it was in this high desert, immaculate. She got a new car and made sure it was spotless.

No one would find fault with her appearances, inside or out.

Not that she had anyone who was looking. She didn't have a boyfriend or a job or a hobby. She didn't have anything except herself.

***

She found herself drawn to the casinos, with their clinking slot machines, musical come-ons, and bright lights. No matter how high tech the places had become, no matter how clean, how "family-oriented," they still had a shady feel.

Or perhaps that was her upbringing, in a state where gambling had been illegal until she was 25, a state where her father used to play a friendly game of poker—even with his friends—with the curtains drawn.

Sin—no matter how sanitized—still had appeal in the brand-new century.

Of course, she was too sensible to gamble away her savings. The slots lost their appeal quickly, and when she sat down at the blackjack tables, she couldn't get past the feeling that she was frittering her money away for nothing.

But she liked the way the cards fell and how people concentrated—as if their very lives depended on this place—and she was good with numbers. One of the pit bosses mentioned that they were always short of poker dealers, so she took a class offered by one of the casinos. Within two months, she was snapping cards, raking pots, and wearing a uniform that made her feel like Carole on a bad night.

It only took a few weeks for her bosses to realize that Grace was a natural poker dealer. They gave her the busy shifts—Thursday through Sunday nights—and she spent her evenings playing the game of cowboys, fancy men, and whores. Finally, there was a bit of an Old West feel to her life, a bit of excitement, a sense of purpose.

When she got off at midnight, she would be too keyed up to go home. She started bringing a change of clothes to work and, after her shift, she would go to the casino next door. It had a great bar upstairs—filled with brass, Victorian furnishings, and a real hardwood floor. She could get a sandwich and a beer. Finally, she felt like she was becoming the woman she wanted to be.

One night, a year after she had run away from home, a man sidled up next to her. He had long blond hair that curled against his shoulders. His face was tanned and lined, a bit too thin. He looked road-hardened—like a man who'd been outside too much, seen too much, worked in the sun too much. His hands were long, slender, and callused. He wore no rings, and his shirt cuffs were frayed at the edges.

He sat beside her in companionable silence for nearly an hour, while they both stared at CNN on the big screen over the bar, and then he said, "Just once I'd like to go someplace authentic."

His voice was cigarette growly, even though he didn't smoke, and he had a Southern accent that was soft as butter. She guessed Louisiana, but it might have been Tennessee or even Northern Florida. She wasn't good at distinguishing Southern accents yet. She figured she would after another year or so of dealing cards.

"You should go up to Virginia City. There's a bar or two that looks real enough."

He snorted through his nose. "Tourist trap."

She shrugged. She'd thought it interesting—an entire historic city, preserved just like it had been when Mark Twain lived there. "Seems to me if you weren't a tourist there wouldn't be any other reason to go."

He shrugged and picked up a toothpick, rolling it in his fingers. She smiled to herself. A former smoker then, and a fidgeter.

"Reno's better than Vegas, at least," he said. "Casinos aren't family friendly yet."

"Except Circus Circus."

"Always been that way. But the rest. You get a sense that maybe it ain't all legal here."

She looked at him sideways. He was at least her age, his blue eyes sharp in his leathery face. "You like things that aren't legal?"

"Gambling's not something that should be made pretty, you know? It's about money, and money can either make you or destroy you."

She felt herself smile, remember what it was like to paw through receipts and tax returns, to make neat rows of figures about other people's money. "What's the saying?" she asked. "Money is like sex—"

"It doesn't matter unless you don't have any." To her surprise, he laughed. The sound was rich and warm, not at all like she had expected. The smile transformed his face into something almost handsome.

He tapped the toothpick on the polished bar, and asked, "You think that's true?"

She shrugged. "I suppose. Everyone's idea of what's enough differs, though."

"What's yours?" He turned toward her, smile gone now, eyes even sharper than they had been a moment ago. She suddenly felt as if she were on trial.

"My idea of what's enough?" she asked.

He nodded.

"I suppose enough that I can live off the interest in the manner in which I've become accustomed. What's yours?"

A shadow crossed his eyes and he looked away from her. "Long as I've got a roof over my head, clothes on my back, and food in my mouth, I figure I'm rich enough."

"Sounds distinctly unAmerican to me," she said.

He looked at her sideways again. "I guess it does, don't it? Women figure a man should have some sort of ambition."

"Do you?"

"Have ambition?" He bent the toothpick between his fore- and middle fingers. "Of course I do. It just ain't tied in with money, is all."

"I thought money and ambition went together."

"In most men's minds."

"But not yours?"

The toothpick broke. "Not any more," he said.

***

Three nights later, he sat down at her table. He was wearing a denim shirt with silver snaps and jeans so faded that they looked as if they might shred around him. That, his hair, and his lean look reminded Grace of a movie gunslinger, the kind that cleaned a town up because it had to be done.

"Guess you don't make enough to live off the interest," he said to her as he sat down.

She raised her eyebrows. "Maybe I like people."

"Maybe you like games."

She smiled and dealt the cards. The table was full. She was dealing 3-6 Texas Hold 'Em and most of the players were locals. It was Monday night and they all looked pleased to have an unfamiliar face at the table.

If she had known him better she might have tipped him off. Instead she wanted to see how long his money would last.

He bought in for $100, although she had seen at least five hundred in his wallet. He took the chips, and studied them for a moment.

He had three tells. He fidgeted with his chips when his cards were mediocre and he was thinking of bluffing. He bit his lower lip when he had nothing, and his eyes went dead flat when he had a winning hand.

He lost the first hundred in forty-five minutes, bought back in for another hundred and managed to hold onto it until her shift ended shortly after midnight. He sat through dealer changes and the floating fortunes of his cards. When she returned from her last break, she found herself wondering if his tells were subconscious after all. They seemed deliberately calculated to let the professional poker players around him think that he was a rookie.

She said nothing. She couldn't, really—at least not overtly. The casino got a rake and they didn't allow her to do anything except deal the game. She had no stake in it anyway. She hadn't lied to him that first night. She loved watching people, the way they played their hands, the way the money flowed.

It was like being an accountant, only in real time. She got to see the furrowed brows as the decisions were made, hear the curses as someone pushed back a chair and tossed in that last hand of cards, watch the desperation that often led to the exact wrong play. Only as a poker dealer, she wasn't required to clean up the mess. She didn't have to offer advice or refuse it; she didn't have to worry about tax consequences, about sitting across from someone else's auditor, justifying choices she had no part in making.

When she got off, she changed into her tightest jeans and a summer sweater and went to her favorite bar.

Casino bars were always busy after midnight, even on a Monday. The crowd wasn't there to have a good time but to wind down from one—or to prepare itself for another. She sat at the bar, as she had since she started this routine, and she'd been about to leave when he sat next to her.

"Lose your stake?" she asked.

"I'm up $400."

She looked at him sideways. He didn't seem pleased with the way the night had gone—not the way a casual player would have been. Her gut instinct was right. He was someone who was used to gambling—and winning.

"Buy you another?" he asked.

She shook her head. "One's enough."

He smiled. It made him look less fierce and gave him a rugged sort of appeal. "Everything in moderation?"

"Not always," she said. "At least, not any more."

***

Somehow they ended up in bed—her bed—and he was better than she imagined his kind of man could be. He had knowledgeable fingers and endless patience. He didn't seem to mind the scar on her breast. Instead he lingered over it, focusing on it as if it were an erogenous zone. His pleasure at the result enhanced hers and when she finally fell asleep, somewhere around dawn, she was more sated than she had ever been.

She awoke to the smell of frying bacon and fresh coffee. Her eyes were filled with sand, but her body had a healthy lethargy.

At least, she thought, *he hadn't left before she awoke.*

At least he hadn't stolen everything in sight.

She still didn't know his name, and wasn't sure she cared. She slipped on a robe and combed her hair with her fingers and walked into her kitchen—the kitchen no one had cooked in but her.

He had on his denims and his hair was tied back with a leather thong. He had found not only her cast iron skillet but the grease cover that she always used when making bacon. A bowl of scrambled eggs steamed on the counter, and a plate of heavily buttered toast sat beside it.

"Sit down, darlin'," he said. "Let me bring it all to you."

She flushed. That was what it felt like he had done the night before, but she said nothing. Her juice glasses were out, and so was her everyday ware, and yet somehow the table looked like it had been set for a *Gourmet* photo spread.

"I certainly didn't expect this," she said.

"It's the least I can do." He put the eggs and toast on the table, then poured her a cup of coffee. Cream and sugar were already out, and in their special containers.

She was slightly uncomfortable that he had figured out her kitchen that quickly and well.

He put the bacon on a paper-towel covered plate, then set that on the table. She hadn't moved, so he beckoned with his hand.

"Go ahead," he said. "It's getting cold."

He sat across from her and helped himself to bacon while she served herself eggs. They were fluffy and light, just like they would have been in a restaurant. She had no idea how he got that consistency. Her home-scrambled eggs were always runny and undercooked.

The morning light bathed the table, giving everything a bright glow. His hair seemed even blonder in the sunlight and his skin darker. He had laugh lines around his mouth, and a bit of blond stubble on his chin.

She watched him eat, those nimble fingers scooping up the remaining egg with a slice of toast, and found herself remembering how those fingers had felt on her skin.

Then she felt his gaze on her, and looked up. His eyes were dead flat for just an instant, and she felt herself grow cold.

"Awful nice house," he said slowly, "for a woman who makes a living dealing cards."

Her first reaction was defense—she wanted to tell him she had other income, and what did he care about a woman who dealt cards, anyway?—but instead, she smiled. "Thank you."

He measured her, as if he expected a different response, then he said, "You're awfully calm considering that you don't even know my name. You don't strike me as the kind of woman who does this often."

His words startled her, but she made sure that the surprise didn't show. She had learned a lot about her own tells while dealing poker, and the experience was coming in handy now.

"You flatter yourself," she said softly.

"Well," he said, reaching into his back pocket, "if there's one thing my job's taught me, it's that people hide information they don't want anyone else to know."

He pulled out his wallet, opened it, and with two fingers removed a business card. He dropped it on the table.

She didn't want to pick the card up. She knew things had already changed between them in a way that she didn't entirely understand, but she had a sense from the fleeting expression she had seen on his face that once she picked up the card she could never go back.

She set down her coffee cup and used two fingers to slide the card toward her. It identified him as Travis

Delamore, a skip tracer and bail bondsman. Below his name was a phone number with a 414 exchange.

Milwaukee, Wisconsin and the surrounding areas. Precisely the place someone from Racine might call if they wanted to hire a professional.

She slipped the card into the pocket of her robe. "Is sleeping around part of your job?"

"Is embezzling part of yours?" All the warmth had left his face. His expression was unreadable except for the flatness in his eyes. What did he think he knew?

She made herself smile. "Mr. Delamore, if I stole a dime from the casino, I'd be instantly fired. There are cameras everywhere."

"I mean your former job, Ms. Mackie. A lot of money is missing from your office."

"I don't have an office." His use of her former name made her hands clammy. What had Michael done?

"Do you deny that you're Grace Mackie?"

"I don't acknowledge or deny anything. When did this become an inquisition, Mr. Delamore? I thought men liked their sex uncomplicated. You seem to be a unique member of your species."

This time he smiled. "Of course we like our sex uncomplicated. That's why we're having this discussion this morning."

"If we'd had it last night, there wouldn't be a this morning."

"That's my point." He downed the last of his orange juice. "And thank you for the acknowledgement, Ms. Mackie."

"It wasn't an acknowledgement," she said. "I don't like to sleep with men who think me guilty of something."

"Embezzlement," he said gently, using the same tone he had used in bed. This time, it made her bristle.

"I haven't stolen anything."

"New house, new name, new town, mysterious disappearance."

The chill she had felt earlier grew. She stood and wrapped her robe tightly around her waist. "I don't know what you think you know, Mr. Delamore, but I believe it's time for you to leave."

He didn't move. "We're not done."

"Oh, yes, we are."

"It would be a lot easier if you told me where the money was, Grace."

"Do you always get paid for sex, Mr. Delamore?" she asked.

He studied her for a moment. "Don't play games with me, honey."

"Why not?" she asked. "You seem to enjoy them."

He shoved his plate away as if it had offended him. Apparently this morning wasn't going the way he wanted it to either. "I'm just telling you what I know."

"And I'm just asking you to leave. It was fun, Travis. But it certainly wasn't worth this."

He stood and slipped his wallet back into his pocket. "You'll hear from me again."

"This isn't high school," she said, following him to the door. "I won't be offended if you fail to call."

"No," he said as he stepped into the dry desert air. "You probably won't be offended. But you will be curious. This is just the beginning, Grace."

"One person's beginning is another person's ending," she said as she closed and locked the door behind him.

***

The worst thing she could do, she knew, was panic. So she made herself clean up the kitchen as if she didn't have a care in the world, and she left the curtains open so that he could see if he wanted to. Then she went to the shower, making it a long and hot. She tried to scrub all the traces of him off of her.

For the first time in her life, she felt cheap.

Embezzlement. Something had happened, something Michael was blaming on her. It would be easy enough, she supposed. She had disappeared. That looked suspicious enough. The new name, the new car, the new town, all of that added to the suspicion.

What had Michael done? And why?

She got out of the shower and toweled herself off. She was tempted to call Michael, but she certainly couldn't do it from the house. If she used her cell, the call would be traceable too. And if she went to a pay phone, she would attract even more suspicion. She had to consider that Travis Delamore was following her, spying on her.

In fact, she had to consider that he had been doing that for some time.

She went over all of their conversation, looking for clues, mistakes she might have made. She had told him very little, but he had asked a lot. Strangely—or perhaps not so strangely any more—all of their conversations had been about money.

Carole would have been proud of her. Grace had finally let her libido get the better of her. Alex would have been disgusted, reminding her that men couldn't be trusted.

What could he do to her besides cast suspicion? He was right. Without the money, he had nothing. And she had a job, no criminal record, and no suspicious investments.

But if he continued to follow her, she could go after him. The bartender had seen them leave her favorite bar together. She had an innocent face, she'd been living here for a year, got promoted, was well liked by her employer. Delamore had obviously flirted with her while he played poker the night before, and the casino had cameras.

They probably had records of all the times he had watched her before she noticed him.

It wouldn't take much to make a stalking charge. That would get her an injunction in the least, and it might scare him off.

Then she could find out why he was so sure he had something on her. Then she could find out what it was Michael had done.

***

The newly remodeled ladies room on the third floor of the casino had twenty stalls and a lounge complete with smoking room. It had once been a small restroom, but the reconstruction had taken out the nearby men's room and replaced it with more stalls. The row of pay phones in the middle stayed, as a convenience to the customers.

Delamore wouldn't know that she called from those pay phones. No one would know.

She started using the third floor ladies room on her break and more than once had picked up the receiver on the third phone and dialed most of her old office number. She'd always stop before she hit the last digit, though. Her intuition told her that calling Michael would be wrong.

What if Delamore had a trace on Michael's line? What if the police did?

A week after her encounter with Delamore, a week in which she used the third floor ladies room more times than she could count, she suddenly realized what was wrong. Delamore didn't have anything on her except suspicion. He had clearly found her—that hadn't been hard, since she really hadn't been hiding from anyone—and he had probably checked her bank records for the money he assumed she had embezzled from her former clients. But the money she had gotten from the sale of the business was still in that hidden numbered account—and would stay there.

Her native caution had served her well once again.

She had nothing to hide. It didn't matter what some good-looking skip trace thought. Her life in Racine was in the past. A part of her past that she couldn't avoid, any more than she could avoid the scar on her breast—the scar that Delamore had clearly used to identify her, the bastard. But past was past, and until it hurt her present, she wasn't going to worry about it.

So she stopped making pilgrimages to the third floor women's room, and gradually, her worries over Delamore faded. She didn't see him for a week, and she assumed—wrongly—that it was all over.

***

He sat next to her at the bar as if he had been doing it every day for years. He ordered a whiskey neat, and another "for the lady," just like men in her fantasies used to do. When he looked at her and smiled, she realized that the look didn't reach his eyes.

Maybe it never had.

"Miss me, darlin'?" he asked.

She picked up her purse, took out a five to cover her drink, and started to leave. He grabbed her wrist. His fingers were warm and dry, their touch no longer gentle. A shiver started in her back, but she willed the feeling away.

"Let go of me," she said.

"Now, Gracie, I think you should listen to what I have to say."

"Let go of me," she said in that same measured tone, "or I will scream so loud that everyone in the place will hear."

"Screams don't frighten me, doll."

"Maybe the police do. Believe me, *hon*, I will press charges."

His smile was slow and wide, but that flat look was in his eyes again, the one that told her he had all the cards. "I'm sure they'll be impressed," he said, reaching into his breast pocket with his free hand. "But I do believe a warrant trumps a tight grip on the arm."

He set a piece of paper down on the bar itself. The bartender, wiping away the remains of another customer's mess, glanced her way as if he were keeping an eye on her.

She didn't touch the paper, but she didn't shake Delamore's hand off her arm, either. She wasn't quite sure what to do.

He picked up the paper, shook it open, and she saw the strange bold-faced print of a legal document, her former name in the middle. "Tell you what, Gracie. How about we finish the talk we started the other morning in one of those dark, quiet booths over there?"

She was still staring at the paper, trying to comprehend it. It looked official enough. But then, she'd never seen a warrant for anyone's arrest before. She had only heard of them.

She had never imagined she'd see her own name on one.

She let Delamore lead her to a booth at the far end of the bar. He slid across the plastic, trying to pull her in beside him, but this time, she shook him off. She sat across from him, perched on the seat with her feet in the aisle, purse clutched on her lap. Flee position, Alex used to call it. You Might Be a Loser and I Reserve the Right to Find Someone Else, was Carole's name for it.

"If I bring you back to Wisconsin," he said, "I get a few thousand bucks. What it don't say on my card is that I'm a bounty hunter."

"What an exciting life you must lead," Grace said dryly.

He smiled. The look chilled her. She was beginning to wonder how she had ever found him attractive. "It's got its perks."

It was at that moment she decided she hated him. He would forever refer to her as a perk of the job, not as someone who had given herself to him freely, someone who had enjoyed the moment as much as he had.

All that gentleness in his fingers, all those murmured endearments. Lies.

She hated lies.

"But," he was saying, "I see a way to make a little more money here. I don't think you're a real threat to society. And you're a lot of fun, more fun than I would've expected, given how you lived before you moved here."

The bartender came over, his bar towel over his arm. "Want anything?"

He was speaking to her. He hadn't even looked at Delamore. The bartender was making sure she was all right.

"I don't know yet," she said. "Can you check back in five minutes?"

"Sure thing." This time he did look at Delamore, who grinned at him. The bartender shot him a warning glare.

"Wow," Delamore said as the bartender moved out of earshot. "You have a defender."

"You keep getting off track," Grace said.

Delamore shrugged. "I like talking to you."

"Well, I find talking with you rather dull."

He raised his eyebrows. "You didn't think so a few days ago."

"As I recall," she said, "we didn't do a lot talking."

His smile softened. "That's my memory too."

She clutched her purse tighter. It always looked so glamorous in the movies, finding the right person, having a night of great sex. And even if he rode off into the sunset never to be seen again, everything still had a glow of perfection to it.

Not the bits of sleaze, the hardness in his expression, the sense that what he wanted from her was something she couldn't give.

"You know, the papers said that Michael Holden went into your old office, and put a gun in his mouth and pulled the trigger. Then the police, after finding the body, discovered that most of the money your clients had entrusted to your firm had disappeared."

She couldn't suppress the small whimper of shock that rose in her throat.

Delamore noted it and his eyes brightened. "Now, you tell me what happened."

She had no idea. She had none at all. But she couldn't tell Delamore that. She didn't even know if the story was true.

It sounded true. But Delamore had lied before. For all she knew he was some kind of con man, out to get her because he smelled money.

He was watching her, his eyes glittering. She could barely control her expression. She needed to get away.

She stood, still clutching her purse like a schoolgirl.

"Planning to leave? I wouldn't do that if I were you." His voice had turned cold. A shiver ran down her spine, but she didn't move, just stared down at him unable to turn away.

"One call," he said softly, "and you'll get picked up by the Nevada police. You should sit down and hear what I have to say."

Her hands were shaking. She sat, feeling trapped. He had finally hooked her, even though she hadn't said a word.

He leaned forward. "Now listen to me, darling. I know you got the money. I been working this one a long time, and I dug up the records. Michael closed all those accounts right after you disappeared. That's not a coincidence."

Her mouth was dry. She wanted to swallow, but couldn't.

"'Member our talk about money? One of those first nights, here in this bar?"

She was staring at him, her eyes wide and dry as if she'd been driving and staring at the road for hours. It felt like she had forgotten to blink.

"I told you I don't need much, and that's true. But I'm getting tired of dragging people back to their parole officers or for their court date, or finding husbands who'd skipped out on their families and then getting paid five grand or two grand. Then people question your expenses, like you don't got a right to spend a night in a motel or eat three squares. Or they demand to know why you took so danged long to find someone who'd been hiding so good no cop could find them."

His voice was so soft she had to strain to hear it. In spite of herself, she leaned forward.

"I'm forty-five years old, doll," he said. "And I'm getting tired. You got one pretty little scar. Did you notice all the ones I got? On the job. Yours is the first case in a while where I didn't get a beating." Then he grinned. "At least, not a painful one."

She flushed, and her fingers tightened on the purse. Her hands were beginning to hurt. Part of her, a part she'd never heard from before, wanted to take that purse and club him in the face. But she didn't move. If she moved, she would lose any control she had.

"So," he said, "here's the deal. I like you. I didn't expect to, but I do. You're a pretty little thing, and smart as a whip, and this is probably going to be the only crime you'll ever commit, because you're one of those girls who just knows better, aren't you?"

She held her head rigidly, careful so that he wouldn't take the most subtle movement for a nod.

"And I think you got a damn fine deal here. The house is nice—lots of light—and the town obviously suits you. I met those friends of yours, the ball-buster and the one who thinks she's God's Gift to Men, and I gotta say it's clear why you left."

Her nails dug into the leather. Pain shot through the tender skin at the top of her fingers.

"I really don't wanna ruin your life. It's time I make a change in mine. You give me fifty grand, and I'll bury everything I found about you."

"Fifty thousand dollars?" Her voice was raspy with tension. "For the first payment?"

His eyes sparkled. "One-time deal."

She snorted. She knew better. Blackmailers never worked like that.

"And maybe I'll stick around. Get to know you a little better. I could fall in love with that house myself."

"Could you?" she asked, amazed at the dry tone she'd managed to maintain.

"Sure." He grinned. That had been the look that had made her go weak less than a week ago. Now it sent a chill through her. "You and me, we had something."

"Yeah," she said. "A one-night stand."

He laughed. "It could be more than that, darlin'. It took you long enough, but you might've just found Mr. Right."

"Seems to me you were the one who was searching." She stood. He didn't protest, and she was glad. She had to leave. If she stayed any longer, she'd say something she would regret.

She tucked her purse under her arm. "I assume the drink's on you," she said, and then she walked away.

He didn't follow her—at least not right away. And she drove in circles before going home, watching for his car behind hers, thinking about everything he had said. Thinking about her break, her freedom, the things she had done to create a new life.

The things that now made her look guilty of a crime she hadn't committed.

**

She didn't sleep, of course. She couldn't. Her mind was too full—and her bed was no longer a private place. He'd been there, and some of him remained, a shadow, a laugh. After an hour of tossing and turning, she moved to the guest room and sat on the edge of the brand new unused mattress, clutching a blanket and thinking.

It was time to find out what had happened. Delamore knew who she was. She couldn't pretend any more. But he wasn't ready to turn her in. That gave her a little time.

She took a shower, made herself a pot of coffee, and a sandwich which she ate slowly. Then she went to her office, sat down in front of her computer and hesitated. The moment she logged on was the moment that all her movements could be traced. The moment she couldn't turn back from.

But she could testify to the conversation she'd had with Delamore, and the bartender would back her up. She wouldn't be able to hide her own identity should the police come for her, and so there was no reason to lie. She would simply say that she was concerned about her former business partner. She wanted to know if any of what Delamore told her was true.

It wouldn't seem like a confession to anyone but him.

She logged on, and used a search engine to find the news.

It didn't take her long. Amazing how many newspapers were online. Michael's death created quite a scandal in Racine, and the pictures of her office—the bloody mess still visible inside—were enough to make the ham on rye that she'd had a few moments ago turn in her stomach.

Michael. He'd been a good accountant. Thorough, exacting. Nervous. Always so nervous, afraid of making any kind of mistake.

Embezzlement? Why would he do that?

But that was what the papers had said. She dug farther, found the follow-up pieces. He'd raised cash, using clients' accounts, to bilk the company of a small fortune.

And Delamore was right. The dates matched up. Michael had stolen from her own clients to pay her for her own business. He had bought the business with stolen money.

She bowed her head, listening to the computer hum, counting her own breaths. She had never once questioned where he had gotten the money. She had figured he'd gotten a loan, had thought that maybe he'd finally learned the value of savings.

Michael. The man who took an advance on his paycheck once every six months. Michael, who had once told her he was too scared to invest on his own.

I wouldn't trust my own judgment, he had said.

Oh, the poor man. He had been right.

The trail did lead to her. The only reason Delamore couldn't point at her exactly was because she had stashed the cash in a blind account. And she hadn't touched it.

Not yet.

She'd been living entirely off her own savings, letting the money from the sale of her business draw interest. The nest egg for the future she hadn't planned yet.

Delamore wanted fifty thousand dollars from her. To give that to him, she'd have to tap the nest egg.

How many times would he make her tap it again? And again? Until it was gone, of course. Into his pocket. And then he'd turn her in.

She wiped her hand on her jeans. It was a nervous movement, meant to calm herself down. She had to think.

If the cops could trace her, they would have. They either didn't have enough on her or hadn't made the leap that Delamore had. And then she had confirmed his leap with the conversation tonight.

She got up and walked away from the computer. She wouldn't let him intrude. He had already taken over her bedroom. She needed to have a space here, in her office, without him.

There was no mention of her in the papers, nothing that suggested she was involved. The police would have contacted the Reno police if they had known where she was. Even if they had hired Delamore to track her, they might still not have been informed about her whereabouts. Delamore wanted money more than he wanted to inform the authorities about where she was.

Grace sat down in the chair near the window. The shade was drawn, but the spot was soothing nonetheless.

The police weren't her problem. Delamore was.

She already knew that he wouldn't be satisfied with one payment. She had to find a way to get rid of him.

She bowed her head. Even though she had done nothing criminal she was thinking like one. How did a woman get rid of a man she didn't want? She could get a court order, she supposed, forcing him to stay away from her. She could refuse to pay him and let the cards fall where they might. Years of legal hassle, maybe even an arrest. She would certainly lose her job. No casino would hire her, and she couldn't fall back on her CPA skills, not after being arrested for embezzlement.

Ignoring him wasn't an option either.

Then, there was the act of desperation. She could kill him. Somehow. She had always thought that murderers weren't methodical enough. Take an intelligent person, have her kill someone in a thoughtful way, and she would be able to get away with the crime.

Everywhere but in her own mind. No matter how hard she tried, no matter how much he threatened her, she couldn't kill Delamore.

There had to be another option. She had to do something. She just wasn't sure what it was.

She went back to the computer and looked at the last article she had downloaded. Michael had stolen from people she had known for years. People who had trusted her, believed in her and her word. People who had thought she had integrity.

She frowned. What must they think of her now? That she was an embezzler too? After all those years of work, did she want that behind her name?

Then again, why should she care about people she would never see again?

But she would see them every time she closed her eyes. Elderly Mrs. Vezzetti and her poodle, trusting Grace to handle her account because her husband, God rest his soul, had convinced her that numbers were too much for her pretty little head. Mr. Heitzkey who couldn't balance a checkbook if his life depended on it. Ms. Andersen, who had taken Grace's advice on ways to legally hide money from the IRS—and who had seemed so excited when it worked.

Grace sighed.

There was only one way to make this right. Only one way to clear her conscience and to clear Delamore out of her life.

She had to turn herself in.

**

She did some more surfing as she ate breakfast and found discount tickets to Chicago. She had to buy them round-trip from Chicago to Reno (God bless the casinos for their cheap airfare deals) and fly only the Reno to Chicago leg. Later she would buy another set, and not use part of it. Both of those tickets were cheaper than buying a single round-trip ticket out of Reno to Racine.

Grace made the reservation, hoping that Delamore wasn't tracking round trips that started somewhere else, and then she went to work. She claimed a family emergency, got a leave of absence, and hoped it would be enough.

She liked the world she built here. She didn't want to lose it because she hadn't been watching her back.

Twenty-four hours later, she and the car she rented in O'Hare were in Racine. The town hadn't changed. More churches than she saw out west, a few timid billboards for Native American Casinos, a factory outlet mall, and bars everywhere. The streets were grimy with the last of the sand laid down during the winter snow and ice. The trees were just beginning to bud, and the flowers were poking through the rich black dirt.

It felt as if she had gone back in time.

She wondered if she should call Alex and Carole, and then decided against it. What would she say to them, anyway? Instead, she checked into a hotel, unpacked, ate a mediocre room service meal, and slept as if she were dead.

Maybe in this city, she was.

***

The district attorney's office was smaller than Grace's bathroom. There were four chairs, not enough for her, her lawyer, the three assistant district attorneys and the DA himself. She and her lawyer were allowed to sit, but the assistant DAs hovered around the bookshelves and desk like children who were waiting for their father to finish business. The DA himself sat behind a massive oak desk that dwarfed the tiny room.

Grace's lawyer, Maxine Jones, was from Milwaukee. Grace had done her research before she arrived and found the best defense attorney in Wisconsin. Grace knew that Maxine's services would cost her a lot—but Grace was gambling that she wouldn't need Maxine for more than a few days.

Maxine was a tall, robust woman who favored bright colors. In contrast she wore debutante jewelry—a simple gold chain, tiny diamond earrings—that accented her toffee-colored skin. The entire look made her seem both flamboyant and powerful, combinations that Grace was certain helped Maxine in court.

"My client," Maxine was saying, "came here on her own. You'll have to remember that, Mr. Lindstrom."

Harold Lindstrom, the district attorney, was in his fifties, with thinning gray hair and a runner's thinness. His gaze held no compassion as it fell on Grace.

"Only because a bounty hunter hired by the police department found her," Lindstrom said.

"Yes," Maxine said. "We'll concede that the bounty hunter was the one who informed her of the charges. But that's all. This man hounded her, harassed her, and tried to extort money out of her, money she did not have."

"Then she should have gone to the Reno police," Lindstrom said.

An assistant DA crossed her arms as if this discussion was making her uncomfortable. It was making Grace uncomfortable. Never before had she been discussed as if she weren't there.

"It was easier to come here," Maxine said. "My client has a hunch, which if it's true, will negate the charges you have against her and against Michael Holden."

"Mr. Holden embezzled from his clients with the assistance of Ms. Reinhart."

"No. Mr. Holden followed standard procedure for the accounting firm."

"Embezzlement is standard procedure?" Lindstrom was looking directly at Grace.

Maxine put her manicured hand on Grace's knee, a reminder to remain quiet.

"No. But Mr. Holden, for reasons we don't know, decided to end his life, and since he now worked alone, no one knew where he was keeping the clients' funds. My client," Maxine added, as if she expected Grace to speak, "would like you to drop all charges against her and to charge Mr. Delamore with extortion. In exchange, she will testify against him, and she will also show you where the money is."

"Where she hid it, huh?" Lindstrom said. "No deal."

Maxine leaned forward. "You don't have a crime here. If you don't bargain with us, I'll go straight to the press, and you'll look like a fool. It seems to me that there's an election coming up."

Lindstrom's eyes narrowed. Grace held her breath. Maxine stared at him as if they were all playing a game of chicken. Maybe they were.

"Here's the deal," he said, "if her information checks out, then we'll drop the charges. We can't file against Delamore because the alleged crimes were committed in Nevada."

Maxine's hand left Grace's knee. Maxine templed her fingers and rested their painted tips against her chin. "Then, Harold, we'll simply have to file a suit against the city and the county for siccing him on my client. A multi-million dollar suit. We'll win, too. Because she came forward the moment she learned of a problem. She hasn't been in touch with anyone from here. Her family is dead, and her friends were never close. She had no way of knowing what was happening a thousand miles away until a man you people sent started harassing her."

"You said he's been harassing you for a month," Lindstrom said to Grace. "Why didn't you come forward before now?"

Grace looked at Maxine who nodded.

"Because," Grace said, "he didn't show me any proof of his claims until the night before I flew out. You can ask the bartender at the Silver Dollar. He saw the entire thing."

Lindstrom frowned at Maxine. "We want names and dates."

"You'll get them," Maxine said.

Lindstrom sighed. "All right. Let's hear it."

Grace's heart was pounding. Here was her moment. She suddenly found herself hoping they would all believe her. She had never lied with so much at stake before.

"Go ahead, Grace," Maxine said softly.

Grace nodded. "We had run into some trouble with our escrow service. Minor stuff, mostly rudeness on the part of the company. It was all irritating Michael. Many things were irritating him at that time, but we weren't close, so I didn't attribute it to anything except work."

The entire room had become quiet. She felt slightly lightheaded. She was forgetting to breathe. She forced herself to take a deep breath before continuing.

"In the week that I was leaving, Michael asked me how he could go about transferring everything from one escrow company to another. It required a lot of paperwork, and he didn't trust the company we were with. I thought he should have let them and the new company handle it, but he didn't want to."

She squeezed her hands together, reminded herself not to embellish too much. A simple lie was always best.

"We had accounts we had initially set up for clients in discreet banks. I told Michael to go to one of those banks, place the money in accounts there, and then when the new escrow accounts were established, to transfer the money to them. I warned him not to take longer than a day in the intermediate account."

"We have no record of such an account," the third district attorney said.

Grace nodded. "That's what I figured when I heard that he was being charged with embezzlement. I can give you the names of all the banks and the numbers of the accounts we were assigned. If the money's in one of them, then my name is clear."

"Depending on when the deposit was made," Lindstrom said. "And if the money's all there."

Grace's lightheadedness was growing. She hadn't realized how much effort bluffing took. But she did know she was covered on those details at least.

"You may go through my client's financial records," Maxine said. "All of her money is accounted for."

"Why wouldn't he have transferred the money to the new escrow accounts quickly, like you told him to?" Lindstrom asked.

"I don't know," Grace said.

"Depression is a confusing thing, Harold," Maxine said. "If he's like other people who've gotten very depressed, I'm sure things slipped. I'm sure this wasn't the only thing he failed to do. And you can bet I'd argue that in court."

"Why did you leave Racine so suddenly?" Lindstrom asked. "Your friends say you just vanished one night."

Grace let out a small breath. On this one she could be completely honest. "I had a scare. I thought I had breast cancer. The lumpectomy results came in the day I left. You can check with my doctor. I was planning to go after that—maybe a month or more—but I felt so free, that I just couldn't go back to my work. Something like that changes you, Mr. Lindstrom."

He grunted as if he didn't believe her. For the first time in the entire discussion, she felt herself get angry. She clenched her fingers so hard that her nails dug into her palms. She wouldn't say any more, just like Maxine had told her to.

"The banks?" Lindstrom asked.

Grace slipped a small leather-bound ledger toward him. She had spent a lot of time drawing that up by hand in different pens. She hoped it would be enough.

"The accounts are identified by numbers only. That's one of the reasons we liked the banks. If he started a new account, I won't know its number."

"If they're in the U.S., then we can get a court order to open them," Lindstrom said.

"Check these numbers first. Most of the accounts were inactive." She had to clutch her fingers together to keep them from trembling.

"All right," Lindstrom said and stood. Maxine and Grace stood as well. "If we discover that you're wrong—about anything—we'll arrest you, Ms. Reinhart. Do you understand?"

Grace nodded.

Maxine smiled. "We're sure you'll see it our way, Harold. But remember your promise. Get that creep away from Grace."

"Right now, your client's the one we're concerned with, Maxine." Lindstrom's cold gaze met Grace's. "I'm sure we'll be in touch."

***

Grace thought the eight o'clock knock on her hotel room door was room service. She'd ordered another meal from them, unable to face old haunts and old friends. Until she had come back, she had never even been in a hotel in Racine, so she felt as if she weren't anywhere near her old home. Now if she could only get the different local channels on the television set, her own delusion would be complete.

She undid the locks, opened the door, and stepped away so that the waiter could bring his cart/table inside.

Instead, Delamore pulled the door back. She was so surprised to see him that she didn't try to close him out. She scuttled away from him toward the nightstand, and fumbled behind her back for the phone.

His cheeks were red, and his eyes sparkling with fury. His anger was so palpable, she could feel it across the room.

"What kind of game are you playing?" he snapped, slamming the door closed.

She got the phone off the hook without turning around. "No game."

"It is a game. You got away from me, and then you come here, telling them that I've been threatening you."

"You have been threatening me." Her fingers found the bottom button on the phone—which she hoped was "0." If the hotel operator heard this, she'd have to call security.

"Of course I'd been threatening you! It's my job. You didn't want to come back here and I needed to drag you back. Any criminal would see that as a threat."

"Here's what you don't understand," Grace said as calmly as she could. "I'm not a criminal."

"Bullshit." Delamore took a step toward her. She backed up farther and the end table hit her thighs. Behind her she thought she heard a tinny voice ask a muted question. The operator, she hoped.

Grace held up a hand. "Come any closer and I'll scream."

"I haven't done anything to you. I've been trying to catch you."

She frowned. What was he talking about? And then she knew. The police had put a wire on him. The conversation was being taped. And they—he—was hoping that she'd incriminate herself.

"You're threatening me now," she said. "I haven't done anything. I talked to the DA today. I explained my situation and what I think Michael did. He's checking my story now."

"Your lies."

"No," Grace said. "You're the one who's lying, and I have no idea why."

"You bitch." He lowered his voice the angrier he got. Somehow she found that even more threatening.

"Stay away from me."

"Stop the act, Grace," he said. "It's just you and me. And we both know you're not afraid of anything."

Then the door burst open and two hotel security guards came in. Delamore turned and as he did, Grace said, "Oh, thank God. This man came into my room and he's threatening me."

The guards grabbed him. Delamore struggled, but the guards held him tightly. He glared at her. "You're lying again, Grace."

"No," she said and stepped away from the phone. He glanced down at the receiver, on its side on the table, and cursed. Even if he hadn't been wired, she had a witness.

The guards dragged him and Grace sank onto the bed, placing her head in her hands. She waited until the shaking stopped before she called Maxine.

***

Grace had been right. Delamore had been wearing a wire, and her ability to stay cool while he attacked had preserved her story. That incident, plus the fact that the DA's office had found the money exactly where she had said it would be, in the exact amount that they had been looking for, went a long way toward preserving her credibility. When detectives interviewed Michael's friends one final time, they all agreed he was agitated and depressed, but he would tell no one why. Without the embezzlement explanation, it simply sounded as if he were a miserable man driven to the brink by personal problems.

She had won, at least on that score. Her old clients would get their money back, and they would be off her conscience. And nothing, not even Delamore, would take their place.

Delamore was under arrest, charged with extortion, harassment, and attempting to tamper with a witness. Apparently, he'd faced similar complaints before, but they had never stuck. This time, it looked as if they would.

Grace would have to return to Racine to testify against him. But not for several months. And maybe, Maxine said, not even then. The hope was that Delamore would plea and save everyone the expense of a trial.

So, on her last night in Racine, perhaps forever, Grace got enough courage to call Alex and Carole. She didn't reach either of them; instead she had to leave a message on their voice mail, asking them to meet her at Oh Kaye's one final time.

Grace got there first. The place hadn't changed at all. There was still a jukebox in the corner and cocktail waitresses in short skirts and ankle boots with big heels. Tin stars and Wild West art on the walls, unstained wood and checkered tablecloths adding to the effect. High bar stools and a lot of lonely people.

Grace ignored them. She sashayed to the bar, slapped her hand on it, and ordered whiskey neat. A group of suits at a nearby table ogled her and she turned away.

She was there to diss men not to meet them.

Carole arrived first, black miniskirt, tight crop top, and cigarette in hand. She looked no different. She hugged Grace so hard that Grace thought her ribs would crack.

"Alex had me convinced you were dead."

Grace shook her head. "I was just sleeping around."

Carole grinned. "Fun, huh?"

Grace thought. The night had been fun. The aftermath hadn't been. But her life was certainly more exciting. She didn't know if the tradeoff was worth it.

Alex arrived a moment later. Her auburn hair had grown, and she was wearing boots beneath a long dress. The boots made her look even taller.

She didn't hug Grace.

"What the hell's the idea?" Alex snapped. "You vanished—kapoof! What kind of friend does that?"

In the past, Grace would have stammered something, then told Alex she was exactly right and Grace was wrong. This time, Grace set her whiskey down.

"I told you about my lumpectomy," Grace said. "You didn't care. I was scared. I told you that, and you didn't care. When I found out I didn't have cancer, I called you to celebrate, and you didn't care. Seems to me you vanished first."

Alex's cheeks were red. Carole stubbed her cigarette in an ashtray on the bar's wooden rail.

"Not fair," Alex said.

"That's what I thought," Grace said.

Carole looked from one to the other. Finally, she said, very softly, "I really missed you, Gracie."

"I thought some misogynistic asshole picked you up and killed you," Alex said.

"Could have happened," Grace said. "Maybe it nearly did."

"Here?" Carole asked. "At Oh Kaye's?"

Grace shook her head. "It's a long story. Are you both finally ready to listen to me?"

Carole tugged her miniskirt as if she could make it longer. "I want to hear it."

Alex picked up Grace's whiskey and tossed it back. Then she wiped off her mouth. "What did I tell you, Grace? Women always tolerate misogyny. You should have fought him off."

"I did," Grace said.

Alex's eyes widened. Carole laughed. "Our Gracie has grown up."

"No," Grace said. "I've always been grown-up. You're just noticing now."

"There's a story here," Alex said, slipping her arm through Grace's, "and I think I need to hear it."

"Me, too." Carole put her arm around Grace's shoulder. "Tell us about your adventures. I promise we'll listen."

Grace sighed. She'd love to tell them everything, but if she did, she'd screw up the case against Delamore. "Naw," Grace said. "Let's just have some drinks and talk about girl things."

"You gotta promise to tell us," Alex said.

"Okay," Grace said. "I promise. Now how about some whiskey?"

"Beer," Alex said.

"You see that cute guy over there?" Carole asked, pointing at the suits.

Grace grinned. Already, her adventure was forgotten. Nothing changed here at Oh Kaye's. Nothing except Cowboy Grace, who'd finally bellied up to the bar.

SPINNING

IDWAY THROUGH that first awful class—when the clock above the mirrors said she had only been on the stationary bike for 22 minutes, but her body told her she had been on it for 2.2 days, when she thought her heart was going to burst through her chest like a creature out of the movie *Alien*, when sweat poured off her in rivers, and her breath came in deep honking gasps—midway through all of that, Patricia bent her head, saw the flab on her thighs go up while her actual legs went down, and heard Tom, her instructor, call over the rock music:

"Good. Real good. Excellent. Keep going. Wonderful. Hmmm. You'll get it. Relax. Wait until it feels good. Good. Relax…."

Something in the rhythm of his voice, in the involuntary nature of the sounds, told her he would sound like this in bed. He would talk, his words meaningless, an accompaniment to the beat his body had established, and the pattern would continue building, building, building, until his voice rose in a cry and everything stopped.

She focused on that, held onto that, because it felt like the only thing that made him real somehow, made him, this Greek god of a man, whose muscles were perfectly sculpted, whose eyes were warm and brown and not-quite-sympathetic-enough, slightly less intimidating. And she needed a reason not to be intimidated.

Two hundred pounds did not fit on her delicate five-four frame. She didn't know how she had let herself go like this. Excuse after excuse, she supposed, a sense of denial, a willingness to believe, at first, that it was her clothes that were shrinking, not her body that was expanding. It had taken two years of failed exercise attempts that had brought her to this class, to this moment, and she had been planning to drop out of this one until he fell into his unconscious personal rhythm, until she realized that he too was human.

And then she looked up, saw those not-quite-sympathetic eyes fall on her with something like disgust. She knew how she looked. The gym had thoughtfully provided a mirror in its exercise room. She saw the five other women in the spinning class: the darling with her tight sculpted 25-year-old body who made it clear that she had never tried this before, and who was so in shape that she managed all the motions with ease; the middle-aged housewives in the middle, looking fine to her, but complaining about that extra ten pounds they always put on in the holidays; the bartender, an older woman who looked strong and solid, who had told Patricia about the class; and the anorexic creature beside Patricia who was having just as much trouble keeping up—apparently her eating habits, like Patricia's, robbed her of the strength to exercise. But none of them looked as disgusting as she did in her sweats, her face red, her new perm damp, her body straining. Why was it that she, a woman who had to struggle to walk across the room, was being treated like the pariah, when she was the one who needed the most courage, the most strength, to be here?

It was because the others were all afraid that some day, somehow, through the same careless inattentiveness that she had shown, they would all end up looking like her.

But *he*, he had no right to look at her that way. He was supposed to be the professional, the one who helped people like her become hard bodies like him. He wasn't supposed to let her see that she disgusted him, even though she did.

It was that look, in combination with her realization about him, that gave her the determination she had lacked. As her legs went round and round, the stationary bike's resistance on its lowest setting, she realized that she now had a goal.

She had been pretty once, eighty pounds and fifteen years ago. She would be pretty again.

And when she was, he would want her. She would take him to bed, and she would find out if he really sounded like that. And if he did, she would look at him with the same disgust she had seen in his eyes only moments before. She would look at him, and she would laugh.

***

Meeting her goal was harder than she thought it would be. After her first spinning class, she had to go immediately to bed and when she got up the next morning, her legs ached so badly that she could barely climb stairs. Over time, she grew used to the class, and she moved onto weights, treadmills, and aerobics.

Within six months, she had lost thirty pounds and her body had definition. The spinning classes were tedious—she had learned the pattern within a few days and knew what he would call out next—and she found herself waiting for a repetition of the moment, the moment that had inspired her. It didn't happen often, and she watched him now. He would catch himself, as if he did know how he sounded, and sometimes, he would catch her looking at him.

She always smiled. She tried to be as congenial as she could.

Fortunately, she didn't have to be congenial anywhere else. She was having trouble being pleasant. The exercise put her in a good mood for an hour or two afterward, but the exhaustion that came with it angered her. She went back to her family doctor, wondering if the exercise was hurting her (even though he claimed, up front, that it would be the best thing for her) and he had calmly, patiently, explained how the human body worked.

She got a sense that he gave this explanation a lot. *You are carrying the weight of a 12-year-old girl in addition to your own body weight. It is as if you are doing these exercises for two, when everyone else in the room was doing them for one.*

She wished she could explain it to them. The looks had stopped, after her second month, except when newcomers entered the gym. Then they stared at her as if she were the freak, or the one that would fail, and eventually, they would disappear.

She remained, tenacious to the last.

***

It was at her job, another twenty pounds later, that she realized she was in a revenge cycle. She worked as a website designer for a local Internet provider. Her brother was her boss, and he would interview the customer on tape, and she would listen to the interview, use the materials, and design the website from there.

In the past two weeks, clients who came to the office (and there were so few of them: most of them as lonely as she was) began to compliment her on her looks. She did look better. The loss of fifty pounds had also taken ten years off her face. The exercise and all the water it forced her to drink had cleared up her skin, and the pretty girl she remembered was beginning to make appearances in her mirror.

The office was a tiny place—a three-room suite with a door opening onto a strip mall sidewalk—that became even tinier whenever someone new came inside.

The wallpaper-thin walls did not shut out any sound, so she usually heard her brother's interviews with potential website clients twice. Those she didn't mind, because she made notes, hearing different things on the first and second listenings. It was the casual conversations, the folks who dropped in just to update their accounts or to gossip with her brother or to see, lately, how different Patricia was looking, that got on her nerves.

She had taken to closing her presswood door and opening the window that overlooked the alley, no matter how cold it was. Sometimes, if she did that, she could focus on the whoosh of traffic on the highway, the crunch of wheels on the gravel, the occasional conversations of people entering other businesses. If she was really lucky, it all became white noise, a sort of background to the tap-tap-tap of her fingers on the keys, her mind not in Seavy Village, but inside the computer, in that vast and somewhat mysterious network of computers known as the internet. There she could float, be someone else, anyone else, and no one seemed to care that she was different except her.

It was in one of those moments when, on a whim, she took the quiz the local psychiatrist had asked her to put on his website. His self-help book, *Negative Thoughts and How to Cure Them*, had been climbing the bestseller list, and he believed he needed a way for his fans to contact him. He thought the quiz was an open door. She hadn't been too sure, but then, she hadn't been too sure about his book either, which seemed to her (when she read it) a '90s rip-off of Napoleon Hill's classic *Think and Grow Rich*. But she, like the suckers she was designing the page for, took the quiz and as she read the paragraph summary of her answers, she saw herself in its analysis:

> *You have a tendency to blame others for your problems. Instead of solving those problems, you hope that others suffer worse than you have. Sometimes you fantasize about causing the suffering yourself. This is not healthy behavior. For a solution, see page 62 in my book...*

And because she had already committed herself that far, she looked up page 62 in the complementary copy of the book that the psychiatrist had given the office, and saw the chapter heading in bold: *The Revenge Cycle: Explanations of Your Obsession and How to Cure it.*

Surprisingly, the advice made sense to her. She had focused—obsessed—on Tom, on the sound of his voice, on the revenge she would get once she had sex with him and more importantly, had laughed at him. Had humiliated him with her voice and her eyes, and the body she had sculpted for just that purpose.

After reading the chapter, she stood up behind her desk, ran her hands down her arms, feeling the skin beneath her cotton blouse. The skin and the muscle and the bone. She hadn't felt bone in years, the sharpness of her elbows, the two bumps on either side of her wrists. She was beginning to like this new self, beginning to accept that it, and not the woman whose thighs brushed together, was who she was.

If she ended her focus on Tom, perhaps the exercise would end too. After all, the book said that all behaviors relating to the revenge cycle had to stop in order for it to be cured.

The only behaviors she had were the good ones; the exercise, the healthy food; the grooming that she had only recently started to do again. Clothes looked good once more. Makeup made her seem older and more mysterious rather than a woman denying her encroaching middle age.

As revenge fantasies went, this was a fairly harmless one. Perhaps she might dent Tom's rather solid self-esteem. Perhaps she might even make him reconsider casual affairs. But those two things might be good for him.

They would certainly be good for her.

It felt, when she looked on that moment later, as if for one brief afternoon, she surfaced from her own thoughts, had a sense of clarity, and then dove back in, like a whale coming to the surface of water to take a breath.

She didn't take another breath for a very long time.

***

At the end of eighteen months, she thought of spinning class as hell. But she hit her ideal weight that month, and actually came to the class in spandex that made her look athletic and not like she had squeezed her bulk into someone else's clothes. As she went through her first class at her perfect weight, she listened for the moment when Tom's voice rose, when it punctuated each word with a gasping sexual rhythm, and when it did, she looked at him and found him looking at her.

The not-quite-sympathetic expression had left his eyes a long time ago, replaced by a kind of pride. She actually overheard him talking to the aerobics instructor, using Patricia as an example of how well spinning worked. She studied him as her legs worked—thighs like steel now, muscles rippling beneath hard skin—and then, slowly, she smiled.

She had been saving her smiles. They had been her best feature even when she was heavy, and she had rationed them, at least for him. She wanted to use them when she was in peak condition, knowing that he would be attracted not so much to her face as to her sculpted form. And so, as their eyes met and the smile creased her face, she saw something new. She saw his eyebrows rise briefly and knew that small movement for something she hadn't seen in years.

Flirting.

She raised her eyebrows in return, and then looked away. First salvo sent and received. Mating dance initiated. Humiliation about to begin.

She went home that night happy for the first time since she had started taking spinning classes. In her two room apartment whose ocean view was the only thing to recommend it, she danced a small jig, and then smiled again.

Her plan would actually work.

***

She didn't know what would happen after she slept with him. That was the problem she was working on as she drove to the gym in her beloved 1974 Volkswagen Bug. It smelled of oil and it vibrated crazily, but she had owned that car since she bought it used in high school and it had been the one thing she had maintained through all the years.

Her job at the IP had begun to pay her real money and she could buy a good car for the first time in her life, but she didn't. She couldn't give up her faithful Bug. She never would. She did her best thinking in it. And as she drove up the hill to the gym, she needed a goal that would last her past her revenge on Tom. And, if she were going to be truly healthy, it had to be one that did not continue to play out her revenge fantasy.

She parked in her usual space, grabbed her gym bag, and got out, startled to see a police car parked beside the bicycle racks. In the two years she had been coming here, she had never seen a police car. But there was that one month when a paramedic tried to fit exercise into his schedule. Sometimes he parked an ambulance outside. That had unnerved her the first time as well.

She pushed her car door shut with her hip, walked around the police car, and headed down the flight of stairs to the club itself. There she saw two policemen at the front desk and the aerobics instructor, a petite thing with too much energy for a human being, sitting on a stool looking stricken. No one was on the machines, and even the hardcore gym rats who spent hours on the free weights, were huddled near the Nautilus equipment. From there, any conversation at the front desk could be heard, loud and clear.

Patricia opened the glass door and came inside. She walked to the desk like she always did, to sign in and pay the extra fee for her special class, when a look from one of the policeman stopped her. The aerobics instructor, whose name she had never learned, raised liquid brown eyes filled with tears.

"There's no class," she said in a shaky voice. "Tom is dead."

The words circled in her head like the wheels on the stationary bike. *Tom. Is. Dead.* He couldn't be dead. She wasn't finished yet. She hadn't had the answer to her question, she hadn't been able to look at him with not-quite-sympathy in her eyes.

The police were watching her reaction. And she looked at them, truly seeing them for the first time. The man closest to her was about her age, fifty pounds overweight and carrying it all in the danger zone around his stomach. The other man was younger, athletic, broad-shouldered. His blue eyes were sharp, his lips thin. He didn't seem to miss anything. Especially the expression that must have crossed her face. What had it looked like? Shock? Disappointment?

Fear?

For her first response, after that flash of what-about-me? was guilt. She could have done it. She *had* done it, a thousand times, in her mind. Not killed him physically, but emotionally. Somehow she thought her contempt would destroy him.

Arrogant, of course, but arrogance was what got her through.

The younger officer stepped forward. "Did you know Tom Ansara?"

Not well enough to know his last name. Maybe not at all. "I saw him three times a week," she said. "But I didn't know him. He instructed my spinning class."

But she had a hunch about how he sounded in bed. It felt as if she had been intimate with him. It felt as if she had lost someone close.

She wanted to put her hand on the wall, on the chair, to use something for support.

Those sharp blue cop eyes watched her, seeing everything. How good an actress was she? She didn't know. Good, she hoped. Good enough.

"And you are?"

"Patricia," she said, giving her first name only as she always did at the gym. Only after a moment, she added, "Taylor. Patricia Taylor."

With that little pause in there, her last name sounded made up, even to her. She fumbled with her purse. "I have ID."

"No need," the cop said. "Just wait with the others."

She carried her gym bag and her coat to the nearest table, littered with out-of-date health and fitness magazines. In her 18 months at the gym, she had never sat here. She had never spent any time sitting on anything that didn't spin or move or have weights attached.

The gym seemed excessively silent. The usual loud rock and roll music had been turned off. Someone had muted all three television sets. A fan whirred in the corner, set to cool whomever had been on the Precor cross-training machine, but that person had been off the machine for so long that the digitized program was running on the computer screen. In the long mirror lining one wall, she could see the racquetball bleachers. The Thursday night wallyball players were seated there, heads bowed, hands threaded and hanging over their knees.

No one spoke. It was as if the cops were playing Agatha Christie, waiting until all the suspects arrived before going through the list and coming up with the killer.

The other members of the spinning class threaded in: the darling, the middle-aged housewives, and the bartender. One by one they all took seats at the table, as if united in the class that no longer existed. The anorexic had given up long ago, and had been replaced by the only man, an accountant with a hairy back and a tendency to take off his shirt at precisely 33 minutes into the session. In street clothes, he looked diminished and not at all like a man who wore a white muscle T and baggy gym shorts cut one size too small.

The aerobics instructor sobbed her line each time a class member entered as if she were a model trying out for a play. The shock seemed similar for all of them. Only the darling asked if it was all right if she exercised while she waited. The incredulous silence that greeted her question was her answer, and even she realized that she had said something wrong.

The clock above the mirror showed that forty-five minutes had passed since Patricia arrived. On a normal night, she would be sweating through the last fifteen minutes of the routine, wondering if he would forget himself again and provide her with enough ammunition to survive another week. Instead, she was sitting as still as she possibly could in a white plastic chair, wondering if the police meant to hold them all night.

Clearly Tom's death was suspicious, and clearly it involved people from the gym. Unless he had no other life but the gym. It surprised her to realize that she knew nothing about him, not really. She hadn't even figured out which car in the driveway was his. She had been able to tell, from the way he spoke in class, that he rode his bicycle a lot outdoors: he knew the coast highway from a rider's perspective—sometimes using actual examples for his class to imagine: *We're going to do an uphill climb. Increase the tension on the bike when I tell you. Pretend this is Cascade Head. Know how good you'll feel when you reach the top.*

She also knew that he preferred jazz to rock and roll, but that the darling had requested peppier music to ride to. Patricia actually missed the Al Jarreau mixed with Branford Marsalis. It had provided a great middle period to the class.

When the spinning hour was up, and all the regulars had come in, the heavyset cop told the aerobics instructor to put a closed sign on the door, and lock it. Then they took people one by one into the manager's office, and asked questions.

The heavyset cop remained out front mostly, to deter conversation, Patricia supposed. He watched them all too closely too, and the mirrors didn't help. They allowed him to see everything in that large exercise area, the slightest gesture, the smallest twitch.

After people spoke to the blue-eyed cop in the office, they were allowed to leave. Exercisers were interviewed in the order that they arrived. Obviously someone had kept very careful track.

What it meant was that by the time Patricia was called, the gym rats were gone, but most of the class remained. The aerobics instructor had called her boss, and he had come down to lock up. Patricia also got a sense that he wanted to speak to the police himself.

When the heavyset cop said her name, Patricia got up, legs wobbly. She almost forgot her purse and gym bag, and grabbed them as an afterthought. Then she walked past the mirrors to the office where she had only been one time: the day she had signed up. That day she had been carrying an extra 80 pounds and even though she had dressed to hide it, it had been painfully obvious in the small room.

This time, the room's contours seemed more suited to her frame. The blue-eyed cop closed the door, asked her if she minded that the conversation was recorded, and then asked her to sit.

"This is just routine," he said.

It didn't seem routine, but she didn't say that. She had promised herself out front that she would volunteer nothing, and if he spent more than five minutes asking questions—the average time he had spent with the others—she would call an attorney just on principle.

"How well did you know Tom Ansara, Ms. Taylor?" The cop sat behind the messy manager's desk and folded his hands on top of a pile of papers that clearly didn't belong to him. His blue eyes seemed even more intense in the small space.

"He was my spinning instructor."

"For how long?"

"Eighteen months."

"You know that number precisely?"

She nodded. "I started my exercise program with his class."

"Was it effective?"

"The program?"

"The class."

She shrugged. "It motivated me."

"I understand you lost a lot of weight due to Mr. Ansara."

She almost choked. She felt a flush climb up her neck, her face, and she couldn't stop it. It was as if this man, this cop, had seen into her mind, had read each secret thought, knew how Tom had inspired her.

Knew about the revenge.

"I don't know if you can blame Tom," she said at last.

Blue-eyes raised his eyebrows ever so slightly. The expression gave his face a warmth it hadn't had before. "Blame? I would think you'd be proud of the loss."

"I am," she said, and almost repeated *I* am. But she didn't. She wasn't going to give anything.

"And Tom helped you."

"The spinning class helped me." The flush had receded from her cheeks. Now her skin was cold. She wondered if she had turned pale, and how he would read this.

"You haven't asked what happened to Tom."

"I figured you would tell me."

He studied her for a moment. "He's still in the workout room. Would you like to take a look?"

"God no!" The response came out of her mouth before she could stop it. What was this man thinking, offering her the chance to look at a dead body? Not just any dead body, but the dead body of a man she had known, and fantasized about, however inappropriately.

"How tall are you, Ms. Taylor?"

The question so startled her that she had to think before responding. "Five-four." How did that relate to Tom's death? How did any of it?

She had forgotten to look at the clock and now she was afraid to, afraid it would seem insensitive, afraid it would make her even more suspicious than she probably already was.

"All right," he said. "We're done."

She remained sitting for a moment, disoriented, as he probably wanted her to be. She opened her mouth once, then closed it.

"Although," he said, "you should probably tell me how to get ahold of you. I'm sure it's here in the gym's records, but it's easier if you tell me."

She did. She told him her work phone and her home phone, and even what hours she would be in both places. He gave her a business card with his name on it. She didn't know policemen had business cards, but apparently they did. This one had the city's symbol on it, and then Detective David Huckleby. It was such a jokey name, a rural cop name, that in any other context, she would have smiled.

Instead she pocketed the card and stood. He stood too, came up beside her, so that he could open the door.

As he reached for the knob, she said, "You still didn't tell me how Tom died."

"I didn't?" He let go of the knob. "Careless of me." When it hadn't been at all. He had wanted her to ask. He had confused her, disoriented her, and then wondered if she would remember to ask. She knew that much. It was some kind of game. Maybe she should have called a lawyer after all.

"Tom's neck was broken, Ms. Taylor," Detective Huckleby said. "We think someone wrapped an arm around his neck and snapped it."

He paused, watching her face. She felt her heart beating hard. She couldn't picture it. She couldn't picture someone grabbing Tom like that.

"You know the grip," Huckleby said. "It's the one they teach in the self defense classes here."

She had taken one of those classes just the month before. The instructor had been from out of town, a burly man who taught self-defense all over the country. He had used her as his model victim. She had stood in front of the class, felt his fingers on her neck as he positioned her, then remained very still while his arm encircled her throat. With a sharp movement of the forearm, and a backward pull on the hair, he had said, a neck could be broken, snapped, in a heartbeat.

She hadn't known why anyone would want this information. But the class had been in self-defense. And sometimes, she knew from her television-watching experience, self-defense meant only one person got out alive.

Huckleby was watching her, waiting for her reaction. He had known she had been in the class. He had obviously seen the sign-up list.

He touched her arm, felt her biceps, the muscle clearly developed beneath a thin layer of skin. His touch was gentle and, if she hadn't been in such a state of heightened awareness, she would have thought it accidental.

"Will you miss him?" Huckleby asked.

Her mouth was dry. The feeling of guilt had grown stronger. "I'll miss his class," she said. It was the only thing she could tell him. It was the only truth she knew.

"What a sad epitaph for a man you've known for eighteen months, a man who was proud of helping you lose weight."

"I didn't know him," she said, hearing as she spoke how defensive the words sounded. "I just took a class from him."

"I hear he had a thing for pretty women."

She laughed without mirth. It was an involuntary reaction, one that had been trained in over all the years, all the weight. "That wouldn't have included me."

"It does now," Huckleby said softly.

She felt the smile, the inappropriate smile, leave her face. "I was obese when I came into his class," she said. "I couldn't even pedal the damn bike with the resistance turned off for more than thirty seconds at a stretch. Then I'd pant for five minutes and try again."

"Tenacity can be attractive."

"Maybe," she said. "But you don't forget how someone looked when you met them."

You don't forget that not-quite-sympathetic look in the eye, the disgust when he thought no one was looking. You don't forget any of that.

She thought those last two sentences, but had enough self control to prevent them from coming out of her mouth.

"I don't think you know how far you've come, Ms. Taylor," Huckleby said softly.

"Oh, I do," she said. "And Tom knew it too." She glanced at the door. "Can I go now?"

His smile was gentle. If she had met him in other circumstances, she might even have thought it kind. "Sure."

She let herself out and glanced at the clock. She had been in there twenty minutes. So much for proper resolutions.

"Ms. Taylor?"

She turned. He was holding her purse and gym bag. She swallowed. "Thanks," she said, taking them from him. She bent her head and walked to the door. The gym's owner, a muscular man who looked as if he spent too much time on the bench press, let her out. She took the stairs, slowly, thinking as she did so, that she would never hear Tom again, never hear that odd hitch in his voice, the way it caught when he got into the rhythm of the workout, the way it soared above the music.

His body was on the floor of the exercise room, his neck tilted at an odd angle. She wondered what he looked like, if he still seemed like a Greek god, even in his death repose. And then she shuddered. She would never be able to go in that room again.

She put her bag and purse in the car, and locked it. Then she took off at a run down the parking lot, not because she was frightened, but because she needed to burn off the fear she had felt.

She needed the exercise, and she had to prove to herself that she could do it without Tom.

***

She woke in the middle of the night with an ache in her heart and tears in her eyes. She wanted a piece of chocolate cake so badly that it hurt. Fortunately, she lived in a small town that didn't have an all night grocery store, and she didn't keep cake mixes in her small apartment.

Comfort food. She wanted comfort food because she needed comforting.

She heard her own voice, speaking to Huckleby: *I didn't know him. I just took a class from him.*

But if it were that simple, why couldn't she sleep? Her mother hadn't been able to sleep in the first few months after her father died. Neither had she, if the truth be told. The brain was busy trying to process the loss. Too busy to sleep more than a few hours at a time.

That had been when she had put on the serious weight. Chocolate cake in the middle of the night, topped with vanilla ice cream. Or Cool Whip. Or Hershey's syrup.

Her mouth watered. She needed something comforting. Now. Never deny the cravings, she knew that much. But she couldn't afford to fall back into bad habits just because her spinning class instructor was dead.

She wondered why the local best-selling psychiatrist would say about this. Probably recommend therapy. Probably report her to the police. She could hear it now: *She had a revenge fantasy about the man. Perhaps she acted it out. Perhaps she stalked him.*

She sat down at the kitchen table she had bought at a Discount Furniture Store and assembled herself, then put her hands in her short-cropped hair. If she were honest with herself, she knew that she could have killed him. If her revenge fantasy had taken a different, more harmful twist. If she had gotten to the acting-out stage—which she had. She had been planning to come in that night, to continue the seduction. She had heard how willing he was to date women at the club. She had known about his preference for the sleek muscular women, the clear athletes. She had planned to use that to her benefit.

And the cop had seen it. He had seen it, and something about her height made him dismiss her.

But he shouldn't have. Patricia hadn't seen the body, but she knew the room, and she knew one thing: Tom liked to sit on the floor and talk to people. She could imagine how someone like her could have killed him:

He would have been sitting cross-legged on the polished wood floor in the center of the room, holding forth on the value of good nutrition or how so many reps burn so much fat, when someone came up behind him, put him in the stranglehold and pulled until he couldn't breathe. Then he fell back, sprawling across the floor, his neck bent at the odd angle. Simple. Easy. So simple and easy even a short person could have done it.

She wished she could mention that to Huckleby without raising suspicion, but she couldn't. All she could do was listen for the gossip, read the local papers, and pretend that Tom's death had no effect on her life.

***

Like a woman who had just fallen off a horse, she made herself go to the gym the following night. Getting back in the saddle, she had whispered to herself, and while that wasn't entirely accurate, it was good enough.

The owner sat behind the desk, paperwork spread in front of him. A big sign, written in black Magic Marker, announced that all classes had been canceled until further notice. He saw her stare at it, and said, "We can't have the room until the investigation's done."

She wasn't sure if that was supposed to make her feel better or worse, so she just nodded, and went into the locker room to change. Another woman was standing near the row of sinks, reading a sign newly taped to the wall. The sign was computer generated and it mentioned a trust fund, set up by the gym, for Tom Ansara's daughter.

Patricia felt a jolt. "I didn't know he had a daughter."

The woman nodded. Patricia had seen her around, but had never bothered to learn her name. "Sixteen. She's being raised by the mother in Seattle. But he was here, trying to earn money for her college. Now she may never go."

Patricia almost asked what happened to scholarships, but thought that too crass. Instead she made a sympathetic noise and changed into her sweats. She went into the gym proper, and used the newest StairMaster set on high for an hour, until sweat poured off her. While she worked out, she noticed that only the regulars were here. The dilettantes, the ones who showed up every January or once a month or after a particularly big meal, hadn't come at all. And that was unusual. Every night usually had one.

As she marched up and down a make-believe flight of stairs, she was conscious of the room behind her, hidden by a row of racquetball courts and bleachers, now cordoned off by the local police. The more she marched and sweated, the more she focused on that room. She wanted to see it, wanted to know, perhaps, if he were really dead.

The room had mirrors covering three walls and a row of windows covering the fourth. The windows overlooked the free weight area. When she got off the StairMaster, and grabbed her sweat towel, wrapping it around her neck, she meandered into the free weight area as if her movement were part of her routine.

The windows showed a darkened room, lit only by the lights reflected in the mirrors. There was no chalk outline of a body on the floor—she had read somewhere that Hollywood made that up and the police never used it. She just hadn't believed it to be true—and the special spinning bikes were lined up against the back wall, just like usual, waiting for class members to wheel them toward the middle. Beside them were the pile of step mats, and next to that the boxy audio system that had threatened to ruin her hearing.

Nothing was different except the yellow police tape covering the door, and the sign attached: *Closed by Order of the Seavy Village Police*. She shuddered, wishing, somehow that she had never heard about his death. That she had stayed away as her weight came down and her revenge fantasy demanded its own conclusion, and when she came back and forgot to ask about Tom, people forgot to tell her about him, so that she would assume he had moved away, or lost his job, or found employment that required use of his mind. But she couldn't pretend those things in retrospect, and she couldn't drop the disappointment she felt that somehow, she had been cheated of something.

"Any clues?" A male voice behind her made her jump.

She turned. Detective Huckleby was standing so close to her that he almost pressed her against the window.

"No," she said.

"Strange," he said. "A room is always a room, even after something awful happened in it. Unless you know, the room is no different."

She had had that thought before. Apartments and hotel rooms always made her wonder when she first arrived if anyone had died in them. She had always thought she would be able to tell by some subtle vibration, something that had altered because of the death.

But she felt no such vibration from the gym, none from the exercise room at all, and she was surprised.

"I didn't think any of the class members would show up tonight," he said.

"I didn't just go to class," she said. "This is my routine."

"Routine." He spoke softly, as if he were musing.

Her heart had started to pound again. "I lost my weight, detective, through exercise. I have to continue that, particularly now—"

"Now that your instructor is dead?"

She nodded.

"So he did have an influence on your weight loss."

She licked her lips. "He inspired me." That much was true.

"Who's going to inspire you now?"

She met his gaze. Electric blue. Neon blue. Like she imagined Paul Newman's eyes would be in person. "I guess I have to," she said.

"Always tough," he said. "It's always better if the motivation comes from the outside."

She wasn't sure if he was speaking of exercise now, or if he was speaking of murder. Would he be happier if the killer came from outside Seavy Village? Or outside the gym? She swallowed. She had been so focused on herself, on Tom's death, that she hadn't thought about the reality of murder. The fact that a murder victim had to have a murderer.

"Are you done with your exercise?" he asked.

"Do you want to interrogate me again?"

To her surprise, he laughed. "If you thought that was an interrogation," he said, "I don't want to put you through a real one."

She saw no humor in it. Yesterday had been a bad day, a day she did not want to repeat.

He must have seen that on her face, for his smile faded. "Sorry," he said. "You're not a suspect."

"At this time," she said.

He half shrugged. "I suppose." He looked around at the empty bleachers, the slouching owner pouring over the papers behind the reception desk. "I was hoping to buy you coffee and ask a few questions about the gym."

"Me?"

He faced her, his eyes meeting hers. "Well," he said. "Actually anyone from the class who bothered to show up tonight. You're the only one."

"I thought you didn't expect any of us to show up tonight."

"I figured it would only be the exercise addicts."

It was her turn to smile, hers rueful. "It is."

He nodded once. "Coffee?"

"Water or Gatorade. Coffee's a diuretic."

"Hmm," he said. "And that's bad?"

She looked at him, uncertain if that were a real joke. She supposed it was. It seemed strange to joke in front of a room where a man had been murdered.

"There's a deli and juice bar upstairs," she said, not sure why she agreed.

"Lead the way," he said.

"Let me change," she said. 'I'll meet you there."

"I suppose you want carrot juice."

"Actually," she said. "I want bottled water. And maybe an apple."

"Done."

She pushed past him and went to the lady's locker room. Her hands were shaking and she was wondering what she was doing. He was a cop investigating a murder, and he wanted to talk to her a second time, informally. She felt as if she were doing something wrong, as if she should get on the phone and ask for a lawyer or not show up or go upstairs and ask what he was charging her with. But all of that seemed melodramatic and unnecessary and a bit rude.

After a quick—very quick—shower, she put on her street clothes—a cheap cotton sweater and a pair of faded jeans. She left on her tennies, and kept her gym bag in the locker. She saw no reason to spend too much time with him.

The restaurant upstairs had gone through many for-mats in the eighteen months she had worked out in the gym. The first and most appalling had been the steak joint that served its meat thick and charbroiled. The next had been a vegetarian restaurant with poorly made, tasteless 1970 cuisine. Then different taverns came in after that, and now, finally, the deli, with its smoothie and juice bars. This new place was the only one that got the regulars from the gym. Sometimes they ran up the stairs, got a small sandwich and a fruit drink and then went back down to work out some more.

She had come up more than once with a novel, usually science fiction, and had eaten, alone, most often the taco deli sandwich made with fat-free refried beans. It had flavor, and it was filling and it didn't have a lot of calories, all of which counted in its favor. The seats were comfortable, and the staff congenial, never asking her to move when she finished her meal.

Now she went up to find herself and Huckleby the only clients. The lights were out in the far section of the deli, and a single employee, an older woman whom Patricia had never seen before, cleaned behind the counter.

A bottled water and the fruit plate waited for her. Huckleby had a cup of coffee and a shortbread cookie.

"That's a lot of food."

"You looked like you could use it."

How many years had she waited for someone to say that only to find it was someone she didn't want to impress. She slipped into the chair, and opened the bottle of water.

"You had questions."

He nodded. "Tell me what you can about Tom."

"We had this conversation yesterday."

"Yesterday I knew less than I do today."

"Oh?" She took a long sip. She had been thirsty, which meant she had let herself get dehydrated. Careless of her.

"Yeah," he said.

"Like what?"

He broke the shortbread cookie in half, then broke a half into smaller pieces. "No," he said. "I get to ask the questions first."

"I already told you about Tom."

"You told me what you know. And that was official. Now I want to know what you suspect."

Suspect. Strange word. Was she supposed to tell this man that she thought Tom Ansara was self-involved and rather stupid, that he had an eye for pretty women, and no real empathy for anyone who wouldn't look like a perfect match for him? Or should she tell him about her suspicions of Tom's performance in bed?

"I think he biked a lot," she said.

Huckleby raised an amused eyebrow. "Gee. We missed that."

She felt color rise in her cheeks. "No," she said. "I mean biked all over the city, maybe over the area."

"That's not gossip."

"You want gossip?"

"Yes."

"Talk to the aerobics instructor then. She collects it."

He leaned back and studied her. "That was harsh. You don't like her?"

"I don't know her."

"It amazes me that you could come to a gym for eighteen months and not know anyone."

"I came to work out."

"People usually make friends in places like this."

"Not with fat people."

"Why? They make friends with fat people everywhere else."

She picked up her fork and stabbed an orange slice with it, feeling a momentary victory when some of the juice shot across the table toward him. "I understand it," she said. "At least I do now. Most people who are more than 20 pounds overweight don't stay. It had nothing to do with discipline and everything to do with effort. It takes a lot of work to move a normal weight, but add extra weight on top of it, and a fat person is working twice, sometimes three times harder than everyone else. Most people don't have the discipline, and they leave."

"So you don't make friends with fat people at the gym either?"

"I thought we already established that I don't make friends," she said.

His gaze seemed a little too sharp for a moment, as if her admission was an admission to something else as well. "I'm sure you do in your personal life."

She had a few friends, people she talked to, but no one she confided in. She hadn't confided in anyone for a very long time. Not even her brother. They talked about casual things. She supposed that counted as friendship.

And she had a lot of acquaintances on-line. She kept a board running behind her work at all time, and answered her e-mail when it showed up. She closed out her nightly sessions in a chat room, each night devoted to a different subject, just to keep her mind active.

The silence between them had grown. Finally, she said, "I thought you wanted to hear about Tom."

"And I thought you didn't gossip."

She ate the orange slice. It was sour. She took a sip of water to cover the taste. "I discovered in the last twenty-four hours how little I knew about him. Like the daughter."

"There is no daughter," Huckleby said.

She set the bottle of water down very deliberately. "But the sign—"

"He told people there was a daughter, and the very kind folks in Seavy Village have started a fund. But I investigated, and I can tell you, there is no daughter. No ex-wife. No acrimonious divorce. There isn't even a Tom Ansara until he came to Seavy Village."

So there was more to this than just the gym. That relieved her somehow, made the thought of murder caused by people who frequented her safe place go away.

"All of his relationships lasted a few weeks at most," Huckleby said, "so consider yourself lucky he didn't make a pass at you."

Such a quaint old-fashioned phrase "make a pass" was. She almost smiled. But a part of her brain, the suspicious part, remained distant.

"Why are you telling me all this?"

"Because," he said. "I figured if I opened up, you would. And you look like a lady who has something to get off her chest."

She felt her eyes widen, and wished she could stop them, wished she had more control than she did. Now, when she lied, he would know it. "I've told you everything I can," she said.

He stared at her for a moment. "Pity."

"I don't hold any keys," she said. "I'd tell you if I did."

"Would you?" he asked, then dropped a ten on the table and stood. By the time she got to her feet, he was gone.

***

All that night and as she ate her solitary bowl of cereal the next morning, she kept telling herself that it was silly to feel like she was failing Huckleby somehow. She didn't even know him, didn't know anything about him. All she knew was that he wanted information on Tom's death, and she had none.

In fact, she had even less than she had had before. She had believed the stories about Tom around the gym, had thought him a divorced man with a conventional past. Now, perhaps, he didn't have one, and he, not the murderer, had violated the safety of the gym, of Seavy Village itself.

Blaming the victim, they called it. But she knew that things were never as clear-cut as they seemed. Apparently, so did Huckleby.

When she got to work, her schedule was light: some routine maintenance of a few sites, and monitoring of a few others. She opened the usual chat room where she hung out when things were slow, but couldn't concentrate.

Her brother was in his office, talking loudly on the phone. He wanted to expand their service beyond the coast, to move into the valley. It would entail hiring additional staff, getting more lines, working more computers. It would be a nightmare for her, but so far she hadn't tried to talk him out of it.

Rather than listen to him argue with another of his friends over his plans, she opened her window. The morning breeze smelled of sea salt and fish. It was cold, but she didn't mind. She needed something else to concentrate on.

But her attention kept wandering back to Huckleby's words about Tom, about his secrets, and she finally succumbed. She knew where he lived: she had followed him there, once, early on, so that she could have a setting to imagine her revenge. Actually sitting in her car on that cold November night, watching him shaded against his window as he moved through his apartment, made her feel like a voyeur, a stalker, something she didn't want to be. So, even though she felt an urge to follow him at other times, she never had.

Still, she used his name and address to access his driver's license. Some schlub had gotten in trouble, in Oregon, for placing all the DMV records on the Internet and, even though he had removed them, Patricia had captured the file, thinking some day it would be useful.

It was. With Tom's driver's license number, she was able to get into his credit report, and that, in turn, gave her his social security number. It didn't belong to Tom Ansara, but to someone else, an elderly woman in Pittsburgh. Apparently he had stolen the number. But he had used it for a very long time and through it, and his credit report, she saw a life of transience, a man of many names and, as she dug, several petty crimes, mostly involving drugs, theft, and a certain roughness with women.

That last made a shudder run through her. Her revenge fantasy had been too subtle for this man. It might have turned on her. No matter how strong she was, she might not have been able to overcome his athlete's quickness. She knew that much.

Her fantasy could have ended badly. For her.

At that, she rested her head on her arms and made herself breathe. How foolish she had become. How obsessed with a man she hadn't even known. She had even mourned him, in her own way, this man she had made up.

The door to her office opened, and her brother came in. She recognized him by his footsteps.

"You okay?"

She raised her head. Her brother still carried all the weight he had put on as he aged. Sometimes he eyed her new form as if it were a reproach to him. But she liked him at this weight. It gave him a cuddly warmth that he hadn't had when he was thinner.

"Yeah," she said. "Just tired."

He nodded. All he knew about Tom was what the rest of the town knew: that he had been murdered in the gym. The next day, her brother had asked her if it was safe for her to return. When she assured him it was, he had said, "I hope so," and she knew, with that terse phrase, that the conversation was closed.

He pulled up the only other chair, a folding chair she kept unfolded in the corner. It squeaked as he sat on it. "Look," he said. "If I manage to get more business, we might have to leave Seavy Village. This just isn't a good place to do business, not if we start focusing on the valley."

Her heart was pounding. She didn't want to leave. She loved it here. "I won't go," she said.

"I know. I was thinking, maybe you could be in charge of our coastal lines."

That meant customer relations. It meant working alone. "Let's wait," she said. "Talk about this when the changes become real."

"It's getting closer every day, Patty," he said. Her brother was the only person who could call her Patty and get away with it.

"I know," she said. "I just don't want to think about it now."

***

And she didn't, not until she was on the silly StairMaster for the second night in a row. Sweat was dripping between her breasts, and the back of her neck was damp. The club's televisions were all tuned to a football game, and their sound was on, as well as the latest Rod Stewart CD at full blast. She was surprised she could hear herself think. But the noise blurred, and she found her mind wandering, going over her brother's words, trying to see if there was any reality in the changes he was discussing for his business.

Then it hit her, what he had said. *Seavy Village isn't a good place to do business.* And it wasn't. The town was small, many of its residents unskilled workers with low-paying jobs or retirees who lived on a fixed income. The tourists were seasonal: summers, mostly, with a few spikes around the holidays. Yet Tom had been here for eighteen months, maybe more. He hadn't had a single arrest, which, considering his record before he arrived, was spectacular, and she remembered nothing that made him seem as if he had been on drugs. What had he found that kept him here? It certainly hadn't been the spinning class. And whatever it had been, someone had considered it worth killing for.

Pretend this is Cascade Head, he would say. *Know how good you'll feel when you reach the top.*

And all the other sites on the coast route. He would mention them, use them in his class. But he always came back to Cascade Head, as if it were important, to them, and to him.

For one long stretch of her workout, she considered buying a bike and exploring the places he had mentioned, searching. But for what, she didn't know. And she had never searched for anything. She had no idea how to go about it.

She had to talk to Huckleby. She wondered if he would think she was crazy, all the work she had done on this. He was going to want to know why and the answer she had was really no answer at all, just a truth she was beginning to discover:

That obsession, once begun, did not end easily. That losing it felt a lot like losing love.

***

The police station, tucked in a back road behind the post office, was a 1960s building, all metal and sand-colored brick. Its gray tile floors were spotless, and the walls had recently been painted white. She felt oddly betrayed by its cleanliness. Somehow she had expected the grit she had seen portrayed on TV.

When she asked for Huckleby, the woman at the desk—statuesque, her uniform accenting rather than hiding her figure—nodded toward the only man sitting in a sea of desks. Patricia wasn't sure how she missed him, except that she hadn't expect this place to be this way, and somehow hadn't expected him to look so lost and all alone, bathed in the fog-gray light filtering in from the cross-hatched windows.

The smell, she noted as she walked toward him, was strong: burned coffee and stale sweat, the kind of smell that a person never got used to. It wasn't until she was standing over him that he looked up, and from the movement of his lips, she guessed he had been planning to make a comment to someone else when he edited himself for her.

"I didn't expect to see you again," he said, and kicked a green and metal desk chair in her direction. She sat gingerly on it, half expecting it to squeal as her folding chair did when her brother sat on it.

His comment was strange given the size of the town they lived in. They would see each other from time to time, probably had already and just hadn't known it, until now.

She licked her lips. "I did some digging."

"Oh?" He was giving her his full attention. The file before him was closed and pushed aside, his hands threaded on the desk like a man who was patiently waiting to hear something he didn't already know.

"The name Ansara is unusual," she said, knowing that this was an inane way to start. "There was a movie star in the late sixties and early seventies named Michael Ansara. He looked something like Tom."

"Yeah," Huckleby said, his tone dry. "I can't decide if Tom's favorite movie was *Sometimes a Great Notion* or that awful television remake of *Dracula*."

In spite of herself, she smiled. She ducked her head so that he wouldn't see how amused she was. This was serious, after all.

"But I did even more digging. I found out about his record."

His eyebrows went up. "You're good," he said. "Care to share with me how you did that?"

She had thought this through before she had come, and now she told him the story she had planned: it was the entire truth minus the driver's license records. Even though anyone could get DMV records simply by writing to the division, she felt almost criminal using them, even more criminal for storing them. Still, if he asked, she would tell him. She only hoped he wouldn't ask.

He didn't, but he was leaning forward now, looking at her with a mixture of puzzlement and respect.

"I would have left it at that," she said, "except I got to wondering, what would a man like that be doing in Seavy Village for so long?"

"Staying clean?" Huckleby said. Clearly he'd thought of that too.

"Maybe," she said. "But when he did spinning class, he outlined bike routes, something we could imagine while our feet were hopelessly circling." She took a piece of paper out of her battered purse. "Here are the places he mentioned, and the way he mentioned them. Cascade Head was the one he focused on, but I always thought that was because it was so high. But he could have used the Van Duzer Corridor for the same thing, or maybe something in the Cascades, and he didn't. He just kept coming back to this one, over and over, like his mind was stuck."

Huckleby glanced at the paper. "You're quite specific. How do you remember what he said?"

She flushed. "I was in his class for a long time. It got boring after a while. You did anything you could to concentrate. I focused on his words. He repeated himself a lot."

He tapped the paper against his hand. "Nice work," he said, tapping the paper against his hand. "I knew you'd remember something if you tried hard enough."

"Is it important?" she asked.

"Important?" He kept a grip on the paper while he reached for the phone. "It's the missing piece."

***

She didn't hear anything for three days. Every time she thought of calling the station, she made herself do something else. The danger with obsession, the website told her, was that once one went away, another sometimes arose in its place. Too many, and a person needed therapy. A single one, and perhaps the person needed more to do with her life.

More than computers, exercise and solitary meals. More than ducking her head to avoid conversations every time she went to the gym.

She joined the aerobics class and made a point, that night, of learning everyone's names. She told her brother that she thought his expansion a bad idea at this stage in their business, and he was so pleased that she used the word "their" that he didn't even try to argue with her. He asked her what she thought the business needed, and she told him all the things she had never said. To her surprise, he made a list and walked out of her office, studying it, ready, he said, to make changes.

On the third day, the local 5:15 newscast announced that a suspect was being held in the murder of Tom Ansara.

A man, with a name Patricia didn't recognize, an out-of-towner, as the announcer called him with obvious relief, who had business with Ansara that predated his arrival in Seavy Village.

She was surprised she hadn't heard from Huckleby. She would have thought that, as a courtesy, he would have told her first.

And then she wondered where that assumption came from. She had provided a small bit of information in an on-going investigation.

He owed her nothing. She owed him nothing. And that's where things would always stand.

***

The details came out bit by bit, not in the local paper which saw itself as a promoter of tourism on the coast and as such tried to cover up the seamier stuff, but in the *Oregonian* which followed the entire case with an interest unusual in their non-Portland coverage.

Tom Ansara's real name was Andrew Thomas. He had arrests in several states for drug crimes, most of which were minor possession violations. But only two states had more serious charges against him. One, in an unlikely connection with a group of art thieves operating in Los Angeles. Ansara fled the area after some Mirós, Picassos, a Jackson Pollack and an original Dali were stolen from a home in Brentwood. He came to Oregon, took a new name, and hid, careful to stay away from Seavy Village's minor drug trade, and managing, somehow, to break off his relations with women before things became too serious.

He hadn't had anything to do with the art heists, had merely stumbled on them in the course of his other shady dealings, and knew, somehow, who was involved. Police assumed he dated one of the thieves, hearing the plans for the Brentwood theft from her. But the heat on that was high, and someone threatened him. When he came to Oregon, he made notes of all he knew, and buried them on Cascade Head.

He had mailed a letter to himself the day he died—obviously he had been worried, perhaps he had seen his killer, a man named Will Garetson. In the letter, Tom explained that he had hidden a box, and how far it was from Highway 101, and he gave a detailed description of the unusual tree and rock formation near the burial site. Unfortunately, he had left out what part of 101 he was talking about. When Patricia—"a private citizen" as the papers called her—had come forward, she had provided the missing piece of information: where exactly the box was. The police looked on Cascade Head at the correct distance from 101, found the distinctive tree and rock formation, and proceeded to dig.

They found the box, and in it, the names of the people involved in the heist, a tape recording with their voices on it planning that heist, and a list of the items that they had hoped to take. Also in the box was a note about the reasons Tom had hidden in Oregon: It wasn't because his conscience had finally gotten to him about the heist or because he had been discovered by the thieves. It was because, on the two jobs the thieves performed before his disappearance, they had killed security guards, and Tom was beginning to fear that killing for sport was becoming the reason behind the heists, not the theft itself.

So he vanished, and it took them a long time to trace him. He made two mistakes: he took a regular job, and he kept the old social security number. Eventually Garetson found him. In fact, the article said, the man who killed Tom had been the self-defense instructor at the gym a few weeks before Tom's death. Because instructors were rarely in the building at the same time, Tom hadn't seen him. Garetson had discovered Tom's routine, where he lived, and who he had offended in Seavy Village and had apparently decided the best way to kill the man was do it at the gym, where all the women he slept with would then become suspects.

It would have worked if it weren't for that letter, and Detective Huckleby, who felt there was something wrong with this case from the beginning.

Patricia read the articles with avid interest, worried when she learned how easy it had been for a killer to infiltrate her small town and target a man, calmer when she realized one of the reasons the man had been targeted was because of his own behavior.

It took a week for the *Oregonian* to print all the articles, but when it was done, and Garetson was in jail awaiting trial, she felt as if it were over. Or at least part of it. She could still remember the touch of his hands on her neck as he held her in place, using her to demonstrate to the rest of the self-defense class how to do the chokehold. When his arm wrapped around her throat, she had thought how easy it would be for him to squeeze, how easy it would be for her to die.

Apparently, he had killed Tom with no struggle. Apparently, she had been right. It had been easy, after all.

***

So she went back to her life, changed as it was. Her brother gave her more responsibility at the IP and she found a jogging partner, a woman whom she had spoken to a few times at the gym and felt an affinity for. They were developing a friendship composed of short conversations followed by a mile or more of gasping silence. She found that she liked talking with someone. She actually looked forward to it.

By the end of the second week, she made it through two days without thinking of Tom. Then Huckleby walked into her office. He leaned against the door, smiled at her, and let his blue eyes draw her in.

"Do you do lunch?" he asked.

"Only on every other Thursday," she said, and was surprised at the tartness of her own reply.

His smile widened into a grin. "I'm buying."

She went with him to the health food restaurant next door. He ordered the only meal with beef in it—a shredded beef taco concoction made with cream cheese instead of sour cream—and she had their homemade tomato soup and fresh sourdough bread.

"You never followed up on the case," he said after the food was served.

"You didn't keep me informed."

He took a bite from the taco, and half the cream cheese fell out. He set the food down. "I was a little busy."

"But you got him," she said.

"We got him. It's up to the L.A. cops to get the rest." He sounded relieved at that.

"More excitement than Seavy Village is used to," she said.

"More than we want," he replied. Then he put an elbow on the table, and watched her. She had never had anyone watch her eat before.

"You know," he said. "In all the times we talked, you never did tell me how you felt about him."

"About Tom?" she asked, stalling. She put her soup spoon down, and picked up the bread, shredding it.

"Yes."

She shrugged. "He was my spinning instructor."

"And?"

There was no harm in telling him now. No harm in saying anything. She felt herself flush. She had to look away. "And I hated him."

He let out a slow whistle, as if he hadn't expected it. "Because he was a drill sergeant?"

She shook her head. The soup was nearly gone. She had made a mess of the bread. There were crumbs on her side of the napkin. She stared at them instead of looking Huckleby in the eye.

"Because of how he looked at me, in the beginning. Like I offended him just by being in his presence."

To her surprise, Huckleby took her hand. She raised her head, saw him looking at her with empathy, not disgust. She wanted to look away, but couldn't.

"Do you know how many times you told me that fat people get treated differently?"

"They do," she said.

"You're no longer fat," he said.

"I always will be." With her free hand she tapped her chest. "Inside. I'll always remember how it feels. Like an alcoholic. I'll always be a fat person crammed into a skinny shell."

"If you want to be," he said. "No one sees you that way any more. No one treats you that way. The loathing I hear when I'm around you comes from you."

He said the words softly, gently, to lessen their sting. But they still hurt. She blinked, startled. No one had ever talked that way to her before. But then, she hadn't let anyone talk to her, really talk to her, for years.

"I don't want to treat anyone else that way," she said.

"But you do," he said. "You assume all the rest of us will look at you with that same disgust that Ansara had, and you hate us in advance."

"I don't hate you," she said.

He smiled and squeezed her hand. "It's a start at least."

"Of what?" she asked.

He shrugged. "I don't know. Friendship, maybe something more. If you're willing."

She had never fantasized about him, not in this way, never imagined what he would sound like in bed, never allowed herself to think a man like this one would even be interested. He was a person to her, not a Greek god who looked down on the less-than-perfect with complete disdain, like Tom had been. Only Tom hadn't been. He had been as imperfect as she was. It just hadn't been apparent from the way he looked, the way he dressed, the way he spoke. Only his eyes had showed it, and only if someone paid attention.

She felt a little floaty hit of adrenaline, like she used get in her early spinning classes after she had been on the bike a while. Just when she thought she would be ready to quit, something in her body would adjust and she would feel slightly dizzy, slightly high. A little afraid and a bit proud of herself at the same time.

Friendship. Something more. If she was willing.

"All right," she said, and squeezed Huckleby's hand.

There was no longer a need for fantasy. The need for fantasy had made her blind to the realities around her. Some of those realities could have harmed her—the arm around her neck, the same arm that had crushed Tom's throat—and others could have helped her, allowed her to see that things were different now, that she was different and perhaps, she always would be.

She was no longer spinning her wheels on a stationary bike. She had been moving forward for a long time; and she had finally noticed.

JURY DUTY

*P*AMELA SAT in the center of the courtroom, not too close to the front because she didn't want to call attention to herself, and not in the back because she didn't want people to think she was hiding. She had done everything she could to blend in: she wore no make-up, and her clothes were Northwest business casual—a pair of brown slacks with an off-white sweater. With her left hand, she fingered her juror number—267—thoughtfully provided on a little wooden keychain so that she wouldn't lose it.

The court clerk pulled numbers out of a box and handed them to the judge. He was balding, and the top of his head shone in the fluorescent lights. His nasal voice boomed through the courtroom without the aid of a microphone, "Five-hundred-and-eighty-one. Five, eight, one."

As the unlucky man rose from his seat on the left side of the courtroom, the remaining members of the jury pool swiveled to watch him walk toward the jury box. Six people sat there already, hands folded, heads down, waiting.

The judge had said they would pick twenty-seven, enough for two juries and three extras. Both juries would listen to the case, although one jury would be designated as "alternate." The remaining three people were alternates also, added protection for a death penalty case that could last over a month.

Pamela had been called up two weeks ago, along with 1,000 others out of this county of 50,000, and she had stood in her kitchen, clutching the letter, feeling an uncomfortable sense of irony.

When she had come to Rickets Rock, a town so small that it seldom showed up on any map, she had decided that she would live as quietly as she could. She didn't want to draw attention to herself, good or bad. That meant getting a driver's license, registering to vote, being a good citizen. It meant concocting a history, and trying to smile at the locals. It meant lying, each and every day.

The jury summons had caught her in the lie: she couldn't back out because she had used a false name on her voter registration form. She had to go along with the fiction that she was Pamela Jackson, and hope that something about Pamela would keep her off the largest and most notorious jury the county had seen in decades.

"Juror thirty-four," the judge said. "Three-four."

A woman two seats from Pamela stood, and nearly tripped as she tried to get out of the row. Pamela kept turning her number over and over, the hard wood edges catching on her fingertips.

She had decided, when she had gone to orientation and received the outrageously long questionnaire, that she wouldn't lie if at all possible: she knew that trying to remember too many lies had tripped up more than one person.

So she had placed her personal views on the pages, thinking that they would disqualify her. Particularly the carefully worded questions on pages 10 through 13, the ones about law, the death penalty, and murder.

Question 33: Do you believe that some acts are so heinous that they can only be punished by death?

To which she had replied: *Yes.*

Question 50: Have you known or are you related to anyone who was murdered?

To which she had replied: *Yes.*

And *Question 117: Do you believe Raymond Northrup is guilty of the crimes of which he has been accused?*

To which she had replied: *I could care less.*

She had felt certain that the defense attorney, going through the questionnaires, would demand she be taken out of the jury pool, especially when she had had to explain her answer to question 50 on a later questionnaire. (*How was the deceased related to you?* Husband; *Explain the circumstances of the death:* He was a jackass. Of course, she didn't write that. Instead, she made up a lie about a beloved uncle who died in a convenience store robbery.)

"Two-sixty-seven," the judge said. "Two, six, seven."

Pamela's hand clenched around the number. She touched her round juror button, pinned to her sweater, and cursed silently. Her luck had abandoned her.

Now her goal was to be dismissed in the voir dire.

She grabbed her book—Patricia Cornwell's treatise on forensics and Jack the Ripper—and slung her purse over her shoulder.

Then Pamela eased out of the row, past the loggers and the truck drivers and the waitresses, and walked, head down, shoulders slumped forward, to the jury box.

Her heart was pounding. She had often pictured herself in a courtroom, but not here, not among the jury.

Instead, she expected to be at the tables, an attorney beside her, defending what was left of her miserable little life.

***

Another half hour went by before the rest of the twenty-seven victims were chosen. Then the questioning began, starting with the first juror picked, a dapper man who was the only person in the room, besides the attorneys, to wear a suit. Fifteen minutes into his voir dire, he was dismissed for claiming he did not have a strong stomach.

As he stepped down, the clerk drew a new number from the box, and another prospective juror took the first juror's place.

Pamela noted the excuse, and apparently so had the second juror. He made the same claim, which caused the judge to issue a gusty sigh.

"If we dismiss everyone with a weak stomach, we'll have no one left." He faced the defense attorney, who had posed the question. "If you believe these crimes are too graphic, we'll make sure there'll be no crime scene photos after lunch and we'll provide sickness bags, just like the airlines. Now, move on."

Pamela was the first up after the luncheon break. She returned to the courtroom loggy from the personal pan she'd had at the nearby Pizza Hut, and exhausted by a morning of listening to other people's lives.

During lunch she had toyed with changing her strategy, possibly saying that she did not approve of the death penalty or that she did not believe a person was innocent until proven guilty. But all of those answers would have contradicted her juror's questionnaire, a questionnaire that had informed her on the top of every page that her answers had the force of answers given under oath.

A new answer would call attention to her. If she was lucky, she would escape without much attention being paid to her at all.

Finally, the attorneys reached her. She had to repeat her name and her address.

"You own a bookstore, Ms. Jackson?" The prosecutor, Daphne Sullivan, stood in front of the jury box. She was a middle-aged woman who wore a stylish black suit that seemed out of place in this small county.

"Yes." Main Street Books, the new-and-used bookstore she had opened in what passed for Rickets Rock's downtown. When she had first received her jury letter, she had hoped that being a small business owner would disqualify her, but the clerk of courts had quizzed her, found out that she had a part-time assistant, and that the store sometimes closed when Pamela planned a day off, and decided that the store could afford to lose Pamela for a few weeks with little or no hardship.

"Do you enjoy reading?" Sullivan asked.

"Yes."

"Do you often read books like that one?" Sullivan nodded at the Cornwell.

"Yes." That was a deliberate lie, one concocted to get Pamela off the jury.

"Would you hold the book up so that everyone can see it?"

Pamela did. Her copy, a hardcover with a shiny dust, looked black and official.

"We won't have to worry about a weak stomach with this one," the judge muttered, even his soft words echoing throughout the courtroom.

"Do you watch *CSI*?" Sullivan asked.

"Sometimes," Pamela said.

"*Cold Case Files*? The forensics programs on The Learning Channel?"

"Sometimes," Pamela said.

"So you feel you have a grasp on the forensic side of police procedure?" Sullivan asked.

Pamela shrugged.

The judge said, "We'll need a verbal response for the record, Ms. Jackson."

"When you say 'a grasp,' I don't know what that means," Pamela said.

"Do you understand it?" Sullivan said.

"It's just science," Pamela said.

"And you understand science?"

Of course, you fool. I have more advanced degrees in biology and chemistry than you can dream up.

Pamela had to bite back the response. She wasn't a scientist now. She owned a bookstore. She was a mousy woman with mousy clothes who tried to disappear when people looked at her.

"I try to understand it," she said, which was as close to the truth as she could come.

"I have no problem with this juror," the prosecutor said, and turned toward the defense attorney, Jake Chivara.

He was too slick for this part of Oregon. His suit had the shine of silk, and his hands were manicured. His black hair had a layered cut that cost more than Pamela's entire outfit, but his eyes shone with an intelligence that she recognized as a match for her own.

He adjusted his suit coat as he walked toward the rail. "Do you consider murder your hobby?"

Her fingers clutched the book, its hard edges biting into her palm. "My *hobby*?"

He nodded toward the book she held. "You read about it. You watch television programs about it. You obviously think about it a lot."

True enough. She didn't like how perceptive he was. "I watch television programs about politics and biography and history, too, but I don't consider them my hobbies. I live alone. I run a bookstore. I read almost everything that comes through the door."

"But you brought that book for a reason, didn't you?" Chivara asked.

"To read while I waited," she said.

"You could have brought a romance novel," he said.

She shrugged. "I would have finished it in the time allowed. I wanted something that would last me all day."

"Be honest, Ms. Jackson. You brought that book so that we'd assume you know police procedure. You wanted to force us to kick you off the jury."

She looked at him in surprise and knew, at that moment, she had been caught. She had never been caught before, at least, not in her manipulations. It was a strange sensation.

Chivara smiled at her. "I don't like being manipulated, Ms. Jackson."

Pamela's hands slid on the book's cover. She was sweating.

"Your questionnaire says you believe that some crimes should be punished by death," Chivara said.

"Yes." She swallowed hard. This was the first time, in all of the questioning, that someone had mentioned the questionnaire.

"Does that mean you believe in the death penalty?" he asked.

"I haven't given it any thought." At least not in that way. The law was the law and she had nothing do with it. She didn't plan it nor could she change it. Human laws weren't immutable like scientific ones, but they existed and nowadays she did her best to live within them.

"Do you have a problem sending a man to his death?" he asked.

"Not in the right circumstances." Her answer had too much of an edge to it. She wished she could take the words back the moment she uttered them.

Chivara smiled again. "What sorts of circumstances, Ms. Jackson?"

Her mouth was dry. "I thought we were talking about the death penalty."

"We are. What circumstances? *These* circumstances?"

"If he did it," she said.

"Do you think he did it?" Chivara asked.

"I could care less," she said, repeating her answer from the questionnaire.

"Really? You don't care one way or another?"

She didn't like this attorney. He was irritating her. "Unless you put me on this jury, this crime has no impact on my life. I don't really care what that man did. I don't really care what the President does either, and he has a lot larger impact on my life than some petty murderer."

"Petty murderer," Chivara repeated softly. "You're quite interesting, Ms. Jackson. You know science and read about the law, but you say this case doesn't concern you. If we put you on the jury, would you care then?"

"Not really," she said. "I'd just be doing this because you're making me."

Chivara's smile became broad. "At least you're honest."

He walked back to his table, examined his notes, and then leaned over the railing, clearly speaking to his jury consultant.

Pamela's heart pounded hard. She tried to keep an impassive expression on her face, but she found it difficult.

For the first time since she'd shown up in this courtroom, she was frightened.

After a moment, Chivara looked up.

"Ms. Jackson, do you know my client?" Chivara swept his arm toward the defendant. Until this moment, Pamela had refrained from looking at him.

She had seen his photograph on the county newspapers and once on the front page of the *Oregonian*, but she hadn't really looked at him. Nor had she looked at him the one or two times he waited on her.

"We've never formally met," she said.

"But you have met," the attorney said.

"He waited on me once at the Sneaker Wave," she said. "And at the Italian Noodle."

"Did you have a conversation?"

She shrugged, then added for the record, "Probably not."

"Probably not?" Chivara repeated.

"I go out alone with a book," she said. "I usually don't have conversations."

Truthful again.

Chivara's eyes narrowed, and she had the sense that he thought she was holding something back.

Chivara turned away, and she hoped he would dismiss her for cause. Instead, he said, "I have no problems with this juror."

The judge turned to her. "Is there any reason you believe you should not sit on this jury?"

Dozens. She had dozens of reasons, but none she could admit to. Neither attorney had given her a way out.

"I don't know if I can be impartial," she said, "given that I've met him."

The judge let out another of his gusty sighs. "The interactions you've had with the defendant are no different than sitting across a courtroom from him day in and day out. So give it a try, Ms. Jackson."

"Your honor," Chivara said, "this is why we wanted the trial moved."

"You made that motion and I dismissed it," the judge said. "If you want to try this case for the court of appeals and not for the jury, go ahead, Mr. Chivara. Otherwise, get over the loss and move on."

Pamela's cheeks were warm. Her ploy hadn't worked, might even have backfired.

"Juror two-six-seven," the judge said, "you'll be sitting on this case."

***

Since it was the off-season, the cut-rate hotel that the court used to sequester juries was happy to have them. The jurors even got to have their own rooms, a luxury for which Pamela was grateful. She didn't like company in the best of circumstances, and this certainly was not the best of circumstances.

That first two days in the courtroom were difficult, especially for the other jurors. The prosecution laid out its case, and the defense gave its own theory of the crime. Most of the jurors were already familiar with the crime, but the details made them squeamish.

Pamela didn't mind the details, but she had trouble wrapping her mind around the crime at all.

Apparently, the defendant, Raymond Northrup, arrived home one afternoon in a rage. He shot his wife, his two daughters, and his infant son, supposedly planning to kill himself as well. In the end, he chickened out (or "came to his senses," as Prosecutor Sullivan said), and called 9-1-1 instead. The paramedics arrived to find a house filled with blood, and Ray Northrup sitting on the couch, watching reruns of *The Simpsons* as if nothing was wrong.

The prosecution promised pictures and the tape of the 9-1-1 call; the defense promised experts showing how the police botched the investigation, figuring that they already had the killer when, of course, the defense claimed, they had not.

Pamela listened with—she thought—clinical detachment, picturing both versions of the crime: a man pushed to his limits by bills, sick children and a nagging wife, hauling the shotgun out of the front closet and turning it on all of them; and the same man pushed to his limits, who arrived home after a hard day's work as a waiter (he could get nothing else in this small town) to find his entire family slaughtered.

But the clinical detachment didn't take, or perhaps it was a façade, designed to fool even herself. For that night, and two nights thereafter, Pamela had the nightmare, the one she had fled when she had come to Oregon.

The images were jumbled: Jason stumbling backwards, his hand up; Jason on the floor, his face gone; Jason's blood staining the wall beside their stove. She started to grab things—her ring, his watch, their checkbook, and then she set them down.

She knew better—even her dreamself knew better—and instead, she took the cash from the drawer, and the bike leaning against the old Billingsly house next door.

More images from before: the water from the shower draining pink; her clothing in the washing machine, the smell of bleach in the air; the half-eaten ham sandwich that had started it all.

She had been clutching it, trying to force it down, when he had walked in. *You can't do anything right*, she had said to him. *I wanted hot mustard, not sweet. Don't you ever listen?*

His voice, meek and soft, infuriated her, and at that moment, she woke up, covered in sweat, shaking, uncertain where she was, figuring at first it was some anonymous hotel on the trip west, then remembering how she had gotten herself into this new predicament years after the fact.

The hotel looked the same as the others: a double-bed barely bigger than the single she'd had in her first apartment; end-tables so cheap that if she leaned on them, they'd crack; a television set bolted to the dresser, and a double-size window with a single pane of glass so thin that it could shatter with the pressure of a determined fist.

Pamela got up and paced, her feet cold against the worn carpet. She was glad she was alone—who knew what she had cried out, what she had actually said?

That first night, she didn't go back to the bed, sleeping instead on the scratchy sofa, an equally scratchy blanket pulled over her scrunched-up form. She didn't sleep much and when she did, she dreamed of being uncomfortable, not of the past.

And she returned to that couch after every day of difficult testimony, after every photograph and replaying of the 9-1-1 call, until the clinical detachment she thought she had achieved that first day became an actual reality.

She could listen, store facts, theories, and opinions in one side of her brain, and kept them separate from the other side.

The emotion side.

The side that had always given her too much trouble.

***

Three-plus weeks of testimony, arguments, breaks and confusion. Three-plus weeks of "retiring" to the jury room to wait while the lawyers and the judge worked something out. Three-plus weeks of small talk with people who probably never would have entered her store, people who probably hadn't voluntarily picked up a book in their lives, people who—with the exception of the transplanted Californian—had never lived anywhere but here.

Small minds with nothing but television and the trial to occupy them. Talk of the trial was off-limits until the testimony was over, so the Small Minds discussed the previous night's *Frasier* or the *Buffy* rerun or the late-night movie they were given on tape so they wouldn't watch the local news and talk shows.

She didn't watch any of it. She didn't discuss any of it either, preferring to read. The guards—at least they felt like guards—let her assistant deliver books, sometimes four and five a day, and Pamela read rather than socialized. So long as her mind was busy, her body remained calm.

The guards would paw through the bags, of course, verifying that everything Pamela's assistant brought were books, verifying that her assistant hadn't hid a newspaper article about the trial as a bookmark, verifying that there was no note advising her how to vote at the end of the trial.

But no one looked at the titles either. She finished the Cornwell, moved onto a history of the fingerprint, then followed that with a history of the corpse. A few tomes on forensics, a study of ballistics, and of course, dozens and dozens of novels—all shapes and sizes.

She read and thought and listened, and wished she had known all of this years ago, before she had come west. She would have done things oh so very differently. How easy it would have been to make it seem like *he* had gotten angry over the sandwich, *he* had hit her repeatedly, *he* had grabbed the gun.

But she hadn't known any of it. She had done the best she could with the little bits of knowledge she had, and she had managed to escape.

She lived here now, a new life she mostly enjoyed, and saw no use re-evaluating every second of the past.

***

Then, finally, the moment arrived. The closing arguments ended, the jury instructions were repeated *ad nauseum*, the defendant staring at jurors as if he were trying to fathom what each and every one of them were thinking.

This time, when they went into the jury room, there was a palpable sense of relief. The restrictions were off: they could discuss anything now, and the Small Minds all started to talk at once, offering opinions, offering advice, discussing what an ordeal they'd been through, how they couldn't stand the pictures.

Pamela couldn't stand the voices. Middle-class, grating, most of them with that slightly dulled speech she'd learned to recognize from locals. She sat in one of the upholstered chairs nearest the door, and wondered how she would get through this.

The jury room itself was small with two exits—one leading back into the courtroom, the other into the hallway. The room had no windows. Whoever had designed this room had certainly visited and obviously enjoyed the ambiance of hell's anteroom, because even the temperature was correct: hot enough to make the already small space seem unbearably stuffy.

"Right, Ms. Jackson?"

She heard her name and looked up. The transplanted Californian was looking at her. He was a wiry blond with a scraggly mustache whose rope-thin body and denim shirt made him look like a man who belonged outdoors, not trapped in a room furnished with modular office chairs and a cheap fake-wood conference table.

"I'm sorry," she said, peering at his name badge. Z. Wilson. She should have learned his name in the past few weeks. She should have learned all of their names, but of course, she hadn't.

"I said, I think we should get around to electing a foreman first, then talk about the case. What do you think?" His blue eyes studied her with an openness she didn't like. Obviously he expected her to be on his side.

"Looks like you're already doing a fine job," she said. "We don't need a vote."

"We'll vote." His voice had that irritated edge Jason used to get when she didn't give him the answer he liked.

She leaned back in her chair, deciding to give Z. Wilson some distance.

The woman who wore the giant silver cross on the front of her blouse each and every day reached to the center of the table and took twelve little pieces of paper from a notepad. Then she grabbed pencils and handed them out as if she were a school teacher.

She gave Pamela her paper and pencil last, smiling at her. Pamela did not smile back.

"Perhaps," said the Silver Cross, "perhaps we should say a small prayer so that God will guide our work."

"A small prayer?" Pamela asked, unable to keep silent in the face of this new irritation. "What kind of guidance do you want? Dearest God, please let us know if you want this killer to go free or if you want the state to fry him. Amen."

"Ms. Jackson," said the Californian. "That's enough."

She shrugged and pressed her lips together, but she had made her point. Two of the Small Minds who hadn't said anything yet—the first man chosen, and one of the other women—glared at Pamela as if she had killed the three children and the namby-pamby wife.

The wife, quite frankly, sounded like she deserved it, but the kids, well, Pamela didn't believe in killing kids. Kids couldn't be blamed for the situations they found themselves in. Only the parents were responsible for that.

"Write down the name of the person you think most suited for jury foreman," the Californian said. "Then put your paper in this little bowl next to the notepad. Don't sign your name."

"Why don't we just have a real election?" Pamela asked, clutching her pencil. "You and whoever else is enough of a control freak to want this idiot job?"

"You mean you?" another Small Mind asked.

"I don't want it," Pamela said.

"Vote for whomever you'd like," the Californian said.

Pamela sighed and shook her head. Then she wrote down *Z. Wilson: Because I believe in validating power grabs*, folded the paper into tiny squares and set it in the bowl.

Hers was the sixth. One Small Mind—a twenty-something man who was already going bald—chewed his pencil and looked from person to person before writing on his paper. He was the eleventh to put his vote in the bowl. The Silver Cross lady was the last, and she looked spooked.

"Mr. Acenan," the Californian said to yet another Small Mind, "would you mind reading the results? Mrs. Dunbar will tally them."

The Dunbar woman took another sheet of paper from the stack and held her pencil poised. The man dug inside the bowl, removed a piece of paper and read the results aloud.

Pamela wished she could take the book out of her purse. Who would've thought that average citizens would take this job so very seriously?

The Small Mind reading the papers had finally gotten to Pamela's. He glanced at her, his face flushed, and only read the name, not the commentary.

"You know," Pamela said mildly, "censorship is against the law."

"And you're a disgrace," the Small Mind said, still clutching her paper. "Can't you be serious about this?"

She thought of answering him honestly, but she knew the word "no" would piss him off. So she said, "I just want to get down to business. I've already lost a month of my life to this mess. I don't want to lose another one because you people dither."

"An election isn't dithering, Ms. Jackson," the Californian said.

"You've already taken over," Pamela said. "Why do we have to bother with the election?"

"Because," the Californian said, "it's part of the instructions. See? Item four. Elect a jury foreperson."

"You said foreman before. Can I change my vote?" Pamela asked. "I didn't consider any women."

Someone made a sound of disgust. Mrs. Dunbar said loudly, "We already have a majority for Mr. Wilson. So he is our foreperson, unless there's an objection."

Pamela almost objected, just out of spite. She had to entertain herself somehow. But she was beginning to realize that her own antics might prolong this already painful situation, so she said nothing.

She crossed her arms and listened to Mr. California-Wilson read the jury instructions that the judge had already read to them, then ask if there were any questions that needed discussion or clarification before they got down to the "nitty-gritty."

Everyone said no, except Pamela, of course, who really didn't like the grade-school way this deliberation session was turning out. But she had decided to be quiet, and so she would be. She listened, or pretended to, while the jury discussed the rules, then reviewed the rules, and then discussed them even more.

Finally, at four o'clock, Mr. California-Wilson suggested that they take a preliminary vote—gosh! Just like the instructions suggested!—to see how far apart they all were. The vote would be anonymous, of course, and all the little pieces of paper would go into that damn bowl again.

She put her little piece of paper on top of her book, a novel called *A Certain Justice* which Pamela had chosen more out of irony than interest, and then paused.

She really hadn't given the fate of Mr. Raymond Northrup much thought, although she had done her part.

She had listened, without prejudice and with that hard-won clinical detachment, to days and days of repetitive testimony, to argumentative lawyers and bad judicial rulings, to witnesses who hadn't known a damn thing and to witnesses who believed they had.

She had listened, she had absorbed, and she had come to no conclusion.

Yet they were asking her for one now. And if she was going to be the good citizen she was pretending to be, she had to give a real opinion. She supposed finding him guilty would get her out of here the quickest. After all, that was what the Small Minds seemed to believe, if their post-trial conversation was any indication.

But she couldn't write *guilty* on her piece of paper. Her hand froze over the page every single time. She was stunned to discover that the decision really did matter to her.

After all, she could have been the person sitting next to Chivara. She could have been pacing some jail cell right now, wondering if 12 disparate people would sentence her to a lifetime of imprisonment. She owed Northrup as much consideration as she had, mostly because she hoped someone would give her the same consideration if (when?) her time came.

She bit her lower lip, then glanced up at the bowl. It looked full. A number of the Small Minds were staring at her again.

Her hand shook over the paper. She gripped the pencil tightly and wrote *Not*, leaving off the guilty. She didn't want Mr. California-Wilson to misconstrue her intent.

She folded her piece of paper in half this time, just like everyone else had, and then she shoved it into the bowl. The Silver Cross woman grabbed it and handed it to California-Wilson as if he weren't capable of grabbing it himself.

He nodded toward the Dunbar woman and she got out yet another piece of paper so that she could tally the results.

Pamela expected more than one not-guilty vote. After all, it was pretty obvious that Northrup didn't have the balls to kill his entire family, no matter how angry and frustrated he got.

But she was the only not-guilty. California-Wilson tried not to ask for names, but she knew they'd find out, so she admitted it.

And that was when the clerk of the courts arrived, and told them to break for the night.

***

The next morning, the Small Minds had game plan ready. They were going to review the evidence to convince her.

"Don't you want to know why I think he didn't do it?" Pamela asked.

"It doesn't matter what you think," Silver Cross said. "You obviously didn't care enough to listen."

"I listened," Pamela said. "I even made notes every evening. Did you people bother doing that?"

No one answered her. No one even looked at her.

"Look," she said. "I could change my vote so that we could get the hell out of here. Lord knows, I don't ever want to see you people again. But I don't think this guy did it, and I'm not going to send him to jail just because I want to sleep in my own bed tonight."

She was rather proud of herself. She sounded like a Real Citizen, like someone who cared about her fellow man.

"So," Mr. California-Wilson said with a notable lack of interest, "why do you think he didn't do it?"

"Because," Pamela said, careful to keep her tone respectful and polite, "he didn't run."

"Most people know better than to run," Wilson said.

"Most people know better than to kill their families," one of the Small Minds muttered.

"What?" Mrs. Dunbar asked.

The man shrugged. "I'm just saying if you're going to apply that kind of logic, then the whole case all falls apart."

The Small Minds argued among themselves for a long time, apparently forgetting that Pamela was the one they had to convince to change her mind. For a while, she thought she had convinced a few of them, but no.

They simply liked arguing.

And another day went by without any progress at all.

***

The week blurred into a series of questions and answers, followed by arguments.

"Ms. Jackson," someone asked at one point, "how can you think he didn't do it? He was covered in blood."

"So was the house," she said. "Didn't you look at the pictures? He sat on the couch, by his own admission. It was soaked in blood. Maybe he even hugged one of the kids like the defense attorney said. What would you do if you came home to your entire family dead?"

Of course, during the ensuing argument, she didn't say that she wouldn't have hugged a dead kid. But the arguments were never really about her, anyway.

"Ms. Jackson," one of the Small Minds said long about day three, "he told everybody at work that he was on edge, that he felt like he was going to explode. It's pretty clear that he did."

"Hell," she snapped. "I'm on edge. Does that mean I'm going to go on a rampage and kill you all to calm myself?"

It sounded tempting, but she knew better. She hadn't hurt anyone—deliberately—since she washed her husband's blood off her skin five years ago.

"Ms. Jackson," the Silver Cross idiot said to her on day five, "who else could have killed that family? Nothing was stolen and no one else even knew them, so no one else had a reason to kill them."

"You mean someone has a reason to kill an infant?" Pamela snapped. She ignored the wife. The wife bothered her. Pamela would have killed the wife given half a chance. Just because the woman hadn't been happy with her reproductive choices and her husband's inability to earn a living didn't give her the right to whine all the damn time.

Like these people were doing. The room really had to be bigger, much bigger, so that Pamela could pace.

She was alone and remained alone on this not-guilty thing. Even when she convinced the entire jury to go back into the courtroom and listen to the read-back of some testimony about the way that Northrup was found. His voice on the 9-1-1 tape, filled with emotion (she knew from personal experience that after killing someone, the emotion drained away), and the way he sat on that couch—as one cop put it—like he had nothing left to live for.

Ten days. Ten days they argued and fought and screamed at each other. (She didn't scream. She hated raised voices.) And they couldn't make her change her mind.

Ten days and three hours. The lunch break was when Mr. California-Wilson, whom she'd taken to calling the remaining Beach Boy to his face because he irritated her, knocked on the court-side door, and told the clerk that the jury was hung.

***

Fascinating word, hung. Past tense of "hang," an active but unhappy word which meant to suspend or to die by hanging or to deadlock. All of those meanings had a little murder in them.

Just a little.

She had committed a killing after all.

And like the one she had committed before, she hadn't given it much thought until she actually completed the act. By then, the deed was done and she had to deal with it. It simply felt wrong to change her mind, as if she had lost a principle or something.

So when the judge polled the jurors—all of them, including her—and asked if there was any way to resolve the deadlock, she had spoken a forceful no.

The judge had no choice but to release the jury from its duty. The case was over, and the prosecutor had lost by one vote. The defense didn't cheer, although Northrup had looked for someone—anyone—to hug and got no volunteers.

Pamela filed back into the jury room with the Small Minds, happy she would never see them again, collected her things, and left the courthouse.

She had to go to the hotel to pack, and then she would be able to go home. Packing took longer than she expected—she had lived in this dive for nearly two months—and when it was over, she found that she would actually miss the place.

She'd learned to sleep in the bed, finally feeling like the ghost of Jason and his hideous death were behind her. The nightmare, completely gone.

It was almost as if she had been on trial and had forgiven herself.

The drive from the hotel to Rickets Rock took her past the courthouse. The cameras and crowds were gone. The place looked almost deserted. She was nearly past it when she realized that she had left her book inside.

She almost thought of donating it, then changed her mind.

She had donated enough to this stupid cause already.

She parked in the lot, just like she had on that very first day, and went inside by the front door. The anteroom was empty except for one of the court employees, sitting behind a counter.

The employee looked up, and clearly didn't recognize her. Pamela had taken off her juror button the moment they had been excused.

"May I help you?"

"I was on the Northrup jury," Pamela said, "and I left a book in the jury room."

The employee swiveled her chair, looked behind her, and reached down, lifting *A Certain Justice.* "This it?"

It was. Pamela had never summoned enough energy to read it. She thanked the woman, took the book, and turned.

"Ms. Jackson?"

The familiar voice sent a shiver through her. She looked over her shoulder. "Mr. Chivara. I thought you'd be off celebrating with your client."

Chivara smiled. It wasn't that predatory smile he used in court, but a rather wistful one. "I had a few things to get out of the courtroom. I see you did too."

She nodded, tucked the book under her arm, and started to leave. He kept pace with her.

"I understand you're the one who hung my jury," he said.

"So?" she asked.

"So," he said as he pushed open the door leading outside, "it surprised me."

"I'm sure it didn't, counselor," she said. "You picked me for some reason and it wasn't my good looks."

He laughed. The sound echoed across the empty street. "That's true. I thought you'd help my client, but not in this part of the case."

She stopped. "What does that mean?"

"It means, Ms. Jackson, we found that you lied on your jury questionnaire."

She felt cold. She knew better than to say anything. If she confirmed or denied, she would play right into his little game, whatever it was.

"And since we found that out, we figured we could use you as the basis for our appeal."

"You planned an appeal?" she asked.

"Every good defense attorney keeps one eye on the current case, and one eye on appeal. You were my ace-in-the-hole."

"I was your ace-in-the-hole when you picked me?"

"Now that wouldn't be quite right, now would it?" This time he gave her the predatory smile. "Of course, no one can prove when we learned that you didn't have a murdered uncle. Nor can they prove when we discovered that Pamela Jackson isn't your real name."

Her chill increased.

"Lying on a jury questionnaire is perjury, Ms. Jackson," Chivara said, "and I'm an officer of the court. Technically, I can't let you get away with that."

She forced herself to breathe. Then she turned around. "I can't say anything to you. You're accusing me and doing it in a do-you-beat-your-wife fashion."

"Am I?" he asked, his arms crossed.

"Besides," she said because she had to, because she couldn't keep silent, "if I did lie, and you discovered it, are you going to serve your client by reporting it? After all, I did hang your jury."

Chivara studied her for a long moment. "If I were still prosecuting, I'd already have you for identity fraud, and perjury. If I keep digging, what else would I find?"

A trail of temper, which had ceased. She had found her own kind of peace here in Seavy County.

"I like fiction, Mr. Chivara," she said. "We established that on the day of jury selection."

"You like crime dramas, Ms. Jackson," he said. "We never established that you liked only fiction."

She remembered the feeling she'd had that first day in the courtroom—that he was the only worthy adversary she had ever found. He was as smart as she was, which was a problem.

"We never established what lengths you'll go to in order to win a case," she said softly. "Looks like we'll learn that one today."

Then she turned around and headed down the steps to her car, feeling his gaze on her back. She half-expected to hear his footsteps following her, to feel his hand grab her arm, to pull her back and take her into that courtroom.

She'd be the one going to jail, and then she'd be the one going to trial, defended by someone like Chivara. Just like she'd imagined.

Just like she'd feared for the past five years.

But Chivara didn't follow her down the stairs. In fact, when she got into her car, and looked out the window, he was still watching her.

He had to choose between letting the client he had clearly thought guilty (after all, why else scheme for the appeal?) go free or letting a woman who had changed her identity and committed at least two small crimes that he knew of go free.

Poor Mr. Chivara. Such choices he had.

Such choices she had. Did she stay and pretend like nothing happened, trust the bastard to do what was in his best interest? Or did she run, again, losing all the money she'd put into her store and her home?

She clutched the key to her car. People who ran were guilty: she had argued that in the jury room, and her argument would come back to him. He'd know she'd done something.

But if she stayed, he'd have only his own conscious to wrestle with.

As a good defense attorney, he did that each and every day.

She put the key in the ignition and started the car. Chivara was still watching her.

She waved at him as she drove out of the parking lot.

Away from the courtroom and juries and the law.

Screw Chivara and his suspicions. She was going back to her store, her home and her life, her solitary life as a model citizen, a woman who did her duty and nothing more, just like everybody else.

THE PERFECT MAN

*P*AIGE RACETTE STARED at herself in the full-length mirror, hands on hips. Golden cap of blond hair expertly curled, narrow chin, high cheekbones, china blue eyes, and a little too much of a figure—thanks to the fact she spent most of her day on her butt and sometimes (usually!) forgetting to exercise. The black cocktail dress with its swirling party skirt hid most of the excess, and the glittering beads around the collar brought attention to her face, always and forever her best asset.

Even with the extra pounds, she was not blind date material. Never had been. Until she quit her day job at the television station, she'd had to turn men away. Ironic that once she became a best-selling romance writer, she couldn't get a date to save her life. Part of the problem was that after she quit, she moved to San Francisco where she'd always wanted to live. She bought a Queen Anne in an old, exclusive neighborhood, set up her office in the bay windows of the second floor, and decided she was in heaven.

Little did she realize that working at home would isolate her, and being in a new city would isolate her more. It had taken her a year to make friends—mostly women, whom she met at the gym not too far from her home.

She saw interesting men, but didn't speak to them. She was still a small town girl at heart, one who was afraid of the kind of men who lurked in the big city, who believed that the only way to meet the right man was after getting to know him through mutual interests—or mutual friends.

In fact, she wouldn't have agreed to this blind date if a friend hadn't convinced her. Sally Myer was her racquetball partner and general confidant who seemed to know everyone in this city. She'd finally tired of Paige's complaining and set her up.

Paige slid on her high heels. Who'd ever thought she'd get this desperate? And then she sighed. She wasn't desperate. She was lonely.

And surely, there was no shame in that.

***

Sally had picked the time and location, and had told Paige to dress up. Sally wasn't going to introduce them. She felt that would be tacky and make the first meeting uncomfortable. She asked Paige for a photograph to give to the blind date— one Josiah Wells—and then told Paige that he would find her.

The location was an upscale restaurant near the Opera House. It was The Place To Go at the moment—famous chef, famous food, and one of those bars that looked like it had come out of a movie set—large and open where Anyone Who Was Someone could see and be seen.

Paige arrived five minutes early, habitually prompt even when she didn't want to be. She adjusted the white pashmina shawl she'd wrapped around her bare shoulders and scanned the bar before she went in.

It was all black and chrome, with black tinted mirrors and huge black vases filled with calla lilies separating the booths. The bar itself was black marble and behind it, bottles of liquor pressed against an untinted mirror, making the place look even bigger than it was.

She had only been here once before, with her Hollywood agent and a movie producer who was interested in her second novel. He didn't buy it—the rights went to another studio for high six figures—but he had bought her some of her most memorable meals in the City by the Bay.

She sat at the bar and ordered a Chardonnay which she didn't plan on touching—she wanted to keep her wits about her this night. Even with Sally's recommendation, Paige didn't trust a man she had never met before. She'd heard too many bad stories.

Of course, all the ones she'd written were about people who saw each other across a crowded room and knew at once that they were soul mates. She had never experienced love at first sight (and sometimes she joked to her editor that it was lust at first sight) but she was still hopeful enough to believe in it.

She took the cool glass of Chardonnay that the bartender handed her and swiveled slightly in her chair so that she would be in profile, not looking anxious, but visible enough to be recognizable. And as she did, she saw a man enter the bar.

He was tall and broad-shouldered, wearing a perfectly tailored black suit that shimmered like silk. He wore a white scarf around his neck—which on him looked like the perfect fashion accent—and a red rose in his lapel. His dark hair was expertly styled away from his chiseled features, and she felt her breath catch.

Lust at first sight. It was all she could do to keep from grinning at herself.

He appeared to be looking for someone. Finally, his gaze settled on her, and he smiled.

Something about that smile didn't quite fit on his face. It was too personal. And then she shook the feeling away. She didn't want to be on a blind date—that was all. She had been fantasizing, the way she did when she was thinking of her books, and she was simply caught off guard. No man was as perfect as her heroes. No man could be, not and still be human.

Although this man looked perfect. His rugged features were exactly like ones she had described in her novels.

He crossed the room, the smile remaining, hand extended. "Paige Racette? I'm Josiah Wells."

His voice was high and a bit nasal. She took his hand, and found the palm warm and moist.

"Nice to meet you," she said, removing her hand as quickly as possible.

He wore tinted blue contacts, and the swirling lenses made his eyes seem shiny, a little too intense. In fact, everything about him was a little too intense. He leaned too close, and he seemed too eager. Perhaps he was just as nervous as she was.

"I have reservations here if you don't mind," he said.

"No, that's fine."

He extended his arm—the perfect gentleman—and she took the elbow in her hand, trying to remember the last time a man had done that for her. Her father maybe, when they went to the father-daughter dinner at her church back when she was in high school. And not one man since.

Although all the men in her books did it. When she wrote about it, the gesture seemed to have an old-fashioned elegance. In real life, it made her feel awkward.

He led her through the bar, placing one hand possessively over hers. This exact scene had happened in her first novel, *Beneath a Lover's Moon*. Fabian Garret and Skye Michaels had met, exchanged a few words, and were suddenly walking together like lovers. And Skye had thrilled to Fabian's touch.

Paige wished Josiah Wells's fingers weren't so clammy.

He led them to the maitre d', gave his name, and let the maitre d' lead them to a table near the back. See and Be Seen. Apparently they weren't important enough.

"I asked for a little privacy," he said, as if reading her thoughts. "I hope you don't mind."

She didn't. She had never liked the display aspect of this restaurant anyway.

The table was in a secluded corner. Two candles burned on silver candlesticks and the table was strewn with miniature carnations. A magnum of champagne cooled in a silver bucket, and she didn't have to look at the label to know that it was Dom Perignon.

The hair on the back of her neck rose. This was just like another scene in *Beneath a Lover's Moon*.

Josiah smiled down at her and she made herself smile at him. Maybe he thought her books were a blueprint to romancing her. She would have said so not five minutes before.

He pulled out her chair, and she sat, letting her shawl drape around her. As Josiah sat across from her, the maitre d' handed her the leather bound menu and she was startled to realize it had no prices on it. A lady's menu. She hadn't seen one of those in years. The last time she had eaten here had been lunch, not dinner, and she had remembered the prices on the menu from that meal. They had nearly made her choke on her water.

A waiter poured the champagne and left discretely, just like the maitre d' did. Josiah was watching her, his gaze intense.

She knew she had to say something. She was going to say how nice this was but she couldn't get the lie through her lips. Instead she said as warmly as she could, "You've read my books."

If anything, his gaze brightened. "I adore your books."

She made herself smile. She had been hoping he would say no, that Sally had been helping him all along.

Instead, the look in his eyes made her want to push her chair even farther from the table. She had seen that look a hundred times at book signings: the too-eager fan who would easily monopolize all of her time at the expense of everyone else in line; the person who believed that his connection with the author—someone he hadn't met—was so personal that she felt the connection too.

"I didn't realize that Sally told you I wrote."

"She didn't have to. When I found out that she knew you, I asked her for an introduction."

An introduction at a party would have done nicely, where Paige could smile at him, listen for a polite moment, and then ease away. But Sally hadn't known Paige that long, and didn't understand the difficulties a writer sometimes faced. Writers rarely got recognized in person—it wasn't their faces that were famous after all but their names—but when it happened, it could become as unpleasant as it was for athletes or movie stars.

"She didn't tell me you were familiar with my work," Paige said, ducking her head behind the menu.

"I asked her not to. I wanted this to be a surprise." He was leaning forward, his manicured hand outstretched.

She looked at his fingers, curled against the linen tablecloth, carefully avoiding the miniature carnations, and wondered if his skin was still clammy.

"Since you know what I do," she continued in that too-polite voice she couldn't seem to shake, "why don't you tell me about yourself?"

"Oh," he said, "there isn't much to tell."

And then he proceeded to describe his work with a software company. She only half listened, staring at the menu, wondering if there was an easy—and polite—way to leave this meal, knowing there was not. She would make the best of it, and call Sally the next morning, warning her not to do this ever again.

"Your books," he was saying, "made me realize that women looked at men the way that men looked at women. I started to exercise and dress appropriately and I…"

She looked over the menu at him, noting the suit again. It must have been silk, and he wore it the way her heroes wore theirs. Right down to the scarf, and the rose in the lapel. The red rose, a symbol of true love from her third novel, *Without Your Love.*

That shiver ran through her again.

This time he noticed. "Are you all right?"

"Fine," she lied. "I'm just fine."

***

Somehow she made it through the meal, feeling her skin crawl as he used phrases from her books, imitated the gestures of her heroes, and presumed an intimacy with her that he didn't have. She tried to keep the conversation light and impersonal, but it was a battle that she really didn't win.

Just before the dessert course, she excused herself and went to the ladies room. After she came out, she asked the maitre d' to call her a cab, and then to signal her when it arrived. He smiled knowingly. Apparently he had seen dates end like this all too often.

She took her leave from Josiah just after they finished their coffees, thanking him profusely for a memorable evening. And then she escaped into the night, thankful that she had been careful when making plans. He didn't have her phone number and address. As she slipped into the cracked backseat of the cab, she promised herself that on the next blind date—if there was another blind date—she would make it drinks only. Not dinner. Never again.

***

The next day, she and Sally met for lattes at an overpriced touristy café on the Wharf. It was their usual spot—a place where they could watch crowds and not be overheard when they decided to gossip.

"How did you meet him?" Paige asked as she adjusted her wrought iron café chair.

"Fundraisers, mostly," Sally said. She was a petite redhead with freckles that she didn't try to hide. From a distance, they made her look as if she were still in her twenties. "He was pretty active in local politics for a while."

"Was?"

She shrugged. "I guess he got too busy. I ran into him in Tower Records a few weeks ago, and we got to talking. That's what made me think of you."

"What did?"

Sally smiled. "He was holding one of your books, and I thought, he's wealthy. You're wealthy. He was complaining about how isolating his work was and so were you."

"Isolating? He works for a software company."

"Worked," Sally said. "He's a consultant now, and only when he needs to be. I think he just manages his investments, mostly."

Paige frowned. Had she heard him wrong then? She wasn't paying much attention, not after she had seen the carnations and champagne.

Sally was watching her closely. "I take it things didn't go well."

"He's just not my type."

"Rich? Good-looking? Good God, girl, what is your type?"

Paige smiled. "He's a fan."

"So? Wouldn't that be more appealing?"

Maybe it should have been. Maybe she had overreacted. She had psyched herself out a number of time about the strange men in the big city. Maybe her overactive imagination—the one that created all the stories that had made her wealthy—had finally betrayed her.

"No," Paige said. "Actually, it's less appealing. I sort of feel like he has photos of me naked and has studied them up close."

"I didn't think books were that personal. I mean, you write romance. That's fantasy, right? Make-believe?"

Paige's smile was thin. It was make-believe. But make-believe on any level had a bit of truth to it, even when little children were creating scenarios with Barbie dolls.

"I just don't think we were compatible," Paige said. "I'm sorry."

Sally shrugged again. "No skin off my nose. You're the one who doesn't get out much. Have you ever thought of going to those singles dinners? They're supposed to be a pretty good place to meet people…"

Paige let the advice slip off her, knowing that she probably wouldn't discuss her love life—or lack of it—with Sally again. Paige had been right in the first place: she simply didn't have the right attitude to be a good blind date. There was probably nothing wrong with Josiah Wells. He had certainly gone to a lot of trouble to make sure she had a good time, and she had snuck off as soon as she could.

And if she couldn't be satisfied with a good-looking wealthy man who was trying to please her, then she wouldn't be satisfied with any other blind date either. She had to go back to that which she knew worked. She had to go about her life normally, and hope that someday, an interesting guy would cross her path.

"…even go to AA to find dates. I mean, that's a little crass, don't you think?"

Paige looked at Sally, and realized she hadn't heard most of Sally's monologue. "You know what? Let's forget about men. It's a brand-new century and I have a great life. Why do we both seem to think that a man will somehow improve that?"

Sally studied her for a moment. "You know what I think? I think you've spent so much time making up the perfect man that no flesh-and-blood guy will measure up."

And then she changed the subject, just like Paige had asked.

***

As Paige drove home, she found herself wondering if Sally was right. After all, Paige hadn't dated anyone since she quit her job. And that was when she really spent most of her time immersed in imaginary romance. Her conscious brain knew that the men she made up were too perfect to be real. But did her subconscious? Was that what was preventing her from talking to men she'd seen at the opera or the theater? Was all this big city fear she'd been thinking about simply a way of preventing herself from remembering that men were as human—and as imperfect—as she was?

She almost had herself convinced as she parked her new VW Bug on the hill in front of her house. She set the emergency brake and then got out, grabbing her purse as she did.

She had a lot of work to do, and she had wasted most of the day obsessing about her unsatisfying blind date. It was time to return to work—a romantic suspense novel set on a cruise ship. She had done a mountain of research for the book—including two cruises—one to Hawaii in the winter, and another to Alaska in the summer. The Alaska trip was the one she had decided to use, and she had spent part of the spring in Juneau.

By the time she had reached the front porch, she was already thinking of the next scene she had to write. It was a description of Juneau, a city that was perfect for her purposes because there was only two ways out of it: by air or by sea. The roads ended just outside of town. The mountains hemmed everything in, trapping people, good and bad, hero and villain, within their steep walls.

She was so lost in her imagination that she nearly tripped over the basket sitting on her porch.

She bent down to look at it. Wrapped in colored cellophane, it was nearly as large as she was, and was filled with flowers, chocolates, wine and two crystal wine goblets. In the very center was a photo in a heart-shaped gold frame. She peered at it through the wrapping and then recoiled.

It was a picture of her and Josiah at dinner the night before, looking, from the outside, like a very happy couple.

Obviously he had hired someone to take the picture. Someone who had watched them the entire evening, and waited for the right moment to snap the shot. That was unsettling. And so was the fact that Josiah had found her house. She was unlisted in the phonebook, and on public records, she used her first name—Giacinta—with no middle initial. And although her last name was unusual, there were at least five other Racettes listed. Had Josiah sent a basket to every one of them, hoping that he'd find the right one and she'd call him?

Or had he had her followed?

The thought made her look over her shoulder. Maybe there was someone on the street now, watching her, wondering how she would react to this gift.

She didn't want to bring it inside, but she felt like she had no choice. She suddenly felt quite exposed on the porch.

She picked up the basket by its beribboned handle and unlocked her door. Then she stepped inside, closed the door as her security firm had instructed her, and punched in her code. Her hands were shaking.

On impulse, she reset the perimeter alarm. She hadn't done that since she moved in, had thought it a silly precaution.

It didn't seem that silly any more.

She set the basket on the deacons bench she had near the front door. Then she fumbled through the ribbon to find the card which she knew had to be there.

Her name was on the envelope in calligraphed script, but the message inside was typed on the delivery service's card.

Two hearts, perfectly meshed.
Two lives, perfectly twined.
Is it luck that we have found each other?
Or does Fate divine a way for perfect matches to meet?

Those were her words. The stilted words of Quinn Ralston, the hero of her sixth novel, a man who finally learned to free the poetry locked in his soul.

"God," she whispered, so creeped out that her hands felt dirty just from touching the card. She picked up the basket and carried it to the back of the house, setting it in the entryway where she kept her bundled newspapers.

She supposed most women would keep the chocolates, flowers, and wine even if they didn't like the man who sent them. But she wasn't most women. And the photograph bothered her more than she could say.

She locked the interior door, then went to the kitchen and scrubbed her hands until they were raw.

***

Somehow she managed to escape to the Juneau of her imagination, working furiously in her upstairs office, getting nearly fifteen pages done before dinner. Uncharacteristically, she closed the drapes, hiding the city view she had paid so much for. She didn't want anyone looking in.

She was cooking herself a taco salad out of Bite-sized Tostitos and bagged shredded lettuce when the phone rang, startling her. She went to answer it, and then some instinct convinced her not to. Instead, she went to her answering machine and turned up the sound.

"Paige? If you're there, please pick up. It's Josiah." He paused and she held her breath. She hadn't given him this number. And Sally had said that morning that she hadn't given Paige's unlisted number to anyone. "Well, um, you're probably working and can't hear this."

A shiver ran through her. He knew she was home, then? Or was he guessing.

"I just wanted to find out of you got my present. I have tickets to tomorrow night's presentation of *La Boheme*. I know how much you love opera and this one in particular. They're box seats. Hard to get. And perfect, just like you. Call me back." He rattled off his phone number and then hung up.

She stared at the machine, with its blinking red light. She hadn't discussed the opera with him. She hadn't discussed the opera with Sally either, after she found out that Sally hated "all that screeching." Sally wouldn't know *La Boheme* from *Don Giovanni*, and she certainly wouldn't remember either well enough to mention to someone else.

Well, maybe Paige's problem was that she had been polite to him the night before. Maybe she should have left. She'd had this problem in the past—mostly in college. She'd always tried to be polite to men who were interested in her, even if she wasn't interested in return. But sometimes, politeness merely encouraged them. Sometimes she had to be harsh just to send them away.

Harsh or polite, she really didn't want to talk to Josiah ever again. She would ignore the call, and hope that he would forget her. Most men understood a lack of response. They knew it for the brush-off it was.

If he managed to run into her, she would just apologize and give him the You're Very Nice I'm Sure You'll Meet Someone Special Someday speech. That one worked every time.

Somehow, having a plan calmed her. She finished cooking the beef for her taco salad and took it to the butcher block table in the center of her kitchen. There she opened the latest copy of *Publishers Weekly* and read it while she ate.

***

During the next week, she got fifteen bouquets of flowers, each one an arrangement described in her books. Her plan wasn't working. She hadn't run into Josiah, but she didn't answer his phone calls. He didn't seem to understand the brush off. He would call two or three times a day to leave messages on her machine, and once an hour, he would call and hang up. Sometimes she found herself standing over the Caller ID box, fists clenched.

All of this made work impossible. When the phone rang, she listened for his voice. When it wasn't him, she scrambled to pick up, her concentration broken.

In addition to the bouquets, he had taken to sending her cards and writing her long e-mails, sometimes mimicking the language of the men in her novels.

Finally, she called Sally and explained what was going on.

"I'm sorry," Sally said. "I had no idea he was like this."

Paige sighed heavily. She was beginning to feel trapped in the house. "You started this. What do you recommend?"

"I don't know," Sally said. "I'd offer to call him, but I don't think he'll listen to me. This sounds sick."

"Yeah," Paige said. "That's what I'm thinking."

"Maybe you should go to the police."

Paige felt cold. The police. If she went to them, it would be an acknowledgement that this had become serious.

"Maybe," she said, but she hoped she wouldn't have to.

***

Looking back on it, she realized she might have continued enduring if it weren't for the incident at the grocery store. She had been leaving the house, always wondering if someone was watching her, and then deciding that she was being just a bit too paranoid. But the fact that Josiah showed up in the grocery store a few moments after she arrived, pushing no grocery cart and dressed exactly like Maximilian D. Lake from *Love at 37,000 Feet* was no coincidence.

He wore a new brown leather bomber jacket, aviation sunglasses, khakis and a white scarf. When he saw her in the produce aisle, he whipped the sunglasses off with an affected air.

"Paige, darling! I've been worried about you." His eyes were even more intense that she remembered, and this time they were green, just like Maximilian Lake's.

"Josiah," she said, amazed at how calm she sounded. Her heart was pounding and her stomach was churning. He had her trapped—her cart was between the tomato and asparagus aisles. Behind her, the water jets, set to mist the produce every five minutes, kicked on.

"You have no idea how concerned I've been," he said, taking a step closer. She backed toward the onions. "When a person lives alone, works alone, and doesn't answer her phone, well, anything could be wrong."

Was that a threat? She couldn't tell. She made herself smile at him. "There's no need to worry about me. There are people checking on me all the time."

"Really?" He raised a single eyebrow, something she'd often described in her novels, but never actually seen in person. He probably knew that no one came to her house without an invitation. He seemed to know everything else.

She gripped the handle on her shopping cart firmly. "I'm glad I ran into you. I've been wanting to tell you something."

His face lit up, a look that would have been attractive if it weren't so needy. "You have?"

She nodded. Now was the time, her best and only chance. She pushed the cart forward just a little, so that he had to move aside. He seemed to think she was doing it to get closer to him. She was doing it so that she'd be able to get away.

"I really appreciate all the trouble you went to for dinner," she said. "It was one of the most memorable—"

"Our entire life could be like that," he said quickly. "An adventure every day, just like your books."

She had to concentrate to keep that smile on her face. "Writers write about adventure, Josiah, because we really don't want to go out and experience it ourselves."

He laughed. It sounded forced. "I'm sure Papa Hemingway is spinning in his grave. You are such a kidder, Paige."

"I'm not kidding," she said. "You're a very nice man, Josiah, but—"

"A nice man?" He took a step toward her, his face suddenly red. "A nice man? The only men who get described that way in your books are the losers, the ones the heroine wants to let down easy."

She let the words hang between them for a moment. And then she said, "I'm sorry."

He stared at her as if she had hit him. She pushed the cart passed him, resisting the impulse to run. She was rounding the corner into the meat aisle when she heard him say, "You *bitch*!"

Her hands started trembling then, and she couldn't read her list. But she had to. He wouldn't run her out of here. Then he'd realize just how scared she was.

He was coming up behind her. "You can't do this, Paige. You know how good we are together. You know."

She turned around, leaned against her cart and prayed silently for strength. "Josiah, we had one date, and it wasn't very good. Now please, leave me alone."

A store employee was watching from the corner of the aisle. The butcher had looked up through the window in the back.

Josiah grabbed her wrist so hard that she could feel his fingers digging into her skin. "I'll make you remember. I'll make you—"

"Are you all right, miss?" The store employee had stepped to her side.

"No," she said. "He's hurting me."

"This is none of your business," Josiah said. "She's my girlfriend."

"I don't know him," Paige said.

The employee had taken Josiah's arm. Other employees were coming from various parts of the store. He must have given them a signal. Some of the customers were gathering too.

"Sir, we're going to have to ask you to leave," the employee said.

"You have no right."

"We have every right, sir," the employee said. "Now let the lady go."

Josiah stared at him for a moment, then at the other customers. Store security had joined them.

"Paige," Josiah said, "tell them how much you love me. Tell them that we were meant to be together."

"I don't know you," she said, and this time her words seemed to get through. He let go of her arm and allowed the employee to pull him away.

She collapsed against her cart in relief, and the store manager, a middle-aged man with a nice face, asked her if she needed to sit down. She nodded. He led her to the back of the store, past the cans that were being recycled and the gray refrigeration units to a tiny office filled with red signs about customer service.

"I'm sorry," she said. "I'm so sorry."

"Why?" The manager pulled over a metal folding chair and helped her into it. Then he sat behind the desk. "It seemed like he was harassing you. Who is he?"

"I don't really know." She was still shaking. "A friend set us up on a blind date, and he hasn't left me alone since."

"Some friend," the manager said. His phone beeped, and he answered it. He spoke for a moment, his words soft. She didn't listen. She was staring at her wrist. Josiah's fingers had left marks.

Then the manager hung up. "He's gone. Our man took his license number and he's been forbidden to come into the store again. That's all we can do."

"Thank you," she said.

The manager frowned. He was looking at her bruised wrist as well. "You know guys like him don't back down."

"I'm beginning to realize that," she said.

***

And that was how she found herself parking her grocery-stuffed car in front of the local precinct. It was a gray cinder-block building built in the late 1960s with reinforced windows and a steel door. Somehow it did not inspire confidence.

She went inside anyway. The front hallway was narrow, and obviously redesigned. A steel door stood to her right and to her left was a window made of bullet-proof glass. Behind it sat a man in a police uniform.

She stepped up to the window. He finished typing something into a computer before speaking to her. "What?"

"I'd like to file a complaint."

"I'll buzz you in. Take the second door to your right. Someone there'll help you."

"Thanks," she said, but her voice was lost in the electronic buzz that filled the narrow hallway. She opened the door and found herself in the original corridor, filled with blond wood and doors with windows. Very sixties, very unsafe. She shook her head slightly, opened the second door, and stepped inside.

She entered a large room filled with desks. It smelled of burned coffee and mold. Most of the desks were empty, although on most of them, the desk lamps were on, revealing piles of papers and files. Black phones as old as the building sat on each desk, and she was startled to see that typewriters outnumbered computers.

There were only a handful of people in the room, most of them bent over their files, looking frustrated. A man with salt and pepper hair was carrying a cup of coffee back to his desk. He didn't look like any sort of police detective she'd imagined. He was squarely built and seemed rather ordinary.

When he saw her, he said, "Help you?"

"I want to file a complaint."

"Come with me." His deep voice was cracked and hoarse, as if he had been shouting all day.

He led her to a small desk in the center of the room. Most of the desks were pushed together facing each other, but this one stood alone. And it had a computer, screen showing the SFPD logo.

"I'm Detective Conover. How can I help you, Miss…?"

"Paige Racette." Her voice sounded small in the large room.

He kicked a scarred wooden chair toward her. "What's your complaint?"

She sat down slowly, her heart pounding. "I'm being harassed."

"Harassed?"

"Stalked."

He looked at her straight on, then, and she thought she saw a world-weariness in his brown eyes. His entire face was rumpled, like a coat that had been balled up and left in the bottom of a closet. It wasn't a handsome face by any definition, but it had a comfortable quality, a trustworthy quality, that was built into the lines.

"Tell me about it," he said.

So she did. She started with the blind date, talked about how strange Josiah was, and how he wouldn't leave her alone.

"And he was taking things out of my novels like I would appreciate it. It really upset me."

"Novels?" It was the first time Conover had interrupted her.

She nodded. "I write romances."

"And are you published?"

The question startled her. Usually when she mentioned her name people recognized it. They always recognized it after she said she wrote romances.

"Yes," she said.

"So you were hoisted on your own petard, aren't you?"

"Excuse me?"

"You write about your sexual fantasies for a living, and then complain when someone is trying to take you up on it." He said that so deadpan, so seriously, that for a moment, she couldn't breathe.

"It's not like that," she said.

"Oh? It's advertising, lady."

She was shaking again. She had known this was a bad idea. Why would she expect sympathy from the police? "So since Donald Westlake writes about thieves, he shouldn't complain if he gets robbed? Or Stephen King shouldn't be upset if someone breaks his ankle with a sledgehammer?"

"Touchy," the detective said, but she noticed a twinkle in his eye that hadn't been there before.

She actually counted to ten, silently, before responding. She hadn't done that since she was a little girl. Then she said, as calmly as she could, "You baited me on purpose."

He grinned—and it smoothed out the care lines in his face, enhancing the twinkle in his eye and, for a moment, making him breathlessly attractive.

"There are a lot of celebrities in this town, Ms. Racette. It's hard for the lesser ones to get noticed. Sometimes they'll stage some sort of crime for publicity's sake. And really, what would be better than a romance writer being romanced by a fan who was using the structure of her books to do it?"

She wasn't sure what she objected to the most, being called a minor celebrity, being branded as a publicity hound, or finding this outrageous man attractive, even for a moment.

"I don't like attention," she said slowly. "If I liked attention, I would have chosen a different career. I hate book signings and television interviews, and I certainly don't want a word of this mess breathed to the press."

"So far so good," he said. She couldn't tell if he believed her, still. But she was amusing him. And that really pissed her off.

She held up her wrist. "He did this."

The smile left Conover's face. He took her hand gently in his own and extended it, examining the bruises as if they were clues. "When?"

"About an hour ago. At San Francisco Produce." She flushed saying the name of the grocery store. It was upscale and trendy, precisely the place a "celebrity" would shop.

But Conover didn't seem to notice. "You didn't tell me about the attack."

"I was getting to it when you interrupted me," she said. "I've been getting calls from him—a dozen or more a day. Flowers, presents, letters and e-mails. I'm unlisted and I never gave him my phone number or my address. I have a private e-mail address, not the one my publisher hands out, and that's the one he's using. And then he followed me to the grocery store and got angry when the store security asked him to leave."

Conover eased her hand onto his desk, then leaned back in his chair. His touch had been gentle, and she missed it.

"You had a date with him—"

"A blind date. We met at the restaurant, and a friend handled the details. And no, she didn't give him the information either."

"—so," Conover said, as if she hadn't spoken, "I assume you know his name."

"Josiah Wells."

Conover wrote it down. Then he sighed. It looked like he was gathering himself. "You have a stalker, Ms. Racette."

"I know."

"And while stalking is illegal under California law, the law is damned inadequate. I'll get the video camera tape from the store, and if it backs you up, I'll arrest Wells. You'll be willing to press charges?"

"Yes," she said.

"That's a start." Conover's world-weary eyes met hers. "but I have to be honest. Usually these guys get out on bail. You'll need a lawyer to get an injunction against him, and your guy will probably ignore it. Even if he gets sent up for a few years, he'll come back and haunt you. They always do."

Her shaking started again. "So what can I do?"

"Your job isn't tied to the community. You can move."

Move? She felt cold. "I have a house." A life. This was her dream city. "I don't want to move."

"No one does, but it's usually the only thing that works."

"I don't want to run away," she said. "If I do that, then he'll be controlling my life. I'd be giving in. I'd be a victim."

Conover stared at her for a long moment. "Tell you what. I'll build the strongest case I can. That might give you a few years. By then, you might be willing to go somewhere new."

She nodded, stood. "I'll bring everything in tomorrow."

"I'd like to pick it up, if you don't mind. See where he left it, whether he's got a hidey hole near the house. How about I come to you in a couple of hours?"

"Okay," she said.

"You got a peephole?"

"Yeah."

"Use it. I'll knock."

She nodded. Then felt her shoulders relax slightly, more than they had for two weeks. Finally, she had an ally. It meant more to her than she had realized it would. "Thanks."

"Don't thank me yet," he said. "Let's wait until this is all over."

All over. She tried to concentrate on the words and not the tone. Because Detective Conover really didn't sound all that optimistic.

***

The biggest bouquet waited for her on the front porch. She could see it from the street, and any hope that the meeting with Conover aroused disappeared. She knew without getting out of the car what the bouquet would be: calla lilies, tiger lilies and Easter lilies, mixed with greens and lilies of the valley. It was a bouquet Marybeth Campbell was designing the day she met Robert Newman in *All My Kisses*, a bouquet he said was both romantic and sad. (Not to mention expensive: the flowers weren't in season at the same time.)

She left the bouquet on the porch without reading the card. Conover would be there soon and he could take the whole mess away. She certainly didn't want to look at it.

After all this, she wasn't sure she ever wanted to see flowers again.

When she got inside, she found twenty-three messages on her machine, all from Josiah, all apologies, although they got angrier and angrier as she didn't answer. He must have thought she had come straight home. What a surprise he would have when he realized that she had gone to the police.

She rubbed her wrist, noting the soreness and cursing him under her breath. In addition to the bruises, her wrist was slightly swollen and she wondered if he hadn't managed to sprain it. Just her luck. He would damage her arm, which she needed to write. She got an ice pack out of the freezer and applied it, sitting at the kitchen table and staring at nothing.

Move. Give up, give in, all because she was feeling lonely and wanted to go on a date. All because she wanted a little flattery, a nice evening, to meet someone safe who could be—if nothing else—a friend.

How big a mistake had that been?

Big enough, she was beginning to realize, to cost her everything she held dear.

***

That night, after dinner, she baked herself a chocolate cake and covered it with marshmallow frosting. It was her grandmother's recipe—comfort food that Paige normally never allowed herself. This time, though, she would eat the whole thing and not worry about calories or how bad it looked. Who would know?

She made some coffee and was sitting down to a large piece, when someone knocked on her door.

She got up and walked to the door, feeling oddly vulnerable. If it was Josiah, he would only be a piece of wood away from her. That was too close. It was all too close now.

She peered through the peephole, just like she promised Conover she would, and she let out a small sigh of relief. He was shifting from foot to foot, looking down at the bouquet she had forgotten she had left there.

She deactivated the security system, then unlocked the three deadbolts and the chain lock she had installed since this nightmare began. Conover shoved the bouquet forward with his foot.

"Looks like your friend left another calling card."

"He's not my friend," she said softly, peering over Conover's shoulder. "And he left more than that."

Conover's glance was worried. What did he imagine?

"Phone calls," she said. "Almost two dozen. I haven't checked my e-mail."

"This guy's farther along than I thought." Conover pushed the bouquet all the way inside with his foot, then closed the door, and locked it. As he did, she reset the perimeter alarm.

Conover slipped on a pair of gloves and picked up the bouquet.

"You could have done that outside," she said.

"Didn't want to give him the satisfaction," Conover said. "He has to know we don't respect what he's doing. Where can I look at this?"

"Kitchen," she said, pointing the way.

He started toward it, then stopped, sniffing. "What smells so good?"

"Chocolate cake. You want some?"

"I thought you wrote."

"Doesn't stop me from baking on occasion."

He glanced at her, his dark eyes quizzical. "This hardly seems the time to be baking."

She shrugged. "I could drink instead."

To her surprise, he laughed. "Yes, I guess you could."

He carried the bouquet into the kitchen and set it on a chair. Then he dug through the flowers to find the card.

It was a different picture of their date. The photograph looked professional, almost artistic, done in black and white, using the light from the candles to illuminate her face. At first glance, she seemed entranced with Josiah. But when she looked closely, she could see the discomfort on her face.

"You didn't like him much," Conover said.

"He was creepy from the start, but in subtle hard-to-explain ways."

"Why didn't you leave?"

"I was raised to be polite. I had no idea he was crazy."

Conover grunted at that. He opened the card. The handwriting inside was the same as all the others.

My future and your future are the same. You
are my heart and soul. Without you, I am nothing.
—Josiah

She closed her eyes, felt that fluttery fear rise in her again. "There'll be a ring somewhere in that bouquet."

"How do you know?" Conover asked.

She opened her eyes. "Go look at the last page of *All My Kisses*. Robert sends a forgive-me bouquet and in it, he puts a diamond engagement ring."

"This bouquet?"

"No. Josiah already used that one. I guess he thought this one is more spectacular."

Conover dug, and then whistled. There, among the stems, was a black velvet ring box. He opened it. A large diamond glittered against a circle of sapphires in a white gold setting.

"Jesus," he said. "I could retire on this thing."

"I always thought that was a gaudy ring," Paige said, her voice shaking. "But it fit the characters."

"Not to your taste?"

"No." She sighed and sank back into her chair. "Just because I write about it doesn't mean I want it to happen to me."

"I think you made that clear in the precinct today." He put the ring box back where he found it, returned the card to its envelope and set the flowers on the floor. "Mind if I have some of that cake?"

"Oh, I'm sorry." She got up and cut him a piece of cake, then poured some coffee.

When she turned around, he was grinning.

"What did I do?" she asked.

"You weren't kidding about polite," he said. "I didn't come here for a tea party, and you could have said no."

She froze in place. "Was this another of your tests? To see if I was really that polite?"

"I wish I were that smart." He took the plate from her hand. "I was getting knocked out by the smell. My mother used to make this cake. It always was my favorite."

"With marshmallow frosting?"

"And that spritz of melted chocolate on top, just like you have here." He set the plate down and took the coffee from her hand. "Although in those days, I would have preferred a large glass of milk."

"I have some—"

"Sit." If anything, his grin had gotten bigger. "Forgive me for being so blunt, but what the hell did you need with a blind date?"

There was admiration in his eyes—real admiration, not the sick kind she'd seen from Josiah. She used her fork to cut a bite of cake. "I was lonely. I don't get out much, and I thought, what could it hurt?"

He shook his head. That weary look had returned to his face. She liked its rumpled quality, the way that he seemed to be able to take the weight of the world onto himself and still stand up. "What a way to get disillusioned."

"Because I'm a romance writer?"

"Because you're a person."

They ate the cake in silence after that, then he gripped his coffee mug and leaned back in the chair.

"Thanks," he said. "I'd forgotten that little taste of childhood."

"There's more."

"Maybe later." And there was no smile on his face any more, no enjoyment. "I have to tell you a few things."

She pushed her own plate away.

"I looked up Josiah Wells. He's got a sheet."

She grabbed her own coffee cup. It was warm and comforting. "Let me guess. The political conferences he stopped going to."

Conover frowned at her. "What conferences?"

"Here in San Francisco. He was active in local politics. That's how my friend Sally met him."

"And he stopped?"

"Rather suddenly. I thought, after all this started, that maybe—"

"I'll check into it," Conover said with a determination she hadn't heard from him before. "His sheet's from San Diego."

"I thought he was from here."

Conover shook his head. "He's not a dot-com million-aire. He made his money on a software system back in the early nineties, before everyone was into this business. Sold his interest for 30 million dollars and some stock, which has since risen in value. About ten times what it was."

Her mouth had gone dry. Josiah Wells had lied to both her and Sally. "Somehow I suspect this is important."

"Yeah." Conover took a sip of coffee. "He stalked a woman in San Diego."

"Oh, God." The news gave her a little too much relief. She had been feeling alone. But she didn't want anyone else to be experiencing the same thing she was.

"He killed her."

"What?" Paige froze.

"When she resisted him, he shot her and killed her." Conover's soft gaze was on her now, measuring. All her relief had vanished. She was suddenly more terrified than she had ever been.

"You know it was him?"

"I read the file. They faxed it to me this afternoon. All of it. They had him one hundred percent. DNA matches, semen matches—"

She winced, knowing what that meant.

"—the fibers from his home on her clothing, and a list of stalking complaints and injunctions that went on for pages."

The cake sat like a lump in her stomach. "Then why isn't he in prison?"

"Money," Conover said. "His attorneys so out-classed the DA's office that by the end of the trial, they could have convinced the jury that the judge had done it."

"Oh, my god," Paige said.

"The same things that happened to you happened to her," Conover said. "Only with her those things took about two years. With you it's taking two weeks."

"Because he feels like he knows me from my books?"

Conover shook his head. "She was a TV business reporter who had done an interview with him. He would have felt like he knew her too."

"What then?" Somehow having the answer to all of that would make her feel better—or maybe she was just lying to herself.

"These guys are like alcoholics. If you take a guy through AA, and keep him sober for a year, then give him a drink, he won't rebuild his drinking career from scratch. He'll start at precisely the point he left off."

She had to swallow hard to keep the cake down. "You think she wasn't the only one."

"Yeah. I suspect if we look hard enough, we'll find a trail of women, each representing a point in the escalation of his sickness."

"You can arrest him, right?"

"Yes." Conover spoke softly. "But only on what he's done. Not on what he might do. And I don't think we'll be any more successful at holding him than the San Diego DA."

Paige ran her hand over the butcher block table. "I have to leave, don't I?"

"Yeah." Conover's voice got even softer. He put a hand on hers. She looked at him. It wasn't world-weariness in his eyes. It was sadness. Sadness from all the things he'd seen, all the things he couldn't change.

"I'm from a small town," she said. "I don't want to bring him there."

"Is there anywhere else you can go? Somewhere he wouldn't think of?"

"New York," she said. "I have friends I can stay with for a few weeks."

"This'll take longer than a few weeks. You might not be able to come back."

"I know. But that'll give me time to find a place to live." Her voice broke on that last. This had been her dream city, her dream home. How quickly that vanished.

"I'm sorry," he said.

"Yeah," she said quietly. "Me, too."

***

He decided to stay without her asking him. He said he wanted to sift through the evidence, listen to the phone messages, and read the e-mail. She printed off all of it while she bought plane tickets on-line. Then she e-mailed her agent and told her that she was coming to the City.

Already she was talking like the New Yorker she was going to be.

Her flight left at 8 a.m. She spent half the night packing and unpacking, uncertain about what she would need, what she should leave behind. The only thing she was certain about was that she would need her laptop, and she spent an hour loading her files onto it. She was writing down the names of some moving and packing services when Conover stopped her.

"We leave everything as is," he said. "We don't want him to get too suspicious too soon."

"Why don't you arrest him now?" she asked. "Don't you have enough?"

Something flashed across his face, so quickly she almost didn't catch it.

"What?" she asked. "What is it?"

He closed his eyes. If anything, that made his face look even more rumpled. "I issued a warrant for his arrest before I came here. We haven't found him yet."

"Oh, God." Paige slipped into her favorite chair. One of many things she would have to leave behind, one of many things she might never see again because of Josiah Wells.

"We have people watching his house, watching yours, and a few other places he's known to hang out," Conover said. "We'll get him soon enough."

She nodded, trying to look reassured, even though she wasn't.

***

About 3 a.m., Conover looked at her suitcases sitting in the middle of the dining room floor. "I'll have to ship those to you. No sense tipping him off if he's watching this place."

"I thought you said—"

"I did. But we need to be careful. One duffel. The rest can wait."

"My laptop," she said. "I need that too."

He sighed. "All right. The laptop and the biggest purse you have. Nothing more."

A few hours earlier, she might have argued with him. But a few hours earlier, she hadn't yet gone numb.

"I need some sleep," she said.

"I'll wake you," he said, "when it's time to go."

***

He drove her to the airport in his car. It was an old bathtub Porsche—with the early seventies bucket seats that were nearly impossible to get into.

"She's not pretty any more," he said as he tucked Paige's laptop behind the seat, "but she can move."

They left at 5, not so much as to miss traffic, but hoping that Wells wouldn't be paying attention at that hour. Conover also kept checking his rearview mirror, and a few times he executed some odd maneuvers.

"We being followed?" she asked finally.

"I don't think so," he said. "But I'm being cautious."

His words hung between them. She watched the scenery go by, houses after houses after houses filled with people who went about their ordinary lives, not worrying about stalkers or death or losing everything.

"This isn't normal for you, is it?" she asked after a moment.

"Being cautious?" he said. "Of course it is."

"No." Paige spoke softly. "Taking care of someone like this."

He seemed even more intent on the road than he had been. "All cases are different."

"Really?"

He turned to her, opened his mouth, and then closed it again, sighing. "Josiah Wells is a predator."

"I know," she said.

"We have to do what we can to catch him." His tone was odd. She frowned. Was that an apology for something she didn't understand? Or an explanation for his attentiveness?

Maybe it was both.

He turned onto the road leading to San Francisco International Airport. The traffic seemed even thicker here, through all the construction and the dust. It seemed like they were constantly remodeling the place. Somehow he made it through the confusing signs to Short Term Parking. He found a space, parked, and then grabbed her laptop from the back.

"You're coming in?" she asked.

"I want to see you get on that plane." He seemed oddly determined.

"Don't you trust me?"

"Of course I do," he said and got out of the car.

San Francisco International Airport was an old airport, built right on the bay. The airport had been trying to modernize for years. The new parts were grafted on like artificial limbs.

Paige took a deep breath, grabbed her stuffed oversized purse, and let Conover lead her inside. She supposed they looked like any couple as they went through the automatic doors, stopping to examine the signs above them pointing to the proper airline. Conover was watching the other passengers. Paige was checking out the lines.

She had bought herself a first class ticket—spending more money than she had spent for her very first car. But she was leaving everything behind. The last thing she wanted was to be crammed into couch next to a howling baby and an underpaid, stressed businessman.

She hurried to the first class line, relieved that it was short. Conover stayed beside her, frowning as he watched the people flow past. He seemed both disappointed and alert. He was expecting something. But what?

Paige stepped to the ticket counter, gave her name, showed her identification, answered the silly security questions, and got her E-ticket with the gate number written on the front.

"You've got an hour and a half," Conover said as she left the ticket counter. "Let's get breakfast."

His hand rested possessively on her elbow, and he pulled her close as he spoke. She glanced at him, but he still wasn't watching her.

"I have to make a stop first," she said.

He nodded.

They walked past the arrival and departure monitors, past the newspaper vending machines and toward the nearest restrooms. This part of the San Francisco airport still had a seventies security design. Instead of a bank of x-ray machines and metal detectors blocking entry into the main part of the terminal, there was nothing. The security measures were in front of each gate: you couldn't enter without going past a security checkpoint. So different from New York, where you couldn't even walk into some areas without a ticket. Conover would have no trouble remaining beside her until it was time for her to take off.

She went into the ladies room, leaving Conover near the departure monitors outside. The line was long—several flights had just arrived—but Paige didn't mind. This was the first time she had a moment to herself since Conover had arrived the night before.

It seemed like weeks ago.

She was going to be sorry to say good-bye to him at the gate. In that short period of time, she had come to rely on him more than she wanted to admit. He made her feel safe for the first time since she had met Josiah Wells.

As she exited the ladies room, a hand grabbed her arm and pulled her sideways. She felt something poke against her back.

"Think you could leave me?"

Wells. She shook her arm, trying to get away, but he clamped harder.

"Scream," he said, "and I will hurt you."

"You can't hurt me," she said. "You can't have weapons in an airport."

"You can bring a gun into an airport," he said softly, right in her ear. "You just can't take it through security."

She felt cold then. He was as crazy as Conover said, then. And as dangerous.

"Josiah." She spoke loudly, hoping that Conover could hear her. She didn't see him anywhere. "I'm going to New York on business. When I come back, we can start planning the wedding."

Wells was silent for a moment. He didn't move at all. She couldn't see his face, but she could feel his body go rigid. "You're playing with me."

"No," she said, letting her voice work for her, hoping it sounded convincing. She kept scanning the crowd, but Conover was gone. "I got your ring last night. I decided I needed to settle a few things in New York before I told you I'd say yes."

Wells put his chin on her shoulder. His breath blew against her hair. "You're not wearing the ring."

"It didn't fit." she said. "But I have it with me. I was going to have it sized in New York."

"Let me see it," he said.

"You'll have to let me dig into my purse."

She wasn't sure he'd believe her. Then, after a moment, he let her go. She brought up her purse, pretended to rummage through it, and took a step toward the ladies room door, praying her plan would work.

He was frowning. He looked like any other businessman in the airport, his suit neat and well tailoredwell-tailored, his trench coat long and expensive, marred only by the way he held his hand in the pocket.

She waited just a split second, until there were a lot of people around from another arriving plane, and then she screamed, "He's got a gun!" and ran toward the ladies room.

Only she didn't make it. She was tackled from behind, and went sprawling across the faded carpet. A gunshot echoed around her, and people started screaming, running. The body on top of hers prevented her from moving, and for a moment, she thought whoever had hit her had been shot.

Then she felt arms around her, dragging her toward the departure monitors.

"You little fool," Conover said in her ear. "I had this under control."

He pushed her against the base of the monitor, then turned around. Half the people around Wells had remained, and two of them had him in their grasp, while another was handcuffing him. Plainclothes airport police officers. More airport police were hurrying to the spot from the front door.

Passengers were still screaming and running out of the airport. Airline personnel were crouched behind their desks. Paige looked to see whether anyone was shot, but she didn't see anyone lying injured anywhere.

Her breathing was shallow, and she suddenly realized how terrified she had been. "What do you mean, under control? This doesn't look under control to me."

Security had Wells against the wall and were searching him for more weapons. One of the uniformed airport police had pulled Wells' head back and was yelling at him. Some of the passengers, realizing the threat was over, were drifting back toward the action.

Conover kept one hand on her, holding her in place. With the other, he pulled out his cell phone. He hit the speed-dial and put the small phone against his ear.

"Wait a minute!" Paige said.

He turned away slightly, as if he didn't want to speak to her. Then he said into the phone, "Frank, do me a favor. Call the news media—everyone you can think of. Tell them something just happened at the airport.... No. I'm not going through official channels. That's why I called you. Keep my name out of it and get them here."

He hung up and glanced at Paige. She had never felt so many emotions in her life. Anger, adrenaline, confusion. Then she saw security lead Wells away.

Conover took her arm and helped her up. "What's going on?" she asked again.

"Outside," he said, and pushed her through the crowd. After a moment, she remembered to check for her laptop. He had it, and somehow she had retained her purse. They reached the front sidewalk only to find it a confusion of milling people—some still terrified from the shots, others just arriving and trying to drop off their luggage. Cabs honked and nearly missed each other. Buses were backing up as the crowd spilled into the street.

"Oh, this is so much better," she said.

He moved her down the sidewalk toward another terminal. The crowd thinned here.

"What the hell was that?" she asked. "Where were you? How did he get past you?"

"He didn't get past me," Conover said softly.

She felt the blood leave her face. "You set me up? I was bait?"

"It wasn't supposed to happen like this."

"Oh, really? He was supposed to drag me onto the nearest flight? Or shoot me?"

"I didn't know he had a gun," Conover said. "He was ballsier than I expected. And he wouldn't have taken you from San Francisco."

"You know this how? Because you're psychic?"

"No, he wanted to control you. He couldn't control you on a plane. I had security waiting outside. A few plainclothes had been around us since we arrived. He was supposed to grab you, but you weren't supposed to try to get away."

"Nice if you would have told me that."

He shook his head slightly. "Most people wouldn't have fought him. Most people would have cooperated."

"Most people would have appreciated an explanation!" Her voice rose and a few stray passengers looked her direction. She made herself take a deep breath before she went on. "You knew he was going to be here. You knew it and didn't tell me."

"I guessed," he said.

"What did you do, tip him off?"

"No," Conover said softly. "You did."

"I did? I didn't talk to him."

"You booked your e-ticket online." His face was close to hers, his voice as soft as possible in all the noise. "He'd hacked into your system weeks ago. That's how he found your address and your phone number. Your public e-mail comes into the same computer as all your other e-mail. He's been following your every move ever since."

"Software genius," she muttered, shaking her head. She should have seen that.

Conover nodded. Across the way, reporters started converging on the building, cameras hefted on shoulders, running toward the doors. Conover shielded her, but she knew they would want to talk to her.

"Why didn't you warn me?" she asked again.

"I thought you'd be too obvious then, and he wouldn't try for you. I didn't expect you to be so cool under pressure. Telling him about the ring, pretending you were interested, was smart."

One of the reporters was working the crowd. People were turning toward the camera.

"Where were you?" she asked. "I looked for you."

"I was behind you all the time."

"So if he took me outside…?"

"I would have followed."

"I don't understand. Why didn't you tell me not to get the ticket on line?"

"The ticket was a gift," Conover said. "I didn't realize you were going to do it that way. You told me when you finished. His file from the previous case mentioned how he had used the internet to spy on his first victim. He was obviously doing that with you."

"But the airport, how did they know?"

"I called ahead, said that I was coming in, expecting a difficult passenger. I faxed his photo from your place while you were asleep. I asked them to wait until I got him outside, unless he did something threatening."

She frowned. More reporters were approaching. These looked like print media. No cameras, but lots of determination. "You could have waited and caught him at home."

"I could have," Conover said. "But this is better."

She turned to him, remembering the feel of the gun against her back, the screaming passengers, the explosive sound when the gun went off. "Someone could have been killed."

"I didn't expect a gun," Conover said. "And I didn't think he'd be rash enough to use it in an airport."

"But he did," she said.

"And it's going to help us." Conover watched another set of reporters run into the building. "First, his assault on you in an airport makes it a federal case. The gun adds to the case, and all the witnesses make it even better. Then there is the fact that airports are filled with security cameras. There's bound to be tape on this."

She frowned, trying to take herself out of this, trying to listen like a writer instead of a potential victim.

"And then," Conover said, "he attacked you. You're nationally known. It'll be big news. Our DA might have lost a stalking case against Wells, but the feds aren't going to let a guy who went nuts in an airport walk, no matter how much money he has."

"You set him up," she said. "If this had failed—"

"At the very least, I would have been fired," Conover said. "But it wouldn't have failed. I wouldn't have let anything happen to you. I didn't let anything happen to you."

"But you took such a risk." She raised her head toward his. "Why?"

He put a finger under her chin, and for a moment, she thought he was going to kiss her.

"Because you didn't want to leave San Francisco," he said softly.

"I get to stay home?" she asked.

He smiled, and let his finger drop. "Yeah."

He stared at her uncertainly, as if he were afraid she was going to yell at him again. But she felt a relief so powerful that it completely overwhelmed her.

She threw her arms around him. For a moment, he didn't move. Then, slowly, his arms wrapped around her and pulled her close.

"I don't even know your first name," she whispered.

"Pete," he said, burying his face in her hair.

"Pete." She tested it. "It suits you."

"I'd ask if I could call you," he said, "but I'm not real good on dates."

That pulled a reluctant laugh from her. "Obviously I'm not either. But I make a mean chocolate cake."

"That's right," he said. "Let's go finish it."

"Don't we have to talk to the press?"

"For a moment." He pulled back just enough to smile at her. "And then I get to take you home."

"Where I get to stay." She couldn't convey how much this meant to her.

"Thank you," she said.

He nodded. "My pleasure."

She leaned her head against his shoulder, feeling his strength, feeling the comfort. It didn't matter how he looked or whether he knew *La Boheme* from *Don Giovanni*. All that mattered was how he made her feel.

Safe. Appreciated. And maybe even loved.

THE SECRET LIVES OF CATS

HOMER ZIFF didn't believe in old adages, but after his long and eventful spring, he couldn't help but think that whoever put the words "curiosity," "cat," and "kill" in the same sentence had to be onto something.

It all began about his own curiosity—about his cats. Homer Ziff lived alone with two indoor cats and six outdoor cats. Well, six he could pet and hold; there were others—the friends, neighbors and hangers-on, he called them—who visited at meal time or for a rest on the back forty in the mid-afternoon sun.

Not that he had a real back forty. But his back yard was an impressive three acres, complete with woods and stream. One of the reasons he bought the house was that it had the best of both worlds: in the front, he had a small lawn that led to a quiet residential street; in the back, he had the acres of property that covered a protected wetland. No one would ever build behind him, the lots next to him were full, and the houses across the street had reached their maximum size according to code.

He knew his neighbors by sight (rather like he knew their cats) and he would nod at them whenever he saw them, but didn't engage in conversation. He couldn't bring himself to talk to them, not after his first attempt, when he'd stuttered at a man several doors down, and the man had rolled his eyes and walked away.

Homer would liked to have blamed his surly neighbor for his own lack of congeniality, but that wouldn't be fair or accurate. Homer didn't engage most people in conversation. He had a stutter that got worse when he was nervous.

Over the years, he'd learned to prefer his own company. He liked being alone with his thoughts and his cats and his property.

And it was his thoughts that made being alone possible. Not that his thoughts were original—sadly, they weren't—but they were organized, and that had given him an edge. Once upon a time, he had been a professor of physics at Oregon State University. A rising star when he was hired, he'd become a stalled star by mid-career—a man for whom the great things expected never materialized.

Which would have been well and good except that stalled stars had to be stellar teachers and he was not. He was pathologically shy, and his stutter got worse in front of large groups. He was better one on one, but stalled stars weren't allowed to teach the smaller classes. He had to teach some large sections as well, and he dreaded them like he dreaded a visit to the dentist.

But he did have one valuable skill. He could explain things clearly. His gift of clarity had gotten him through graduate school and into an important teaching position, but that gift also stalled him. And it made him into something of a rebel.

Because of his gift, he threw out the suggested text for 101 Physics (a more confusing book he'd never seen) and wrote a series of notes that sold in the campus bookstore—not just to his students, but to students from other physics classes. The bookstore owner called him one day to ask whether students at the nearby University of Oregon could purchase the notes. Then students from some of the private colleges made the drive from McMinnville and Portland to get his notes, and finally, the chairman of his department said, "Y'know, Ziff, you could make a fortune on those notes if you just turned them into a book."

So he did. It became the number one 101 physics text in the country, which led his publisher to ask if he would write a simple physics book for the masses, which he did, and another for children, which he did, and suddenly Homer Ziff no longer needed to worry about being a stalled star. He had become a rising star again—or maybe even an established one—and could have his pick of the courseload within his department.

Only the books had given him another gift. Financial independence. He no longer had to teach. And since standing in front of students made him so nervous that he sometimes spent the hour before class in the restroom, he decided that the prudent move would be to quit.

He bought his marvelous house, made sure his finances were in order, and then retired to write a half dozen more popular science books, with more under contract.

Some days, the cats were his only companions. He didn't mind, really. He never stuttered when he spoke to cats, and they didn't care that he lacked original thought.

They were happy that he provided food and shelter and a bit of companionship.

He was happy to have them purr.

Because of them, he had become a little cat-obsessed.

He had been surfing the net one night when he discovered a website designed by a man in Germany. The man sounded like a kindred spirit. He lived with a cat to whom he devoted an inordinate amount of time. That cat was an indoor-outdoor cat, and the German man wondered how his cat spent his time outside the house.

So the man, who appeared to be some kind of engineer, modified a digital camera, put it around his cat's neck, set it up to take pictures every minute and a half, and sent the cat on its way. The resulting photographs were charming and inspiring.

Homer found himself staring at his outdoor friends, wondering how their days went. One cat's routine illuminated the life of one cat. Six cats' routines might actually be the beginning of some kind of scientific study.

At least, that was what he told himself as he used the instructions on the German man's website to build six catcams. After some struggle, Homer managed to attach them to five of his outdoor favorites (he gave up on the wily old tom—who not only drew blood, but managed to slice him up badly enough to require fifteen stitches on his left hand).

Then he sent the five on their mission, hoping to discover the secret lives of cats.

***

And he did. He discovered all sorts of marvelous things.

He saw the same feline faces in his yard, in his neighbor's yard, at the century-old schoolhouse down the street. He realized that each cat had not only its own routine, but shared a neighborhood routine as well.

Mornings began at his house, with a treat of kibble and soft food, followed by a trek to the dumpster behind the local Burger King, then to a long rest under the bleachers at the old school.

The ground beneath his neighbors' cars and his own Ford pick-up served as sites for daily conferences. A house three blocks away provided an afternoon snack, usually followed by a dumpster diving at a local fish market and the nearby Diary Queen.

On warm days, the cats tromped down to the wetlands for drinks from the springs that prevented anyone from building behind Homer's property.

He would have blessed those springs, if he hadn't seen something curious.

On the earliest photos the springs looked like a primeval swampland. Cats, due to their low-to-the-ground perspective, took the most amazing photographs. Apparently the wetlands at dawn (or was it dusk?) had ground fog, which made everything opaque and surreal.

The swamp (he didn't know what else to call it) had tree limbs and branches and sticks rising from the muck, all hidden by the ghost-like grayness of the fog. To his surprise, the cats didn't drink from the water here. They sat in front of it—all five of them—as if they were watching something.

Subsequent photos on different days showed something that resembled an elephant's graveyard. What he'd initially thought were tree branches were bones sticking out of the mud. Some of the bones were covered in moss. Others had ivy growing around them like large green cobwebs.

The ivy gave him some perspective, but not enough. He couldn't tell what kind of bones these were. Cats are small creatures and the cameras took photographs from that small perspective. Bones which seemed huge in some photographs seemed tiny in others.

Those others, he soon realized, were taken from some kind of height. Either that particular feline photographer had climbed a tree or it sat on a bank or it watched from a stump.

Homer found it curious that the cats never got close to the elephant's graveyard. They always sat back. But as the weeks went on and the photographs accumulated, Homer realized that the graveyard was a spring haunt, just like the school had been in the winter.

The cats weren't interested in food; they were observing something.

And that intrigued him.

Because cats, like humans, had a scientific turn of mind.

***

He had noticed that scientific frame of mind from the day he brought home his first kitten. Cats not only studied things, but they made a study of things. One of his cats decided to probe the mysteries of ice cubes—how they turned into water, whether they could be carried, why they sometimes shattered. Another spent an entire week learning how the front door knob turned. Eventually that cat learned how to turn the knob herself; fortunately she never did figure out the necessity of pulling the door open.

Or maybe opening the door didn't interest her. The front door was the only one with a cut glass door knob. It refracted light. Maybe the cat had been more interested in the prisms inside the knob than in using that knob to go outside.

Homer never mentioned these thoughts to anyone else. He often felt as if he put too much time into his cats. And then he discovered that German man's website, and realized he was not alone in his obsession with cat thought.

But, Homer would have wagered, the German man did not have an entire second computer devoted to the photographs that the cats created. Nor, Homer suspected, did the German man spend as much time trying to figure out what his cats were thinking as they stared—not just at the elephant graveyard, but also from underneath cars or beside Dumpsters.

The cats seemed involved in a part of life that Homer had somehow missed.

***

As the spring went on, he realized the cats were studying the elephant graveyard the same way that his indoor cat had studied that doorknob. They just hadn't gotten to the touching stage yet.

He would know when they did. Daily, he got a series of photos of the back of pink tongues, lapping water from a puddle or a stream or a bowl that someone had placed outside. He would get photographs of near-dead prey wriggling out of a mouth.

But he saw nothing like that near the bones.

Only cats, watching the swampy water as if it held the secret of the universe.

***

Then, one Sunday afternoon, everything changed.

A little white female he called Mata Hari because of her attractiveness to the males (even after she was fixed) and her tendency to wander off on dangerous and secretive missions of her own brought home a defining photograph.

Every day, she sat in the same spot near the swamp. The little camera around her neck took a variation of the same photograph—a bone fragment sticking out of the primordial ooze. Sometimes the fragment was brown with mud and sometimes it looked almost white. But, over time, he realized it was the same fragment, which meant she sat in the same spot daily, studying something that she felt was important.

Only that Sunday, the fragment was covered by a human hand.

The hand loomed in the photograph, the fingers dominating the scene. They rose upward toward the sky, the ridges of the knuckles visible against the blackness of the muck. Dried cuts marred the flesh along the back, and the fingernails—clipped short—had dirt embedded all the way down to the skin.

Mata Hari had brought home ten pictures of the hand, which meant she spent fifteen minutes contemplating it, twice as long as she usually spent at that spot. The cat had managed to get several different angles, and oddly, each was farther away than the previous one.

The hand put the other bones in perspective. He returned to his photo files, opened the relevant pictures next to the photo of the hand and compared.

His breath caught. What had seemed like animal bones—small and fragile, old, abandoned, like elephants in their graveyard—were not. They were too large. He had been more accurate with the foggy photos when he'd thought of the bones as branches and logs.

These bones were large. No domesticated animal, except maybe a Husky or a Rotweiller, would have bones like that. Nor would most of the wild animals around here. This area was too populated for bears, even with the wetlands below. Maybe a deer or two had died down there, but certainly not a bunch of them. The coyotes were the size of raccoons, and barely larger than the cats, and there were no wolves here.

Which left only one other creature that could have provided the bones.

Humans.

And the latest victim had just arrived.

***

He needed to know if any of the other cats had photographs of the hand.

He got up and peered out his window. Two of the other cats had returned.

He stepped outside and removed the memory card from both cameras, careful to put in a new card before he shut the cameras off. He'd tried night photos before, but the flash had scared the cat so badly that it had run in circles, screaming.

He hadn't known cats could scream.

He gave each cat some pets and a small treat, then went back inside and downloaded the photographs.

In every bunch, a handful were duds—blurs, unrecognizable objects, a paw in front of the lens. These two batches were no different. But he set aside the blurs and unrecognizable objects this time, deciding they might be useful.

Then he scanned the images until he got to the swamp.

These cats had come to the graveyard as well, and at about the same time as Mata Hari. In fact, one of the unrecognizable objects might have been her haunch as the other cat sniffed her in greeting.

These cats stayed even farther away. He got found photographs of an entire arm, covered in bruises, and a bit of shoulder. His hands were shaking as he magnified the images.

The arm and hand had clearly come from the same place. He could see the bone fragment, the moss-covered bones, the ivy-covered bones and the brackish water. Now he knew why the cats didn't drink here.

He wasn't even sure why they came—they were well fed, so they didn't need to eat decaying flesh. Were they watching something decompose? Or were they hunting the rats or some other creature that frequented the wetlands?

For the first time since he started this experiment, he felt frustrated that he couldn't ask.

And then he found the money shot.

Or what would have been a money shot had he been a photographer along the lines of Weegee—the man who photographed corpses at crime scenes.

This shot was worthy of Weegee as well: a naked woman, her back arched, arms and legs splayed over what he had once thought were branches, her face turned toward the camera.

His shaking grew worse as he magnified this image. Her face had no real expression. The mouth was open, battered and bloody, the nose flattened, the cheeks covered in either blood or dirt.

But the eyes got to him. The eyes didn't look human. They looked like something out of a bad horror movie—filmed over with white, unfocused, and empty. It wasn't even fair to say that they were staring, because they weren't. There was no intelligence behind them, no thought, no anything. No staring happened because there was no intelligence inside those eyes to stare.

He leaned away from the computer and frowned. Something about the image was familiar. At first he thought it was simply the way the woman had fallen, and then he realized what it was.

She had come to his door. Four days ago. She'd parked her SUV against the curb, the windows open, her daughter—who was ten, maybe eleven—crying inside.

The woman had knocked, and he almost didn't answer because she looked so angry. But when he pulled the door open, she smiled at him.

"My daughter is selling candy so that her band can go to the regional tournaments." She opened the box. "Would you like to buy something?"

He didn't look at the candy. He looked at the crying girl in the SUV, wondering what her story was. He could probably guess. She didn't want to sell the candy, but her mother tried to force her. And when that hadn't worked, the mother decided to do it herself.

"She's shy," her mother said, as if confirming his thoughts.

He couldn't condone this kind of behavior, not from an adult. He hated bullying in all its forms, having been a victim of it when he was young and skinny and too nerdy for his own good.

But the woman made him nervous, and he couldn't say what he wanted to, which was, *Let your daughter be herself. Not everyone is a good salesperson.* Or good with people. Or even good one-on-one.

Instead, he struggled with, "N-N-No th-th-thanks."

And shut the door.

The woman remained on the porch for a moment, as if she couldn't believe he'd been that rude, and then she'd walked back to the SUV. She'd tossed the box of candy at her poor daughter before getting inside, and driving away.

If she was here, in this swamp, somewhere in the neighborhood, where was the little girl?

He was reaching for the phone before he even realized what he was doing, and dialed 911. When the operator answered, he said, "I think there's a dead body in my neighborhood."

And that brought the detectives to his door.

***

They were in plain clothes, but they showed him badges. He recognized both detectives from the local paper. They had been working on some kind of task force, and they had their pictures in the Metro section often enough that he could almost remember their names.

Fortunately for him, he didn't need to. They introduced themselves.

The man with the silver hair trimmed so close to his neck that it looked like whiskers was Detective DeCarovich. His partner, a woman who looked like she could bench-press Homer without any effort, was Detective Ortiz.

They came inside Homer's house without invitation, and wanted to know where he had seen the body. He brought them the photograph which he'd printed out on his laser printer, and they asked again where he had seen her.

So he had to explain—slowly because his stutter acted up—about the cat cameras and the experiment. The detectives stared at him as if he were crazy, so he finally waved them over to the computer and showed them the German man's home page, complete with instructions on how to build the camera.

Ortiz was the one who finally realized that Homer was serious. She turned to him, her dark eyes wide and stunned. "You did this with your own cats?"

Then she turned toward Princess, his pampered white Persian who looked like she had starred in the Fancy Feast commercials. Princess was lying on top of the red satin pillow he had placed on his couch as a joke, and she looked about as indolent as a cat could get.

"Not her," he said. "The outdoor cats. The more or less feral ones."

DeCarovich crossed his arms. He clearly didn't believe Homer and might even think Homer had something to do with the woman's disappearance.

Homer crooked a finger. "Come with me," he said. "But quietly."

He led them into the kitchen which overlooked the back forty. Fortunately, Mata Hari was in her afternoon spot, on top of a rock near an overgrown rhododendron, stretched out and sound asleep.

"See that box around her neck?" he said. "It has her camera. There are four other cats with cameras as well."

"For godsake," DeCarovich said and shook his head. He clearly wasn't impressed. He acted more like a man who had thought he'd seen it all, only to be surprised by something this weird. "Why would you do that?"

"Curiosity," Homer said. "I wondered what they do all day."

"Eat and sleep," Ortiz said.

"Actually, no," Homer said. "They're quite active…"

And then he let his voice trail off. The detectives weren't interested in his cats. They were interested in the photographs. DeCarovich was looking at the dead woman again.

"You really don't know where this is," DeCarovich said.

"No," Homer said. "And I'm not even sure it's on my property. It could be anywhere in the neighborhood."

"Or farther," Ortiz said. "Cats can have a territory of twenty acres or more."

DeCarovich turned toward her as if she had suddenly gone as crazy as Homer.

She shrugged. "I grew up around cats."

DeCarovich let out a small laugh, the kind a person used when he discovered he was among people he thought beneath him. Homer had heard that laugh a lot as a kid, and he didn't miss it.

His face heated, and his throat tightened. The stutter would get even worse. He knew the symptoms. He had to struggle just to start his next sentence, but he knew the tricks: don't get stuck on one word. Instead, recast your sentence into something else.

"M-M-Maybe I can reconstruct where they go," he said. He led the detectives back into his study so that he could open the computer photo files. "I have d-d-days worth of photos. Maybe th-th-there are l-l-landmarks."

He called up the files and started with the swamp and elephant graveyard photos, working backwards through each cat's imagery file. He wished now he hadn't thrown out most of the blurred and unfocused photos. They might tell him something.

Ortiz was leaning over his shoulder as he worked. DeCarovich walked through the room, studying Homer's books and his framed awards.

"You wrote these?" he asked after a moment.

"Y-Y-Yes," Homer said.

"Science guy, huh?"

He wanted to go for a self-deprecating "kinda" but the "k" would give him trouble. He had to settle for another stammered "yes."

"I guess guys like you would do stuff like this. Experiments, huh?"

But Homer was careful not to answer that vague a question. He still had the sense DeCarovich believed he was involved in that woman's death.

"Th-Th-The p-p-pictures?"

"Yeah." DeCarovich looked at him.

Homer nodded. His throat had tightened so badly he knew he wouldn't be able to easily get out another sentence.

"Damn," Ortiz said beside him. "These cats go underneath everything."

They did too. Under leaves, between bushes, under rocks. There was no clear trail, nothing recognizable, at least to human eyes.

"You actually think this guy's onto something?" DeCarovich asked, no longer trying to hide his contempt.

"I think we finally found the bone yard," Ortiz said, and Homer was the one who shuddered.

He remembered the articles now. These detectives had just formed a task force to investigate a series of missing persons cases, all of women in their thirties who disappeared in broad daylight.

"Except we didn't find it, not yet," Ortiz was saying. "These cats can't tell us where it is and if we try to follow them, we'll make sure they never go there again."

"We'll have to do a grid search," DeCarovich said.

"And destroy a lot of physical evidence along the way." Ortiz sighed. "At least now we know what happened to Ann Kemmel."

"Th-Th-That's the woman?" Homer asked.

Ortiz nodded.

"Wh-Wh-What about her daughter?"

Both detectives stared at him as if he had just confessed. He swallowed and forced himself to tell them about the incident with the candy bars and the SUV.

"F-F-Four days ago," he said.

"That's when she disappeared," DeCarovich said. "Only her kid wasn't with her. Her kid was at home the whole time."

Homer shook his head. "I saw her. She was in th-th-the c-c-car."

"How would you know?" DeCarovich asked.

"She was c-c-crying real hard." He felt his face get even redder. "I th-th-thought her mother was b-b-being mean."

DeCarovich's eyes narrowed, but Ortiz didn't seem to notice. She turned toward him.

He raised his eyebrows. "I thought we were too easy on her."

"I can't believe she was lying," Ortiz said. "She must have seen something. I'll bet she was scared."

DeCarovich shook his head. "She was just another—."

He waved his hand at Homer, and Homer wondered what word DeCarovich left out.

"She st-st-st…" Homer couldn't say the word. He never could under stress. "She has a speech d-d-defect?"

"Like you," DeCarovich said.

Homer nodded. He had been right then. The mother had been treating her like his mother had treated him, believing that he could overcome his problems with just a little more hard work.

"She wasn't in the car," Ortiz said. "She was lying."

"Lying," Homer said slowly so that he wouldn't stutter any more, "makes a speech problem worse. Any stress, even small stress, will make the problem worse."

He got it out without a single mistake. His cheeks grew even hotter. DeCarovich frowned at him, but it was no longer the frown of the impatient. It was a frown of consideration.

"You think the kid saw something?" he asked Homer, and Homer got that sense again that DeCarovich still suspected him.

Homer's throat tightened, so he shrugged.

"I'll bet she did," Ortiz said. "We need to reinterview."

"With the photographic evidence." DeCarovich picked up the print-out. "Can we keep that?"

Homer nodded.

"She's going to be just as afraid of us as she was the last time." Ortiz sighed.

Homer knew what she was imagining. Trying to interview a child whose mouth continually betrayed her would be difficult at best.

Ortiz took the photograph from DeCarovich. "Too bad you can't put a video camera on those cats. Then we could just find the body and the evidence. There's bound to be some if he's been using that spot for the past five years."

Five years. Homer started. They were investigating five years worth of disappearances. Five years of dumping dead women into a primeval swamp.

"It c-c-can't be t-t-too cl-cl-close," Homer said. "We'd smell it. Me and the neighbors. Bodies…"

He didn't have to finish his sentence. Ortiz was nodding.

"You're right," she said. "We need a topo map."

"You want wind charts too?" DeCarovich was being sarcastic.

"I'm serious," Ortiz said. "If we can find the body without talking to that kid—"

"We have to talk to her," DeCarovich said. "We have to know why she lied."

Homer knew DeCarovich was right. But the two thoughts—the video camera and that little girl—gave him an idea.

"D-D-Don't show her the photograph," he said. "She won't be able t-t-to t-t-talk after th-th-that."

"Listen, buddy," DeCarovich said, but Ortiz put a hand on his arm.

Homer made himself take a deep breath. "What I meant was I might b-b-be able t-t-to modify the c-c-cameras. Instead of every 90 seconds, I might be able t-t-to have images every five."

"Which just show us more leaves and trees and rocks," DeCarovich said. "Nice try, but that's going to give us more of the same."

"No," Ortiz said. "It won't. It might show us where the cats go into the woods. Can you set up a time stamp too?"

"Yes," Homer said. "If we know where they go in, the angle of the sun might tell us what direction they're going."

He realized after he spoke that he was no longer nervous. He liked the female detective. She didn't intimidate him.

"These cats aren't looking up," DeCarovich said. "We can't see sunlight."

"Through the leaves, on the ground, we'll get some stuff. C'mon, Rick," Ortiz said. "You've done similar things with shadow."

"I still think we do a grid."

"Let's give Mr. Ziff a chance," Ortiz said. "His cats might help us."

DeCarovich snorted. "Like they can do that."

"They already have," Ortiz said. "They gave us Ann Kemmel, and a reason to reinterview her daughter."

DeCarovich glared at Homer. "You get one day for this nonsense. One day. After that, we do a grid."

As if Homer had a stake in not having a grid search. He just wanted them to find this poor woman's body. And figure out what else was down in that swamp.

Near his house.

Someone had been dumping bodies near his house. Near the safest place he knew.

He shuddered.

"Would you like a c-c-copy of th-th-the photo files?" he asked Ortiz.

"Yeah," she said. "We have some computer whizzes who might find some answers here. And give me the URL for that German website, so they know this is legit."

He nodded, made copies onto a CD, and wrote down the web address for her.

She tapped him on the arm as a thank you. "This is kinda cool," she said, holding up the CD in the jewel case he'd given her. "Who knew that cats did such interesting things?"

"Yeah," DeCarovich said as he led her out the door. "Like staring at dead bodies. Who knew?"

***

Homer couldn't let DeCarovich's sarcasm and attitude get to him, even though it brought back not only Homer's high school days, but his teaching days as well. More than once, he'd caught his students in the hall, making fun of his stutter. Often they were the students from his 101 Physics class, and it was right after the unit on particles.

He had no trouble discussing electrons and protons or baryons and mesons. But quarks. Quarks caught him every time. That "ka" sound tripped him up and it got worse the longer he taught. The closer he got to the discussion of elementary particles, the more difficulty he would have.

Just like that little girl. He wished he could interview her. His stutter would put her at ease. She would be able to tell him what she saw or didn't see. She would be able to tell him how she survived when her mother hadn't.

He sighed and turned to the project at hand. He was glad he still had that sixth camera, the one the old tom had fought off. Homer was able to experiment with it. He couldn't set the timer for five seconds—it simply didn't work—but it could go off every ten seconds.

The problem was that it used a lot of energy when it took that many pictures. He found some larger memory cards, but he didn't have adequate batteries, and it was too late to buy any new ones.

So he would have to pick his times, hoping he got the right part of the day.

Then he checked his cupboards. He had a lot of canned salmon and tuna. He would need it. He would have to catch each of his feral photographers, remove their cameras, modify them, and reattach them. Then he'd have to catch the group again tomorrow and remove the memory card.

Twenty-four hours really wasn't enough.

But it was all he had.

***

By dawn, he had replaced the cameras on all of the cats.

Mata Hari was the first to return. She brought him a lovely series of photographs of the undercarriage of every car on the street. Just as the memory of the camera filled, she had crawled under a fence near the school.

He wondered if that was where she would go to get to the swamp, but he had no way of knowing.

He removed the camera, reset its automatic timer to beginning shooting later the following day, but knew it would do no good.

DeCarovich would hold to the twenty-four hour rule. The man probably still suspected Homer. Homer knew that by now, his fingerprints would have been removed from the jewel case to see if he had a criminal record (he did not) and the computer crimes unit would make sure that he hadn't dummied up the German website. They would find that he hadn't faked the website and that his cats had been taking pictures now for more than a month.

DeCarovich would also check Homer's work history, his phone usage (which was almost nil) and his bank records, which would probably surprise the detective. Popular science books made money—even if men like DeCarovich weren't interested.

Although Homer didn't know how someone like DeCarovich couldn't be interested. His job was all about science. Just on this case alone, they'd be using topographic maps and sunlight angles; they'd be removing fingerprints and studying computer records; they'd probably be using DNA to identify what was left of the other bodies.

Just by that quick reckoning, Homer figured their work would touch on geography, physics, computer science, biology, and chemistry. And all of it—even the deductive reasoning that DeCarovich was probably using to continue to blame Homer—required a meticulousness that only the best scientists could achieve.

So Homer had to hope that the other cats would bring him something, something recognizable.

Something good.

***

The answers he sought came, surprisingly, from Einstein—a small shy male with a shock of white hair over his tiny furrowed brow. Einstein had been difficult to conquer: it had taken weeks to catch him to neuter him, and weeks after that to regain his trust. That he wore a camera at all was amazing; that he actually showed Homer the trail to the body was a shock.

Homer thought Einstein was one of the few cats who didn't make a daily pilgrimage to the swamp. Apparently he did go, just didn't stay as long as the others, and so sometimes he didn't get a good photograph. Also, Einstein was the cat whose photos were most likely to blur because he ran almost everywhere.

But on this morning, he meandered toward the swamp—through the hole in the fence that Mata Hari had found, around a stone with the year 1908 carved into the top, and then down an embankment into a copse of trees.

Einstein actually followed a tiny trail. Homer hadn't noticed it on the previous shots because it looked like a bare line in the earth, nothing spectacular. But on the ten-second shots, it was clear that the bare line was connected to other bare lines—a rabbit path that wound from the 1908 rock and into the trees.

There he saw a moss-covered old-growth stump, some ancient logging, and several late-blooming irises in front of a ruined log that Einstein crawled on top of to peer into the swamp.

The body looked worse today; less like the woman Homer had met and more like a corpse. Einstein had gotten several good pictures of it, and Homer didn't study any of them.

Instead, he copied the entire memory card onto a CD, printed the files, and called Ortiz.

She wasn't at the station. The dispatch patched him into her cell. She answered on the fourth ring, sounding annoyed.

Homer identified himself, then said, "I think I know where the path is."

"Thank God," she said. "We'll be right there."

And they were. Within fifteen minutes, they had parked in front of his house. DeCarovich looked less dyspeptic today, but Ortiz seemed frustrated.

They had been talking to the little Kemmel girl when Homer called, although "talking," DeCarovich said, "isn't really the word for it."

Homer didn't ask about it. He figured they'd tell him if they wanted to. It wasn't his investigation after all. He was just helping with one small part.

He put the printed photographs in a line, with little gaps between them. Next to them, he put a map of this section of the neighborhood.

"See this?" he said, pointing to the fence. "That's part of this house."

He pointed to a house not far from the school.

"And this rock?" he said. "It's behind the school. They christened it last year as part of a rededication. It's been there since the school was built."

He had highlighted what he believed to be the path leading into the trees.

"I figure you can use the landmarks—the irises, the old-growth stump, the log—to find her."

"You didn't look?" DeCarovich asked.

Homer frowned at him. No one in his right mind would investigate this one on his own, not when he understood the science of trace and the importance of keeping a crime scene uncontaminated.

"No," Homer said. "I figure th-th-that's your job."

The stutter surprised him. He thought he was confident enough in his map not to tighten up. But that hint of a threat in DeCarovich's voice had been enough to bring back the stutter.

"We need to go down there," DeCarovich said.

"Let's send a team," Ortiz said studying the photos.

"Let's not waste taxpayer dollars until we know we're in the right place."

For once, Homer agreed with DeCarovich. They didn't say much more to him. They took the printed photographs, the map, and the CD, and then they left.

He felt at loose ends. Despite his sensible thoughts about the crime scene, he did want to investigate it himself. He wished he were more involved.

After all, his cats had been the one to discover what Ortiz had called the body dump. If only they were trained cats. He could send them down the path to the swamp with cameras around their neck and watch as the detectives officially found Ann Kemmel's body.

But he couldn't assign the cats anything, and he could only view what they wanted to look at. Mostly, all they cared about was the undercarriage of cars.

Then he frowned and headed toward his computer. The cats loved the undercarriage of SUVs more than actual cars. SUVs had big tires and a wider frame, but a lower undercarriage than a truck. That gave the cat a lot of places to hide and even more places to visit with little feline friends, all in the comfort of a shady spot on the street.

But one photo had come to mind. A photo taken by yet another cat—Galileo—somewhere around the time of the candy selling incident. It had been a blur photo, and Homer had tossed it, but he hadn't yet cleared off the memory card.

He grabbed all the cards that needed clearing and started cycling through them one by one. He didn't find any more images of the path to the swamp—he knew he wouldn't—but he did find several of a parked SUV with unfamiliar tires.

And then he found the photograph he was looking for. Two photographs, actually. One of a skinny leg with a single pink girl's tennis shoe about to touch the pavement—and another of a pink-and-blue blur disappearing behind a bench across the street.

He closed his eyes, trying to remember what that crying girl had been wearing that afternoon. He just remembered her face, splotchy and humiliated, her eyes swollen from all the tears she'd shed. He could also remember the SUV, with its blue and silver metallic sides.

Silver, like the side where the pants leg brushed.

He opened his eyes and studied the next two frames. He didn't see any more pink and blue blurs, but he did know where that bench was. It was several doors down from his, right across the street from his surly neighbor, the man who had rolled his eyes when he'd heard the ferocity of Homer's stutter.

Homer went cold.

He wondered if he should call Ortiz. He didn't want to bother her, not when she was looking at the crime scene.

Instead, he opened a file on his computer, looked at the neighborhood map he'd downloaded earlier and studied the wetlands.

They not only ran behind his house, they ran the entire length of this side of the street, ending (or beginning depending on your point of view) at the century-old school house.

Anyone who wanted to could carry a body from their own personal back forty into the wetlands and walk through the overgrown wooded area to the swamp without being seen.

No wonder DeCarovich had suspected Homer. Homer fit all kinds of profiles. He was reclusive. He lived alone. He had access to the so-called body dump. He even inserted himself in the investigation.

His hands were shaking again. He wasn't sure if he had important information or not. The two detectives were still having trouble talking to the daughter. But Homer had evidence she left the SUV on her own and ran away.

Before or after her mother had disappeared?

He logged onto the internet and looked up what he could find on the disappearance of Ann Kemmel. She only ranked a few paragraphs in the paper on the day after her disappearance. But those few paragraphs were enough.

She and the SUV were missing.

She was last seen here on his quiet block in the middle of the afternoon on the day she disappeared, selling band candy for her daughter.

Just like he'd said.

He sank deeper into his chair. His mouth was dry. He was innocent. Ortiz knew that or she would have confiscated his computer. They would have come into his house with a warrant.

Or maybe they were waiting to find the body.

Maybe they needed just a little more for probable cause.

***

A knock on the door snapped him out of his reverie. His heart was pounding and his face was already flushed. He knew he looked guilty. For all his caution, he had done so much wrong.

It would only be a matter of time before someone would come to arrest him.

He managed to leave his study, walk across his living room and peer through the glass in the door.

Ortiz stood there, arms folded behind her back. There was no sign of DeCarovich.

When she saw Homer, she nodded. She didn't smile.

Here it was: fair warning. She had come to ask if she could search his house. He would tell her to get a warrant. He would use his small fortune to hire the best criminal defense attorney in the state. He might even get his publisher's publicist to get him some interviews on his good Samaritan deed gone wrong.

He pulled open the door.

"We found her." Ortiz sounded tired. "And the others, most likely. I just wanted you to know. Your cats were right."

He waited for her to say the next part, the part about searching his house or getting a warrant. But she didn't.

She seemed to be done.

"Wow," he said. "The photos worked?"

"There was a cat path," she said. "The lab techs are down there now. It's a mess. But no one would have smelled it. Too far from houses. Too far from that school."

"The cats had to know."

"The cats must have smelled something decaying, but it didn't interest them. None of them are starving."

He smiled in spite of himself. Her comment had echoed his thoughts.

And besides, she'd seen his outdoor cats. They clearly weren't starving.

"Um," he said. "I was wondering one other thing. Th-th-that girl? Did she run away from her mother?"

Ortiz frowned at him. "How did you know?"

"I th-th-think I found some more pictures."

She came inside without asking, but she did take off her shoes. They had a swampy smell—or maybe she did— the beginnings of decay.

Princess and his other indoor cat, King, came out of the bedroom, sniffing the air. So that smell did attract them.

"I think I found pictures of the SUV," he said, and told her about the underbellies of cars, how cats socialized there, and how much they seemed to like a shady spot on the road.

"We were talking to her when you called," Ortiz said. "Poor kid. She's going to need therapy for the rest of her life."

He looked at the detective. She was already peering at the photographs on his computer.

"Why?"

"She says her mother went inside a house to sell band candy, and she ran away. She went to her grandmother's, but her grandmother brought her home."

"And no one saw the mother again."

"That's right," Ortiz said. "Missing Persons wasn't even that interested since the SUV was gone too. They figured the mother had run off."

He pointed out the skinny leg, the pink shoes, the blur of blue-and-pink across the street.

"And you know where this is, don't you?" Ortiz said.

He nodded.

She grinned at him. "Too bad we can't put those cats of yours on payroll."

"You wouldn't like them as employees," he said. "They go their own way."

And it wasn't until after she left, with more printed photographs and more files on CD, that he realized he had had an entire conversation with a woman he liked and hadn't stammered.

At least, not much.

He thought of it as a victory.

He didn't realize it was also the beginning of an odyssey.

***

Ortiz and DeCarovich got a search warrant for the surly neighbor's house and found blood in the basement, and all sorts of other grisly things. The man had done exactly what Homer had hypothesized: killed the women (after abusing them sexually), then waited until dark and carried their bodies through the wetlands to the wider swampy area, dumping them there. Sometimes he would move their cars before he killed them, sometimes afterwards.

DeCarovich believed that there was a car dump like there was a body dump, but so far, no one had found it.

Ortiz kept Homer apprised of all of it. She even visited him a few times, always asking about his cats. Finally she told him she wanted to go to dinner with him, but she couldn't, not until the trial was over.

The trial. He hadn't thought of it. The grand jury, the testimony. The cross-examination.

He could already see what was coming:

He was a central part of the case—actually, his cats were—and he would feel like a failing professor all over again. Stammering his way through his stories, wishing that he could find a way to mitigate the talking part, and still explain—meticulously—his role in the arrest.

He decided to write out his testimony, to plan it, detail by detail. And as he did, he threaded the photographs through the text.

It only took him a week to figure out what he had.

A true crime book.

An unusual true crime book.

No one else had ever written anything like it.

He summoned up his courage and showed it to his agent. She loved it. She proposed a few other books as well—one just a book of photography by his cats. She showed him some curious coffee-table book from several years before of cats painting (actually just sweeping their paint-covered paws over walls and floors) and told him it had been a bestseller.

He agreed to do it all, but prosecutors wanted him to wait until his testimony was finished so that he wouldn't be accused of helping the police for money.

He wondered how anyone would think he had rigged his cameras to his feral cats for money, but he knew that people could believe anything.

So he waited. And he testified. And he did feel humiliated.

Until Detective Ortiz—her first name was Susan—took him out for a celebratory steak dinner. She had praised him, called him brilliant, and even said he was interesting.

He didn't feel interesting.

But he liked her attention.

He liked her.

He was so glad that the case had wrapped up quickly. He had been a star witness—not *the* star witness, though. That proved to be the little girl, with her father at her side, pointing out the man she'd last seen with her mother.

The surly neighbor, who no longer rolled his eyes at people who stuttered.

They had convicted him, two of the people he held in contempt. They had ended his life on the outside.

Two stammerers—two momentary stars—and five wandering cats, reluctantly sharing their secret lives bit by tiny bit.

DISCOVERY

"OVER THERE." Pita Cardenas waved a hand at the remaining empty spot on the floor of her office. The Federal Express deliveryman rested a hand on top of the stack of boxes on his handcart.

"I don't think it'll fit."

It probably wouldn't. Her office was about the size of the studio apartment she'd had when she went to law school in Albuquerque. She could have had a cubicle with more square footage if she'd taken the job that La Jolla, Webster, and Garcia offered her when she graduated from law school five years before.

But her mother had been dying, and had refused to leave Rio Gordo. So Pita had come back to the town she thought she'd escaped from, put out her shingle, and had gotten a handful of cases, enough to pay the rent on this sorry excuse for an office. If she'd wanted something bigger, she would have had to buy, and even at Rio Gordo's depressed prices, she couldn't afford payments on the most dilapidated building in town.

She stood up. The Fed Ex guy, who drove here every day from Lubbock, was looking at her with pity. He was trim and tanned, with a deep West Texas accent. If she had been less tired and overwhelmed, she would have flirted with him.

"Let's put this batch in the bathroom," she said and led the way through the rabbit path she'd made between the boxes. The Fed Ex guy followed, dragging the six boxes on his hand truck and probably chafing at the extra time she was costing him.

She opened the door. He put the boxes inside, tipped an imaginary hat to her, and left. She'd have to crawl over them to get to the toilet, but she'd manage.

Six boxes today, twenty yesterday, thirty the day before. Dwyer, Ralbotten, Seacur and Czolb was burying her in paper.

Of course, she had expected it. She was a solo practitioner in a town whose population probably didn't equal the number of people who worked at DRS&C.

People had told her she was crazy to take this case. But she was crazy like an impoverished attorney. Every other firm in New Mexico had told her client, Nan Hughes, to settle. The problem was that Nan didn't want to settle. Settling meant losing everything she owned.

Pita took the case and charged Nan two thousand dollars, with more due and owing when (if) the case went to trial. Pita didn't plan on taking the case to trial. At trial, she wouldn't just get creamed, she'd be pureed, sautéed and recycled.

But she did plan to work for that two grand. She would spend exactly one month filing motions, doing depositions, and listening to offers. She figured once she had actual numbers, she'd be able to convince Nan to take a deal.

If not, she'd resign and wish Nan luck finding a new attorney.

Her actions wouldn't hurt Nan. Nan had a spectacular loser of a case. She was taking on the railroads and two major insurance companies. She had no idea how bad things could get.

Pita would show her. Nan wouldn't exactly be happy with her lot—how could she be, when she'd lost her husband, her business, and her home on the same day?—but she would finally understand how impossible the winning was.

Pita was doing her a favor and making a little money besides.

And what was wrong with that?

***

At its heart, the case was simple. Ty Hughes tried to beat a train and failed. He survived long enough to leave his wife a voice mail message, which Pita had heard in all its heartbreaking slowness:

"Nan baby, I tried to beat it. I thought I could beat it."

Then his diesel truck engine caught fire and he died, horribly alive, in the middle of the wreck.

The accident occurred on a long stretch of brown nothingness on the New Mexico side of the Texas/New

Mexico border. A major highway ran a half mile parallel to the tracks. On the opposite side of the tracks stood the Hughes ranch and all its outbuildings.

Nan Hughes and the people who worked her spread watched the accident. She didn't answer her cell because she'd left it on the kitchen counter in her panic to get down the dirt road where her husband's cattle truck had been demolished by a fast-moving train.

And not just any train.

This train pulled dozens of oil tankers.

It was a miracle the truck engine fire hadn't spread to the tankers and the entire region hadn't exploded into one great fireball.

Pita had been familiar with the case long before Nan Hughes came to her. For weeks, the news carried stories about dead cattle along the highway, the devastated widow, the ruined ranch, and the angry railroad officials who had choice (and often bleeped) words about the idiots who tried to race trains.

It didn't matter that the crossing was unmarked. Even if Ty hadn't left that confession on Nan's voice mail (which she had deleted but which the cell company was so thoughtfully able to retrieve), trains in this part of the country were visible for miles in either direction.

The railroads wanted the ranch, the cattle (what was left of them), the life insurance money, and millions from the ranch's liability insurance. The liability insurance company was willing to settle for a simple million, and the other law firms had told Nan to sell the ranch, and pay the railroads from the proceeds. That way she could live on Ty's life insurance and move away from the site of the disaster.

But Nan kept saying that Ty would haunt her if she gave in. That he had never raced a train in his life. That he knew how far away a train was by its appearance against the horizon—and that he had taught her the same trick.

When Pita gently asked why Ty had confessed to trying to beat the train, Nan had burst into tears.

"Something went wrong," she said. "Maybe he got stuck. Maybe he hadn't looked up. He was in shock. He was dying. He was just trying to talk to me one last time."

Pita could hear any good lawyer tear that argument to shreds, just using Ty's wording. If Ty wanted to talk with her, why hadn't he told her he loved her? Why had he talked about the train?

Pita had gently asked that too. Nan had looked at her from across the desk, her wet cheeks chapped from all the tears she'd shed.

"He knew I saw what happened. He wanted me to know he never would have done that to me on purpose."

In this context, "on purpose" had a lot of different definitions. Ty Hughes probably didn't want his wife to see him die in a train wreck, certainly not in a train wreck he caused. But he had crossed a railroad track with a double-decker cattle truck filled carrying two hundred head. He had no acceleration, and no maneuverability.

He'd taken a gamble, and he'd lost.

At least, Nan hadn't seen the fire in the cab. The truck had flipped over the train, landing on the highway side of the tracks, and had been impossible to see from the ranch side. Whatever Ty Hughes's last few minutes had looked like, Nan had missed them.

She had only her imagination, her anger at the railroads, and her unshakeable faith in her dead husband.

Those were not enough to win a case of this magnitude.

If someone asked Pita what her case really was (and if this imaginary someone could get her to answer honestly), what she'd say was that she was going to try Ty Hughes before his wife, and show her how impossible a defense of the man's actions that morning would be in court.

And Pita believed her own powers of persuasion were enough to convince her jury of one to settle.

***

But the boxes were daunting. In them were bits and pieces of information, reproduced letters and memos that probably showed some kind of railroad duplicity, however minor. A blot on an engineer's record, for example, or an accident at that same crossing twenty years before.

If Pita had the support of a giant law firm like La Jolla, Webster, and Garcia, she might actually delve into that material. Instead, she let it stack up like unread novels in the home of an obsessive compulsive.

The only thing she did do was take out the witness list, which had come in its own envelope as part of court-ordered discovery. The list had the witnesses' names along with their addresses, phone numbers, and the dates of their depositions. DRS&C was so thorough that each witness had a single line notation at the bottom of the cover sheet describing the reason the witness had been deposed in this case.

The list would help Pita in her quest to recreate the accident itself. She had dozens of questions. Had someone inspected the truck to see if it malfunctioned at the time of the accident? Why had Ty stayed in the truck when it was clear that it was going to catch fire? How badly had he been injured? How good was Ty's eyesight? And how come no one helped him before the truck caught fire?

She was going to cover all her bases. All she needed was one argument strong enough to let Nan keep the house.

She was afraid she might not even find that.

DRS&C's categories were pretty straightforward. They had categories for the ranch, the railroad, and the eyewitnesses.

A number of the witnesses belonged to separate lawsuits, started because of the fender benders on the nearby highway. About a dozen cars had damage—some while they were stopped beside the road, and others because they'd been going too fast to stop when the train accident occurred.

Pita started charting the location of the cars as she figured this category out, and realized all of them had been in the far inside lane, going east. People who had pulled over to help Ty and the railroad employees had instead been dealing with accidents involving their own cars.

A separate group of accident victims had resolved insurance claims: their vehicles had been hit or had hit a cow that had escaped from the cattle truck. One poor man had had his SUV gored by an enraged bull.

Cars heading west had had an easier time of things. None had hit each other and a few had stopped. Of those who had stopped, some were listed as 911 callers. One had grabbed a fire extinguisher and eventually tried to put out the truck cab fire. That person had prevented the fire from spreading to the tankers.

But the category that caught Pita's attention was a simple one. Several people on the list had been marked "Witness," with no accompanying explanation.

One had an extra long zip code, and as she entered it into her own computer data base, she realized that the last three digits weren't part of the zip code at all.

They were a previous notation, one that hadn't been deleted.

Originally, this witness had been in the 911 category.

She decided to start with him.

***

C.P. Williams was a Texas financier of the Houston variety, even though his offices were in Lubbock. He wore cowboy boots, but they were custom made, hand-tooled jobbies that wouldn't last fifteen minutes on a real ranch. He had an oversized silver belt buckle and he wore a bolo tie, but his shiny suit was definitely not off the rack and neither was the silk shirt underneath it. His cufflinks matched his belt buckle and he twisted them as he led Pita into his office.

"I already gave a deposition," he said.

"Before I was on the case," Pita said.

His office was big, with original oil paintings of the Texas Hill Country, and a large but not particularly pretty view of downtown Lubbock.

"Can't you just read it?" He slipped behind a custom-made desk. The chair in front was made of hand-tooled leather that made her think of his impractical boots.

She sat down. The leather pattern bit through the thin pants of her best suit.

"I have a few questions of my own." She took out a small tape recorder. "I may have to call you in for a second deposition, but I hope not."

Mostly because she would have to rent space as well as a court reporter in order to conduct that deposition. Right now, she simply wanted to see if any testimony was worth the extra cost.

"I don't have that much time. I barely have enough time to see you now." He glanced at his watch for emphasis.

She clicked on the recorder. "Then let's do this quickly. Please state your name and occupation for the record."

He did.

When he finished, she said, "On the morning of the accident—"

"I never saw that damn accident," he said. "I told the other lawyers that."

She was surprised. Why had they talked with him then? She was interviewing blind. So she went with the one fact she knew.

"You called 911. Why?"

"Because of the train," he said.

"What about the train?"

"Damn thing was going twice as fast as it should have been."

For the first time since she'd taken this case, she finally felt a flicker of real interest. "Trains speed?"

"Of course trains speed," he said. "But this one wasn't just speeding. It was going well over a hundred miles an hour."

"You know that because…?"

"I was going 70. It passed me. I had nothing else to do, so I figured out the rate of passage. Speed limits for trains on that section of track is 65. Most weeks, the trains match me, or drop back just a bit. This one was leaving me in the dust."

She was leaning forward. If the train was speeding—and if she could prove it—then the accident wasn't Ty's fault alone. He wouldn't have been able to judge how fast the train was going. And if it was going twice as fast as usual, it would have reached him two times quicker than he expected.

"So why call 911?" she asked. "What can they do?"

"Not damn thing," he said. "I just wanted it on record when the train derailed or blew through a crossing or hit some kid on the way to school."

"You could have contacted the railroad or maybe the NTSB," she said. "They could have fined the operators or pulled the engineers off the train."

"I could have," he said. "I didn't want to."

She frowned. "Why not?"

"Because I wanted the record."

And because he repeated that sentence, she felt a slight shiver. "Have you done this before? Clocked trains going too fast, I mean."

"Yeah." He sounded surprised at the question. "So?"

"Do you call 911 on people speeding in cars?"

His eyes narrowed. "No."

"So why do you call on trains?"

"I told you. The potential damage—"

"Did you contact the police after the accident, then?" she asked.

"No. It was already on record. They could find it. That attorney did."

"I wouldn't know how to compute how fast a train was going while I was driving," she said. "I mean, if we were going the same speed or something close, sure. But not an extra thirty miles an hour or more. That's quite a trick."

"Simple math," he said. "You had to do problems like that in school. We all did."

"I suppose," she said. "But it's not something I would think to do. Why did you?"

For the first time, he looked down. He didn't say anything.

"Do you have something against the railroad?" she asked.

His head shot up. "Now you sound like them."

"Them?"

"Those other lawyers."

She started to nod, but made herself stop. "What did they say?"

His lips thinned. "They said that I'm just making stuff up to get the railroad in trouble. They said that I'm pathetic. Me! I out earn half those walking suits. I make money every damn day, and I do it without investing in any land holdings or railroad companies. They have no idea who I am."

Neither did she, really, but she thought she'd humor him.

"You're a good citizen," she said.

"Damn straight."

"Trying to protect other citizens."

"That's right."

"From the railroads."

"They think they can run all over the countryside like they're invulnerable. That train pulling oil tankers, imagine if it had derailed in that accident. You'd've heard the explosion in Rio Gordo."

Probably seen it too. He had a point.

"Tell me," she said. "Is there any way we can prove the train was going that fast?"

"The 911 call," he said.

"Besides the 911 call," she said.

He leaned back as he considered her question. "I'm sure a lot of people saw it. Or you could examine that truck. You know, it's just basic physics. If you vary the speed of an incoming train in an impact with a similar truck frame, you'll get differing results. I'm sure you can find some experts to testify."

You could find experts to testify on anything. But she didn't say that. She was curious about his expertise, though. He seemed to know a lot about trains.

She asked, "Wouldn't a train derail at that speed when it hit a truck like that?"

"Actually, no. It would be less likely to derail when it was going too fast. That truck was a cattle truck, right? If the train hit the cattle car and not the cab, then the train would've treated that truck like tissue. Most cattle cars are made of aluminum. At over a hundred miles per hour, the train would have gone through it like paper."

Interesting. She would check that.

"One last question, Mr. Williams. When did the railroad fire you?"

He blinked at her, stunned. She had caught him. That's why DRS&C's attorneys had called him pathetic. Because he had a reason for his train obsession.

A bad reason.

"That was a long time ago," he whispered.

But she still might be able to use him if he had some kind of expertise. If his old job really did require that he clock trains by sight alone.

"What did you do for them?"

He coughed, then had the grace to finally meet her gaze. "I was a security guard at the station here in Lubbock."

Security guard. Not an engineer, not anyone with special training. Just a guy with a phony badge and a gun.

"That's when you learned to clock trains," she said.

He smiled. "You have to do something to pass the time."

She bit back her frustration. For a few minutes, he'd given her some hope. But all she had was a fired security guard with a grudge.

She wrapped up the interview as politely as she could, and headed into the bright Texas sunshine.

And allowed herself one small moment to wish that C.P. Williams had been a real witness, one that could have opened this case wide.

Then she sighed, and went back to preparing her case for her jury of one.

***

Most everyone else in the witness category on DRS&C's list was either a rubbernecker or someone who had made a false 911 call. Pita had had no idea how many people reported a crime or an accident *after* seeing coverage of it on television, but she was starting to learn.

She was also learning why the police didn't fine or arrest these people. Most of them were certifiably crazy.

Pita was beginning to think the list was worthless. Then she interviewed Earl Jessup Jr.

Jessup was a contractor who had been on his way to Lubbock to pick up a friend from the airport when he'd seen the accident. He'd pulled over, and because he was so well known in Rio Gordo, someone had remembered he was there.

When Pita arrived at his immaculate house in one of Rio Gordo's failed housing developments, she promised herself she wouldn't interview any more witnesses. Then Jessup pulled the door open. He smiled in recognition. So did she.

She had talked with him in the hospital cafeteria during her mother's final surgery. He'd been there for his brother, who'd been in a particularly horrendous accident, and who had somehow managed to survive.

They hadn't exchanged names.

He was a small man with brown hair in need of a good trim. His house smelled faintly of cigarette smoke and aftershave. The living room had been modified—lowered furniture, and wide paths cut through what had once been wall-to-wall carpet.

"Your brother moved in with you, huh?" she asked.

"He needed somebody," Jessup said with a finality that closed the subject.

He led her into the kitchen. On the right side of the room, the cabinets had been pulled from the walls. A dishwasher peeked out of the debris. On the left were frames for lowered countertops. Only the sink, the stove and the refrigerator remained intact, like survivors in a war zone.

He pulled a chair out for her at the kitchen table. The table was shorter than regulation height. An ashtray sat near the end of the table, but no chair. That had to be where his brother usually parked.

Pita pulled out her tape recorder and a notebook. She explained again why she was there, and asked Jessup to state some information for the record. She implied, as she had with all the others, that this informal conversation was as good as being under oath.

Jessup smiled as she went through her spiel. He seemed to know that his words would have no real bearing on the case unless he was giving a formal deposition.

"I didn't see the accident," he said. "I got there after."

He'd missed the fender benders and the first wave of the injured cows. He'd pulled up just as the train stopped. He'd been the one to organize the scene. He'd sent two men east and two men west to slow traffic until the sheriff arrived.

He'd made sure people in the various accidents exchanged insurance information, and he got the folks who'd suffered minor bumps and bruises to the side of the road. He directed a couple of teenagers to keep an eye on the injured animals, and make sure none of them made for the road again.

Then he'd headed down the embankment toward the overturned truck.

"It wasn't on fire yet?"

"No," he said. "I have no idea how it got on fire."

She frowned. "It overturned. It was leaking diesel and the engine was on."

"So the fancy Dallas lawyers tell me," he said.

"You don't believe them?"

"First thing any good driver does after an accident is shut off his engine."

"Maybe," she said. "If he's not in shock. Or seriously injured. Or both."

"Ty had enough presence of mind to make that phone call." Everyone in Rio Gordo knew about that call. Some even cursed it, thinking Nan could own the railroads if Ty hadn't picked up his cell. "He would've shut off his engine."

Pita wasn't so sure.

"Besides, he wasn't in the cab."

That caught her attention. "How do you know?"

"I saw him. He was sitting on some debris halfway up the road. That's why I was in no great hurry to get down there. He'd gotten himself out, and there wasn't much I could do until the ambulance arrived."

Jessup had a construction worker's knowledge of injuries. He knew how to treat bruises and he knew what to do for trauma. He'd talked with her about that in the cafeteria, when he'd told her how helpless he'd felt coming on his brother's car wrapped around a utility pole. He hadn't been able to get his brother out of the car—the ambulance crew later used the jaws of life—and he was afraid his brother would bleed out right there.

"But you went to help Ty anyway," Pita said.

Jessup got up, walked to the stove, and lifted up the coffee pot. He'd been brewing the old-fashioned way, in a percolator, probably because he didn't have any counter space.

"Want some?" he asked.

"Please," she said, thinking it might get him to talk.

He pulled two mugs out of the dishwasher, then set them on top of the stove. "I thought he was going to be fine."

"You're not a doctor. You don't know." She wasn't acting like a lawyer now. She was acting like a friend, and she knew it.

He grabbed the pot, and poured coffee into both mugs. Then he brought them to the table.

"I did know," he said. "I knew there was trouble, and I left."

"Sounds like you did a lot before you left," she said, trying to move him past this. She remembered long talks about his guilt over his brother's accident. "Organizing the people, making sure Ty was okay. Seems to me that you did more than most."

He shook his head.

"What else could you have done?" she asked.

"I could've gone down there and helped him," he said. "If nothing else, I could've defended him against those men with guns."

She went cold. Men with guns. She hadn't heard about men with guns.

"Who had guns?" she asked.

He gave her a self-deprecating smile, apparently realizing how dramatic he had sounded. "Everyone has guns. This is the Texas-New Mexico border."

He'd said too much, and he clearly wanted to backtrack. She wouldn't let him.

"Not everyone uses them at the scene of an accident," she said.

"If they'd've been smart, they might have. That bull was mighty scary."

"Who had guns?" she asked.

He sighed, clearly knowing she wouldn't back down. "The engineers. They carried their rifles out of the train."

She raised her eyebrows, not sure what to say.

He seemed to think she didn't believe him, so he went on. "I figured they were carrying the guns to shoot any livestock that got in their way. Made me want my gun. I'd been thinking about the accident, not a bunch of injured animals that weighed eight times what I did."

"Why did you leave?" she asked.

"It was a judgment call," he said. "I was watching those engineers walk. With purpose."

As she listened to Jessup recount the story, she realized the purpose had nothing to do with cattle. These men carried their rifles like they intended to use them. They weren't looking at the carnage. After they'd finished inspecting the train for damage, they didn't look at the train either.

Instead, they stared at Ty.

"For the entire two-mile walk?" she asked.

"I don't know," Jessup said. "That's when I decided not to stay. I thought Ty was going to be fine."

He paused. She waited, knowing if she pushed him, he might not say any more.

Jessup ran a hand through his hair. "I knew that in situations like this tempers get out of hand. I couldn't be the voice of reason. I might even get some of the blame."

He wrapped his hands around his coffee mug. He hadn't touched the liquid.

"Besides," he said, "I could see Ty's cowboys. They were riding around the train and heading toward the loose cattle near the highway. If things got ugly, they could help him. I headed back up the embankment, went to my truck, and drove on to Lubbock."

"Then I don't understand why this is bothering you," she said. "You did as much as you could, and then you left it to others, the ones who needed to handle the problem."

"Yeah," he said softly. "I tell myself that."

"But?"

He tilted his head, as if shaking some thoughts loose. "But a couple of things don't make sense. Like why did Ty go back into the cab of that truck? And how come no one smelled the diesel? Wouldn't it bother them so close to the oil tankers?"

She waited, watching him. He shrugged.

"And then there's the nightmares."

"Nightmares?" she asked.

"I get into my truck, and as I slam the door, I hear a gunshot. It's half a second behind the sound of the door slamming, but it's clear."

"Did you really hear that?" she asked.

"I like to think if I did, I would've gone back. But I didn't. I just drove away, like nothing had happened. And a friend of mine died."

He didn't say anything else. She took another sip of her coffee, careful not to set the mug to close to her recorder.

"No one else reported gunshots," she said.

He nodded.

"No one else saw Ty outside that cab," she said.

"He was in a gully. I was the only one who went down the embankment. You couldn't see him from the road."

"And the truck? Could you see it?"

He shook his head.

"What do you think happened?" she asked.

"I don't know," he said, "and it's driving me insane."

***

It bothered her too, but not in quite the same way.

She found Jessup in DRS&C's list of 911 nutcases. He'd been buried among the crazies, just like important information was probably hidden in the boxes that littered her office floor.

No one else had seen the angry engineers or Ty out of the truck, but no one could quite figure out how he'd made that cell phone call either. If he'd been sitting on some debris outside the cab, that made more sense than calling from inside, while bleeding, with the engine running and diesel dripping.

But Jessup was right. It raised some disturbing questions.

They bothered her, enough so that she called Nan on her cell phone during the drive back to her office.

"Do you have a copy of the autopsy report for Ty?" Pita asked.

"There was no autopsy," Nan said. "It's pretty clear how he died."

Pita sighed. "What about the truck? What happened to it?"

"Last I saw, it was in Digger's Salvage Yard."

So Pita pulled into the salvage yard, and parked near a dented Toyota. Digger was a good ole boy who salvaged parts, and when he couldn't, he used a crusher to demolish the vehicles into metal for scrap.

But he still had the cab of that truck—insurance wouldn't release it until the case was settled.

For the first time, she looked at the cab herself, but couldn't see anything except charred metal, a steel frame, and a ruined interior. She wasn't an expert, and she needed one.

It took only a moment to call an old friend in Albuquerque who knew a good freelance forensic examiner. The examiner wanted $500 plus expenses to travel to Rio Gordo and look at the truck.

Pita hesitated. She could've—and should've—called Nan for the expense money.

But the examiner's presence would raise Nan's hopes. And right now, Pita couldn't do that. She was trusting a man she'd met late night at the hospital, a man who talked her through her mother's last illness, a man she couldn't quite get enough distance from to examine his veracity.

She needed more than Jessup's nightmares and speculations. She needed something that might pass for proof.

***

"I can't tell you when it got there," said the examiner, Walter Shepard. He was a slender man with intense eyes. He wore a plaid shirt despite the heat and tan trousers that had pilled from too many washings.

He was sitting in Pita's office. She had moved some boxes aside so that the path into the office was wider.

She'd also found a chair that had been buried since the case began.

He pushed some photographs onto her desk. The photographs were close-ups of the truck's cab. He'd thoughtfully drawn an arrow next to the tiny hole in the door on the driver's side.

"It's definitely a bullet hole. It's too smooth to be anything else," he said. "And there's another in the seat. I was able to recover part of a bullet."

He shifted the photos so that she could see a shattered metal fragment.

"The problem is I can't tell you anything else, except that the bullet holes predate the fire. I can't tell you how long they were there or how they got there. They could be real old. Or brand new. I can't tell."

"That's all right." A bullet hole, along with Jessup's testimony, was enough to cast doubt on everything. She felt like she could go to DRS&C and ask for a settlement.

She wasn't even regretting that she hadn't worked on contingency. This case was proving easier than she had thought it would be.

"I know you asked me to look for evidence of shooting or a fight," Shepard said, "but I wouldn't be doing my job if I let it go at that. The anomaly here isn't the bullets. It's the fire itself."

She looked up from the photos, surprised. Shepard wasn't watching her. He was still studying the photographs. He put a finger on one of them.

"The diesel leaked. There's runoff along the tank and a drip pattern that trails to the passenger side of the cab."

The cab had landed on its passenger side.

"But the fire started here." He was touching the photo of the interior of the cab. He pushed his finger against the image of the ruined seat. "See how the flames spread upwards. You can see the burn pattern. And fuel fed it. It burned around something—probably the body—so it looks to me like someone poured fuel onto the body itself and lit it on fire. I didn't find a match, but I found the remains of a Bic lighter on the floor of the cab. It melted but it's not burned the way everything else is. I think it was tossed in after the fire started."

Pita was having trouble wrapping her mind around what he was saying. "You're saying someone deliberately started the fire? So close to oil tankers?"

"I think that someone knew the truck wouldn't explode. The fire was pretty contained."

"Some people from the highway had a fire extinguisher in their car. It was too late to save Ty."

"You'll want your examiner to look at the body again," Shepard said. "I have a hunch you'll find that your client's husband was dead before he burned, not after."

"Based on this pattern."

"A man doesn't sit calmly and let himself burn to death," Shepard said. "He was able to make a phone call. He was conscious. He would have tried to get out of that cab. He didn't."

Pita was shaking. If this was true, then this case went way beyond a simple accident. If this was true, then those engineers shot Ty and tried to cover it up.

Ballsy, considering how close to the road they had been.

But the other drivers had been preoccupied with their own accidents and the injured cows and stopping traffic. No one except Jessup had even tried to come down the embankment.

And the engineers, who drove the route a lot, would have known how hard that truck was to see from the road.

They would have figured that the burning cab would get put out once someone saw the smoke. No wonder they'd lit the body. They didn't want to risk catching the cab on fire, and leaving the bullet-ridden corpse untouched.

"You're sure?" Pita asked.

"Positive." Shepard gathered the photos. "If I were you, I'd take this to the state police. You don't have an accident here. You have cold-blooded murder."

***

The next few weeks became a blur. DRS&C dropped the suit, becoming the friendliest big law firm that Pita had ever known. Which made her wonder when they'd realized that the engineers had committed murder.

Either way, it didn't matter. DRS&C was willing to work with her, to do whatever it took to "make Mrs. Hughes happy."

Nan wouldn't be happy until her husband's killers were brought to justice. She snapped into action the moment the state coroner confirmed Shepard's hunches. Ty had been shot in the skull before he died, and then his body had been burned to cover up the crime.

If Nan hadn't worked so hard and believed in her husband so much, no one would have known.

The story came out slowly. The train had been speeding when Ty crossed the tracks. Williams' estimate of more than 100 miles per hour was probably correct—enough for the railroads to have liability right there.

But the engineers, both frightened by the accident itself and terrified for their jobs, had walked the length of the train to Ty's overturned truck and, finding him alive and relatively unhurt, let their anger explode.

They'd threatened him with the loss of everything if he didn't confess that he had failed to beat the train. He'd made the call to satisfy them. But it hadn't worked. Somehow—and neither man was going to admit how (not even more than a year later at sentencing)—one of the rifles had gone off, killing him. Then they'd stuffed him in the cab—whose ignition was off—poured some diesel from the spill on him, and lit him on fire.

They watched him burn for a few minutes before going up the embankment to see if anyone had a fire extinguisher in his car. Fortunately someone did. Otherwise, they planned to have someone drive them the two miles to the engine for the train's fire extinguishers.

The engineers were eventually convicted, Nan got to keep her ranch and her husband's reputation, and the railroads kept trying to settle.

But Pita insisted that Nan hire an attorney who specialized in cases against big companies. Pita helped with the hire, finding someone with a great reputation who wasn't afraid of a thousand boxes of evidence and, more importantly, would work on contingency.

"You sure you don't want it?" Nan had asked, maybe two dozen times.

And each time, Pita had said, "Positive. The case is too big for me."

Although it wasn't. She could have gone to La Jolla, Webster, and Garcia as a rainmaker, someone who brought in a huge case and made millions for the company.

But she didn't.

Because this case had taught her a few things.

She'd learned that she hated big cases with lots and lots of evidence.

She'd learned that she really didn't care about the money. (Although the ten thousand dollar bonus that Nan had paid her—a bonus Pita hadn't asked for—had come in very handy.)

And she learned how valuable it was to know the people of her town. If she hadn't spent all those evenings in the cafeteria with Jessup, she wouldn't have trusted his story, and she never would have hired the forensic examiner.

Her mom had been right, all those years ago. Rio Gordo wasn't a bad place. Yeah, it was impoverished. Yeah, it was filled with dust, and didn't have a good nightlife or a great university.

But it did have some pretty spectacular people.

People who congratulated Pita for the next year on her success in the Hughes case. People who now came to her to do their wills or their prenups. People who asked her advice on the smallest legal matters, and believed her when she gave them an unvarnished opinion.

Her biggest case had helped her discover her calling: She was a small town attorney—someone who cared more about the people around her than the money their cases could bring in.

She wouldn't be rich.

But she would be happy.

And that was more than enough.

PATRIOTIC GESTURES

*P*AMELA KINNEY heard the noise in her sleep—
giggles, followed by the crunching of leaves. Later,
she smelled smoke, faint and acrid, and realized that her
neighbors were burning garbage in their fireplace again.
She got up long enough to close the window and silently
curse them; she hated it when they did illegal burning.

She forgot about it until the next morning. She stepped
out her back door into the crisp fall morning, and found
charred remains of her flag in the middle of her driveway.
There'd been no wind during the night, fortunately, or all
the evidence would have been gone.

Instead, there was a pile of burned fabric and a burn
stain on the pavement. There were even footprints outlined in leaves.

She noted all of that with a professional's detachment—she'd eyeballed more than a thousand crime
scenes—before the fabric itself caught her attention. Then
the pain was sudden and swift, right above her heart,
echoing through the breastbone and down her back.

Anyone else would have thought she was having a heart attack. But she wasn't, and she knew it. She'd had this feeling twice before, first when the officers came to her house and then when the chaplain handed her the folded flag which just a moment before had draped over her daughter's coffin.

Pamela had clung to that flag like she'd seen so many other military mothers do, and she suspected she had looked as lost as they had. Then, when she stood, that pain ran through her, dropping her back to the chair.

Her sons took her arms, and when she mentioned the pain, they dragged her to the emergency room. She had been late for her own daughter's wake, her chest sticky with adhesive from the cardiac machines and her hair smelling faintly of disinfectant.

And the feeling came back now, as she stared at the massacre before her. The flag, Jenny's flag, had been ripped from the front door and burned in her driveway.

Pamela made herself breathe. Then she rubbed that spot above her left breast, felt the pain spread throughout her body, burning her eyes and forming a lump in the back of her throat. But she held the tears back. She wouldn't give whoever had done this awful thing the satisfaction.

Finally she reached inside her purse for her cell, called Neil—she had trouble thinking of him as the sheriff after all the years she'd known him—and then she protected the scene until he arrived.

***

It only took him five minutes. Halleysburg was still a small town, no matter how many Portlanders sprawled into the community, willing to make the one and a half hour one-way daily commute to the city's edge. Pamela had told the dispatch to make sure that Neil parked across the street so that any wind from his vehicle wouldn't move the leaves.

And she had asked for a second scene-of-the-crime kit because she didn't want to go inside and get hers. She didn't want to risk losing the crime scene with a moment of inattention.

Neil pulled onto the street. His car was an unwieldy Olds with a souped up engine and a reinforced frame. It could take a lot of punishment, and often did.

As a result, the paint covering the car's sides was fresh and clean, while the hood, roof and trunk looked like they were covered in dirt.

The sheriff was the same. Neil Karlyn was in his late fifties, balding, with a face that had seen too much sun. But his uniform was always new, always pristine, and never wrinkled. He'd been that way since college, a precise man with precise opinions about a difficult world.

He got out of the Olds and did not reach around back for a scene-of-the-crime kit. Annoyance threaded through her.

"Where's my kit?" she asked.

"Pam," he said gently, "it's a low-level property crime. It'll never go to trial and you know it."

"It's arson with malicious intent," she snapped. "That's a felony."

He sighed and studied her for a moment. He clearly recognized her tone. She'd used it often enough on him when they were students at the University of Oregon. When they were lovers on different sides of the political fence, and constantly on the verge of splitting up.

When they finally did, it had taken years for them to settle into a friendship. But settle they did. They hardly even fought any more.

He went back to the car, opened the back seat and removed the kit she'd requested. She crossed her arms, waiting as he walked toward her. He stopped at the edge of the curb, holding the kit tight against his leg.

"Even if you somehow get the D.A. to agree that this is a cockamamie felony, you know that processing the scene yourself taints the evidence."

"Why do you care so much?" she asked, hearing an edge in her voice that usually wasn't there. The challenge, unspoken: *It's my daughter's flag. It's like murdering her all over again.*

To his credit, Neil didn't try to soothe her with a platitude.

"It's the eighth flag this morning," he said. "It's not personal, Pam."

Her chin jutted out. "It is to me."

Neil looked down, his cheek moving. He was clenching his jaw, trying not to speak.

He didn't have to.

She understood the irony of the statement. Somewhere in her pile of college paraphernalia was a badly framed newspaper clipping that had once been the front page of the Portland *Oregonian*. She'd framed the clipping so that a photo dominated, a photo of a much-younger Pamela with long hair and a tie-dye t-shirt, front and center in a group of students, holding an American flag by a stick, watching as it burned.

God, she could still remember how that felt, to hold a flag up so that the wind caught it. How fabric had its own acrid odor, and how frightened she'd been at the desecration, even though she'd been the one to light the flag on fire.

She had been protesting the Vietnam War. It was that photo and the resulting brouhaha it caused, both on campus and in the State of Oregon itself, that had led to the final break-up with Neil.

He couldn't believe what she had done. Sometimes she couldn't either. But she felt her country was worth fighting for. So had he. He joined up not two months later.

To his credit, Neil didn't say anything about her own flag-burning as he handed her the kit. Instead he watched as she took photographs of the scene, scooped up the charred bits of fabric, and made a sketch of the footprint she found in the leaves.

She found another print in the yard, and that one she made a cast of. Then she dusted her front door for prints, trying not to cry as she did so.

"A flag is a flag is a flag," she used to say.

Until it draped over her daughter's coffin.

Until it became all she had left.

***

"I called the local VFW, Mom," her son Stephen said over dinner that night. Stephen was her oldest and had been her support for thirty years, since the day his father walked out, never to return. "They're bringing another flag."

She stirred the mashed potatoes into the creamed corn on her plate. The meal had come from KFC: her sons had brought a bucket with her favorite sides, and told her not to argue with them about the fast food meal.

She wasn't arguing, but she didn't have much of an appetite.

They sat in the dining room, at the table that had once held four of them. Pamela had slid the fake rose centerpiece in front of Jenny's place, so she wouldn't have to think about her daughter.

It wasn't working.

"Another flag isn't the same, dumbass," Travis said. At thirty, he was the youngest, unmarried, still finding himself, a phrase she had come to hate.

The hell of it was, Travis was right. It wasn't the same. That flag these people had burned, that flag had comforted her. She had clung to it on the worst afternoon of her life, her fingers holding it tight, even at the emergency room, when the doctors wanted to pry it from her hands.

It had taken almost a week for her to let it go. Stephen had come over, Stephen and his pretty wife Elaine and their teenage daughters, Mandy and Liv. They'd brought KFC then, too, and talked about everything but the war.

Until it came time to take the flag away from Pamela.

Stephen had talked to her like she was a five-year-old who wanted to take her blankie to kindergarten. In the end, she'd handed the flag over. He'd been the one to find the old flagpole, the one she'd taken down when she bought the house, and he'd been the one to place the pole in the hanger outside the front door.

"The VFW says they replace flags all the time," Stephen said to his brother.

"Because some idiot burned one?" Travis asked.

Pamela's cheeks flushed.

"Because people lose them. Or moths eat them. Or sometimes, they get stolen," Stephen said.

"But not burned," Travis persisted.

Pamela swallowed. Travis didn't remember the newspaper photo, but Stephen probably did. It had hung over the console stereo she had gotten when her mother died, and it had been a teacher—Neil's first grade teacher? Pamela couldn't remember—who had seen it at a party and asked if she really wanted her children to see that before they could understand what it meant.

"I don't want another one," Pamela said.

"Mom…." Stephen started in his most reasonable voice.

She shook her head. "It's been a year. I need to move on."

"You don't move on from that kind of loss," Travis said, and she wondered how he knew. He didn't have children.

Then she looked at him, a large broad-shouldered man with tears in his eyes, and remembered that Jenny had been the one who walked him to school, who bathed him at night, who usually tucked him in. Jenny had done all that because Stephen at thirteen was already working to help his mom make ends meet, and Pamela was working two jobs herself, as well as attending community college to get her degree in forensic science and criminology. A pseudoscience degree, one of her almost-boyfriends had said. But it wasn't. She used science every day. She needed science like she needed air.

Like she needed to find out who had destroyed her daughter's flag.

"You don't move on," Pamela said.

Her boys watched her. Sometimes she could see the babies they had been in the lines of their mouths and the shape of their eyes. She still marveled at the way they had grown into men, large men who could carry her the way she used to carry them.

"But," she added, "you don't have to dwell on it, every moment of every day."

And yet she was dwelling. She couldn't stop. She never told her sons or anyone else, not even Neil who had become a closer friend in the year since Jenny had died. Neil, a widower now, a man who understood death the way that Pamela did. Neil, whose grandson had enlisted after 9/11 and had somehow made it back.

She was dwelling and there was only one way to stop. She had to use science to solve this. She couldn't think about it emotionally. She had to think about it clinically.

She had her evidence and she needed even more.

The next morning, the local paper ran an article on the burnings, and listed the addresses in the police log section. So Pamela visited the other crime scenes with her kit and her camera, identifying herself as an employee of the State Crime Lab.

Since *CSI* debuted on television, that identification opened doors for her. She didn't have to tell the other victims that she had been a victim too.

She took pictures of scorch marks on pavement and flag holders wrenched loose of their sockets. She removed flag bits from garbage cans, and studied footprints in the leaf-covered grass to see if they looked similar to the ones on her lawn.

And late that afternoon, as she stepped back to photograph yet another twisted flag holder beside a front door, she saw the glint of a camera hiding in a cobwebby corner of the door frame. The house was a starter, maybe 1200 square feet total. She wouldn't have expected a camera here.

"Do you have a security system?" she asked the homeowner, a woman Travis's age who looked like she hadn't slept in weeks. Her name was Becky something. Pamela hadn't really heard her last name in the introduction.

"My husband put it up," Becky said, her voice shaking a little. "I have no idea how it works."

"When will he be back?" Pamela asked.

Becky shrugged. "When they cancel stop-loss, I guess."

Pamela felt her breath slide out of her body. "He's in Iraq?"

Becky nodded. "I put the flag up for him, you know? And I haven't told him what happened to it. I've gotta find someone to fix the holder, and I have to get another flag."

Pamela looked at the house more closely. It needed paint. The bushes in front were overgrown. There were cobwebs all over the windows, and dry rot on the sills. Obviously the couple had purchased it expecting someone to work on it.

Either the money wasn't there, or the husband had planned to do the work himself.

"I can fix the holder," Pamela said. "If you have a few tools."

"My husband does," Becky said. "I can show them to you."

"I have a few things to finish, and then you can show me," Pamela said.

She dusted for prints, and then, for comparison, took Becky's and some off the husband's comb, which hadn't been touched since he left. Then Pamela went into his workroom, which also hadn't been touched, and took a hammer, some screws, and a screwdriver.

It took only ten minutes to repair the flag holder. But in that time, she'd made a friend.

"How'd you learn how to do that?" Becky asked.

"Raised three kids alone," Pamela said. "You realize there's not much you can't do, if you just try."

Becky nodded.

Pamela glanced at the camera. Untended since the husband left. It was probably in the same state of disrepair as the rest of the house.

"Can I see the security system?" she asked.

"It's not really a system," Becky said. "Just the cameras, and some motion sensors that're supposed to alert us when someone's on the property. But they clearly don't work any more."

"Let me see anyway," Pamela said.

Becky took her past the workroom, into a small closet filled with electronics. The closet was warm from the heat the panels gave off. Lights still blinked.

Pamela stared at it all, then touched the rewind button on the digital recorder. On the television monitor, she watched an image of herself fixing the flag holder.

"It looks like the camera's still working," she said. "Mind if I rewind farther?"

"Go ahead."

Backwards, she watched darkness turn to day. Saw Neil inspect the hanger. Saw Becky crying, then the tears evaporate into a stare of disbelief before she backed off the porch and away from the scene.

Back to the previous night. No porch light. Just images blurred in the darkness. Faces, not quite real, mostly turned away from the camera.

"Got a recordable DVD?" Pamela asked.

"Somewhere." Becky vanished into the house. Pamela studied the system, hoping that she wouldn't erase the information as she tried to record it.

She rewound again. Studied the faces, the half turned heads. She saw crew cuts and piercings and hoodies. Slouchy clothes worn by half the young people in Halleysburg.

Nothing to identify them. Nothing to separate them from everyone else in their age group.

Like her, her hair long, her jeans torn, as she stood front and center at the U of O, a burning flag before her.

She made herself study the machine, and figured out how to save the images to the disk's hard drive so that they wouldn't be erased. Then she inspected the buttons near the machine's DVD slot.

"Here," Becky said, thrusting a packet at her.

DVD-Rs, unopened, dust-covered. Pamela used a fingernail to break the seal, then pulled one out, and inserted it in the slot. She managed to record, but had no way to test. So she made a few more copies, feeling somewhat reassured that she could come back and try to download the images from the hard drive again.

"Will this catch them?" Becky asked while she watched the process.

"I don't know," Pamela said. "I hope so."

"It's just, they got so close, you know." Becky's voice shook. "I didn't know anyone could get that close."

It took Pamela a moment to understand what she meant. Becky meant that they had gotten close to the house. Close to her. The burning hadn't just upset her, it had frightened her, and made her feel vulnerable.

Odd. All it had done to Pamela was make her angry.

"Just lock up at night," Pamela said after a minute. "Locks deter ninety-percent of all thieves."

"And the remaining ten percent?"

They get in, Pamela almost said, but thought the better of it.

"They don't usually come to places like Halleysburg," she said. "Why would they? We all know each other here."

Becky nodded, seemingly reassured. Or maybe she just wanted to abandon an uncomfortable topic.

Pamela certainly did. She wanted to play with the images, see what she could find.

She wanted a solid image of the culprits, one that she could bring to Neil.

Maybe then, he would stop complaining that this was a petty property crime. Maybe then he might understand how important this really was.

***

But it was her own words that replayed in her head later that night as she sat in front of her computer.

They don't usually come to places like Halleysburg.... We all know each other here.

She had lied to make Becky feel better, but the words hadn't felt like a lie. Thieves really didn't come here. There was no need. There was richer pickings in Portland or Salem or the nearby bedroom communities.

Besides, it was hard to commit a crime here without someone seeing you.

Except under cover of darkness.

Her home office was quiet. It overlooked the back yard, and she had never installed curtains on the window, preferring the view of the year-round flower garden she had planted. At the moment, her garden was full of browns and oranges, fall plants blooming despite the winter ahead. She had little lights beneath the plants, lights she usually kept off because they spiked her energy bill.

But she had them on now. She would probably have them on for some time to come.

Maybe Becky wasn't the only one who felt vulnerable.

Pamela put one of the DVDs in her computer, and opened the images. They played, much to her relief, so she copied the images to her hard drive and removed the DVD.

Her computer at home wasn't as good as her computer at work. But it would have to do.

She didn't want to do any work on this case at the State Crime Lab if she could help it. The lab was so understaffed and so overworked that it usually took four months to get something tested. When she last checked, more than 600 cases were backlogged, some of them dating back more than nine months.

Those cases were bigger than hers. The backlogs were semen samples from possible rapists and blood droplets from the scene of a multiple murder case.

She couldn't, in good conscience, bring something personal and private to the lab. She would work here as long as she could. Then if she couldn't finish here, she might be able to convince herself that the time she took at the lab would go toward an arson case—a serious one, not a petty property crime, as Neil had called it.

Petty property crime.

Funny that they would be on opposite sides of this issue too.

Pamela went through the images frame by frame, looking for clear faces. Her computer didn't have the face recognition software that one of the computers at the lab had, but she had installed a home version of image sharpening software. She used it to clean out the fuzz and to lighten the darkness, trying to find more than a chin or the corner of an ear.

Finally she got a small face just behind the flag, a serious white face with a frown—of disapproval? She couldn't tell—and a bit of an elongated chin. Enough to see the wisp of a beard—a boy's beard, more a wish of a beard than the real thing—and a tattooed hand coming up to catch the flag as the person almost blocking the camera yanked the pole out of the holder.

She blew up the image, softened it, fixed it, and then felt tears prick her eyes.

They don't usually come to places like Halleysburg.

No. They grew up here. And worked at the grocery store down the street to pay for their football uniforms at the underfunded high school. They collected coins in a can on Sunday afternoons for Boosters, and they smiled when they saw her and respectfully called her Mrs. Kinney and asked, with a little too much interest, how her granddaughters were doing.

"Jeremy Stallings," she whispered. "What the hell were you thinking?"

And she hoped she knew.

***

Neil wouldn't let her sit in while he questioned Jeremy Stallings. He was appalled she'd even asked.

"That sort of thing belongs on TV and you know it," he'd said.

But she also knew he probably wouldn't do much more than slap the boy on the wrist, so what would be the harm? She hadn't made that argument, though.

Instead, she waited on the bench chair outside the sheriff's office conference room, which doubled as an interview room on days like this, and watched the parade of parents and lawyers as they trooped past.

No one acknowledged her. No one so much as looked at her. Not Reg Stallings, whose brother had sold her the house, or his wife June, who had taken over the PTA just before Travis got out of high school. No one mentioned the friendly exchanges at the high school football games or the hellos at the diner behind the movie theater. It was easier to forget all that and pretend they weren't neighbors than it was to acknowledge what was going on inside that room.

Then, finally, Jeremy came out. He was wearing his baggy pants with a Halo t-shirt hanging nearly to his knees. He wore that same frown he'd had as he took the flag off from Becky's front door.

He glanced at Pamela, then looked away, a blush working its way up the spider tattoo on his neck into his crew cut.

His parents and the lawyers led him away, as Neil reminded all of them to be in court the following morning.

Neil waited until they went through the front doors before coming over to Pamela.

She stood, her knees creaky from sitting so long. "He confess?"

Neil nodded. "And gave me the names of his buddies."

Pamela bit her lower lip. "Funny," she said, "he didn't strike me as the type to be a war protestor."

Neil rubbed his hands on his pristine shirt. "Is that what you thought?"

"Of course," Pamela said. "Every house he hit, we're all military families."

"Who happened to be flying flags, even at night." There was a bit of judgment in Neil's voice.

She knew what he was thinking. People who knew how to handle flags took them down at dusk. But she couldn't bear to touch hers. She hadn't asked Becky why hers remained up, but she would wager the reason was similar.

And it probably was for every other family Jeremy and his friends had targeted.

"That's the important factor?" she asked. "Night?"

"And beer," Neil said. "They lost a football game, went out and drank, and that fueled their anger. So they decided to act out."

"By burning flags?" Her voice rose.

"A few weeks before, they knocked down mailboxes. I'm going to hate to charge them. There won't be much left of the football team."

"That's all right," Pamela said bitterly. "Petty property crimes shouldn't take them off the roster long."

"It's going to be more than that," Neil said. "They're showing a destructive pattern. This one isn't going to be fun."

"For any of us," Pamela said.

***

Her hands were shaking as she left. She had wanted the crime to mean something. The flag had meant something to her. It should have meant something to them too.

God, Mom, for an old hippie, you're such a prude. Jenny's voice, so close that Pamela actually looked around, expecting to see her daughter's face.

"I'm not a prude," she whispered, and then realized she was reliving an old argument between them.

Sure you are. Judgmental and dried up. I thought you protested so that people could do what they wanted.

Pamela sat in the car, her creaky knees no longer holding her.

No, I protested so that people wouldn't have to die in another senseless war, she had said to her daughter on that May afternoon.

What year was that?

It had to be 1990, just before Jenny graduated from high school.

I'm not going to die in a stupid war, Jenny had said with such conviction that Pamela almost believed her. *We don't do wars any more. I'm going to get an education. That way, you don't have to struggle to pay for Travis. I know how hard it's been with Steve.*

Jenny, taking care of things. Jenny, who wasn't going to let her cash-strapped mother pay for her education. Jenny, being so sure of herself, so sure that the peace she'd known most of her life would continue.

To Jenny, going into the military to get a free education hadn't been a gamble at all.

Things'll change, honey, Pamela had said. *They always do.*

And by then I'll be out. I'll be educated, and moving on with my life.

Only Jenny hadn't moved on. She'd liked the military. After the First Gulf War, she'd gone to officer training, one of the first women to do it.

I'm a feminist, Mom, just like you, she'd said when she told Pamela.

Pamela had smiled, keeping her response to herself. She hadn't been that kind of feminist. She wouldn't have stayed in the military. She wasn't sure she believed in the military—not then.

And now? She wasn't sure what she believed. All she knew was that she had become a military mother, one who cried when a flag was burned.

Not just a flag.

Jenny's flag.

And that's when Pamela knew.

She wanted the crime to mean something, so she would make sure that it did.

***

She brought her memories to court. Not just the scrapbooks she'd kept for Jenny, like she had for all three kids, but the pictures from her own past, including the badly framed front page of the *Oregonian*.

Five burly boys had destroyed Jenny's flag. They stood in a row, their lawyers beside them, and pled to misdemeanors. Their parents sat on the blond bench seats in the 1970s courtroom. A reporter from the local paper took notes in the back. The judge listened to the pleadings.

Otherwise, the room was empty. No one cheered when the judge gave the boys six months of counseling. No one complained at the nine months of community service and even though a few of them winced when the judge announced the huge fines that they (and not their parents) had to pay, no one said a word.

Until Pamela asked if she could speak.

The judge—primed by Neil—let her.

Only she really didn't speak. She showed them Jenny. From the baby pictures to the dress uniform. From the brave eleven-year-old walking her brother to school to the dust-covered woman who had smiled with some Iraqi children in Baghdad.

Then Pamela showed them her *Oregonian* cover.

"I thought you were protesting," she said to the boys. "I thought you were trying to let someone know that you don't approve of what your country is doing."

Her voice was shaking.

"I thought you were being patriotic." She shook her head. "And instead you were just being stupid."

To their credit, they watched her. They listened. She couldn't tell if they understood. If they knew how her heart ached—not that sharp pain she'd felt when she found the flag, but just an ache for everything she'd lost.

Including the idealism of the girl in the picture. And the idealism of the girl she'd raised.

When she finished, she sat down. And she didn't move as the judge gaveled the session closed. She didn't look up as some of the boys tried to apologize. And she didn't watch as their parents hustled them out of court.

Finally, Neil sat beside her. He picked up the framed *Oregonian* photograph in his big, scarred hands.

"Do you regret it?" he asked.

She touched the edge of the frame.

"No," she said.

"Because it was a protest?"

She shook her head. She couldn't articulate it. The anger, the rage, the fear she had felt then. Which had been nothing like the fear she had felt every day her daughter had been overseas.

The fear she felt now when she looked at Stephen's daughters and wondered what they'd chose in this never-ending war.

"If I hadn't burned that flag," she said, "I wouldn't have had Jenny."

Because she might have married Neil. And even if they had made babies, none of those babies would have been

Jenny or Stephen or Travis. There would have been other babies who would have grown into other people.

Neil wasn't insulted. They had known each other too long for insults. Instead, he put his hand over hers. It felt warm and good and familiar. She put her head on his shoulder.

And they sat like that, until the court reconvened an hour later, for another crime, another upset family, and another broken heart.

DETAILS

NO MORE ALCOHOL, no more steak. In the end, it's the little things that go, and you miss them like you miss a lover at odd times, at comfort times, at times when you need something small that means a whole lot more.

I've been thinking about the little things a lot since my granddaughter drove me to the glass-and-chrome hospital they built on the south side of town. Maybe it was the look the doctor gave me, the one that meant *you should've listened to me, George.* Maybe it was the sight of Flaherty's, all made over into a diner.

Or maybe it's the fact that I'm seventy-seven years old and not getting any younger. Every second becomes a detail then. An important one, and I can hear the details ticking away quicker than I would like.

It gets a man to thinking, all those details. I mentioned it to Sarah on the way back, and she said, in that dry way of hers, "Maybe you should write some of those details down."

So I am.

***

I know Sarah wanted me to start with what she considers the beginning: my courting—and winning—of her grandmother. Then she'd want me to cover the early marriage, and of course the politics, all the way to the White House years.

But Flaherty's got me thinking—details again—and Flaherty's got me remembering.

They don't make gas stations like that no more. You know the kind: the round-headed pumps, the Coke machine outside—the kind that dispenses bottles and has a bottle opener built in—and the concrete floor covered with gum and cigarette butts and oil so old it looks like it come out of the ground.

But Flaherty's hasn't been a gas station for a long time. For years it was closed up, the pumps gone, plywood over the windows. Then just last summer some kids from Vegas came in, bought the land, filled the pits, and made the place into a diner. For old folks like me, it looks strange—kinda like people being invited to eat in a service station—but everyone else thinks it looks authentic.

It isn't.

The authentic Flaherty's exists only in my mind now, and it won't leave me alone. It never has. And so I'm starting with my most important memory of Flaherty's—maybe my most important memory period—not because it's the prettiest or even the best, but because it's the one my brain sticks on, the one I see when I close my eyes at night and when I wake bleary eyed in the morning. It's the one I mull over on sunny mornings, or catch myself daydreaming about as I take those walks the doctor has talked me into.

You'd think instead I'd focus on the look in Sally Anne's eyes the first time I kissed her, or the way that pimply faced German boy moaned when he sank to his knees with my knife in his belly outside of Argentan.

But I don't.

Instead, I think about Flaherty's in the summer of 1946, and me fresh home from the war.

***

I got home from the war later than most.

Part of that was because of my age, and part of it was that I'd signed up for a second tour of duty, World War II being that kinda war, the kind where a man was expected to fight until the death, not like that police action in Korea, that strange mire we called Vietnam, or that video war them little boys fought in the Gulf.

I came back to McCardle in my uniform. I'd left a scrawny teenager, allowed to sign up because old Doc Elliot wanted to go himself and didn't want to deny anyone anything, and I'd come back a twenty-five year old who'd killed his share of men, had his share of drunken nights, and slept with women who didn't even know his name let alone speak his language. I'd seen Europe, even if much of it'd been bombed, and I knew how its food tasted, its people smelled, and its women smiled.

I was somebody different and I wanted the whole world to know.

The whole world, in those days, was McCardle, Nevada. My grandfather'd come west for the Comstock Load, but made his money selling dry goods, and when the Load petered, came to McCardle. He survived the resulting depression, and when the boom hit again around the turn of the century, he doubled his money. My father got into government early on, using the family fortune to control the town, and expected me to do the same.

When I came home, I wasn't about to spend my whole life in Nevada. I had the GI Bill and a promise of a future, a future I planned on taking.

I had the summer free, and then in September, I'd be allowed to go East. I'd got accepted to Harvard, but I'd met some of those boys, and decided a pricey snobby school like that wasn't a place for me. Instead, I went to Boston College because I'd heard of it and because it wasn't as snobby and because it was far away.

It turned out to be an okay choice, but not the one I'd dreamed of. Nothing ever quite turns out like you dream.

I should've known that the day I drove into McCardle in '46, but I didn't. For years, I'd imagined myself coming back all spit-polished and shiny, the conquering hero. Instead I was covered in the dust that rolled into the windows of my ancient Ford truck, and the sweat that made my uniform cling to my skinny shoulders. The distance from Reno to McCardle seemed twice as long as it should have, and when I hit Clark

County, I realized those short European distances had worked their way into my soul.

Back then, Clark County was so different as to be another country. Gambling had been legal since I was a boy, but it hadn't become the business it is now. Bugsy Siegel's dream in the desert, the Flamingo, wouldn't be completed for another year, and while Vegas was going through a population boom the likes of which Nevadans hadn't seen since the turn of the century, it wasn't nowhere near Nevada's biggest city.

McCardle got its share of soldiers and drifters and cons looking for a great break. Since gambling was in the hands of local and regional folks, its effects were different around the state. McCardle's powers that be, including my father, took one look at Siegel and his ilk and knew them for what they were. Those boys couldn't buy land, they couldn't even get no one to talk to them, and they moved on to Vegas, which was farther from California, but much more willing to be bought. Years later, my father would brag that he stared down gangsters, but the truth of it was that the gangsters were looking for a quick buck and they knew that they'd be fighting unfriendlies in McCardle for generations when Vegas would have them for a song.

Nope. We had our casino, but our biggest business was divorces. For a short period after the war, McCardle was the divorce capitol of the US of A.

You sure could recognize the divorce folks. They'd come into town in their fancy cars, wearing too many or too few clothes, and then they'd go to McCardle's only hotel, built by my grandfather's dry goods money long about 1902, and they'd cart in enough luggage to last most people a year. Then they'd visit the casino, look for the local watering holes, and attempt to chat up a local or two for the requisite two weeks, and then they'd drive off, marriage irretrievably broken. Some would go back to Reno where they'd sign a new marriage license. Others would go about their business, never to be thought of again.

In those days, Flaherty's was on the northern-eastern side of town, just at the edge of the buildings where the highway started its long trek toward forever. Now, Flaherty's is dead center. But in those days, it was the first sign you were coming into civilization, that and the way the city spread before you like a vision. You had about five minutes of steady driving after you left Flaherty's before you hit the main part of McCardle, and I decided, on that hot afternoon, that five minutes was five too many.

I pulled into Flaherty's and used one thin dime to buy myself an ice-cold Coca-Cola.

I remember it as if it happened an hour ago: getting out of that Ford, my uniform sticking to my legs, the sweat pouring down my chest and back, the grit of sand in my eyes. I walked past several cars to get to the concrete slab they'd built Flaherty's on. A bell ting-tinged near me as someone's tank got filled, and in the cool darkness of the station proper, a little bell pinged before the cash register popped open. Flaherty himself stood behind the register in those days, although like as not by '46, you'd find him drunk.

The place smelled of gasoline and motor oil. A greasy Philco perched on a metal filing cabinet near the cash register, and it was broadcasting teen idol Frankie Sinatra live, a pack of screaming girls ruining the song. In the bay, a green car was half disassembled, the legs of some poor kid sticking out from under its side as he worked underneath. Another mechanic, a guy named Jed, a tough who'd been a few years behind me in school, leaned into the hood. I remembered Jed real well. Rumor had it he'd knifed an Indian near a roadside stand. I'd stopped him from hitting one of the girls in my class when she'd laughed at him for asking her on a date. After that, Jed and I avoided each other when we could and were coldly polite when we couldn't.

The Coke bottle—one of the small ones that they don't make any more—popped out of the machine. I grabbed its cold wet sides, and used the built-in bottle opener to pop the lid. Brown fizz streamed out the top, and I bent to catch as much of it as I could without getting it on my uniform.

The Coke was ice-cold and delicious, even if I was drinking foam. In those days, Coke was sweet and lemony and just about the best non-alcoholic drink money could buy. I finished the bottle in several long gulps, then dug in my pocket for another dime. I hadn't realized how thirsty I was or how tired; being this close to home brought out every little ache, even the ones I had no idea that I had. I stuck the dime in the machine, and took my second bottle, this time waiting until the contents settled before opening it.

"Hey, soldier. Mind if I have a sip?"

The voice was sultry and sexy and very female. I jumped just a little at the sound. I hadn't seen anyone besides Flaherty and the grease monkeys inside, even though I had known, on some level, that other folks were around me. I kept a two-fingered grip on the chilly bottle as I looked up.

A woman was leaning against the building. She wore a checked blouse tied beneath her breasts, tight pants that gathered around her calves, and Keds. She finished off an unfiltered cigarette and flicked it with her thumb and forefinger into the sand on the building's far side. Her hair was a brownish red, her skin so dark it made me wonder if she were a devotee of that crazy new fad that had women lying in the sun all hours trying to get tan. Her eyes were coal-black but her features were delicate, almost as if someone had taken the image from a Dresden doll and changed its coloring to something else entirely.

"Well?" she said. "I'm outta dimes."

I opened the bottle and handed it to her. She put its mouth between those lips and sucked. I felt a shiver run down my back. For a moment, it felt as if I hadn't left Italy.

Then she pulled the bottle down, handed it back to me, and wiped the condensation on her thighs. "Thanks," she said. "I was getting thirsty."

"That your car in there?" I managed.

She nodded. "It made lots of pretty blue smoke and a helluva groan when I tried to start it up. And here I thought it only needed gas."

Her laugh was deep and self-deprecating, but beneath it I thought I heard fear.

"How long they been working on it?"

"Most of the day," she said. "God knows how much it's going to cost."

"Have you asked?"

"Sure." She held out her hand, and I gave the bottle back to her, even though I hadn't yet taken a drink. "They don't know either."

She tipped the bottle back and took another swig. I watched her drink and so did most of the men in the place. Jed was leaning on the car, his face half hidden in the shadows. I could sense rather than see his expression. It was that same flatness I'd seen just before he lit into the girl outside school. I didn't know if I was causing the look just by being there, or if he'd already made a pass at this woman, and failed.

"You're not from McCardle," I said.

She wiped her mouth with the back of her hand, and gave the bottle back to me. "Does it show?" she asked, grinning.

The grin transformed all her strange features, making her into one of the most beautiful women I'd ever seen. I took a sip from the bottle simply to buy myself some time, and tasted her on the glass rim. Suddenly it seemed as if the heat of the day had grown more intense. I drank more than I intended, and pulled the bottle away only when my body threatened to burp the liquid back up.

"You just visiting?" I asked which was the only way I could get the answer I really wanted. She wasn't wearing a ring; I suspected she was here for a quickie divorce.

"Taking in the sights, starting with Flaherty's here," she said. "Anything else I shouldn't miss?"

I almost answered her seriously before I caught that grin again. "There's not much to the place," I said.

"Except a soldier boy, going home," she said.

"Does it show?" I asked and we both laughed. Then I finished the second bottle, put it in the wooden crate with the first, and flipped her a dime.

"The next one's on me," I said, as I made my way back to the Ford.

"You're the first hospitable person I've met here," she said and I should've heard it then, that plea, that subtle request for help.

Instead, I smiled. "I'm sure you'll meet others," I said and left.

***

Kinda strange I can remember it detail for detail, word for word. If I close my eyes and concentrate, the taste of her mingled with Coke comes back as if I had just experienced it; the way her laugh rasped and the sultry warmth of her voice are just outside my earshot.

Only now the memory has layers: the way I felt it, the way I remembered it at various times in my life, and the understanding I have now.

None of it changes anything.

It can't.

No matter what, she's still dead.

**

I was asleep when Sheriff Conner showed up at the door at ten a.m. two mornings later. I was usually up with the dawn, but after two nights in my childhood bed, I'd finally found a way to be comfortable. Seems the bed was child-sized, and I had grown several inches in my four years away. The bed was a sign to me that I didn't have long in my parents' home, and I knew it. I didn't belong here any-way. I was an adult full grown, a man who'd spent his time away from home. Trying to fit in around these people was like trying to sleep in my old bed: every time I moved I realized I had grown beyond them.

When Sheriff Conner arrived, my mother woke me with a sharp shake of the shoulder. She frowned at me, as if I had embarrassed her, and then she vanished from my room. I pulled on a pair of khakis that were wrinkled from my overnight case, and combed my hair with my fingers. I grabbed a shirt as I wandered barefoot into the living room.

Sheriff Conner was a big man with skin that turned beet-red in the Nevada sun. His blond hair was cropped so short that the top of his head sunburned. He hadn't changed since I was a boy. He was still too large for his uniform, and his watch dug red lines into the flesh of his wrist. I always wondered how he could be comfortable in those tight clothes in that heat, but, except for the dots of perspiration around his face, he never seemed to notice.

"You grew some," he said as the screen door slammed behind my mother.

"Yep," I said.

"Your folks say you saw action."

"A bit."

He grunted and his bright blue eyes skittered away from mine. In that moment, I realized he had been too young for World War I, and too old for this war, and he was one of those men who wanted to serve, no matter what the cause. I wasn't that kind of man, only I learned it later when I contemplated Korea and the mess we were making there.

"I guess you just got to town," he said.

"Two days ago."

"And when you drove in, you stopped at Flaherty's first, but didn't get no gas." His tone had gotten sharper. He was easing into the questions he felt he needed to ask me.

"I was thirsty. It's a long drive across that desert."

He smiled then, revealing a missing tooth on his upper left side. "You bought a soda."

"Two," I said.

"And shared one."

So that was it. Something to do with the girl. I stiffened, waiting. Sometimes girls who came onto a man like that didn't like the rejection. I hadn't gone looking for her over to the hotel. Maybe she had taken offense and told a lie or two about me. Or maybe her soon-to-be ex-husband had finally arrived and had taken an instant dislike to me. Maybe Sheriff Conner had come to warn me about that.

"You make it your policy to share your drinks with a nigra?"

"Excuse me?" I asked. I could lie now and say I was shocked at his word choice, but this was 1946, long before political correctness came into vogue, almost a decade before the official start of the Civil Rights movement, although the seeds of it were in the air.

No. I wasn't shocked because of his language. I was shocked at myself. I was shocked that I had shared a drink with a black woman—although in those days, I probably would have called her colored not to give too much offense.

"A whole buncha people saw you talk to her, share a Coke with her, and buy her another one. A few said it looked like there was an attraction. Couple others coulda sworn you was flirting."

I had been flirting. I hadn't seen her as black—and yes, back then, it would have made a difference to me. I've learned a lot about racial tolerance since, and a lot more about intolerance. I wasn't an offensive racist in those days, just a passive one. A man who kept to his own side of the street and didn't mingle, just as he was supposed to do.

I would never have flirted if I had known. No matter how beautiful she was. But that hair, those features all belied what I had been taught. I had thought the darkness of her skin due to tanning not to heredity.

I had seen what I had wanted to see.

Sheriff Conner was watching me think. God knows what kind of expressions had crossed my face, but whatever they were, they weren't good.

"Well?" he asked.

"Is it against the law now to buy a woman a drink on a hot summer day?" I asked.

"Might be," he said, "if that woman shows up dead the next day."

"Dead?" I whispered.

He nodded.

"I never saw her before," I said.

"So you usually just go up and share a drink with a nigra woman you never met."

"I didn't know she was colored," I said.

He raised his eyebrows at me.

"She was in the shade," I said and realized how weak that sounded.

The Sheriff laughed. "And all pussy's the same in the dark, ain't it?" he said, and slapped my leg. I'd heard worse, much worse, in the army but it didn't shock me like he just had. I'd never heard Sheriff Conner be crude, although my father always said he was. Apparently the Sheriff was only crude to adults. To children he was the model of decorum.

I wasn't a child any longer.

"How'd she die?" I asked.

"Blow to the head."

"At the station?"

"In the desert. Her pants was gone, and that scrap of fabric that passed for a blouse was underneath her."

The desert. Someone had to take her there. I felt myself go cold.

"I didn't know her," I said, and if she had been a white woman, he might have believed me. But in McCardle, in those years and before, a man like me didn't flirt with—hell, a man like me didn't talk to—a woman like her.

"Then what was she doing here?" he asked.

"Getting a divorce?"

"Girls like her don't get a divorce."

That rankled me, even then. "So what do they do?"

He didn't answer. "She wasn't here for no divorce."

"Have you investigated it?"

"Hell, no. Can't even find her purse."

"Well, did you trace the license on the car?"

He frowned at me then. "What car?"

"The ones the guys were fixing, the green car. They had it nearly taken apart."

"And it was hers?"

"That's what she said." At least, that was what I thought she said. I suddenly couldn't remember her exact words, although they would come to me later.

The whole scene would come to me later, like it was something I made up, like a dream that was only half there upon waking and then came, full-blown and unbidden, into the mind.

That your car? I said to her, and she didn't answer, at least not directly. She didn't say yes or no.

"Did you check with the boys at the station?" I asked.

"They didn't say nothing about a car."

"Did you ask Jed?"

The sheriff frowned at me. I'd forgotten until then that he and Jed were drinking buddies. "Yeah, of course I did."

"Well, I can't be the only one to remember it," I said. "They had it torn apart."

"Izzat so?" he asked, stroking his chin. "You think that's important?"

"If it tells you who she is, it is," I said, a bit stunned at his denseness.

"Maybe," he said, but he didn't seem to be thinking of that. He seemed focused on something else altogether. The look that crossed his face was half sad, half worried. Then he heaved himself out of the chair, and left without even a good-bye.

I sat on the sofa, wondering what, exactly, that all meant. I was still shaken by my own blindness, and by the Sheriff's willingness to accuse me of a crime that seemed impossible to me.

It seemed impossible that a woman that vibrant could be dead.

It seemed impossible that a woman that vibrant had been black.

It seemed impossible, but there it was. It startled me.

I was more shocked at her color than at her death.

And that was the hell of it.

***

I tried not to think of it.

I'd learned how to do that during the war—it's what helped me survive Normandy—and it had been effective during my tour.

But it stopped working about a week later when her family showed up.

They came for the body, and they seemed a lot more out of place than she had. Her father was a big man, the kind most folks in McCardle would have crossed the street to avoid or would have bullied out of fear. Her mother was delicate, with the same Dresden features as her daughter but on much darker skin. The auburn hair didn't seem to come from either of them.

And with them was her husband. He wore a uniform, like I did, and his eyes were red as if he'd been crying for a long, long time. I saw them come out of the mortuary, the parents with their arms around each other, the husband walking alone.

The husband threw me, and made me even more uncomfortable than I had already been.

I thought she had flirted with me.

I usually didn't mistake those things.

But, it seemed, I made a whole lot of mistakes in that short half hour I had known her.

They drove out that night with her body in the back of their truck. I knew that because my conscience forced me over to the hotel to talk to them, to ask them about the green car, and to tell them I was sorry.

When I got there, I learned that the only hotel in McCardle—my family's hotel—didn't take their kind. Maybe that, more than an assumption, explained the Sheriff's remark: Girls like her didn't get a divorce.

Maybe they didn't, at least not in McCardle, because the town made sure they couldn't, unless they had some place to stay.

And there weren't blacks in McCardle then. The blacks didn't start arriving for another year.

***

The next day, I moved, over my mother's protests, into my own apartment. It was a single room with a hot plate and a small icebox over the town's only restaurant. I shared a bathroom with three other tenants, and counted myself fortunate to have two windows. The place came furnished, and the Murphy bed was long enough for me, although even with fans I had trouble sleeping. The building kept the heat of the day, and not even the temperature drop after sunset could ease it. On those unbearable summer nights, I lay in tangled sheets, the smell of greasy hamburgers and chicken-fried steak carried on the breeze. I counted it better than being at home.

Especially after the nightmares started.

Strangely they weren't about her. Nor were they about the war. I didn't have nightmares about that war for twenty years, not until I started seeing images from Vietnam on television. Then a different set of nightmares came, and I went to the VA where I was diagnosed with a delayed stress reaction and given a whole passel of drugs that I eventually pitched.

No. Those early nightmares were about him. Her husband. The man with the olive green uniform and the red eyes. I knew guys like him. They walked with their backs straight, their faces impassive. They didn't move unless they had to, and they never talked back, and if they showed emotion, it was because they thought guys like me weren't looking.

He hadn't cared about hiding any more. His emotion had been too deep.

And once Sheriff Conner figured out I had nothing to do with it, he'd declared the case closed. Over dinner the night before I left, my father speculated that Conner'd just shown up to show my father who was boss. Mother'd ventured that Conner hoped I was guilty, so it'd bring down the whole power structure of the town.

Instead, I think, it just brought Conner down. He was out of office by the following year, and the year after that he was dead, a victim of a slow-speed single vehicle drunken car crash in the days before seat belts.

I think no one would have known what happened if it hadn't been for those nightmares. I'd dream in that dry, dry heat of him just standing there, looking at me, eyes red, face impassive. Her body was in the green car beside us, and he would stare at me, as if I knew something, as if I were keeping something from him.

But how could I have known anything? I'd shared a Coke with her and gone on.

I hadn't even bothered to learn her name.

***

In the sixties they called what I was feeling white liberal guilt. Not that I had done anything wrong, mind you, but if I had known what she was—who she was—I would have acted differently. I knew it, and it bothered me.

It almost bothered me more than the fact she was dead.

Although that bothered me too. That, and the dreams. And the green car.

I went to Flaherty's soon after the dreams started and filled up my tank. I got myself another Coke and I stared at the spot where I had seen her. The shadows were dark there, but not that dark. The air was cool but not that cool, and only someone who was waiting for a car would choose to wait in that spot, on that day, with a real town nearby. She must have been real thirsty to ask me for a drink.

Real thirsty and real scared.

And maybe she took one look at my uniform, and thought I'd be able to help her.

She even tried to ask.

You're the first hospitable person I've met here, she'd said. *I'm sure you'll meet others.*

What she must have thought of that sentence.

How wrong I'd been.

I took my Coke and walked around the place, seeing lots of cars half finished, and even more car parts, but nothing of that particular shade of green.

Her family had taken her home in a truck.

The car was missing.

And as I leaned on the back of that brick building, the bottle cold in my hand, I wondered. Had the mechanics started working on the car because they too hadn't realized who she was? Had she gotten all the way to Nevada traveling white highways and hiding her darker-than-expected skin under a trail of moxie?

I went into the mechanic's bay, and Jed was there, putting oil into a 1937 Ford truck that had seen better days. A younger man stood beside him, and I wagered from the cut of his pants and the constant movement of his feet, that he'd been the guy under the car that day.

I leaned against the wall, sipping my Coke, and watched them.

They got quiet when they saw me. I grinned at them. I wasn't wearing my uniform that day, just a pair of grimy dungarees and a t-shirt. Even so, I was hot and miserable, and probably looked it.

I tilted my bottle toward them in a kinda salute. The younger man, the one I didn't recognize, nodded back.

"You seen that girl the other day?" I asked. I might have said more. I try not to remember. I can't believe the language we used then: Japs and niggers and wops; the way we got gypped or jewed down; laughing at the pansies and whistling at the dames. And we didn't think nothing of it, at least I didn't. Each word had to be unlearned, just as—I guess—it had to be learned.

Jed put a hand on his friend's arm, a small subtle movement I almost didn't see. "Why're you askin'?" And I could feel it, that old antipathy between us. Every word we'd ever exchanged, every look we had was buried in those words.

He wouldn't talk to me, not really. He wouldn't tell me what I needed to know. But his friend might. I had to play that at least.

"I was wondering if she's living around here." I said with an intentional leer.

"You don't know?" the younger asked.

My heart triple-hammered. I knew then that the sheriff hadn't told anyone he'd come after me. "Know what?"

"They found her in the desert with her face bashed in."

"Jesus," I said softly, then whistled for good measure. "What happened?"

"Dunno," Jed said, his hand squeezing the other boy's arm. Jed saw my gaze drop to his fingers, and then go back to his face. He grinned, like we were sharing a secret. And I didn't like what I was thinking.

It seemed simple. Too simple. Impossibly simple. A man couldn't just sense that another man had done something wrong. He needed proof.

"Too damn bad," I said, taking another swig of my Coke. "I woulda liked a piece of that."

"You and half the town," the younger one said, and laughed nervously.

Jed didn't laugh with him, but stared at me with narrowed green eyes. "I can't believe you didn't hear of it," he said. "The whole town's been talking."

I shrugged. "Maybe I wasn't listening." I set the Coke down beside the radio and scanned the bay. "What're they gonna do with that car of hers? Sell it?"

"Ain't no one found it," the younger boy said.

"She drove it outta here?" I asked. "She said it seemed hopeless."

Finally Jed grinned. He actually looked merry, as if we were talking about the weather instead of a murder. "Women always say that."

I didn't smile back. "What was wrong with it?"

"You name it," the younger one said. "She'd driven that thing to death."

I knew one more question would be too many, but I couldn't stop myself. "She say why?"

"You gotta reason for all this interest, George?" Jed asked. "You can't get nothing from her now."

"Guess not," I said. "Just seems curious somehow. Woman comes here, to this town, and ends up dead."

"Don't seem curious to me," Jed said. "She didn't belong here."

I stared at him a moment. "People don't belong a lotta places but that don't mean they need to die."

He shrugged and turned away, ending the conversation.

I picked up my Coke bottle. It had gotten warm already. I took another sip, letting the sweet lemony taste and the carbonation make up for the lack of coolness.

Then I went outside.

What did I want with all this? To get rid of some guilt? To make the dreams go away?

I didn't know, and it angered me.

"Hey." It was the younger one. He'd come out into the sun, ostensibly to smoke. He lit up a Chesterfield and offered me one. I took it to be companionable, and we lit off the same match.

Jed peeked out of the bay and watched for a moment, then disappeared, apparently satisfied that nothing was going to be said, probably thinking he had the kid under his thumb. Only Jed was wrong.

The younger one spoke softly, so softly I had to strain to hear, and I was standing next to him. "She said she was driving from Mississippi to California to join her husband. Said he'd got back from Europe and got a job in some plant in Los Angeles. Said they'd make good money there, but they didn't have it now, and could we do as little as possible on the car, so that it'd be cheap."

"Did you?" I asked. And when he looked confused, I added for clarification, "Keep it cheap?"

He took a long drag off the cigarette, and let the smoke out his nose. "We didn't finish," he said.

I felt that triple-hammer again. A little bit of adrenaline, something to let me know that I was going somewhere. "So where's the car?"

"We left it in the bay. Next morning, we come back and it's gone. Jed, there, he cusses her out, says all them people are like that, you can't trust 'em for nothing, and that was that. Till the sheriff showed up, saying she was dead."

The car I saw couldn't have been driven, and the woman I saw couldn't have fixed it. She would not have stopped here if she could.

"You left the car in pieces?" I asked. "And it was gone the next day? Someone drove it out of here?"

He shrugged. "Guess they finished it."

"That would've taken some know-how, wouldn't it?"

"Some," he said. He flicked his cigarette butt onto the sandy gravel. I glanced up. Jed was staring us from the bay. I felt the hair on the back of my neck rise.

I took another drag off my cigarette and watched a heat shimmer work its way down the highway. The boy started walking away from me.

"Where was she?" I asked. "When you left? Where was she?"

And I think he knew then that my interest wasn't really casual. Up until that point, he could have pretended it was. But at that moment, he knew.

"I dunno," he said, and his voice was flat.

"Sure you do," I said. I spoke softly so Jed couldn't overhear me.

The man looked at my face. His had turned bright red, and beads of sweat I hadn't noticed earlier were dotting his skin. "I—left her outside. Near the Coke machine."

With a car that didn't run, and no place to take her in for the night.

"Did you offer to give her a lift somewhere?"

He shook his head.

"Was the station still open when you left?"

"For another hour," he said.

"Did you tell the sheriff this?"

He shook his head again.

"Why not?"

He glanced at Jed, who had crossed his arms and was leaning against the bay doors. "I didn't think it was none of his business," the boy whispered.

"You didn't think, or Jed there, he didn't think."

"Neither of us," the boy said. "Jed told her she could sleep in there by the car. But it woulda been an oven, even during the night. I think she knew that."

"Is that where she slept?"

"I dunno." This time the boy did not meet my gaze. Sweat ran off his forehead, onto his chin, and dripped on his shirt. He didn't know, and he was sorry.

And so was I.

If I was going to pursue this logically, then I had to think logically. And it seemed to me that whoever killed the girl had known about the car. I couldn't believe she would have talked to anyone else—I suspected she only spoke to me because I was in uniform. And if I made that assumption, then the only other people who would have known about her, about the car, about the entire business were the people who worked the station.

"Who was working that night?" I asked.

"Mr. Flaherty," he said.

Mr. Flaherty. Mac Flaherty, whom I'd known since I was a boy. He was a hard decent man who expected work out of his employees, payment from his customers, and good money for a job well done. I'd seen Mac Flaherty in his station, at church, and at school getting his son, and I couldn't believe he had killed someone.

But then, I had. I had killed a lot of boys overseas, and I would have killed more if Hitler hadn't proved he was a coward and did the world a favor by dying by his own hand.

And the Mac Flaherty who ran the station now wasn't the same man as the one I'd known. I'd learned that much in my few short days in McCardle.

A shiver ran down my back. Then I headed inside, looking for Mac Flaherty, and finding him.

**

Mac Flaherty was drunk. Not falling down, noticeable drunk, but his daily drunk, the kind that made a man a bit blurry around the edges, kept him from feeling the pain of day-to-day living, and kept him working a job he no longer liked.

Once Flaherty'd loved his work. It had been obvious in the booming way he'd greet new customers, in the smile he wore every day whether going or coming from work.

But then he left for the war, like I did, only he came back in '43 minus three fingers on his left hand to find his wife shacking up with the local undertaker, and a half-sibling for his son baking in the oven. The wife, not him, took advantage of the McCardle's divorce laws, and Flaherty was never the same. She and the undertaker left that week, and apparently, Flaherty never saw his kid again.

I went inside the service station's main area, and the smell of beer mixed with the stench of gasoline. Flaherty was clutching a can, staring at me.

"You harassing the kid?" he asked.

"No," I said, even though I felt that wasn't entirely true. "I was just curious about the woman who died."

"She something to you?" Flaherty asked.

"Only met her the once," I said.

"Then what's the interest?"

"I don't know," I said, and we both seemed surprised by my honesty. "Your boy says he left her sitting outside. That true?"

Flaherty shrugged. "I never saw her. Not when I locked up."

"What about her car?"

"Her car," he repeated dully. "Her car. I had it towed."

"At night?"

"That morning," he said. "When it became clear she skipped out on me."

"Towed where?" I asked.

"My place," he said. "For parts."

And those parts had probably already been taken, along with anything incriminating. I didn't say that aloud, though.

"You have any idea who killed her?" I asked.

"What do you care?" he asked, gaze suddenly back on me, and sharper than I would have expected.

I thought of Jed then, Jed as I'd seen him that day, staring at me, that flat look on his face. "If Jed killed her—"

"I didn't see Jed touch nobody," Flaherty said. "And I wouldn't say if I did."

I froze. "Why not?"

Flaherty frowned, his eyes small and bloodshot. "He's the best mechanic I got."

"But if he killed someone—"

"He didn't kill no one."

"How can you be so sure?"

"What happened, happened," Flaherty said. "Let's not go wrecking more lives." Then he grabbed the bottle of beer he'd been nursing, and took a sip, his crippled hand looking unbalanced in the grimy afternoon light.

***

By the time I got back with the sheriff, Jed was gone. Not that it mattered. The case went down on the books as unsolved. What else could it have been with the other kid denying he'd even talked to me, and Mac Flaherty swearing that the girl'd been fine when he drove by at midnight, fine and unwilling to leave her post near the Coke machine. He'd winked at the sheriff when he'd told that story, and the sheriff seemed to accept it all.

I went to Jed's apartment, and found the door open, all his clothes missing, and a neighbor who said that Jed had run in, not even bothering to change, and packed a bag, took some money from a jam jar he'd had under his bed, and disappeared down the highway, never to be seen again.

He'd been driving one of Flaherty's rebuilds.

When I found out, I told the sheriff, and the sheriff'd been unimpressed. "Man can leave town if'n he wants," the sheriff said. "Don't mean he killed nobody."

No, I suppose it didn't. But it seemed like a huge coincidence to me, the girl getting beaten to death, Jed watching us talk, and then, when he knew I'd left for the law, disappearing like he did.

It was just the sheriff saw no percentage in pursing the case. It'd been interesting when he could come after me because of my family, because of the power we had, but it soon lost its appeal when the girl's family took her away. Took her away, and pointed the finger at a good local boy, a mechanic who could down some beers and tell great jokes, who'd gone off to serve his country same as the rest of us. Jed had had worth to the sheriff; the girl had had none.

***

I don't know why he killed her. We'll never know now. Jed disappeared but good, and wasn't heard from until five years ago, when what was left of his family got an obituary mailed to them from somewhere in Canada. He'd died not saying a word—

***

Sorry. Got interrupted there. Was going to come back to it this afternoon, but things changed this morning.

About nine a.m., I walked into my front room, buttoning one of my best shirts in preparation for yet another meeting with that pretty doctor down at the glass-and-chrome White Elephant, when I saw Sarah sitting in my best chair, feet on the footstool my granny hand-stitched, and all forty hand-written pages of this memory in her hands. She was reading raptly which I found flattering for the half second it took to realize what she was doing. I didn't want any one to read this stuff until I was dead, and here was my granddaughter staring at the pages as if they were something outta Stephen King.

She looked up at me, her heart-shaped face so like Sally Anne's at that age that it made my breath catch, and said, "So you think you're some bad guy for failing this woman."

I shook my head, but the movement didn't stop her.

"You," she says, "who've done more for people—black, white or purple—than anyone else in this town. You, who went and opened that civil rights law practice back east, who fought every racist law and every racist politician you could find. For godssake, Gramps, you marched with Dr. King, and you were a presidential advisor on Civil Rights. You're the kinda man who shows the rest of us how to live our lives, and you're feeling like this? You're being silly."

"You don't understand," I said.

"Damn straight," she said, and I winced, as I always do, at the sailor language she uses. "You shouldn't be mulling over this any more. You did what you could, and more, it seems, than anyone else."

"And even that wasn't enough."

"Sometimes," she said, "that happens, Gramps. You know that. Hell, you taught it to me."

Seems I did. But that wasn't the point either, and I didn't know how to tell her. So I didn't. I took the papers from her, put them back on my desk where they belonged, and let her drive me to the doctor so that they both could feel useful.

And all the way there and all the way back, I thought about how to make my point so that girls like her would understand. You see, the world is so different now, and yet it's still the same. Just the faces change, and a few of the rules.

These days, Jed would've been arrested, or the sheriff would've been bounced out of office, or the press'd make some huge scandal over the whole thing.

But it wouldn't be that simple, because pretty women don't approach strange men any more, especially if the strange men are in uniform, and pretty women certainly don't wait alone in gas stations while their cars are being repaired.

But they're still dying, because they're women or because they're black or because they're in the wrong place at the wrong time, and there's so damn many of them we just shrug and move on, shaking our heads as we go.

But that isn't my point. My point is this:

I wouldn't have marched with Dr. King if it weren't for that poor girl, and I wouldn't have made it my life's work to stamp out all the things that cause the condition I found myself in that hot afternoon, the condition that would have led me to ignore a girl if I'd noticed the true color of her skin.

Because I think I know why she died that day. I think she died because she'd flirted with me.

And that just wasn't done between girls like her and men like me.

Jed wouldn't have taken her to the desert if she were white. He would've thought she had family, she had someone who missed her. He might have roughed her up for talking to me. He might have had a few words with me.

But he didn't. I did something unspeakable to people of our generation, and he saw a way to get back at me. If I'd talked to her, then I'd want to do what was probably done to her before she died. And if she'd fought, then I'd have bashed her. That's what the sheriff was thinking. That's what Jed wanted him to think.

And all because of who she was, and who I was, and who Jed was.

The sad irony is that if I'd kept my place, she'd be alive, and because I didn't, she was dead. That had bothered me then, and bothers me now. Seems a man—any man—should be able to talk to whomever he wants. But what bothered me worse was the fact that when I learned, on the same morning, that she was black and that she was dead, it bothered me more that she was black and that I had talked to her.

It just wasn't done.

And I was more worried about my own blindness than I was about one woman's life.

Since that day, hers is the face I see every morning when I wake up, and every night when I doze. And, if God gave me the chance to relive any day in my life, it'd be that one, not, strangely, the day I enlisted or the day I deliberately misunderstood that German kid asking for clemency, but the day I inadvertently led a pretty girl to her death.

White liberal guilt maybe.

Or maybe it was the last straw, somehow.

Or maybe it was the fact that I had so much trouble learning her name.

Learning her name was harder than learning the identity of the man who killed her. It took me three more weeks and a bribe to the twelve-year-old son of the owner of the funeral home.

Not that her name really mattered. To me or to anyone else.

But it mattered to her, and to that man in uniform with the red, red eyes. Because it was the only bit of her that couldn't be sold for parts. The only bit she could call completely hers.

Lucille Johnson.

Not quite as exotic as I would have thought, or as fitting to a woman as beautiful as she was. But it was hers. And in the end, it was all she had.

It was a detail.

An important detail.

And one I'll never forget.

G-MEN

"There's something addicting about a secret."
—J. Edgar Hoover

THE SQUALID LITTLE ALLEY smelled of piss. Detective Seamus O'Reilly tugged his overcoat closed and wished he'd worn boots. He could feel the chill of his metal flashlight through the worn glove on his right hand.

Two beat cops stood in front of the bodies, and the coroner crouched over them. His assistant was already setting up the gurneys, body bags draped over his arm. The coroner's van had blocked the alley's entrance, only a few yards away.

O'Reilly's partner, Joseph McKinnon, followed him. McKinnon had trained his own flashlight on the fire escapes above, unintentionally alerting any residents to the police presence.

But they probably already knew. Shootings in this part of the city were common. The neighborhood teetered between swank and corrupt. Far enough from Central Park for degenerates and muggers to use the alleys as corridors, and, conversely, close enough for new money to want to live with a peak of the city's most famous expanse of green.

The coroner, Thomas Brunner, had set up two expensive, battery-operated lights on garbage can lids placed on top of the dirty ice, one at the top of the bodies, the other near the feet. O'Reilly crouched so he wouldn't create any more shadows.

"What've we got?" he asked.

"Dunno yet." Brunner was using his gloved hands to part the hair on the back of the nearest corpse's skull. "It could be one of those nights."

O'Reilly had worked with Brunner for eighteen years now, since they both got back from the war, and he hated it when Brunner said it could be one of those nights. That meant the corpses would stack up, which was usually a summer thing, but almost never happened in the middle of winter.

"Why?" O'Reilly asked. "What else we got?"

"Some colored limo driver shot two blocks from here." Brunner was still parting the hair. It took O'Reilly a minute to realize it was matted with blood. "And two white guys pulled out of their cars and shot about four blocks from that."

O'Reilly felt a shiver run through him that had nothing to do with the cold. "You think the shootings are related?"

"Dunno," Brunner said. "But I think it's odd, don't you? Five dead in the space of an hour, all in a six-block radius."

O'Reilly closed his eyes for a moment. Two white guys pulled out of their cars, one Negro driver of a limo, and now two white guys in an alley. Maybe they were related, maybe they weren't.

He opened his eyes, then wished he hadn't. Brunner had his finger inside a bullet hole, a quick way to judge caliber.

"Same type of bullet," Brunner said.

"You handled the other shootings?"

"I was on scene with the driver when some fag called this one in."

O'Reilly looked at Brunner. Eighteen years, and he still wasn't used to the man's casual bigotry.

"How did you know the guy was queer?" O'Reilly asked. "You talk to him?"

"Didn't have to." Brunner nodded toward the building in front of them. "Weekly party for degenerates in the penthouse apartment every Thursday night. Thought you knew."

O'Reilly looked up. Now he understood why McKinnon had been shining his flashlight at the upper story windows. McKinnon had worked vice before he got promoted to homicide.

"Why would I know?" O'Reilly said.

McKinnon was the one who answered. "Because of the standing orders."

"I'm not playing twenty questions," O'Reilly said. "I don't know about a party in this building and I don't know about standing orders."

"The standing orders are," McKinnon said as if he were an elementary school teacher, "not to bust it, no matter what kind of lead you got. You see someone go in, you forget about it. You see someone come out, you avert your eyes. You complain, you get moved to a different shift, maybe a different precinct."

"Jesus." O'Reilly was too far below to see if there was any movement against the glass in the penthouse suite. But whoever lived there—whoever partied there—had learned to shut off the lights before the cops arrived.

"Shot in the back of the head," Brunner said before O'Reilly could process all of the information. "That's just damn strange."

O'Reilly looked at the corpses—really looked at them—for the first time. Two men, both rather heavy set. Their faces were gone, probably splattered all over the walls. Gloved hands, nice shoes, one of them wearing a white scarf that caught the light.

Brunner had to search for the wound in the back of the head, which made that the entry point. The exit wounds had destroyed the faces.

O'Reilly looked behind him. No door on that building, but there was one on the building where the party was held. If they'd been exiting the building and were surprised by a queer basher or a mugger, they'd've been shot in the front, not the back.

"How many times were they shot?" O'Reilly asked.

"Looks like just the once. Large caliber, close range. I'd say it was a purposeful headshot, designed to do maximum damage." Brunner felt the back of the closest corpse. "There doesn't seem to be anything on the torso."

"They still got their wallets?" McKinnon asked.

"Haven't checked yet." Brunner reached into the back pants pocket of the corpse he'd been searching and clearly found nothing. So he grabbed the front of the overcoat and reached inside.

He removed a long thin wallet—old fashioned, the kind made for the larger bills of forty years before. Hand-tailored, beautifully made.

These men weren't hurting for money.

Brunner handed the wallet to O'Reilly, who opened it. And stopped when he saw the badge inside. His mouth went dry.

"We got a feebee," he said, his voice sounding strangled.

"What?" McKinnon asked.

"FBI," Brunner said dryly. McKinnon had only moved to homicide the year before. Vice rarely had to deal with FBI. Homicide did only on sensational cases. O'Reilly could count on one hand the number of times he'd spoken to agents in the New York bureau.

"Not just any feebee either," O'Reilly said. "The Associate Director. Clyde A. Tolson."

McKinnon whistled. "Who's the other guy?"

This time, O'Reilly did the search. The other corpse, the heavier of the two, also smelled faintly of perfume. This man had kept his wallet in the inner pocket of his suit coat, just like his companion had.

O'Reilly opened the wallet. Another badge, just like he expected. But he didn't expect the bulldog face glaring at him from the wallet's interior.

Nor had he expected the name.

"Jesus, Mary and Joseph," he said.

"What've we got?" McKinnon asked.

O'Reilly handed him the wallet, opened to the slim paper identification.

"The Director of the FBI," he said, his voice shaking. "Public Hero Number One. J. Edgar Hoover."

***

Francis Xavier Bryce—Frank to his friends, what few of them he still had left—had just dropped off to sleep when the phone rang. He cursed, caught himself, apologized to Mary, and then remembered she wasn't there.

The phone rang again and he fumbled for the light, knocking over the highball glass he'd used to mix his mom's recipe for sleepless nights, hot milk, butter and honey. It turned out that, at the tender age of 36, hot milk and butter laced with honey wasn't a recipe for sleep; it was a recipe for heartburn.

And for a smelly carpet if he didn't clean the mess up.

He found the phone before he found the light.

"What?" he snapped.

"You live near Central Park, right?" A voice he didn't recognize, but one that was clearly official, asked the question without a hello or an introduction.

"More or less." Bryce rarely talked about his apartment. His parents had left it to him and, as his wife was fond of sniping, it was too fancy for a junior G-Man.

The voice rattled off an address. "How far is that from you?"

"About five minutes." If he didn't clean up the mess on the floor. If he spent thirty seconds pulling on the clothes he'd piled onto the chair beside the bed.

"Get there. Now. We got a situation."

"What about my partner?" Bryce's partner lived in Queens.

"You'll have backup. You just have to get to the scene. The moment you get there, you shut it down."

"Um." Bryce hated sounding uncertain, but he had no choice. "First, sir, I need to know who I'm talking to. Then I need to know what I'll find."

"You'll find a double homicide. And you're talking to Eugene Hart, the Special Agent in Charge. I shouldn't have to identify myself to you."

Now that he had, Bryce recognized Hart's voice. "Sorry, sir. It's just procedure."

"Fuck procedure. Take over that scene. *Now*."

"Yes, sir," Bryce said, but he was talking into an empty phone line. He hung up, hands shaking, wishing he had some BromoSeltzer.

He'd just come off a long, messy investigation of another agent. Walter Cain had been about to get married when he remembered he had to inform the Bureau of that fact and, as per regulation, get his bride vetted before walking down the aisle.

Bryce had been the one to investigate the future Mrs. Cain, and had been the one to find out about her rather seamy past—two Vice convictions under a different name, and one hospitalization after a rather messy backstreet abortion. Turned out Cain knew about his future wife's past, but the Bureau hadn't liked it.

And two nights ago, Bryce had to be the one to tell Cain that he couldn't marry his now-reformed, somewhat religious, beloved. The soon-to-be Mrs. Cain had taken the news hard. She had gone to Bellevue this afternoon after slashing her wrists.

And Bryce had been the one to tell Cain what his former fiancée had done. Just a few hours ago.

Sometimes Bryce hated this job.

Despite his orders, he went into the bathroom, soaked one of Mary's precious company towels in water, and dropped the thing on the spilled milk. Then he pulled on his clothes, and finger-combed his hair.

He was a mess—certainly not the perfect representative of the Bureau. His white shirt was stained with marinara from that night's take-out, and his tie wouldn't keep a crisp knot. The crease had long since left his trousers and his shoes hadn't been shined in weeks. Still, he grabbed his black overcoat, hoping it would hide everything.

He let himself out of the apartment before he remembered the required and much hated hat, went back inside, grabbed the hat as well as his gun and his identification. Jesus, he was tired. He hadn't slept since Mary walked out. Mary, who had been vetted by the FBI and who had passed with flying colors. Mary, who had turned out to be more of a liability than any former hooker ever could have been.

And now, because of her, he was heading toward something big, and he was one-tenth as sharp as usual.

All he could hope for was that the SAC had overreacted. And he had a hunch—a two in the morning, get-your-ass-over-there-now hunch—that the SAC hadn't overreacted at all.

***

Attorney General Robert F. Kennedy sat in his favorite chair near the fire in his library. The house was quiet even though his wife and eight children were asleep upstairs. Outside, the rolling landscape was covered in a light dusting of snow—rare for McLean, Virginia even at this time of year.

He held a book in his left hand, his finger marking the spot. The Greeks had comforted him in the few months since Jack died, but lately Kennedy had discovered Camus.

He had been about to copy a passage into his notebook when the phone rang. At first he sighed, feeling all of the exhaustion that had weighed on him since the assassination. He didn't want to answer the phone. He didn't want to be bothered—not now, not ever again.

But this was the direct line from the White House and if he didn't answer it, someone else in the house would.

He set the Camus book face down on his chair and crossed to the desk before the third ring. He answered with a curt, "Yes?"

"Attorney General Kennedy, sir?" The voice on the other end sounded urgent. The voice sounded familiar to him even though he couldn't place it.

"Yes?"

"This is Special Agent John Haskell. You asked me to contact you, sir, if I heard anything important about Director Hoover, no matter what the time."

Kennedy leaned against the desk. He had made that request back when his brother had been president, back when Kennedy had been the first attorney general since the 1920s who actually demanded accountability from Hoover.

Since Lyndon Johnson had taken over the presidency, accountability had gone by the wayside. These days Hoover rarely returned Kennedy's phone calls.

"Yes, I did tell you that," Kennedy said, resisting the urge to add, but *I don't care about that old man any longer.*

"Sir, there are rumors—credible ones—that Director Hoover has died in New York."

Kennedy froze. For a moment, he flashed back to that unseasonably warm afternoon when he'd sat just outside with the federal attorney for New York City, Robert Morganthau and the chief of Morganthau's criminal division, Silvio Mollo, talking about prosecuting various organized crime figures.

Kennedy could still remember the glint of the sunlight on the swimming pool, the taste of the tuna fish sandwich

Ethel had brought him, the way the men—despite their topic—had seemed lighthearted.

Then the phone rang, and J. Edgar Hoover was on the line. Kennedy almost didn't take the call, but he did and Hoover's cold voice said, *I have news for you. The President's been shot.*

Kennedy had always disliked Hoover, but since that day, that awful day in the bright sunshine, he hated that fat bastard. Not once—not in that call, not in the subsequent calls—did Hoover express condolences or show a shred of human concern.

"Credible rumors?" Kennedy repeated, knowing he probably sounded as cold as Hoover had three months ago, and not caring. He'd chosen Haskell as his liaison precisely because the man didn't like Hoover either. Kennedy had needed someone inside Hoover's hierarchy, unbeknownst to Hoover, which was difficult since Hoover kept his hand in everything. Haskell was one of the few who fit the bill.

"Yes, sir, quite credible."

"Then why haven't I received official contact?"

"I'm not even sure the President knows, sir."

Kennedy leaned against the desk. "Why not, if the rumors are credible?"

"Um, because, sir, um, it seems Associate Director Tolson was also shot, and um, they were, um, in a rather suspect area."

Kennedy closed his eyes. All of Washington knew that Tolson was the closest thing Hoover had to a wife.

The two old men had been life-long companions. Even though they didn't live together, they had every meal together. Tolson had been Hoover's hatchet man until the last year or so, when Tolson's health hadn't permitted it.

Then a word Haskell used sank in. "You said shot."

"Yes, sir."

"Is Tolson dead too then?"

"And three other people in the neighborhood," Haskell said.

"My God." Kennedy ran a hand over his face. "But they think this is personal?"

"Yes, sir."

"Because of the location of the shooting?"

"Yes, sir. It seems there was an exclusive gathering in a nearby building. You know the type, sir."

Kennedy didn't know the type—at least not through personal experience. But he'd heard of places like that, where the rich, famous and deviant could spend time with each other, and do whatever it was they liked to do in something approaching privacy.

"So," he said, "the bureau's trying to figure out how to cover this up."

"Or at least contain it, sir."

Without Hoover or Tolson. No one in the bureau was going to know what to do.

Kennedy's hand started to shake. "What about the files?"

"Files, sir?"

"Hoover's confidential files. Has anyone secured them?"

"Not yet, sir. But I'm sure someone has called Miss Gandy."

Helen Gandy was Hoover's long-time secretary. She had been his right hand as long as Tolson had operated that hatchet.

"So procedure's being followed," Kennedy said, then frowned. If procedure were being followed, shouldn't the acting head of the bureau be calling him?

"No, sir. But the Director put some private instructions in place should he be killed or incapacitated. Private emergency instructions. And those involve letting Miss Gandy know before anyone else."

Even me, Kennedy thought. *Hoover's nominal boss.* "She's not there yet, right?"

"No, sir."

"Do you know where those files are?" Kennedy asked, trying not to let desperation into his voice.

"I've made it my business to know, sir." There was a pause and then Haskell lowered his voice. "They're in Miss Gandy's office, sir."

Not Hoover's like everyone thought. For the first time in months, Kennedy felt a glimmer of hope. "Secure those files."

"Sir?"

"Do whatever it takes. I want them out of there, and I want someone to secure Hoover's house too. I'm acting on the orders of the President. If anyone tells you that they are doing the same, they're mistaken. The President made his wishes clear on this point. He often said if anything happens to that old queer—" And here Kennedy deliberately used LBJ's favorite phrase for Hoover "—then we need those files before they can get into the wrong hands."

"I'm on it, sir."

"I can't stress to you the importance of this," Kennedy said. In fact, he couldn't talk about the importance at all. Those files could ruin his brother's legacy. The secrets in there could bring down Kennedy too, and his entire family.

"And if the rumors about the Director's death are wrong, sir?"

Kennedy felt a shiver of fear. "Are they?"

"I seriously doubt it."

"Then let me worry about that."

And about what LBJ would do when he found out. Because the president upon whose orders Kennedy acted wasn't the current one. Kennedy was following the orders of the only man he believed should be president at the moment.

His brother, Jack.

***

The scene wasn't hard to find; a coroner's van blocked the entrance to the alley. Bryce walked quickly, already cold, his heartburn worse than it had been when he had gone to bed.

The neighborhood was in transition. An urban renewal project had knocked down some wonderful turn of the century buildings that had become eyesores. But so far, the buildings that had replaced them were the worst kind of modern—all planes and angles and white with few windows.

In the buildings closest to the park, the lights worked and the streets looked safe. But here, on a side street not far from the construction, the city's shady side showed. The dirty snow was piled against the curb, the streets were dark, and nothing seemed inhabited except that alley with the coroner's van blocking the entrance.

The coroner's van and at least one unmarked car. No press, which surprised him. He shoved his gloved hands in the pockets of his overcoat even though it was against FBI dress code, and slipped between the van and the wall of a grimy brick building.

The alley smelled of old urine and fresh blood. Two beat cops blocked his way until he showed identification. Then, like people usually did, they parted as if he could burn them.

The bodies had fallen side by side in the center of the alley. They looked posed, with their arms up, their legs in classic P position—one leg bent, the other straight. They looked like they could fit perfectly on the dead body diagrams the FBI used to put out in the 1930s. He wondered if they had fallen like this or if this had been the result of the coroner's tampering.

The coroner had messed with other parts of the crime scene—if, indeed, he had been the one who put the garbage can lids on the ice and set battery-powered lamps on them. The warmth of the lamps was melting the ice and sending runnels of water into a nearby grate.

"I hope to hell someone thought to photograph the scene before you melted it," he said.

The coroner and the two cops who had been crouching beside the bodies stood up guiltily. The coroner looked at the garbage can lids and closed his eyes. Then he took a deep breath, opened them, and snapped his fingers at the assistant who was waiting beside a gurney.

"Camera," he said.

"That's Crime Scene's—." the assistant began, then saw everyone looking at him. He glanced at the van. "Never mind."

He walked behind the bodies, further disturbing the scene. Bryce's mouth thinned in irritation. The cops who stood were in plain clothes.

"Detectives," Bryce said, holding his identification, "Special Agent Frank Bryce of the FBI. I've been told to secure this scene. More of my people will be here shortly."

He hoped that last was true. He had no idea who was coming or when they would arrive.

"Good," said the younger detective, a tall man with broad shoulders and an all-American jaw. "The sooner we get out of here the better."

Bryce had never gotten that reaction from a detective before. Usually the detectives were territorial, always reminding him that this was New York City and that the scene belonged to them.

The other detective, older, face grizzled by time and work, held out his gloved hand. "Forgive my partner's rudeness. I'm Seamus O'Reilly. He's Joseph McAllister and we'll help you in any way we can."

"I appreciate it," Bryce said, taking O'Reilly's hand and shaking it. "I guess the first thing you can do is tell me what we've got."

"A hell of a mess, that's for sure," said McAllister. "You'll understand when…."

His voice trailed off as his partner took out two long, old-fashioned wallets and handed them to Bryce.

Bryce took them, feeling confused. Then he opened the first, saw the familiar badge, and felt his breath catch. Two FBI agents, in this alley? Shot side-by-side? He looked up, saw the darkened windows.

There used to be rumors about this neighborhood. Some exclusive private sex parties used to be held here, and his old partner had always wanted to visit one just to see if it was a hotbed of Communists like some of the agents had claimed. Bryce had begged off. He was an investigator, not a voyeur.

The two detectives were staring at him, as if they expected more from him. He still had the wallet open in his hand. If the dead men were New York agents, he would know them. He hated solving the deaths of people he knew.

But he steeled himself, looked at the identification, and felt the blood leave his face. His skin grew cold and for a moment he felt lightheaded.

"No," he said.

The detectives still stared at him.

He swallowed. "Have you done a visual i.d.?"

Hoover was recognizable. His picture was on everything. Sometimes Bryce thought Hoover was more famous than the president—any president. He'd certainly been in power longer.

"Faces are gone," O'Reilly said.

"Exit wounds," the coroner added from beside the bodies. His assistant had returned and was taking pictures, the flash showing just how much melt had happened since the coroner arrived.

"Shot in the back of the head?" Bryce blinked. He was tired and his brain was working slowly, but something about the shots didn't match with the body positions.

"If they came out that door," O'Reilly said as he indicated a dark metal door almost hidden in the side of the brick building, "then the shooters had to be waiting beside it."

"Your crime scene people haven't arrived yet, I take it?" Bryce asked.

"No," the coroner said. "They think it's a fag kill. They'll get here when they get here."

Bryce clenched his left fist and had to remind himself to let the fingers loose.

O'Reilly saw the reaction. "Sorry about that," he said, shooting a glare at the coroner. "I'm sure the director was here on business."

Funny business. But Bryce didn't say that. The rumors about Hoover had been around since Bryce joined the FBI just after the war. Hoover quashed them, like he quashed any criticism, but it seemed like the criticism got made, no matter what.

Bryce opened the other wallet, but he already had a guess as to who was beside Hoover, and his guess turned out to be right.

"You want to tell me why your crime scene people believe this is a homosexual killing?" Bryce asked, trying not to let what Mary called his FBI tone into his voice. If Hoover was still alive and this was some kind of plant, Hoover would want to crush the source of this assumption. Bryce would make sure that the source was worth pursuing before going any farther.

"Neighborhood, mostly," McAllister said. "There're a couple of bars, mostly high-end. You have to know someone to get in. Then there's the party, held every week upstairs. Some of the most important men in the city show up at it, or so they used to say in Vice when they told us to stay away."

Bryce nodded, letting it go at that.

"We need your crime scene people here ASAP, and a lot more cops so that we can protect what's left of this scene, in case these men turn out to be who their identification says they are. You search the bodies to see if this was the only identification on them?"

O'Reilly started. He clearly hadn't thought of that. Probably had been too shocked by the first wallets that he found.

The younger detective had already gone back to the bodies. The coroner put out a hand, and did the searching himself.

"You think this was a plant?" O'Reilly asked.

"I don't know what to think," Bryce said. "I'm not here to think. I'm here to make sure everything goes smoothly."

And to make sure the case goes to the FBI. Those words hung unspoken between the two of them. Not that O'Reilly objected, and now Bryce could understand why. This case would be a political nightmare, and no good detective wanted to be in the middle of it.

"How come there's no press?" Bryce asked O'Reilly. "You manage to get rid of them somehow?"

"Fag kill," the coroner said.

Bryce was getting tired of those words. His fist had clenched again, and he had to work at unclenching it.

"Ignore him," O'Reilly said softly. "He's an asshole and the best coroner in the city."

"I heard that," the coroner said affably. "There's no other identification on either of them."

O'Reilly's shoulders slumped, as if he'd been hoping for a different outcome. Bryce should have been hoping as well, but he hadn't been. He had known that Hoover was in town. The entire New York bureau knew, since Hoover always took it over when he arrived—breezing in, giving instructions, making sure everything was just the way he wanted it.

"Before this gets too complicated," O'Reilly said, "you want to see the other bodies?"

"Other bodies?" Bryce felt numb. He could use some caffeine now, but Hoover had ordered agents not to drink coffee on the job. Getting coffee now felt almost disrespectful.

"We got three more." O'Reilly took a deep breath. "And just before you arrived, I got word that they're agents too."

***

Special Agent John Haskell had just installed six of his best agents outside the Director's suite of offices when a small woman showed up, key clutched in her gloved right hand. Helen Gandy, the Director's secretary, looked up at Haskell with the coldest stare he'd ever seen outside of the Director's.

"May I go into my office, Agent Haskell?" Her voice was just as cold. She didn't look upset, and if he hadn't known that she never stayed past five unless directed by Hoover himself, Haskell would have thought she was coming back from a prolonged work break.

"I'm sorry, Ma'am," he said. "No one is allowed inside. President's orders."

"Really?" God, that voice was chilling. He remembered the first time he'd heard it, when he'd been brought to this suite of offices as a brand-new agent, after getting his "Meet the Boss" training before his introduction to the Director. She'd frightened him more than Hoover had.

"Yes, Ma'am. The President says no one can enter."

"Surely he didn't mean me."

Surely he did. But Haskell bit the comment back. "I'm sorry, Ma'am."

"I have a few personal items that I'd like to get, if you don't mind. And the Director instructed me that in the case of..." and for the first time she paused. Her voice didn't break nor did she clear her throat. But she seemed to need a moment to gather herself. "In case of emergency, I was to remove some of his personal items as well."

"If you could tell me what they are, Ma'am, I'll get them."

Her eyes narrowed. "The Director doesn't like others to touch his possessions."

"I'm sorry, Ma'am," he said gently. "But I don't think that matters any longer."

Any other woman would have broken down. After all, she had worked for the old man for forty-five years, side-by-side, every day. Never marrying, not because they had a relationship—Helen Gandy, more than anyone, probably knew the truth behind the Director's relationship with the Associate Director—but because for Helen Gandy, just like for the Director himself, the FBI was her entire life.

"It matters," she said. "Now if you'll excuse me…"

She tried to wriggle past him. She was wiry and stronger than he expected. He had to put out an arm to block her.

"Ma'am," he said in the gentlest tone he could summon, "the President's orders supersede the Director's."

How often had he wanted to say that over the years? How often had he wanted to remind everyone in the Bureau that the President led the Free World, not J. Edgar Hoover.

"In this instance," she snapped, "they do not."

"Ma'am, I'd hate to have some agents restrain you." Although he wasn't sure about that. She had never been nice to him or to anyone he knew. She'd always been sharp or rude. "You're distraught."

"I am not." She clipped each word.

"You are because I say you are, Ma'am."

She raised her chin. For a moment, he thought she hadn't understood. But she finally did.

The balance of power had shifted. At the moment, it was on his side.

"Do I have to call the president then to get my personal effects?" she asked.

But they both knew she wasn't talking about her personal things. And the President was smart enough to know that as well. As hungry to get those files as the Attorney General had seemed despite his Eastern reserve, the President would be utterly ravenous. He wouldn't let some old skirt, as he'd been known to call Miss Gandy, get in his way.

"Go ahead," Haskell said. "Feel free to use the phone in the office across the hall."

She glared at him, then turned on one foot and marched down the corridor. But she didn't head toward a phone—at least not one he could see.

He wondered who she would call. The President wouldn't listen. The Attorney General had issued the order in the president's name. Maybe she would contact one of Hoover's Assistant Directors, the four or five men that Hoover had in his pocket.

Haskell had been waiting for them. But word still hadn't spread through the Bureau. The only reason he knew was because he'd received a call from the SAC of the New York office. New York hated the Director, mostly because the old man went there so often and harassed them.

Someone had probably figured out that there was a crisis from the moment that Haskell had brought his people in to secure the Director's suite. But no one would know that the Director was dead until Miss Gandy made the calls or until someone in the Bureau started along the chain of command—the one designated in the book Hoover had written all those years ago.

Haskell crossed his arms. Sometimes he wished he hadn't let the A.G. know how he felt about the Director. Sometimes he wished he were still a humble assistant, the man who had joined the FBI because he wanted to be a top cop like his hero J. Edgar Hoover.

A man who, it turned out, never made a real arrest or fired a gun or even understood investigation.

There was a lot to admire about the Director—no matter what you said, he'd built a hell of an agency almost from scratch—but he wasn't the man his press made him out to be.

And that was the source of Haskell's disillusionment. He'd wanted to be a top cop. Instead, he snooped into homes and businesses and sometimes even investigated fairly blameless people, looking for a mistake in their past.

Since he'd been transferred to FBIHQ, he hadn't done any real investigating at all. His arrests had slowed, his cases dwindled.

And he'd found himself investigating his boss, trying to find out where the legend ended and the man began.

Once he realized that the old man was just a bureaucrat who had learned where all the bodies were buried and used that to make everyone bow to his bidding, Haskell was ripe for the undercover work the A.G. had asked him to do.

Only now he wasn't undercover any more. Now he was standing in the open before the Director's cache of secrets, on the President's orders, hoping that no one would call his bluff.

***

As O'Reilly led him to the limousine, Bryce surreptitiously checked his watch. He'd already been on scene for half an hour, and no back-up had arrived. If he was supposed to secure everything and chase off the NYPD, he'd need some manpower.

But for now, he wanted to see the extent of the problem. The night had gotten colder, and this street was even darker than the street he'd walked down. All of the streetlights were out. The only light came from some porch bulbs above a few entrances. He could barely make out the limousine at the end of the block, and then only because he could see the shadowy forms of the two beat cops standing at the scene, their squad cars parking the limo in.

As he got closer, he recognized the shape of the limo. It was thicker than most limos and rode lower to the ground because it was encased in an extra frame, making it bulletproof. Supposedly, the glass would all be bullet-proof as well.

"You said the driver was shot inside the limo?" Bryce asked.

"That's what they told me," O'Reilly said. "I wasn't called to this scene. We were brought in because of the two men in the alley. Even then we were called late."

Bryce nodded. He remembered the coroner's bigotry. "Is that standard procedure for cases involving minorities?"

O'Reilly gave him a sideways glance. Bryce couldn't read O'Reilly's expression in the dark.

"We're overtaxed," O'Reilly said after a moment. "Some cases don't get the kind of treatment they deserve."

"Limo drivers," Bryce said.

"If he'd been killed in the parking garage under the Plaza maybe," O'Reilly said. "But not because of who he was. But because of where he was."

Bryce nodded. He knew how the world worked. He didn't like it. He spoke up against it too many times, which was why he was on shaky ground at the Bureau.

Then his already upset stomach clenched. Maybe he wasn't going to get back-up. Maybe they'd put him on his own here to claim he'd botched the investigation, so that they would be able to cover it up.

He couldn't concentrate on that now. What he had to do was take good notes, make the best case he could, and keep a copy of every damn thing—maybe in more than one place.

"You were called in because of the possibility that the men in the alley could be important," Bryce said.

"That's my guess," O'Reilly said.

"What about the others down the block? Has anyone taken those cases?"

"Probably not," O'Reilly said. "Those bars, you know. It's department policy. The coroner checks bodies in the suspect area, and decides, based on...um...evidence of...um...

activity...whether or not to bring in detectives."

Bryce frowned. He almost asked what the coroner was checking for when he figured out that it was evidence on the body itself, evidence not of the crime, but of certain kinds of sex acts. If that evidence was present, apparently no one thought it worthwhile to investigate the crime.

"You'd think the city would revise that," Bryce said. "A lot of people live dual lives—productive and interesting people."

"Yeah," O'Reilly said. "You'd think. Especially after tonight."

Bryce grinned. He was liking this grizzled cop more and more.

O'Reilly spoke to the beat cops, then motioned Bryce to the limo. As Bryce approached, O'Reilly trained his flashlight on the driver's side.

The window wasn't broken like Bryce had expected. It had been rolled down.

"You got here one James Crawford," said one of the beat cops. "He got identification says he's a feebee, but I ain't never heard of no colored feebee."

"There's only four," Bryce said dryly. And they all worked for Hoover as his personal housekeepers or drivers. "Can I see that identification?"

The beat cop handed him a wallet that matched the ones on Tolson and Hoover. Inside was a badge and identification for James Crawford as well as family photographs. Neither Tolson nor Hoover had had any photographs in their wallets.

Bryce motioned O'Reilly to move a little closer to the body. The head was tilted toward the window. The right side of the skull was gone, the hair glistening with drying blood. With one gloved finger, Bryce pushed the head upright. A single entrance wound above the left ear had caused the damage.

"Brunner says the shots are the same caliber," O'Reilly said.

It took Bryce a moment to realize that Brunner was the coroner.

Bryce carefully searched Crawford but didn't find the man's weapon. Nor could he find a holster or any way to carry a weapon.

"It looks like he wasn't carrying a weapon," Bryce said.

"Neither were the two in the alley," O'Reilly said, and Bryce appreciated his caution in not identifying the other two corpses. "You'd think they would have been."

Bryce shook his head. "They were known for not carrying weapons. But you'd think their driver would have one."

"Maybe they had protection," O'Reilly said.

And Bryce's mouth went dry. Of course they did. The office always joked about who would get HooverWatch on each trip. He'd had to do it a few times.

Agents on HooverWatch followed strict rules, like everything else with Hoover. Remain close enough to see the men entering and exiting an area, stop any suspicious characters, and yet somehow remain inconspicuous.

"You said there were two others shot?"

"Yeah. A block or so from here." O'Reilly waved a hand vaguely down the street.

"Pulled out of one car or two?"

"Not my case," O'Reilly said.

"Two," said the beat cop. "Black sedans. Could barely see them on this cruddy street."

HooverWatch. Bryce swallowed hard, that bile back. Of course. He probably knew the men who were shot.

"Let's look," he said. "You two, make sure the coroner's man photographs this scene before he leaves."

"Yessir," said the second beat cop. He hadn't spoken before.

"And don't let anyone near this scene unless I give the o.k.," Bryce said.

"How come this guy's in charge?" the talkative beat cop asked O'Reilly.

O'Reilly grinned. "Because he's a feebee."

"I'm sorry," the beat cop said automatically turning to Bryce. "I didn't know, sir."

Feebee was an insult—or at least some in the Bureau thought so. Bryce didn't mind it. Any more than he minded when some rookie said "Sack" when he meant "Ess-Ay-Cee." Shorthand worked, sometimes better than people wanted it to.

"Point me in the right direction," he said to the talkative cop.

The cop nodded south. "One block down, sir. You can't miss it. We got guys on those scenes too, but we weren't so sure it was important. You know. We coulda missed stuff."

In other words, they hadn't buttoned up the scene immediately. They'd waited for the coroner to make his verdict, and he probably hadn't, not with the three new corpses nearby.

Bryce took one last look at James Crawford. The man had rolled down his window, despite the cold, and in a bad section of town.

He leaned forward. Underneath the faint scent of cordite and mingled with the thicker smell of blood was the smell of a cigar.

He took the flashlight from O'Reilly and trained it on the dirty snow against the curb. It had been trampled by everyone coming to this crime scene.

He crouched, and poked just a little, finding three fairly fresh cigarette butts.

As he stood, he said to the beat cops, "When the scene of the crime guys get here, make sure they take everything from the curb."

O'Reilly was watching him. The beat cops were frowning, but they nodded.

Bryce handed O'Reilly back his flashlight and headed down the street.

"You think he was smoking and tossing the butts out the window?" O'Reilly asked.

"Either that," Bryce said, "or he rolled his window down to talk to someone. And if someone was pointing a gun at him, he wouldn't have done it. This vehicle was armored. He had a better chance starting it up and driving away than he did cooperating."

"If he wasn't smoking," O'Reilly said, "he knew his killer."

"Yeah," Bryce said. And he was pretty sure that was going to make his job a whole hell of a lot harder.

***

Kennedy took the elevator up to the fifth floor of the Justice Department. He probably should have stayed home, but he simply couldn't. He needed to get into those files and he needed to do so before anyone else.

As he strode into the corridor he shared with the Director of the FBI, he saw Helen Gandy hurry in the other direction. She looked like she had just come from the beauty salon. He had never seen her look anything less than completely put together but he was surprised by her perfect appearance on this night, after the news that her long-time boss was dead.

Kennedy tugged at the overcoat he'd put on over his favorite sweater. He hadn't taken the time to change or even comb his hair. He probably looked as tousled as he had in the days after Jack died.

Although, for the first time in three months, he felt like he had a purpose. He didn't know how long this feeling would last, or how long he wanted it to. But this death had given him an odd kind of hope that control was coming back into his world.

Haskell stood in front of the Director's office suite, arms crossed. The Director's suite was just down the corridor from the Attorney General's offices. It felt odd to go toward Hoover's domain instead of his own.

Haskell looked relieved when he saw Kennedy.

"Was that the dragon lady I just saw?" Kennedy asked.

"She wanted to get some personal effects from her office," Haskell said.

"Did you let her?"

"You said the orders were to secure it, so I have."

"Excellent." Kennedy glanced in both directions and saw no one. "Make sure your staff continues to protect the doors. I'm going inside."

"Sir?" Haskell raised his eyebrows.

"This may not be the right place," Kennedy said. "I'm worried that he moved everything to his house."

The lie came easily. Kennedy would have heard if Hoover had moved files to his own home. But Haskell didn't know that.

Haskell moved away from the door. It was unlocked. Two more agents stood inside, guarding the interior doors.

"Give me a minute, please, gentlemen," Kennedy said.

The men nodded and went outside.

Kennedy stopped and took a deep breath. He had been in Miss Gandy's office countless times, but he had never really looked at it. He'd always been staring at the door to Hoover's inner sanctum, waiting for it to open and the old man to come out.

That office was interesting. In the antechamber, Hoover had memorabilia and photographs from his major cases. He even had the Plaster of Paris death mask of John Dillinger on display. It was a ghastly thing, which made Kennedy think of the way that English kings used to keep severed heads on the entrance to London Bridge to warn traitors of their potential fate.

But this office had always looked like a waiting room to him. Nothing very special. The woman behind the desk was the focal point. Jack had been the one who nicknamed her the dragon lady and had even called her that to her face once, only with his trademark grin, so infectious that she hadn't made a sound or a grimace in protest.

Of course, she hadn't smiled back either.

Her desk was clear except for a blotter, a telephone, and a jar of pens. A typewriter sat on a credenza with paper stacked beside it.

But it wasn't the desk that interested him the most. It was the floor-to-ceiling filing cabinets and storage bins. He walked to them. Instead of the typical system—marked by letters of the alphabet—this one had numbers that were clearly part of a code.

He pulled open the nearest drawer, and found row after row of accordion files, each with its own number, and manila folders with the first number set followed by another. He cursed softly under his breath.

Of course the old dog wouldn't file his confidentials by name. He'd use a secret code. The old man liked nothing more than his secrets.

Still, Kennedy opened half a dozen drawers just to see if the system continued throughout. And it wasn't until he got to a bin near the corner of the desk that he found a file labeled "Obscene."

His hand shook as he pulled it out. Jack, for all his brilliance, had been sexually insatiable. Back when their brother Joe was still alive and no one ever thought Jack would be running for president, Jack had had an affair with a Danish émigré named Inga Arvad. Inga Binga, as Jack used to call her, was married to a man with ties to Hitler. She'd even met and liked Der Fuhrer, and had said so in print.

She'd been the target of FBI surveillance as a possible spy, and during that surveillance who should turn up in her bed but a young naval lieutenant whose father had once been Ambassador to England. The Ambassador, as he preferred to be called even by his sons, found out about the affair, told Jack in no uncertain terms to end it, and then to make sure he did by getting him assigned to a PT boat in the Pacific, as far from Inga Binga as possible.

Kennedy had always suspected that Hoover had leaked the information to the Ambassador, but he hadn't known for certain until Jack became President when Hoover told them. Hoover had been surveilling all of the Kennedy children at the Ambassador's request. He'd given Kennedy a list of scandalous items as a sample, and hoped that would control the president and his brother.

It might have controlled Jack, but Hoover hadn't known Kennedy very well. Kennedy had told Hoover that if any of this information made it into the press, then other things would appear in print as well, things like the strange FBI budget items for payments covering Hoover's visits to the track or the fact that Hoover made some interesting friends, mobster friends, when he was vacationing in Palm Beach.

It wasn't quite a Mexican stand-off—Jack was really afraid of the old man—but it gave Kennedy more power than any Attorney General had had over Hoover since the beginnings of the Roosevelt administration.

But now Kennedy needed those files, and he had a hunch Hoover would label them obscene.

Kennedy opened the file, and was shocked to see Richard Nixon's name on the sheets inside. Kennedy thumbed through quickly, not caring what dirt they'd found on that loser. Nixon couldn't win an election after his defeat in 1960. He'd even told the press after he lost a California race that they wouldn't have him to kick around any more.

Yet Hoover had kept the files, just to be safe.

That old bastard really and truly had known where all the bodies were buried. And it wouldn't be easy to find them.

Kennedy took a deep breath. He stood, shoved his hands in his pockets, and surveyed the walls of files. It would take days to search each folder. He didn't have days. He probably didn't have hours.

But he was Hoover's immediate supervisor, whether the old man had recognized it or not. Hoover answered to him. Which meant that the files belonged to the Justice Department, of which the FBI was only one small part.

He glanced at his watch. No one pounded on the door. He probably had until dawn before someone tried to stop him. If he was really lucky, no one would think of the files until mid-morning.

He went to the door and beckoned Haskell inside.

"We're taking the files to my office," he said.

"All of them, sir?"

"All of them. These first, then whatever is in Hoover's office, and then any other confidential files you can find."

Haskell looked up the wall as if he couldn't believe the command. "That'll take some time, sir."

"Not if you get a lot of people to help."

"Sir, I thought you wanted to keep this secret."

He did. But it wouldn't remain secret for long. So he had to control when the information got out—just like he had to control the information itself.

"Get this done as quickly as possible," he said.

Haskell nodded and turned the doorknob, but Kennedy stopped him before he went out.

"These are filed by code," he said. "Do you know where the key is?"

"I was told that Miss Gandy had the keys to everything from codes to offices," Haskell said.

Kennedy felt a shiver run through him. Knowing Hoover, he would have made sure he had the key to the Attorney General's office as well.

"Do you have any idea where she might have kept the code keys?" Kennedy asked.

"No," Haskell said. "I wasn't part of the need-to-know group. I already knew too much."

Kennedy nodded. He appreciated how much Haskell knew. It had gotten him this far.

"On your way out," Kennedy said, "call building maintenance and have them change all the locks in my office."

"Yes, sir." Haskell kept his hand on the doorknob. "Are you sure you want to do this, sir? Couldn't you just change the locks here? Wouldn't that secure everything for the President?"

"Everyone in Washington wants these files," Kennedy said. "They're going to come to this office suite. They won't think of mine."

"Until they heard that you moved everything."

Kennedy nodded. "And then they'll know how futile their quest really is."

***

The final crime scene was a mess. The bodies were already gone—probably inside the coroner's van that blocked the alley a few blocks back. It had taken Bryce nearly a half an hour to find someone who knew what the scene had looked like when the police had first arrived.

That someone was Officer Ralph Voight. He was tall and trim, with a pristine uniform despite the fact that he'd been on duty all night.

O'Reilly was the one who convinced him to talk with Bryce. Voight was the first to show the traditional animosity between the NYPD and the FBI, but that was because Voight didn't know who had died only a few blocks away.

Bryce had Voight walk him through the crime scene. The buildings on this street were boarded up, and the lights burned out. Broken glass littered the sidewalk—and it hadn't come from this particular crime. Rusted beer cans, half buried in the ice piles, cluttered each stoop like passed-out drunks.

"Okay," Voight said, using his flashlight as a pointer, "we come up on these two cars first."

The two sedans were parked against the curb, one behind the other. The sedans were too nice for the neighborhood—new, black, without a dent. Bryce recognized them as FBI issue—he had access to a sedan like that himself when he needed it.

He patted his pocket, was disgusted to realize he'd left his notebook at the apartment, and turned to O'Reilly. "You got paper? I need those plates."

O'Reilly nodded. He pulled out a notebook and wrote down the plate numbers.

"They just looked wrong," Voight was saying. "So we stopped, figuring maybe someone needed assistance."

He pointed the flashlight across the street. The squad had stopped directly across from the two cars.

"That's when we seen the first body."

He walked them to the middle of the street. This part of the city hadn't been plowed regularly and a layer of ice had built over the pavement. A large pool of blood had melted through that ice, leaving its edges reddish black and revealing the pavement below.

"The guy was face down, hands out like he'd tried to catch himself."

"Face gone?" Bryce asked, thinking maybe it was a head shot like the others.

"No. Turns out he was shot in the back."

Bryce glanced at O'Reilly, whose lips had thinned. This one was different. Because it was the first? Or because it was unrelated?

"We pull our weapons, scan to see if we see anyone else, which we don't. The door's open on the first sedan, but we didn't see anyone in the dome light. And we didn't see anyone obvious on the street, but it's really dark here and the flashlights don't reach far." Voight turned his light toward the block with the parked limousine, but neither the car nor the sidewalk was visible from this distance.

"So we go to the cars, careful now, and find the other body right there."

He flashed his light on the curb beside the door to the first sedan.

"This one's on his back and the door is open. We figure he was getting out when he got plugged. Then the other guy—maybe he was outside his car trying to help this guy with I don't know what, some car trouble or something, then his buddy gets hit, so he runs for cover across the street and gets nailed. End of story."

"Did you check to see if the cars start?" O'Reilly asked. Bryce nodded that was going to be his next question as well.

"I'm not supposed to touch the scene, sir," Voight said with some resentment. "We secured the area, figured everything was okay, then called it in."

"Did you hear the other shots?"

"No," Voight said. "I know we got three more up there, and you'd think I'd've heard the shooting if something happened, but I didn't. And as you can tell, it's damn quiet around here at night."

Bryce could tell. He didn't like the silence in the middle of the city. Neighborhoods that got quiet like this so close to dawn were usually among the worst. The early morning maintenance workers, and the delivery drivers stayed away whenever they could.

He peered in the sedan, then pulled the door open. The interior light went on, and there was blood all over the front seat and steering wheel. There were styrofoam coffee cups on both sides of the little rise between the seats. And the keys were in the ignition. Like all Bureau issue, the car was an automatic.

Carefully, so that he wouldn't disturb anything important in the scene, he turned the key. The sedan purred to life, sounding well-tuned just like it was supposed to.

"Check to see if there are other problems," Bryce said to O'Reilly. "A flat maybe."

Although Bryce knew there wouldn't be one. He shut off the ignition.

"You didn't see the interior light when you pulled up?" he asked Voight.

"Yeah, but it was dim," Voight said. "That's why I figured there was car problems. I figured they left the lights on so they could see."

Bryce nodded. He understood the assumption. He backed out of the sedan, then walked around it, shining his own flashlight at the hole in the ice, and then back at the first sedan.

Directly across.

He walked to the second sedan. Its interior was clean—no styrofoam cups, no wadded up food containers, no notebooks. Not even some tools hastily pulled to help the other drivers in need.

He let out a small sigh. He finally figured out what was bothering him.

"You find weapons on the two men?" he asked Voight.

"Yes, sir."

"Holstered?"

"The guy by the car. The other one had his in his right hand. We figured we just happened on the scene or someone would have taken the weapon."

Or not. People tended to hide for a while after shots were fired, particularly if they had nothing to do with the shootings but might get blamed anyway.

Bryce tried to open the passenger door on the second sedan, but it was locked. He walked around to the driver's door. Locked as well.

"No one looked inside this car?"

"No, sir. We figured crime scene would do it."

"But they haven't been here yet?" Bryce asked.

"It's the neighborhood, sir. Right there—" Voight aimed his flashlight at stairs heading down to a lower level "—is one of those men-only clubs, you know? The kind that you go to when you're…you know…looking for other men."

Bryce felt a flash of irritation. He'd been running into this all night. "Okay. What I'm hearing in a sideways way from every representative of the NYPD on this scene is that crimes in this neighborhood don't get investigated."

Voight sputtered. "They get investigated—"

"They get investigated," O'Reilly said, "enough to tell the families they probably want to back off. You heard Brunner. That's what most in the department call it. The rest of us, we call them lifestyle kills. And we get in trouble if we waste too many resources on them."

"Lovely," Bryce said dryly. His philosophy, which had gotten him in trouble with the Bureau more than once, was that all crimes deserved investigation, no matter how distasteful you found the victims. Which was why he kept getting moved, from communists to reviewing wire-taps to digging dirt on other agents.

And that was probably why he was here. He was expendable.

"Did you find car keys on either of the victims?" Bryce asked.

"No, sir," Voight said. "And I helped the coroner when he first arrived."

"Then start looking. See if they got dropped in the struggle."

Although Bryce doubted they had.

"I got something to jimmy the lock in my car," O'Reilly said.

Bryce nodded. Then he stood back, surveying the whole thing. He didn't like how he was thinking. It was making his heartburn grow worse.

But it was the only thing that made sense.

Agents worked HooverWatch in pairs. There were two dead agents and two cars. If the second sedan was back-up, there should have been four agents and two cars.

But it didn't look that way. It looked like someone had pulled up behind the HooverWatch vehicle, and got out, carefully locking the door.

Then he went to the door of the HooverWatch car. The driver had got out to talk to him, and the new guy shot him.

At that point, the second HooverWatch agent was an easy target. He scrambled out of the car, grabbed his own weapon, and headed across the street—maybe shooting as he went. The shooter got him, and then casually walked up the street to the limo, which he had to know was there even though he couldn't see it.

As he approached the limo, the limo driver lowered his window. He would have recognized the approaching man, and thought he was going to report on the danger.

Instead, the man shot him, then went to lie in wait for Hoover and Tolson.

Bryce shivered. It would have happened very fast, and long before the beat cops showed up.

The guy in the street had time to bleed out. The limo driver couldn't warn his boss. And the beat cops hadn't heard the shots in the alley, which they would have on such a quiet night.

O'Reilly brought the jimmy, shoved it into the space between the window and the lock, and flipped the lock up with a single movement. Then he opened the door.

No keys in the ignition.

Bryce flipped open the glovebox. Nothing inside but the vehicle registration. Which, as he expected, identified it as an FBI vehicle.

The shooter had planned to come back. He'd planned to drive away in this car. But he got delayed. And by the time he got here, the two beat cops were on scene. He couldn't get his car.

He had to improvise. So he probably walked away or took the subway, hoping the cops would think the extra car belonged to one of the victims.

And that was his mistake.

"How come you guys were here in the middle of the night?" Bryce asked Voight.

Voight swallowed. It was the first sign of nervousness he'd shown. "This is part of our beat."

"But?" Bryce asked.

Voight looked away. "We're supposed to go up Central Park West."

"And you don't."

"Yeah, we do. Just not every time."

"Because?"

"Because I figure, you know, when the bars let out, we could, you know, let our presence be known."

"Prevent a lifestyle kill."

"Yes, sir."

"And you care about this because…?"

"Everyone should," Voight snapped. "Serve and protect, right, sir?"

Voight was touchy. He thought Bryce was accusing him of protecting the lifestyle because he lived it.

"Does your partner like this drive?" Bryce asked.

"He complains, sir, but he lets me do it."

"Have you stopped any crimes?"

"Broken up a few fights," Voight said.

"But not something like this."

"No, sir."

"You don't patrol every night, do you, Voight?"

"No, sir. We get different regions different nights."

"Do you think our killer would have thought that this street was unprotected?"

"It usually is, sir."

O'Reilly was frowning, but not at Voight. At Bryce. "You think this was planned?" O'Reilly asked.

Bryce didn't answer. This was a Bureau matter, and he wasn't sure how the Bureau would handle it.

But he did think the killing was planned. And he had a hunch it would be easy to solve because of the abandoned sedan.

And that abandoned sedan bothered him more than he wanted to admit. Because the presence of that sedan meant only one thing: that the person who had shot all five FBI agents was—almost without a doubt—an FBI agent himself.

***

Kennedy looked at the bins and the filing cabinets stacked around his office and allowed himself one moment to feel overwhelmed. People ribbed him about the office; he had taken the reception area and made it his, rather than use the standard size office in the back.

As a result, his office was as long as a football field, with stunning windows along the walls. The watercolors painted by his children had been covered by the cabinets. His furniture was pushed aside to make room for the bins, and for the first time, this space felt small.

He put his hands on his hips and wondered how to begin.

Since six agents began moving the filing cabinets across the corridor more than an hour ago, Kennedy had received five phone calls from LBJ's chief of staff. Kennedy hadn't taken one of them. The last had been a direct order to come to the Oval Office.

Kennedy ignored it.

He also ignored the ringing telephone—the White House line—and the messages his own assistant (called in after a short night's sleep) had been bringing to him.

Helen Gandy stood in the corridor, arms crossed, her purse hanging off her wrist, and watching with deep disapproval. Haskell was trying to find out if there were remaining files and where they were. But Kennedy had found the one thing he was looking for: the key.

It was in a large, innocuous index file box inside the lowest drawer of Helen Gandy's desk. Kennedy had brought it into his office and was thumbing through it, hoping to understand it before he got interrupted again.

A man from building maintenance had changed the lock on the door leading into the interior offices, and was working on the main doors now that the files were all inside. Kennedy figured he'd have his own office secure by seven a.m.

Then he heard a rustling in the hallway, a lot of startled, "Mr. President, sir!" followed by official, "Make way for the President," and instinctively he turned toward the door. The maintenance man was leaning out of it, the door knob loose in his hand.

"Where the fuck is that bastard?" Lyndon Baines Johnson's voice echoed from the corridor. "Doesn't anyone in this building have balls enough to tell him that he works for me?"

Even though the question was rhetorical, someone tried to answer. Kennedy heard something about "your orders, sir."

"Horseshit!" Then LBJ stood in the doorway. Two secret service agents flanked him. He motioned with one hand at the maintenance man. "I suggest you get out."

The man didn't have to be told twice. He scurried away, still carrying the doorknob. LBJ came inside alone, pushed the door closed, then grimaced as it popped back open. He grabbed a chair and set it in front of the door, then glared at Kennedy.

The glare was effective in that hang-dog face, despite LBJ's attire. He wore a plaid silk pajama top stuffed into a pair of suitpants, finished with dress shoes and no socks. His hair—what remained of it—hadn't been Brilcremed down like usual, and stood up on the sides and the back.

"I get a phone call from some weasel underling of that Old Cocksucker, informing me that he's dead, and you're stealing from his tomb. I try to contact you, find out that you are indeed removing files from the Director's office, and that you won't take my calls. Now, I should've sent one of my boys over here, but I figured they're still walking on tip-toe around you because you're in fucking mourning, and this don't require tip-toe. Especially since you got to be wondering about now what the hell you did to deserve all of this."

"Deserve what?" Kennedy had expected LBJ's anger, but he hadn't expected it so soon. He also hadn't expected it here, in his office, instead of in the Oval Office a day or so later.

"Well, there's only two things that tie J. Edgar and your brother. The first is that someone was gunning for them and succeeded. The second is that they went after the mob on your bidding. There's a lot of shit running around here that says your brother's shooting was a mob hit, and I know personally that J. Edgar was doing his best to make it seem like that Oswald character acted alone. But now Edgar is dead and Jack is dead and the only tie they have is the way they kow-towed to your stupid prosecution of the men that got your brother elected."

Kennedy felt lightheaded. He hadn't even thought that the deaths of his brother and J. Edgar were connected. But LBJ had a point. Maybe there was a conspiracy to kill government officials. Maybe the mob was showing its power. He'd had warning.

Hell, he'd had suspicions. He hadn't let himself look at any of the evidence in his brother's assassination, not after he secured the body and prevented a disastrous autopsy in Texas. If those doctors at Parkland had done their job, they would've seen just how advanced Jack's Addison's disease was. The best kept secret of the Kennedy Administration—an administration full of secrets—was how close Jack was to incapacitation and death.

Kennedy clutched the file box. But LBJ knew that. He knew a lot of the secrets—had even promised to keep a few of them. And he wanted the files as badly as Kennedy did.

There had to be a lot in here on LBJ too. Not just the women, which was something he had in common with Jack, but other things, from his days in Congress.

"From what I heard," Kennedy said, making certain his voice was calm even though he wasn't, "all they know is someone shot Hoover. Did you get more details than that? Something that mentions organized crime in particular?"

"I'm sure it'll come out," LBJ said.

"You're sure that saying such things would upset me," Kennedy said. "You're after the files."

"Damn straight," LBJ said. "I'm the head of this government. Those files are mine."

"You're the head of this government for another year. Next January, someone'll take the oath of office and it might not be you. Do you really want to claim these in the name of the presidency? Because you might be handing them over to Goldwater come January."

LBJ blanched.

Someone knocked on the door, and startled both men. Kennedy frowned. He couldn't think of anyone who would have enough nerve to interrupt him when he was getting shouted at by LBJ. But someone had.

LBJ pulled the door open. Helen Gandy stood there.

"You boys can be heard in the hallway," she said, sweeping in as if the leader of the free world wasn't holding the door for her. "And it's embarrassing. It was precisely this kind of thing the Director hoped to avoid."

Then she nodded at LBJ. Kennedy watched her. The dragon lady. Jack, as usual, had been right with his jibes. Only the dragon lady would walk in here as if she were the most important person in the room.

"Mr. President," she said, "these files are the Director's personal business. He wanted me to take care of them, and get them out of the office, where they do not belong."

"Personal files, Miss Gandy?" LBJ asked. "These are his secret files."

"If they were secret, Mr. President, then you wouldn't be here. Mr. Hoover kept his secrets."

Mr. Hoover used his secrets, Kennedy thought, but didn't say.

"These are just his confidential files," Miss Gandy was saying. "Let me take care of them and they won't be here to tempt anyone. That's what the Director wanted."

"These are government property," LBJ said with a sly look at Kennedy. For the first time, Kennedy realized his Goldwater argument had gotten through. "They belong here. I do thank you for your time and concern, though, ma'am."

Then he gave her a courtly little bow, put his hand on the small of her back, and propelled her out of the room.

Despite himself Kennedy was impressed. He'd never seen anyone handle the dragon lady that efficiently before.

LBJ grabbed one of the cabinets and slid it in front of the door he had just closed. Kennedy had forgotten how strong the man was. He had invited Kennedy down to his Texas ranch before the election, trying to find out what Kennedy was made of, and instead, Kennedy had realized just what LBJ was made of—strength, not bluster, brains *and* brawn.

He'd do well to remember that.

"All right," LBJ said as he turned around. "Here's what I'm gonna offer. You can have your family's files. You can watch while we search for them and you can have everything. Just give me the rest."

Kennedy raised his eyebrows. He hadn't felt this alive since November. "No."

"I can fire your ass in five minutes, put someone else in this fancy office, and then you can't do a goddamn thing," LBJ said. "I'm being kind."

"There's historical precedent for a cabinet member barricading himself in his office after he got fired," Kennedy said. "Seems to me it happened to a previous president named Johnson. While I'm barricaded in, I'll just go through the files and find out everything I need to know."

LBJ crossed his arms.

It was a stand-off and neither of them had a good play. They only had a guess as to what was in those files—not just theirs but all of the others as well. They did know that whatever was in those files had given Hoover enough power to last in the office for more than forty years.

The files had brought down presidents. They could bring down congressmen, supreme court justices, and maybe even the current president. In that way, Helen Gandy was right.

The best solution was to destroy everything.

Only Kennedy wouldn't. Just like he knew LBJ wouldn't. There was too much history here, too much knowledge.

And too much power.

"These are our files," Kennedy said after a moment, although the word "our" galled him, "yours and mine. Right now we control them."

LBJ nodded, almost imperceptibly. "What do you want?"

What did he want? To be left alone? To have his family left alone? At midnight, he might have said that. But now, his old self was reasserting itself. He felt like the man who had gone after the corrupt leaders of the Teamsters, not the man who had accidentally gotten his brother murdered.

Besides, there might be things in that file that could head off other problems in the future. Other murders. Other manipulations.

He needed a bullet-proof position. LBJ was right: the Attorney General could be fired. But there was one position, constitutionally, that the president couldn't touch.

"I want to be your Vice President," Kennedy said. "And in 1972, when you can't run again, I want your endorsement. I want you to back me for the nomination."

LBJ swallowed hard. Color suffused his face and for a moment, Kennedy thought he was going to shout again.

But he didn't.

Instead he said, "And what happens if we don't win?"

"We move these to a location of our choosing. And we do it with trusted associates. We get this stuff out of here."

LBJ glanced at the door. He was clearly thinking of what Helen Gandy had said, how it was better to be rid of all of this than it was to have it corrupting the office, endangering everyone.

But if LBJ and Kennedy controlled the entire cache, they also controlled their own files. LBJ could destroy his and Kennedy could preserve his family's legacy.

If it weren't for the fact that LBJ hated him almost as much as Kennedy hated LBJ, the decision would be easy.

"You'd trust me to a gentleman's agreement?" LBJ asked, not disguising the sarcasm in his tone. He knew Kennedy thought he was too uncouth to ever be considered a gentleman.

"You know where your interests lie. Just like I do," Kennedy said. "If we don't let Miss Gandy have the files, then this is the only choice."

LBJ sighed. "I hoped to be rid of the Kennedys by inauguration day."

"And what if I planned to run against you?" Kennedy asked, even though he knew he wouldn't. Already the party stalwarts had been approaching him about a 1964 presidential bid, and he had put them off. He had been too shaky, too emotionally fragile.

He didn't feel fragile now.

LBJ didn't answer that question. Instead, he said, "You can be an incautious asshole. Why should I trust you?"

"Because I saved Jack's ass more times than you can count," Kennedy said. "I'm saving yours too."

"How do you figure?" LBJ asked.

"Your fear of those files brought you to me, Mr. President." Kennedy put an emphasis on the title, which he usually avoided using around LBJ. "If I barricade myself in here, I'll have the keys to the kingdom and no qualms about letting the information free when I go free. If you work with me, your secrets remain just secrets."

"You're a son of bitch, you know that?" LBJ asked.

Kennedy nodded. "The hell of it is you are too or you wouldn't've brought up Jack's death before we knew what really happened to Hoover. So let's control the presidency for the next sixteen years. By then the information in these files will probably be worthless."

LBJ stared at him. It took Kennedy a minute to realize that although he'd won the argument, he wouldn't get an agreement from LBJ, not if Kennedy didn't make the first move.

Kennedy held out his hand. "Deal?"

LBJ stared at Kennedy's extended hand for a long moment before taking it in his own big clammy one.

"You goddamn son of a bitch," LBJ said. "You've got a deal."

***

It took Bryce only one phone call. The guy who ran the motorpool told him who checked out the sedan without asking why Bryce want to know. And Bryce, as he leaned in the cold telephone booth half a block from the first crime scene, instantly understood what had happened and why.

The agent who checked out the sedan was Walter Cain. He should've been on extended leave. Bryce had recommended it after he had told Cain that his ex-fiancé had tried to commit suicide. On getting the news, Cain had just had that look, that blank, my-life-is-over look.

And it had scared Bryce. Scared him enough that he asked Cain be put on indefinite leave. How long ago had that been? Less than twelve hours.

More than enough time to get rid of the morals police—the one man who made all the rules at the FBI. The man who had no morals himself.

J. Edgar Hoover.

Bryce had spent the past week studying Cain's file. Cain had had HooverWatch off and on throughout the past year. Cain knew the procedure, and he knew how to thwart it.

He'd killed five agents.

Because no one would listen to Bryce about that vacant look in Cain's eye.

Bryce let himself out of the phone booth. He walked back to the coroner's van. If he didn't have back up by now, he'd call for some all over again. They couldn't leave him hanging on this. They had to let him know, if nothing else, what to do with the Director's body.

But he needn't've worried. When he got back to the alley, he saw five more sedans, all FBI issue. And as he stepped into the alley proper, the first person he saw was his boss, crouching over Hoover's corpse.

"I thought I told you to secure the scene," said the SAC for the District of New York, Eugene Hart. "In fact, I ordered you to do it."

"The scene extends over six blocks. I'm just one guy," Bryce said.

Hart walked over to him. He looked tired.

"I need to speak to you," Bryce said. He walked Hart back to the two sedans, explained what he'd learned, and watched Hart's face.

The man flinched, then, to Bryce's surprise, put his hand on Bryce's shoulder. "It's good work."

Bryce didn't thank him. He was worried that Hart hadn't asked any questions. "I'd heard Cain bitch more than once about Hoover setting the moral values for the office. And with what happened this week—"

"I know." Hart squeezed his shoulder. "We'll take care of it."

Bryce turned so quickly that he made Hart lose his grip. "You're going to cover it up."

Hart closed his eyes.

"You weren't hanging me out to dry. You were trying to figure out how to handle this. Son of a bitch. And you're going to let Cain walk."

"He won't walk," Hart said. "He'll just…be guilty of something else."

"You can't cover this up. It's too important. So soon after President Kennedy—"

"That's precisely why we're going to handle it," Hart said. "We don't want a panic."

"And you don't want anyone to know where Hoover and Tolson were found. What're you going to say? That they died of natural causes in their beds? Their *separate* beds?"

"It's not your concern," Hart said. "You've done well for us. You'll be rewarded."

"If I keep my mouth shut."

Hart sighed. He didn't seem to have the energy to glare. "I don't honestly care. I'm glad to have the old man gone. But I'm not in charge of this. We've got orders now, and everything'll get taken care of at a much higher level than either you or me.

You should be grateful for that."

Bryce supposed he should be. It took the political pressure off him. It also took the personal pressure off.

But he couldn't help feeling if someone had listened to him before, if someone had paid attention, then none of this would have happened.

No one cared that an FBI agent was going to marry a former prostitute. If the Bureau knew—and it did, then not even the KGB could use that as blackmail.

It was all about appearances. It would always be about appearances. Hoover had designed a damn booklet about appearances, and it hadn't stopped him from getting shot in a back alley after a party he would never admit attending.

Hoover had been so worried about people using secrets against each other, he hadn't even realized how his own secrets could be used against him.

Bryce looked at Hart. They were both tired. It had been a long night. And it would be an even longer few weeks for Hart. Bryce would get some don't-tell promotion and he'd stay there for as long as he had to. He had to make sure that Cain got prosecuted for something, that he paid for five deaths.

Then Bryce would resign.

He didn't need the Bureau, any more than he had needed Mary, his own pre-approved wife. Maybe he'd talk to O'Reilly, see if he could put in a good word with the NYPD. At least the NYPD occasionally investigated cases.

If they happened in the right neighborhood.

To the right people.

Bryce shoved his hands in his pockets and walked back to his apartment. Hart didn't try to stop him. They both knew Bryce's work on this case was done. He wouldn't even have to write a report.

In fact, he didn't dare write a report, didn't dare put any of this on paper where someone else might discover it. The wrong someone. Someone who didn't care about handling and the proper information.

Someone who would use that information to his own benefit.

Like the Director had.

For more than forty-five years.

Bryce shook the thought off. It wasn't his concern. He no longer had concerns. Except getting a good night's sleep.

And somehow he knew that he wouldn't get one of those for a long, long time.

THE RETRIEVAL ARTIST

1

I HAD JUST COME OFF a difficult case, and the last thing I wanted was another client. To be honest, not wanting another client is a constant state for me. Miles Flint, the reluctant Retrieval Artist. I work harder than anyone else in the business at discouraging my clients from seeking out the Disappeared. Sometimes the discouragement fails and I get paid a lot of money for putting a lot of lives in danger, and maybe, just maybe, bringing someone home who wants to come. Those are the moments I live for, the moments when it becomes clear to a Disappeared that home is a safe place once more.

Usually though, my clients and their lost ones are more trouble than they're worth. Usually, I won't take their cases for any price, no matter how high.

I do everything I can to prevent client contact from the start. The clients who approach me are the courageous ones or the really desperate ones or the ones who want to use me to further their own ends.

I try not to take my cases personally. My clients and their lost ones depend on my objectivity. But every once in a while, a case slips under my defenses—and never in the way I expect.

This was one of those cases. And it haunts me still.

2

*M*Y OFFICE is one of the ugliest dives on the Moon. I found an original building still made of colonial permaplastic in the oldest section of Armstrong, the Moon's oldest colony. The dome here is also made of permaplastic, the clear kind, although time and wear have turned it opaque. Dirt covers the dome near the street level. The filtration system tries to clean as best it can, but ever since some well-meaning dome governor pulled the permaplastic flooring and forgot to replace it, this part of Armstrong Dome has had a dust problem. The filtration systems have been upgraded twice in my lifetime, and rebuilt at least three times since the original settlement, but they still function at one-tenth the level of the state-of-the-art systems in colonies like Gagarin Dome and Glenn Station. Terrans newly off the shuttle rarely come to this part of Armstrong; the high-speed trains don't run here, and the unpaved streets strike most Terrans as unsanitary, which they probably are.

The building that houses my office had been the original retail center of Armstrong, or so says the bronze plaque that someone had attached to the plastic between my door and the rent-a-lawyer's beside me. We are an historic building, not that anyone seems to care, and rent-a-lawyer once talked to me about getting the designation changed so that we could upgrade the facilities.

I didn't tell him that if the designation changed, I would move.

You see, I like the seedy look, the way my door hangs slightly crookedly in its frame. It's deceptive. A careless Tracker would think I'm broke, or equally careless. Most folks don't guess that the security in my little eight-by-eight cube is state of the art. They walk in, and they see permaplastic, and a desk that cants slightly to the right, and only one chair behind it. They don't see the recessed doors that hide my storage in the wall between the rent-a-lawyer's cube and my own, and they don't see the electronics because they aren't looking for them.

I like to keep the office empty. I own an apartment in one of Armstrong's better neighborhoods. There I keep all the things I don't care about. Things I do care about stay in my ship, a customized space yacht named *The Emmeline*. She's my only friend and I treat her like a lover. She's saved my life more times than I care to think about, and for that (and a few other things), she deserves only the best.

I can afford to give her the best, and I don't need any more work although, as I said, I sometimes take it. The cases that catch me are usually the ones that catch me in my Sir Galahad fantasy—the one where I see myself as a rescuer of all things worthy of rescue—although I've been known to take cases for other reasons.

But, as I'd said, I'd just come off a difficult case, and the last thing I needed was another client. Especially one as young and innocent as this one appeared to be.

She showed up at my door wearing a dress, which no one wears in this part of Armstrong any more, and regular shoes, which had to have been painful to walk in. She also had a personal items bag around her wrist, which, in this part of town, was like wearing a giant *Mug Me!* sign. The bags were issued on shuttles and only to passengers who had no idea about the luggage limitations.

She was tall and raw-boned, but slender, as if diet and exercise had reduced her natural tendency toward lushness. Her dress, an open and inexpensive weave, accented her figure in an almost unconscious way. Her features were strong and bold, her eyes dark, and her hair even darker.

My alarm system warned me she was outside, staring at the door or the plaque or both. A small screen popped up on my desk revealing her and the street beyond. I shut off the door alarm, and waited until she knocked. Her clutched fist, adorned with computer and security enhancements that winked like diamonds in the dome's fake daylight, rapped softly on the permaplastic. The daintiness of the movement startled me. I wouldn't have thought her a dainty woman.

I had been cleaning up the final reports, notations and billings from the last case. I closed the file and the keyboard (I never use voice commands for work in my office—too easily overheard) folded itself into the desk. Then I leaned back in the chair, and waited.

She knocked three times, before she tried the door. It opened, just like it had been programmed to do in instances like this.

"Mr. Flint?" Her voice was soft, her English tinted with a faintly Northern European accent.

I still didn't say anything. She had the right building and the right name. I would wait to see if she was the right kind of client.

She squinted at me. I was never what clients expected. They expected a man as seedy as the office, maybe one or two unrepaired scars, a face toughened by a hard life and space travel. Even though I was thirty-five, I still had a look some cultures called angelic: blond curls, blue eyes, a round and cherubic face. A client once told me I looked like the pre-Raphaelite paintings of Cupid. I had smiled at him and said, *Only when I want to.*

"Are you Mr. Flint?" The girl stepped inside, then slapped her left hand over the enhancements on her right. She looked faintly startled, as if someone had shouted in her ear.

Actually, my security system had cut in. Those enhancements linked her to someone or something outside herself, and my system automatically severed such links, even if they had been billed as unseverable.

"You want to stay in here," I said, "you stay in here alone. No recording, no viewing, and no off-site monitoring."

She swallowed, and took another step inside. She was playing at being timid. The real timid ones, severed from their security blankets, bolt.

"What do you want?" I asked.

She flinched, and took another step forward. "I understand that you—find—people."

"Where did you hear that?"

"I was told in New York." One more step and she was standing in front of my desk. She smelled faintly of lavender soap mixed with nervous sweat. She must have come here directly from the shuttle. A woman with a mission, then.

"New York?" I asked as if I'd never heard of it.

"New York City."

I had several contacts in New York, and a handful of former clients. Anyone could have told her, although none were supposed to. They always did though; they always saw their own desperation in another's eyes, figured it was time to help, time to give back whatever it was they felt they had gained.

I sighed. "Close the door."

She licked her lips—the dye on them was either waterproof or permanent—and then walked back to the door. She looked into the street as if she would find help there, then gently pushed the door closed.

I felt a faint hum through my wrist as my computer notified me that it had turned the door security back on.

"What do you want?" I asked before she turned around.

"My mother," she said. "She's—"

"That's enough." I kept my tone harsh, and I didn't stand. I didn't want this girl/woman to be too comfortable. It was always best to keep potential clients off balance.

Children, young adults, and the elderly were the obvious choices of someone trying to use my system for the wrong purposes, and yet they were the ones most likely to contact me. They never seemed to understand the hostility I had to show clients, the insistence I put on identity checks, and they always balked at the cost. *It feels as if I'm on trial, Mr. Flint*, they would say, and I wouldn't respond. They were. They had to be. I always had to be sure they were only acting on their own interests. It was too easy for a Tracker to hire someone to play off a Retrieval Artist's sympathies, and initiate a search that would get the Disappeared killed—or worse.

The girl turned. Her body was so rigid that it looked as if I could break her in half.

"I don't find people," I said. "I uncover them. There's a vast difference. If you don't understand that, then you don't belong here."

That line usually caused half my potential clients to exit. The next line usually made most of the remaining fifty percent excuse themselves, never to darken my door again.

"I charge a minimum of two million credits, Moon issue, not Earth issue—" which meant that they were worth triple what she was used to paying—"and I can charge as much as ten million or more. There is no upper limit on my costs nor is there one on my charges. I charge by the day, with expenses added in. Some investigations take a week, some take five years. You would be my exclusive employer for the period of time it takes to find your— mother—or whomever I'd be looking for. I have a contract. Several of my former clients have tried to have the courts nullify it. It holds up beautifully. I do not take charity cases, no matter what your sob story is, and I do not allow anyone to defer payment. The minute the money stops, so do I."

She threaded her fingers together. Her personal items bag bumped against her hip as she did so. "I'd heard about your financial requirements." Which meant that one of my former clients had recommended me to her. Dammit. "I have limited funds, but I can afford a minor investigation."

I stood. "We're done talking. Sorry I can't help you." I walked past her and pulled open the door. Security didn't mind if I did that. It would have minded if she had.

"Can't you do a limited search, Mr. Flint?" Her eyes were wide and brown. If she was twenty, she was older than I thought. I checked for tears. There were none. She could be legit, and for that I was sorry.

I closed the door so hard the plastic office shook. "Here's what you're asking me," I said. "If the money runs out, I quit searching, which is no skin off my nose. But I'll have dug a trail up to that particular point, and your mother—or whomever I'm looking for—"

She flinched again as I said that. A tender one. Or a good actress.

"—would be at more of a risk than she is now. Right now, she's simply disappeared. And since you've come to me, you've done enough research to know that one of six government programs—or one of fifteen private corporations—have gone to considerable expense to give her a new life somewhere else. If the cover on that existence gets blown, your mother dies. It's that simple. And maybe, just maybe, the people who helped her will die too, or the people who are now important to her, or the people who were hidden with her, for whatever reason. Half an investigation is a death sentence. Hell, sometimes a full investigation is a death sentence. So I don't do this work on whim, and I certainly don't do it in a limited fashion. Are we clear?"

She nodded, just once, a rabbit-like movement that let me know I'd connected.

"Good," I said and pulled the door back open. "Now get out."

She scurried past me as if she thought I might physically assault her, and then she hurried down the street. The moon dust rose around her, clinging to her legs and her impractical dress, leaving a trail behind her that was so visible, it looked as if someone were marking her as a future target.

I closed the door, had the security system take her prints and DNA sample off the jamb just in case I needed to identify her someday, and then tried not to think of her again.

It wouldn't be easy. Clients were rare and, if they were legit, they always had an agenda. By the time they found me, they were desperate, and there was still a part of me that was human enough to feel sympathy for that.

Sympathy is rare among Retrieval Artists. Most Retrieval Artists got into this line of work because they owed a favor to the Disty, a group of aliens who'd more or less taken over Mars. Others got into it because they had discovered, by accident, that they were good at it, usually making that discovery in their jobs for human corporations or human crime syndicates.

I got in through a different kind of accident. Once I'd been a space cop assigned to Moon Sector. A lot of the Disappeared come through here on their way to new lives, and over time, I found myself working against a clock, trying to save people I'd never met from the people they were hiding from. The space police frowned on the work—the Disappeared are often reformed criminals and not worth the time, at least according to the Moon Sector—and so, after one of the most horrible incidents of my life, I went into business on my own.

I'm at the top of my profession, rich beyond all measure, and usually content with that. I chose not to have a spouse or children, and my family is long-dead, which I actually consider to be a good thing. Families in this business are a liability. So are close friends. Anyone who can be broken to force you to talk. I don't mind being alone.

But I do hate to be manipulated, and I hate even more to take revenge, mine or anyone else's. I vigilantly protect myself against both of those things.

And this was the first time I failed.

3

*A*FTER THE GIRL LEFT, I stayed away from the office for two days. Sometimes snubbed clients come back. They tell me their stories, the reasons they're searching for their parent/child/spouse, and they expect me to understand. Sometimes they claim they've found more money. Sometimes they simply try to cry on my shoulder, believing I will sympathize.

Once upon a time maybe I would have. But Sir Galahad has calluses growing on his heart. I am beginning to hate the individuals. They always take a level of judgment that drains me. The lawyers trying to find a long-lost soul to meet the terms of a will; the insurance agents, required by law to find the beneficiaries, forced by the government to search "as far as humanly possible without spending the benefits"; the detective, using government funds to find the one person who could put a career criminal, serial killer, or child molester, away for life; these people are the clients I like the most. Almost all are repeat customers. I still have to do background checks, but I have my gut to rely on as well. With individuals, I can never go by gut, and even armed with information, I've been burned.

I've gotten to the point where coldness is the way of the game for me, at least at first. Once I sign on, I become the most intense defender of the Disappeared. The object of my search also becomes the person I protect and care about the most. It takes a lot of effort to maintain that caring, and even more to manage the protection.

Sometimes I'll go to extremes.

Sometimes I have no other choice.

On the third day, I went back to my office, and of course, the girl was waiting. This time she was dressed appropriately, a pair of boots, cargo pants that cinched at the ankles, and a shirt the color of sand. Her personal items bag was gone—obviously someone, probably the maitre d at the exclusive hotel she was most likely staying at, told her it made her a mark for pickpockets and other thieves. Thin mesh gloves covered her enhancements. Only her long hair marked her as a newcomer. If she stayed longer than a month, she'd cut it off just like the rest of us rather than worry about keeping it clean.

She was leaning against my locked door, her booted feet sticking into the street. In that outfit, she looked strong and healthy, as if she were hiring me to take her on one of those expeditions outside the dome. The rent-a-lawyer next door, newly out of Armstrong Law, was eyeing her out of his scarred plastic window, a sour expression on his thin face. He probably thought she was scaring away business.

I stopped in the middle of the street. It was hot and airless as usual. There was no wind in the dome, of course, and the recycled air got stale real fast. Half the equipment in this part of town had been on the fritz for the last week, and the air here wasn't just stale, it was thin and damn near rancid. I hated breathing bad air. The shallow breaths, and the increased heartbeat made me feel as if there was danger around when there probably wasn't. If the air got any thinner, I'd have to start worrying about my clarity of thought.

She saw me when I was still several meters from the place. She stood, brushed the dust off her pants, and watched me. I pretended as if I were undecided about my next move, even though I knew I'd have to confront her sooner or later. Her kind only went away when chased.

"I'm sorry," she said as I approached. "I was told that you expected negotiation, so I—"

"Lied about the money, did you?" I asked, knowing she was lying now too. If she knew enough to find me, she also knew that I didn't negotiate. All the lie proved was that she had an ego big enough to believe that the rules were different for her.

I shoved past her to use my palm to unlock the door. I only used a palm scan when someone else was present. It let us in, but initiated a higher level of security monitoring.

She started to follow me, but I slammed the door in her face. Then I went to my desk, and switched on my own automatic air. It was illegal, and it wouldn't be enough, but

I wasn't planning to stay long. I would finish the reports from the last case, get the final fees, and then maybe I'd take a vacation. I had never taken one before. It was past time.

I wish, now, that I had listened to my gut and gone. But there was just enough of Sir Galahad left in me to make me watch the door. And of course, it opened just like I expected it to.

She came inside, a little downtrodden but not defeated. Her kind seldom were. "My name is Anetka Sobol," she said as if I should know it. I didn't. "I really do need your help."

"You should have thought of that before," I said. "This isn't a game."

"I'm not trying to play one."

"So what was that attempt at negotiation?"

She shook her head. "My source—"

"Who is your source?"

"He said I wasn't—"

"Who is it?"

Again she licked that lower lip just like she had the day before, a movement that was too unconscious to be planned. The nervousness, then, wasn't feigned. "Norris Gonnot."

Gonnot. Sobol was the third client he'd sent to me in the last year. The other two checked out, and both cases had been easy to solve. But he was making himself too visible, and I would have to deal with that, even though I hated to do so. He was extremely grateful that I had found his daughter and granddaughter alive (although they hadn't appreciated it), and he'd been even more grateful when I was able to prove that the Disty were no longer looking for them.

"And how did you find him?"

She frowned. "Does it matter?"

I leaned back in my chair. It squeaked and the sound made her jump ever so slightly. "Either you're up front with me now or the conversation ends."

The frown grew deeper, and she clutched her left wrist with her right hand, holding the whole mess against her stomach. The gesture looked calculated. "Do you treat everyone like this?"

"Nope. Some people I treat worse."

"Then how do you get any work?"

I shrugged. "Just lucky."

She stared at me for a moment. Then she glanced at the door. Was she letting her thoughts be that visible on purpose or was she again acting for my benefit? I wasn't sure.

"A cop told me about him. Norris, that is." She sounded reluctant. "I wasn't supposed to tell you."

"Of course not. Gonnot wasn't supposed to talk to anyone. This cop, was he a rent-a-cop, a real cop, a Federal cop, or with the Earth Force?"

"She," she said.

"Okay," I said. "Was she a—"

"She was a New York City police officer who had her own detective agency."

"That's illegal in New York."

She shrugged. "So?"

I closed my eyes. Ethics had disappeared everywhere. "You hired her?"

"She was my fifth private detective. Most would work for a week and then quit when they realized that searching for an interstellar Disappeared is a lot harder than finding a missing person."

I waited. I'd heard that sob story before. Most detectives kept the case and simply came to someone like me.

"Of course," she said, "my father's looming presence doesn't help either."

"Your father?"

She was staring at me as if I had just asked her what God was.

"I'm Anetka Sobol," she said as if that clarified everything.

"And I'm Miles Flint. My name doesn't tell you a damn thing about my father."

"My father is the founding partner of the Third Dynasty."

I had to work to hide my surprise. I knew what the Third Dynasty was, but I didn't know the names of its founders. The Dynasty itself was a formidable presence all over the galaxy. It was a megacorp with its fingers in a lot of pies, mostly to do with space exploration, establishing colonies in mineral rich areas, and exploitation of new resources. My contacts with the Third Dynasty weren't on the exploration level, but within its narrow interior holdings. The Third Dynasty was the parent company for Privacy Unlimited, one of the services which helped people disappear.

Privacy Unlimited had been developed, as so many of the corporate disappearance programs had, when humans discovered the Disty, and realized that in some alien cultures, there was no such word as forgiveness. The Disty were the harshest of our allies. The Revs, the Wygnin, and the Fuetrer also targeted certain humans, and our treaties with these groups allowed the targeting if the aliens could show cause.

The balance was a delicate one, allowing them their cultural traditions while protecting our own. Showing cause had to happen before one of eighteen multicultural tribunals, and if one of those tribunals ruled in the aliens' favor, the humans involved were as good as dead. We looked the other way most of the time. Most of the lives involved were, according to our government, trivial ones. But of course, those people whose lives had been deemed trivial didn't feel that way, and that was when the disappearance services cropped up. If a person disappeared and could not be found, most alien groups kept an outstanding warrant, but stopped searching.

The Disty never did.

And since much of the Third Dynasty's business was conducted in Disty territory, its disappearance service, Privacy Unlimited, had to be one of the best in the galaxy.

Something in my face must have given my knowledge away, because she said, "Now do you understand my problem?"

"Frankly, no," I said. "You're the daughter of the big kahuna. Go to Privacy Unlimited and have them help you. It's usually not too hard to retrace steps."

She shook her head. "My mother didn't go to Privacy Unlimited. She used another service."

"You're sure?"

"Yes." She brushed a hand alongside her head, to move the long hair. "It's my father she's running from."

A domestic situation. I never get involved in those. Too messy and too complicated. Never a clear line. "Then she didn't need a service at all. She probably took a shuttle here, then a transport for parts unknown."

Anetka Sobol crossed her arms. "You don't seem to understand, Mr. Flint. My father could have found her with his own service if she had done something like that. It's simple enough. My detectives should have been able to find her. They can't."

"Let me see if I can understand this," I said. "Are you looking for her or is your father?"

"I am."

"As a front for him?"

Color flooded her face. "No."

"Then why?"

"I want to meet her."

I snorted. "You're going to a lot of expense for a 'hello, how are you.' Aren't you afraid Daddy will find out?"

"I have my own money."

"Really? Money Daddy doesn't know about? Money Daddy doesn't monitor?"

She straightened. "He doesn't monitor me."

I nodded. "That's why the mesh gloves. Fashion statement?"

She glanced at her enhancements. "I got them. They have nothing to do with my father."

My smile was small. "Your father has incredible resources. You don't think he'd do something as simple as hack into your enhancement files. Believe me, one of those pretty baubles is being used to track you, and if my security weren't as good as it is, another would have been monitoring this conversation."

She put her left hand over her right as if covering the enhancements would make me forget them. All it did was remind me that this time, she didn't react when my security shut down her links. This was one smart girl, and one I didn't entirely understand.

"Go home," I said. "Deal with Daddy. If you want family ties, get married, have children, hire someone to play your mother. If you need genetic information or disease history, see your family doctors. I suspect they'll have all the records you need and probably some you don't. If you want Daddy to leave you alone, I'd ask him first before I go to any more expense. He might just do what you want. And if you're trying to make him angry, I'll bet you've gone far enough. You'll probably be hearing from him very soon."

Her eyes narrowed. "You're so sure of yourself, Mr. Flint."

"It's about the only thing I am sure of," I said, and waited for her to leave.

She didn't. She stared at me for a long moment, and in her eyes, I saw a coldness, a hardness I hadn't expected. It was as if she were evaluating me and finding me lacking.

I let her stare. I didn't care what she thought one way or another. I did wish she would get to the point so that I could kick her out of my office.

Finally she sighed and pursed her lips as if she had eaten something sour. She looked around, probably searching for some place to sit down. She didn't find one. I don't like my clients to sit. I don't want them to be comfortable in my presence.

"All right," she said, and her voice was somehow different. Stronger, a little more powerful. I knew the timidity had been an act. "I came to you because you seem to be the only one who can do this job."

My smile was crooked and insincere. "Flattery."

"Truth," she said.

I shook my head. "There are dozens of people who do this job, and most are cheaper." I let my smile grow colder. "They also have chairs in their offices."

"They value their clients," she said.

"Probably at the expense of the people they're searching out."

"Ethics," she said. "That's why I've come here. You're the only one in your profession who seems to have any."

"You have need of ethics?" Somehow I had trouble believing the woman with that powerful voice had need of anyone with ethics. "Or is this simply another attempt at manipulation?"

To my surprise, she smiled. The expression was stunning. It brought life to her eyes, and somehow seemed to make her even taller than she had been a moment before.

"Manipulation got me to you," she said. "Your Mr. Gonnot seems to have a soft spot for people who are missing family."

"Everyone who's missing is a member of a family," I said, but more to the absent Gonnot than to her. I could see how he could be manipulated, and that made it more important than ever to stop him from sending customers my way.

She shrugged at my comment, then she sat on the edge of my desk. I'd never had anyone do that, not in all my years in the business. "I do have need of ethics," she said. "If you breathe a single word of what I'm going to tell you…"

She didn't finish the sentence, on purpose of course, probably figuring that whatever I could imagine would be worse than what she could come up with.

I sighed. This girl—this woman—liked games.

"If you want the sanctity of a confessional," I said, "see a priest. If you want a profession that requires its practitioners to practice confidentiality as a matter of course, see a psychiatrist. I'll keep confidential whatever I deem worthy of confidentiality."

She folded her slender hands on her lap. "You enjoy judging your clients, don't you?"

I stared at her—up at her—which actually put me at a disadvantage. She was good at intimidation skills, even better than she had been as an actress. It made me uncomfortable, but somehow it seemed more logical for the daughter of the man who ran the Third Dynasty.

"I have to," I said. "A lot of lives depend on my judgments."

She shook her head slightly. It was as if my earlier answer stymied her, prevented her from continuing. She had to learn that we would do this on my terms or we wouldn't do it at all.

I waited. I could wait all day if I had to. Most people didn't have that kind of patience no matter what sort of will they had.

She clearly didn't. After a few moments, she brushed her pants, adjusted the flap on one of the pockets, and sighed again. She must have needed me badly.

Finally, she closed her eyes, as if summoning strength. When she opened them, she was looking at me directly. "I am a clone, Mr. Flint."

Whatever I had thought she was going to say, it wasn't that. I worked very hard at keeping the surprise off my face.

"And my father is dying." She paused, as if she were testing me.

I knew the answer, and the problem. When her father died, she couldn't inherit. Clones were barred from familial inheritance by interstellar law. The law had been adapted universally after several cases where clones created by a non-family member and raised far from the original (wealthy) family inherited vast estates. The basis of the inheritance was a shared biology that anyone could create. Rather than letting large fortunes get leached off to whoever was smart enough to steal a hair from a hairbrush and use it to create a copy of a human being, legislators finally decided to create the law. The courts upheld it. It was rigid.

"Your father could change his will," I said, knowing that she had probably broached this with him already.

"It's too late," she said. "He's been ill for a while. The change could easily be disputed in court."

"So you're not an only child?" I had to work to keep from asking if she were an only copy.

"I am the only clone," she said. "My father had me made, and he raised me himself. I am, for all intents and purposes, his daughter."

"Then he should have changed his will long ago."

She waved a hand, as if the very idea were a silly one. And it probably was. A clone had to come from somewhere. So either she was the copy of a real child or a copy of the woman she wanted me to find. Perhaps the will was unchanged because the original person was still out there.

"My mother vanished with the real heir," she said.

I waited.

"My father always expected to find them. My sister is the one who inherits."

I hated clone terminology. "Sister" was such an inaccurate term, even though clones saw themselves as twins. They weren't. They weren't raised that way or thought of that way. The Original stood to inherit. The clone before me did not.

"So you, out of the goodness of your heart, are searching for your missing family." I laid the sarcasm on thick. I've handled similar cases before. Where money was involved, people were rarely altruistic.

"No," she said, and her bluntness surprised me. "My father owns 51% of the Third Dynasty. When he dies, it goes into the corporation itself, and can be bought by other shareholders. I am not a shareholder, but I have been raised from birth to run the Dynasty. The idea was that I would share my knowledge with my sister, and that we would run the business together."

This made more sense.

"So I need to find her, Mr. Flint, before the shares go back into the corporation. I need to find her so that I can live the kind of life I was raised to live."

I hated cases like this. She was right. I did judge my clients. And if I found them the least bit suspicious, I didn't take on the case. If I believed that what they would do would jeopardize the Disappeared, I wouldn't take the case either. But if the reason for the disappearance was gone, or if the reason for finding the missing person benefited or did not harm the Disappeared, then I would take the case.

I saw benefit here, in the inheritance, and in the fact that the reason for the disappearance was dying.

"Your father willed his entire fortune to his missing child?"

She nodded.

"Then why isn't he searching for her?"

"He figured she would come back when she heard of his death."

Possible, depending on where she had disappeared to, but not entirely probable. The girl might not even know who she was.

"If I find your mother," I said, "then will your father try to harm her?"

"No," she said. "He couldn't if he wanted to. He's too sick. I can forward the medical records to you."

One more thing to check. And check I would. I guess I was taking this case, no matter how messily she started it. I was intrigued, just enough.

"Your father doesn't have to be healthy enough to act on his own," I said. "With his money, he could hire someone."

"I suppose," she said. "But I control almost all of his business dealings right now. The request would have to go through me."

I still didn't like it, but superficially, it sounded fine. I would, of course, check it out. "Where's your clone mark?"

She frowned at me. It was a rude question, but one I needed the answer to before I started.

She pulled her hair back, revealing a small number eight at the spot where her skull met her neck. The fine hairs had grown away from it, and the damage to the skin had been done at the cellular level. If she tried to have the eight removed, it would grow back.

"What happened to the other seven?" I asked.

She let her hair fall. "Failed."

Failed clones were unusual. Anything unusual in a case like this was suspect.

"My mother," she said, as if she could hear my thoughts, "was pregnant when she disappeared. I was cloned from sloughed cells found in the amnio."

"Hers or the baby's?"

"The baby's. They tested. But they used a lot of cells to find one that worked. It took a while before they got me."

Sounded plausible, but I was no expert. More information to check.

"Your father must have wanted you badly."

She nodded.

"Seems strange that he didn't alter his will for you."

Her shoulders slumped. "He was afraid any changes he made wouldn't have been lawyer-proof. He was convinced I'd lose everything because of lawsuits if he did that."

"So he arranged for you to lose everything on his own."

She shook her head. "He wanted the family together. He wanted me to work with my sister to—"

"So he said."

"So he says." She ran a hand through her hair. "I think he hopes that my sister will cede the company to me. For a percentage, of course."

There it was. The only loophole in the law. A clone could receive an inheritance if it came directly from the person whose genetic material the clone shared, provided that the Original couldn't die under suspicious circumstances. Of course, a living person could, in Anetka's words, "cede" that ownership as well, although it was a bit more difficult.

"You're looking for her for money," I said in my last ditch effort to get out of the case.

"You won't believe love," she said.

She was right. I wouldn't have.

"Besides," she said. "I have my own money. More than enough to keep me comfortable for the rest of my life. Whatever else you may think of my father, he has provided that. I'm searching for her for the corporation. I want to keep it in the family. I want to work it like I was trained. And this seems to be the only way."

It wasn't a very pretty reason, and I'd learned over the years, it was usually the ugly reasons that were the truth. Not, of course, that I could go by gut. I wouldn't.

"My retainer is two million credits," I said. "If you're lucky, that's all this investigation will cost you. I have a contract that I'll send to you or your personal representative, but let me give you the short version verbally."

She nodded.

I continued, reciting, as I always did, the essential terms so that no client could ever say I'd lied to her. "I have the right to terminate at any time for any reason. You may not terminate until the Disappeared is found, or I have concluded that the Disappeared is gone for good. You are legally liable for any lawsuits that arise from any crimes committed by third parties as a result of this investigation. I am not. You will pay me my rate plus expenses whenever I bill you. If your money stops, the investigation stops, but if I find you've been withholding funds to prevent me from digging farther, I am entitled to a minimum of ten million credits. I will begin my investigation by investigating you. Should I decide you are unworthy as a client before I begin searching for the Disappeared, I will refund half of your initial retainer. There's more but those are the salient points. Is all of that clear?"

"Perfectly."

"I'll begin as soon as I get the retainer."

"Give me your numbers and I'll have the money placed in your account immediately."

I handed her my single printed card with my escrow account embedded into it. The account was a front for several other accounts, but she didn't need to know that. Even my money went through channels. Someone who is good at finding the Disappeared is also good at making other things disappear.

"Should you need to reach me in an emergency," I said, "place 673 credits into this account."

"Strange number," she said.

I nodded. The number varied from client to client, a random pattern. Sometimes, past clients sent me their old amounts as a way to contact me about something new. I kept the system clear.

"I'll respond to the depositing computer from wherever I am, as soon as I can. This is not something you should do frivolously nor is it something to be done to check up on me. It's only for an emergency. If you want to track the progress of the investigation, you can wait for my weekly updates."

"And if I have questions?"

"Save them for later."

"What if I think I can help?"

"Leave me mail." I stood. She was watching me, that hard edge in her eyes again. "I've got work to do now. I'll contact you when I'm ready to begin my search."

"How long will this investigation of me take?"

"I have no idea," I said. "It depends on how much you're hiding."

4

LIENTS NEVER tell the truth. No matter how much I instruct them to, they never do. It seems to be human nature to lie about something, even it's something small. I had a hunch, given Anetka Sobol's background, she had lied about a lot. The catch was to find out how much of what she had lied about was relevant to the job she had hired me for. Finding out required research.

I do a lot of my research through public accounts, using fake i.d. It is precautionary, particularly in the beginning, because so many cases don't pan out. If a Disappeared still has a Tracker after her, repeated searches from me will be flagged. Searches from public accounts—especially different public accounts—will not. Often the Disappeared are already famous or become famous when they vanish, and are often the subject of anything from vidspec to school reports.

My favorite search site is a bar not too far from my office. I love the place because it serves some of the best food in Armstrong, in some of the largest quantities. The large quantities are required, given the place's name. The Brownie Bar serves the only marijuana in the area, baked into specially marked goods, particularly the aforementioned brownies. Imbibers get the munchies, and proceed to spend hundreds of credits on food. The place turns quite a profit, and it's also comfortable; marijuana users seem to like their creature comforts more than most other recreational drug types.

Recreational drugs are legal on the Moon, as are most things. The first settlers came in search of something they called "freedom from oppression" which usually meant freedom to pursue an alternative lifestyle. Some of those lifestyles have since become illegal or simply died out, but others remain. The only illegal drugs these days, at least in Armstrong, are those that interfere with the free flow of air. Everything from nicotine to opium is legal—as long as its user doesn't smoke it.

The Brownie Bar caters to the casual user as well as the hard-core and, unlike some drug bars, doesn't mind the non-user customer. The interior is large, with several sections. One section, the party wing, favors the bigger groups, the ones who usually arrive in numbers larger than ten, spend hours eating and giggling, and often get quite obnoxiously wacky. In the main section, soft booths with tables shield clients from each other. Usually the people sitting there are couples or groups of four. If one group gets particularly loud, a curtain drops over the open section of the booth, and their riotous laughter fades into nearly nothing.

My section caters to the hard-core, who sometimes stop for a quick fix in the middle of the business day, or who like a brownie before dinner to calm the stress of a hectic afternoon. Many of these people have only one, and continue work while they're sitting at their solitary tables. It's quiet as a church in this section, and many of the patrons are plugged into the free client ports that allow them access to the Net.

The access ports are free, but the information is not. Particular servers charge by the hour in the public areas, but have the benefit of allowing me to troll using the server or the bar's identicodes. I like that; it usually makes my preliminary searches impossible to trace.

That afternoon, I took my usual table in the very back. It's small, made of high grade plastic designed to look like wood—and it fools most people. It never fooled me, partly because I knew the Brownie Bar couldn't afford to import, and partly because I knew they'd never risk something that valuable on a restaurant designed for stoners. I sat cross-legged on the thick pillow on the floor, ordered some turkey stew—made here with real meat—and plugged in.

The screen was tabletop, and had a keyboard so that the user could have complete privacy. I'd heard other patrons complain that using the Brownie Bar's system required them to read, but it was one of the features I liked.

I started with Anetka, and decided to work my way backwards through the Sobol family. I found her quickly enough; her life was well covered by the tabs, which made no mention of her clone status. She was twenty-seven, ten to twelve years older than she looked. She'd apparently had those youthful looks placed in stasis surgically. She'd look girlish until she died.

Another good fact to know. If there was an original, she might not look like Anetka. Not any more.

Anetka had been working in her father's corporation since she was twelve. Her IQ was off the charts—surgically enhanced as well, at least according to most of the vidspec programs—and she breezed through Harvard and then Cambridge. She did postdoc work at the Interstellar Business School in Islamabad, and was out of school by the time she was twenty-five. For the last two years, she'd been on the corporate fast-track, starting in lower management and working her way to the top of the corporate ladder.

She was, according to the latest feeds, her father's main assistant.

So I had already found Possible Lie Number One: She wasn't here for herself. She was, as I had suspected, a front for her father. Not to find the wife, but to find the real heir.

I wasn't sure how I'd feel if that were true. I needed to find out if, indeed, the Original was the one who'd inherit. If she wasn't, I wouldn't take the case. There'd be no point.

But I wasn't ready to make judgments yet. I had a long way to go. I looked up Anetka's father, and discovered that Carson Sobol had never remarried, although he'd been seen with a bevy of beautiful women over the years. All were close to his age. He never dated women younger than he was. Most had their own fortunes, and many their own companies. He spent several years as the companion to an acclaimed Broadway actress, even funding some of her more famous plays. That relationship, like the others, had ended amicably.

Which led to Possible Lie Number Two: a man who terrorized his wife so badly that she had to run away from him also terrorized his later girlfriends. And while a man could keep something like that quiet for a few years, eventually the pattern would become evident. Eventually one of the women would talk.

There was no evidence of terrorizing in the stuff I found. Perhaps the incidences weren't reported. Or perhaps there was nothing to report. I would vote for the latter. It seemed, from the vidspec I'd read, everyone knew that the wife had left him because of his cruelty. My experience with vidspec reporters made me confident that they'd be on the lookout for more proof of Carson Sobol's nasty character. And if they found it, they'd report it.

No one had.

I didn't know if that meant Sobol had learned his lesson when the wife ran off, or perhaps Sobol had learned that mistreatment of women was bad for business. I couldn't believe that a man could terrify everyone into silence. If that were his methodology, there would be a few leaks that were quickly hushed up, and one or two dead bodies floating around, bodies belonging to folks who hadn't listened. Also, there would be rumors, and there were none.

Granted, I was making assumptions on a very small amount of information. Most of the reports I found about Sobol weren't about his family or his love life, but about the Third Dynasty as it expanded in that period to new worlds, places that human businesses had never been before.

The Third Dynasty had been the first to do business with the Fuetrers, the HDs, and the chichers. It opened plants on Korsve, then closed them when it realized that the Wygnin, the dominant life forms on Korsve, did not—and apparently could not—understand the way that humans did business.

I shuddered at the mention of Korsve. If a client approached me because a family member had been taken by the Wygnin, I refused the case. The Wygnin took individuals to pay off debt, and then those individuals became part of a particular Wygnin family. For particularly heinous crimes, the Wygnin took firstborns, but usually, the Wygnin just took babies—from any place in the family structure—at the time of birth, and then raised them. Occasionally they'd take an older child or an adult. Sometimes they'd take an entire group of adults from offending businesses. The adults were subject to mind control, and personality destruction as the Wygnin tried to remake them to fit into Wygnin life.

All of that left me with no good options. Children raised by the Wygnin considered themselves Wygnin and couldn't adapt to human cultures. Adults who were taken by the Wygnin were so broken that they were almost unrecognizable. Humans raised by the Wygnin did not want to return. Adults who were broken always wanted to return, and when they did, they signed a death warrant for their entire family—or worse, doomed an entire new generation to kidnap by the Wygnin.

But Wygnin custom didn't seem relevant here. Despite the plant closings, the Third Dynasty had managed to avoid paying a traditional Wygnin price. Or perhaps someone had paid, down the line, and that information was classified.

There were other possibles in the files. The Third Dynasty seemed to have touched every difficult alien race in the galaxy. The corporation had an entire division set aside for dealing with new cultures. Not that the division was infallible. Sometimes there were unavoidable errors.

Sylvy Sobol's disappearance had been one of those. It had caused all sorts of problems for both Sobol and the Third Dynasty. The vidspecs, tabs, and other media had had a field day when she had disappeared. The news led to problems with some of the alien races, particularly the Altaden. The Altaden valued non-violence above all else, and the accusations of domestic violence at the top levels of the Third Dynasty nearly cost the corporation its Altade holdings.

The thing was, no one expected the disappearance—or the marriage, for that matter. Sylvy Sobol had been a European socialite, better known for her charitable works and her incredible beauty than her interest in business. She belonged to an old family with ties to several still existing monarchies. It was thought that her marriage would be to someone else from the accepted circle.

It had caused quite a scandal when she had chosen Carson Sobol, not only because of his mixed background and uncertain lineage, but also because some of his business practices had taken large fortunes from the countries she was tied to and spent them in space instead.

He was controversial; the marriage was controversial; and it looked like, from the vids I watched, that the two of them had been deeply in love.

I felt a hand on my shoulder. A waitress stood behind me, holding a large ceramic bowl filled with turkey stew. She smiled at me.

"Didn't want to set it on your work."

"It's fine," I said, indicating an empty spot near the screen. She set my utensils down, and then the bowl. The stew smelled rich and fine, black beans and yogurt adding to the aroma. My stomach growled.

The waitress tapped one of the moving images. "I remember that," she said. "I was living in Vienna. The Viennese thought that marriage was an abomination."

I looked up. She was older than I was, without the funds to prevent the natural aging process. Laugh lines crinkled around her eyes, and her lips—unpainted and untouched—were a faint rose. She smiled.

"Guess it turned out that way, huh? The wife running off like that? Leaving that message?"

"Message?" I asked. I hadn't gotten that far.

"I don't remember exactly what it was. Something like 'The long arm of the Third Dynasty is impossible to fight. I am going where you can't find me. Maybe then I'll have the chance to live out my entire life.' I guess he nearly beat her to death." The waitress laughed, a little embarrassed. "In those days I had nothing better to do than study the lives of more interesting people."

"And now?" I asked.

She shrugged. "I figured out that everybody's interesting. I mean, you've got to try. You've got to live. And if you do, you've done something fascinating."

I nodded. People like her were one of the reasons I liked this place.

"You want something to drink?" she asked.

"Bottled water."

"Got it," she said as she left.

By the time she brought my bottled water, I had indeed found the note. It had been sent to all the broadcast media, along with a grainy video, taken from a hidden camera, of one of the most brutal domestic beatings I'd ever seen. The images were sometimes blurred and indistinct, but the actions were clear. The man had beat the woman senseless.

There was no mention of the pregnancy in any of this. There was, however, notification of Anetka's birth six months before her mother had disappeared.

Which led me to Possible Lie Number Three. Anetka had said her mother traveled pregnant. Perhaps she hadn't. Or, more chillingly, someone had altered the record either before or after the clones were brought to term. There had to be an explanation of Anetka in the media or she wouldn't be accepted. If that explanation had been planted before, something else was going on. If it were planted afterwards, Sobol's spokespeople could have simply said that reporters had overlooked her in their rush to other stories.

I checked the other media reports and found the same story. It was time to go beneath those stories and see what else I could find. Then I would confront Anetka about the lies before I began the search for her mother.

5

I CONTACTED HER and we met, not at my office, but at her hotel. She was staying in Armstrong's newest district, an addition onto the dome that caused a terrible controversy before it was built. Folks in my section believe the reason for the thinner air is that the new addition has stretched resources. I know they aren't right—with the addition came more air and all the other regulation equipment—but it was one of those arguments that made an emotional kind of sense.

I thought of those arguments, though, as I walked among the new buildings, made from a beige material not even conceived of thirty years before, a material that's supposed to be attractive (it isn't) and more resistant to decay that permaplastic. This entire section of Armstrong smelled new, from the recycled air to the buildings rising around me. They were four stories high and had large windows on the dome side, obviously built with a view in mind.

This part of the dome is self-cleaning and see-through. Dust does not slowly creep up the sides as it does in the other parts of Armstrong. The view is barren and stark, just like the rest of the Moon, but there's a beauty in the starkness that I don't see anywhere else in the universe.

The hotel was another large four story building. Most of its windows were glazed dark, so no one could see in, but the patrons could see out. It was part of a chain whose parent company was, I had learned the day before, the Third Dynasty. Anetka was doing very little to hide her search from her father.

Inside, the lobby was wide, and had an old-fashioned feel. The walls changed images slowly, showing the famous sites from various parts of the galaxy where the hotels were located. I had read before the hotel opened that the constantly changing scenery took eight weeks to repeat an image. I wondered what it was like working in a place where the view shifted constantly, and then decided I didn't want to know.

The lobby furniture was soft and a comforting shade of dove gray. Piano music, equally soft and equally comforting, was piped in from somewhere. Patrons sat in small groups as if they were posing for a brochure. I went up to the main desk and asked for Anetka. The concierge led me to a private conference room down the main hallway.

I expected the room to be monitored. That didn't bother me. At this point, I still had nothing to hide. Anetka did, but this was her company's hotel. She could get the records, shut off the monitors, or have them destroyed. It would all be her choice.

To my surprise, she was waiting for me. She was wearing another dress, a blue diaphanous thing that looked so fragile I wondered how she managed to move from place to place. Her hair was up and pinned, with diamonds glinting from the soft folds. She also had diamonds glued to the ridge beneath her eyebrows, and trailing down her cheeks. The net effect was to accent her strength. Her broad shoulders held the gown as if it were air, and the folds parted to reveal the muscles on her arms and legs. She was like the diamonds she wore; pretty and glittering, but able to cut through all the objects in the room.

"Have you found anything?" she asked without preamble.

I shut the door and helped myself to the carafe of water on the bar against the nearest wall. There was a table in the center of the room—made, it seemed—of real wood, with matching chairs on the side. There was also a workstation, and a one-way mirror with a view of the lobby.

I leaned against the bar, holding my water glass. It was thick and heavy, sturdy like most things on the Moon. "Your father's will has been posted among the Legal Notices on all the nets for the last three years."

She nodded. "It's common for CEOs to do that to allay stockholder fears."

"It's common for CEOs to authorize the release after they've died. Not before."

Her smile was small, almost patronizing. "Smaller corporations, yes. But it's becoming a requirement for major shareholders in megacorps to do this even if they are not dead. Investigate further, Mr. Flint, and you'll see that all of the Third Dynasty's major shareholders have posted their wills."

I had already checked the other shareholders' wills, and found that Anetka was right. I also looked for evidence that Carson Sobol was dead, and found none.

She took my silence to be disbelief. "It's the same with the other megacorps. Personal dealings are no longer private in the galactic business world."

I had known that the changes were taking place. I had known, for example, that middle managers signed loyalty oaths to corporations, sometimes requiring them to forsake family if the corporation had called for it. This, one pundit had said, was the hidden cost of doing business with alien races. You had to be willing to abandon all you knew in the advent of a serious mistake. The upshot of the change was becoming obvious. People to whom family was important were staying away from positions of power in the megacorps.

I said, "You're not going to great lengths to hide this search from your father."

She placed a hand on the wooden chair. She was not wearing gloves, and mingled among the enhancements were more diamonds. "You seem obsessed with my father."

"Your mother disappeared because of him. I'm not going to find her only to have him kill her."

"He wouldn't."

"Says you."

"This is your hesitation?"

"Actually, no," I said. "My hesitation is that, according to all public records, you were born six months before your mother disappeared."

I didn't tell her that I knew all the databases had been tampered with, including the ones about her mother's disappearance. I couldn't tell if the information had been altered to show that the disappearance came later or that the child had been born earlier. The tampering was so old that the original material was lost forever.

"My father wanted me to look like a legitimate child."

"You are a clone. He knew cloning laws."

"But no one else had to know."

"Not even with his will posted?"

"I told you. It's only been posted for the last three years."

"Is that why you're not mentioned?"

She raised her chin. "I received my inheritance before—already," she said. I found the correction interesting. "The agreement between us about my sister is both confidential and binding."

"'All of my worldly possessions shall go to my eldest child,'" I quoted. "That child isn't even listed by name."

"No," she said.

"And he isn't going to change the will for you?"

"The Disty won't do business with clones."

"I didn't know you had business with the Disty," I said.

She shrugged. "The Disty, the Emin, the Revs. You name them, we have business with them. And we have to be careful of some customs."

"Won't the stockholders be suspicious when you don't inherit?"

Her mouth formed a thin line. "That's why I'm hiring you," she said. "You need to find my sister."

I nodded. Then, for the first time in the meeting, I sat down. The chair was softer than I had expected it would be. I put my feet on the nearest chair. She glanced at them as if they were a lower life form.

"In order to search for people," I said, "I need to know who they're running from. If they're running from the Disty, for example, I'll avoid the Martian colonies, because they're overrun with Disty. No one would hide there. It would be impossible. If they were running from the Revs, I would start looking at plastic surgeons and doctors who specialize in genetic alteration because anyone who looks significantly different from the person the Revs have targeted is considered, by the Revs, to be a different being entirely."

She started to say something, but I held up my hand to silence her.

"Human spouses abuse each other," I said. "It seems to be part of the human experience. These days, the abused spouse moves out, and sometimes leaves the city, sometimes the planet, but more often than not stays in the same area. It's unusual to run, to go through a complete identity change, and to start a new life, especially in your parents' income bracket. So tell me, why did your mother really leave?"

Nothing changed in Anetka's expression. It remained so immobile that I knew she was struggling for control.

The hardness that had been so prevalent the day before was gone, banished, it seemed, so that I wouldn't see anything amiss.

"My father has a lot of money," she said.

"So do other people. Their spouses don't disappear."

"He also controls a powerful megacorp with fingers all over the developing worlds. He has access to more information than anyone. He vowed to never let my mother out of his sight. My father believed that marriage vows were sacred, and no matter how much the parties wanted out, they were obligated by their promises to each other and to God to remain." Anetka's tone was flat too. "If she had just moved out, he would have forced her to move back in. If she had moved to the Moon, he would have come after her. If she had moved to some of the planets in the next solar system, he would have come for her. So she had no choice."

"According to your father."

"According to anyone who knew her." Anetka's voice was soft. "You saw the vids."

I nodded.

"That was mild, I guess, for what he did to her."

I leaned back in the chair, lifting the front two legs off the ground. "So how come he didn't treat his other women that way?"

Something passed through her eyes so quickly that I wasn't able to see what the expression was. Suspicion? Fear? I couldn't tell.

"My father never allowed himself to get close to anyone else."

"Not even his Broadway actress?"

She frowned, then said, "Oh, Linda? No. Not even her. They were using each other to throw off the media. She had a more significant relationship with one of the major critics, and she didn't want that to get out."

"What about you?" I asked that last softly. "If he hurt your mother, why didn't he hurt you?"

She put her other hand on the chair as if she were steadying herself. "Who says he didn't?"

And in that flatness of tone, I heard all the complaints I'd ever heard from clones. She had legal protection, of course. She was fully human. But she didn't have familial protection. She wasn't part of any real group. She didn't have defenders, except those she hired herself.

But I didn't believe it, not entirely. She was still lying to me. She was still keeping me slightly off balance. Something was missing, but I couldn't find it. I'd done all the digging I could reasonably do. I had no direction to go except after the missing wife—if I chose to continue working on this case. This was the last point at which I could comfortably extricate myself from the entire mess.

"You're not telling me everything," I said.

Again, the movement with the eyes. So subtle. So quick. I wondered if she had learned to cover up her emotions from her father.

"My father won't harm her," she said. "If you want, I'll even sign a waiver guaranteeing that."

It seemed the perfect solution to a superficial problem. I had a hunch there were other problems lurking below.

"I'll have one sent to you," I said.

"Are you still taking the case?"

"Are you still lying to me?"

She paused, the dress billowing around her in the static-charged air. "I need you to find my sister," she said.

And that much, we both knew to be true.

6

M Y WORK is nine-tenths research and one-tenth excitement. Most of the research comes in the beginning, and it's dry to most people, although I still find the research fascinating. It's also idiosyncratic and part of the secret behind my reputation. I usually don't describe how I do the research—and I never explain it to clients. I usually summarize it, like this:

It took me four months to do the preliminary research on Sylvy Sobol. I started from the premise that she was pregnant with a single girl child. A pregnant woman did one of three things: she carried the baby to term, she miscarried, or she aborted. After dealing with hospital records for what seemed like weeks, I determined that she carried the baby to term. Or at least, she hadn't gotten rid of it before she disappeared.

A pregnant woman had fewer relocation options than a non-pregnant one. She couldn't travel as far or on many forms of transport because it might harm the fetus. Several planets, hospitable to humans after they'd acclimatized, were not places someone in the middle of pregnancy was allowed to go. The pregnancy actually made my job easier, and I was glad for it.

Whoever had hidden her was good, but no disappearance service was perfect. They all had cracks in their systems, some revealing themselves in certain types of disappearance, others in all cases past a certain layer of complexity. I knew those flaws as well as I knew the scars and blemishes on my own hands. And I exploited them with ease.

At the end of four months, I had five leads on the former Mrs. Sobol. At the end of five months, I had eliminated two of those leads. At the end of six months, I had a pretty good idea which of the remaining three leads was the woman I was looking for.

I got in my ship, and headed for Mars.

7

*I*N THE HUNDRED YEARS since the Disty first entered this solar system, they have taken over Mars. The human-run mineral operations and the ship bases are still there, but the colonies are all Disty run, and some are Disty built.

The Emmeline has clearance on most planets where humans make their homes. Mars is no difference. I docked at the Dunes, above the Arctic Circle, and wished I were going elsewhere. It was the Martian winter, and here, in the largest field of sand dunes in the solar system, that meant several months of unrelenting dark.

I had never understood how the locals put up with this. But I hadn't understood a lot of things. The domes here, mostly of human construction, had an artificial lighting system built in, but the Disty hated the approximation of a twenty-four hour day. Since the Disty had taken over the northern most colonies, darkness outside and artificial lights inside were the hallmarks of winter.

The Disty made other alterations as well. The Disty were small creatures with large heads, large eyes, and narrow bodies. They hated the feeling of wide open spaces, and so in many parts of the Sahara Dome, as Terrans called this place, false ceilings had been built in, and corridors had been compressed. Buildings were added into the wider spaces, getting rid of many passageways and making the entire place seem like a rat's warren. Most adult humans had to crouch to walk comfortably through the city streets and some, in disgust, had bought small carts so that they could ride. The result was a congestion that I found claustrophobic at the best of times. I hated crouching when I walked, and I hated the stink of so many beings in such a confined space.

Many Terran buildings rose higher than the ceiling level of the street, but to discourage that wide-open spaces feel, the Disty built more structures, many of them so close together that there was barely enough room for a human to stick his arm between them. Doors lined the crowded streets, and the only identifying marks on most places were carved into the frame along the door's side. The carvings were difficult to see in the weird lighting, even if there weren't the usual crowds struggling to get through the streets to God knew where.

My candidate lived in a building owned by the Disty. It took me two passes to find the building's number, and another to realize that I had found the right place. A small sign, in English, advertised accommodations fit for humans, and my back and I hoped that the sign was right.

It was. The entire building had been designed with humans in mind. The Disty had proven themselves to be able interstellar traders, and quite willing to adapt to local customs when it suited them. It showed in the interior design of this place. Once I stepped through the door, I was able to stand upright, although the top of my head did brush the ceiling. To my left, a sign pointed toward the main office, another pointed to some cramped stairs, and a third pointed to the recreation area.

I glanced at the main office before I explored any farther. The office was up front, and had the same human-sized ceilings. In order to cope, the Disty running the place sat on its desk, its long feet pressed together in concentration. I passed it, and went to the recreation area. I would look for the woman here before I went door to door upstairs.

The recreation area was about half the size of a human-made room for the same purpose. Still, the Disty managed to cram a lot of stuff in here, and the closeness of everything—while comfortable for the Disty—made it uncomfortable for any human. All five humans in the room were huddled near the bar on the far end. It was the only place with a walking path large enough to allow a full-grown man through.

To get there, I had to go past the ping-pong table, and a small section set aside for Go players. Several Disty were playing Go—they felt it was the best thing they had discovered on the planet Earth, with ping-pong a close second—sitting on the tables so that their heads were as near the ceiling as they could get. Two more Disty were standing on the table, playing ping-pong. None of them paid me any attention at all.

I wound my way through the tight space between the Go players and the ping-pong table, ducking once to avoid being whapped in the head with an out-of-control ping-pong ball. I noted three other Disty watching the games with rapt interest. The humans, on the other hand, had their backs to the rest of the room. They were sitting on the tilting bar stools, drinking, and not looking too happy about anything.

A woman who could have been anywhere from thirty to seventy-five sat at one end of the bar. Her black hair fell to the middle of her back, and she wore makeup, an affectation that the Disty seemed to like. She was slender—anyone who wanted to live comfortably here had to be—and she wore a silver beaded dress that accented that slimness. Her legs were smooth, and did not bear any marks from mining or other harsh work.

"Susan Wilcox?" I asked as I put my hand on her shoulder and showed her my license.

I felt the tension run through her body, followed by several shivers, but her face gave no sign that anything was wrong.

"Want to go talk?"

She smiled at me, a smooth professional smile that made me feel a little more comfortable. "Sure."

She stood, took my hand as if we'd been friends a long time, and led me onto a little patio someone had cobbled together in a tiny space behind the recreation area. I didn't see the point of the thing until I looked up. This was one of the few places in Sahara where the dome was visible, and through its clear surface, you could see the sky. She pulled over a chair, and I grabbed one as well.

"How did you find me?" she asked.

"I'm not sure I did." I held out my hand. In it was one of my palmtop. "I want to do a DNA check."

She raised her chin slightly. "That's not legal."

"I could get a court order."

She looked at me. A court order would ruin any protection she had, no matter who—or what—she was running from.

"I'm not going to see who you are. I want to see if you're who I'm looking for. I have comparison DNA."

"You're lying," she said softly.

"Maybe," I said. "If I am, you're in trouble either way."

She knew I was right. She could either take her chances with me, or face the court order where she had no chance at all.

She extended her hand. I ran the edge of the computer along her palm, removing skin cells. The comparison program ran, and as I turned the palmtop face-up, I saw that there was no match. The only thing this woman shared in common with the former Mrs. Sobol was that they were both females of a similar age, and that they had both disappeared twenty-nine years ago while pregnant. Almost everything else was different.

I used my wrist-top for a double-check, and then I sighed. She was watching me closely, her dark eyes reflecting the light from inside.

I smiled at her. "You're in the clear," I said. "But if it was this easy for me to find you, chances are that it'll be as easy for someone else. You might want to move on."

She shook her head once, as if the very idea were repugnant.

"Your child might appreciate it," I said.

She looked at me as if I had struck her. "She's not who—"

"No," I said. "She's safe. From me at least. And maybe from whoever's after you. But you've survived out here nearly thirty years. You know the value of caution."

She swallowed, hard. "You know a lot about me."

"Not really." I stood. "I only know what you have in common with the woman I'm looking for." I slipped the palmtop into my pocket and bowed slightly. "I appreciate your time."

Then I went back inside, slipped through the recreation area, walked past two more Disty in the foyer, and headed into the narrow passageway they called a street. There I shuddered. I hated the Disty. I'd worked so many cases in which people ran to avoid being caught by the Disty that I'd become averse to them myself.

At least, that was my explanation for my shudder. But I knew that it wasn't a real explanation. I had put a woman's life in jeopardy, and we both knew it. I hoped no one had been paying attention. But I was probably wrong. The only solace I had was that since she was hiding amongst the Disty, she probably wasn't being sought by one of them. If she had been pursued by a Disty, my actions probably would have signed her death warrant.

I spent a night in a cramped hotel room since the Disty didn't allow take-offs within thirty-six hours of landing. And then I got the hell away from Sahara Dome—and Mars.

8

*M*Y SECOND POSSIBILITY was in New Orleans, which made my task a lot easier. I had former clients there who felt they owed me, some of whom were in related businesses. I had one of those clients break into the Disappeared's apartment, remove a strand of hair, and give it to another former client. A third brought me the strand in my room in the International Space Station. Because the strand proved not to be a match, and because I was so certain it would be, I repeated the procedure once more, this time getting another old friend to remove another hair strand from the suspect's person. Apparently, he passed her in a public place, and plucked. The strand matched the first one, but didn't belong to Sylvy Sobol.

I didn't warn this woman at all because I didn't feel as if I had put her in danger. If she were suspicious about the hair pulling incident, I felt it was her responsibility to leave town on her own.

The third candidate was on the Moon, in Hadley. I had no trouble finding her, which seemed odd, but she didn't check out either. I returned to Armstrong, both stumped and annoyed.

The logical conclusion was that my DNA sample was false—that it wasn't the sample for Sylvy Sobol. I had taken the sample from the Interstellar DNA database, and there was the possibility that the sample had been changed or tainted. I had heard of such a thing being done, but had always dismissed it as impossible. Those samples were the most heavily guarded in the universe. Even if someone managed to get into the system, they would encounter back-ups upon back-ups, and more encryption than I wanted to think about.

So I contacted Anetka and asked her to send me a DNA sample of her mother. She did, and I ran it against the sample I had. Mine had been accurate. The women I had seen were not Sylvy Sobol.

I had never, in my entire career, made an error of this magnitude. One of those women should have been the former Mrs. Sobol. Unless my information was wrong. Unless I was operating from incorrect assumptions. Still, the assumptions shouldn't have mattered in this search. A pregnant woman wasn't that difficult to hide, not when she was taking transport elsewhere. I'd even found the one who'd remained on Earth.

No. The incorrect assumption had to come after the pregnancy ended. The children. Transport registries always keep track of the sex of the fetus, partly as a response to a series of lawsuits where no one could prove that the woman who claimed she'd lost a fetus on board a transport had actually been pregnant. The transports do not do a DNA check—such things are considered violations of privacy in all but criminal matters—but they do require pregnant women to submit a doctor's report on the health of the mother and the fetus before the woman is allowed to board.

I'd searched out pregnant women, but only those carrying a single daughter. Not twins or multiples. And no males.

Anetka had mentioned failed clones. Clones failed for a variety of reasons, but they only failed in large numbers when someone was using a defective gene or was trying to make a significant change on the genetic level. If the changes didn't work at the genetic level, surgery was performed later to achieve the same result and the DNA remained the same.

I had Anetka's DNA. I'd taken it that first day without her knowing it. I ran client DNA only when I felt I had no other choice; sometimes to check identity, sometimes to check for past crimes. I hadn't run Anetka's—photographic, vid, and those enhancements made it obvious that she was who she said she was. I knew she wasn't concealing her identity, and there was no way she was fronting for a Disty or any other race. She had told me she was a clone. So I felt a DNA check was not only redundant, it was also unnecessary because it didn't give me the kind of information I was searching for.

But now things were different. I needed to check it to see if she was a repaired child, if there had been some flaw in the fetus that couldn't have been altered in the womb. I hadn't looked for repaired children when I'd done the hospital records scans. I hadn't looked for anything that complicated at all.

So I ran the DNA scan. It only took a second, and the results were not what I expected.

Anetka Sobol wasn't a repaired child, at least not in the sense that I had been looking for. Anetka Sobol was an altered child.

According to her DNA, Anetka Sobol had once been male.

9

*I*F THE TRAIL hadn't been so easy to follow once I realized I was looking for a woman pregnant with a boy, I wouldn't have traced it. I would have gone immediately to Anetka and called her on it. But the trail was easy to follow, and any one of my competitors would have done so—perhaps earlier because they had different methods than I did. I knew at least three of them that ran DNA scans on clients as a matter of course.

If Anetka went to any of them after I refused to complete the work, they would find her mother. It would take them three days. It took me less, but that was because I was better.

10

SYLVY SOBOL ran a small private university in the Gagarin Dome on the Moon. She went by the name Celia Walker, and she had transferred from a school out past the Disty homeworld where she had spent the first ten years of her exile. She had run the university for fifteen years.

Gagarin had been established fifty years after Armstrong, and was run by a governing board, the only colony that had such a government. The board placed covenants on any person who owned or rented property within the interior of the dome. The covenants covered everything from the important, such as oxygen regulators, to the unimportant, such as a maintenance schedule for each building, whether the place needed work or not. Gagarin did not tolerate any rules violations. If someone committed three such violations—whether they be failing to follow the maintenance schedule or murder—that person was banned from the dome for life.

The end result was that residents of Gagarin were quiet, law-abiding, and suspicious. They watched me as if I were a particularly distasteful bug when I got off the high speed train from Armstrong. I learned later that I didn't meet the dome's strict dress code.

I had changed into something more appropriate after I got my hotel room, and then went to the campus. The university was a technical school for undergraduates, most of them local, but a few came in from other parts of the Moon. The administrative offices were in a low building with fake adobe facades. The classrooms were in some of Gagarin's only high rises, and were off limits to visitors.

I didn't care about that. I went straight to the Chancellor's office, and buzzed myself in, even though I didn't have an appointment. Apparently, the open campus policy that the on-line brochures proudly proclaimed extended to the administrative offices as well.

Sylvy Sobol sat behind a desk made of Moon clay. Ancient southwestern tapestries covered the walls, and matching rugs covered the floor. The permaplastic here had been covered with more fake adobe, and the net effect was to make this seem like the American Southwest hundreds of years before.

She looked no different than the age-enhancement programs on my computer led me to believe she'd look. Her dark hair was laced with silver, her eyes had laugh lines in the corners, and she was as slender as she had been when she disappeared. She wore a blouse made of the same weave as the tapestries, and a pair of tan cargo pants. Beneath the right sleeve of her blouse a stylish wrist-top glistened. When she saw me, she smiled. "May I help you?"

I closed the door, walked to her desk, and showed her my license. Her eyes widened ever so slightly, and then she covered the look.

"I came to warn you," I said.

"Warn me?" She straightened almost imperceptibly, but managed to look perplexed. Behind the tightness of her lips, I sensed fear.

"You and your son need to use a new service, and disappear again. It's not safe for you anymore."

"I'm sorry, Mr.—Flint?—but I'm not following you."

"I can repeat what I said, or we can go somewhere where you'd feel more comfortable talking."

She shook her head once, then stood. "I'm not sure I know what we'd be talking about."

I reached out my hand. I had my palm scanner in it. Anyone who'd traveled a lot, anyone who had been on the run, would recognize it. "We can do this the old-fashioned way, Mrs. Sobol, or you can listen to me."

She sat down slowly. Her lower lip trembled. She didn't object to my use of her real name. "If you're what your identification says you are, you don't warn people. You take them in."

I let my hand drop. "I was hired by Anetka Sobol," I said. "She wanted me to find you. She claimed that she wanted to share her inheritance with her Original. She's a clone. The record supports this claim."

"So, you want to take us back." Her voice was calm, but her eyes weren't. I watched her hands. They remained on the desktop, flat, and she was without enhancement. So far, she hadn't signaled anyone for help.

"Normally, I would have taken you back. But when I discovered that Anetka's Original was male, I got confused."

Sylvy licked her lower lip, just like her cloned daughter did. A hereditary nervous trait.

I rested one leg on the corner of the desk. "Why would a man change the sex of a clone when the sex didn't matter? Especially if all he wanted was the child. A man with no violent tendencies, who stood accused of attacking his wife so savagely all she could do was leave him, all she could do was disappear. Why would he do that?"

She hadn't moved. She was watching me closely. Beads of perspiration had formed on her upper lip.

"So I went back through the records and found two curious things. You disappeared just after his business on Korsve failed. And once you moved to Gagarin, you and your son were often in other domed Moon colonies at the same time as your husband. Not a good way to hide from someone, now is it, Mrs. Sobol?"

She didn't respond.

I picked up a clay pot. It was small and very, very old. It was clearly an original, not a Moon-made copy. "And then there's the fact that your husband never bothered to change his will to favor the child he had raised. It wouldn't have mattered to most parents that the child was a clone, especially when the Original was long gone. He could have arranged a dispensation, and then made certain that the business remained in family hands." I set the pot down. "But he had already done that, hadn't he? He hoped that the Wygnin would forget."

She made a soft sound in the back of her throat, and backed away from me, clutching at her wrist. I reached across the desk and grabbed her left arm, keeping her hand away from her wrist-top. I wasn't ready for her to order someone to come in here. I still needed to talk to her alone.

"I'm not going to turn you in to the Wygnin," I said. "I'm not going to let anyone know where you are. But if you don't listen to me, someone else will find you, and soon."

She stared at me, the color high in her cheeks. Her arm was rigid beneath my hand.

"The will was your husband's only mistake," I said. "The Wygnin never forget. They targeted your firstborn, didn't they? The plants on Korsve didn't open and close without a fuss. Something else happened. The Wygnin only target firstborns for a crime that can't be undone."

She shook her arm free of me. She rubbed the spot where my hand had touched her flesh, then she sighed. She seemed to know I wouldn't go away. When she spoke, her voice was soft. "No Wygnin were on the site planning committee. We bought the land, and built the plants according to our customs. At that point, the Wygnin didn't understand the concept of land purchase."

I noted the use of the word "we." She had been involved with the Third Dynasty, more involved than the records said.

"We built on a haven for nestlings. You understand nestlings?"

"I thought they were a food source."

She shook her head. "They're more than that. They're part of Wygnin society in a way we didn't understand. They become food only after they die. It's the shells that are eaten, not the nestlings themselves. The nestlings themselves are considered sentient."

I felt myself grow cold. "How many were killed?"

She shrugged. "The entire patch. No one knows for sure. We were told, when the Wygnin came to us, that they were letting us off easily by taking our firstborn—Carson's and mine. They could easily take all the children of anyone who was connected with the project, but they didn't."

They could have too. It was the Third Dynasty that acted without regard to local custom, which made it liable to local laws. Over the years, no interstellar court had overturned a ruling in instances like that.

"Carson agreed to it," she said. "He agreed so no one else would suffer. Then we got me out."

"And no one came looking for you until I did."

"That's right," she said.

"I don't think Anetka's going to stop," I said. "I suspect she wants her father to change the will—"

"What?" Sylvy clenched her collar with her right hand, revealing the wrist-top. It was one of the most sophisticated I'd seen.

"Anetka wants control of the Third Dynasty, and I was wondering why her father hadn't done a will favoring her. Now I know. She was probably hoping I couldn't find you so that her father would change the will in her favor."

"He can't," Sylvy said.

"I'm sure he might consider it, if your son's life is at stake," I said. "The Wygnin treat their captives like family—indeed, make them into family, but the techniques they use on adults of other species are—"

"No," she said. "It's too late for Carson to change his will."

She was frowning at me as if I didn't understand anything. And it took me a moment to realize how I'd been used.

Anetka Sobol had tricked me in more ways than I cared to think about. I wasn't half as good as I thought I was. I felt the beginnings of an anger I didn't need. I suppressed it. "He's dead, isn't he?"

Sylvy nodded. "He died three years ago. He installed a personal alarm that notified me the moment his heart stopped. My son has been voting his shares through a proxy program my husband set up during one of his trips here."

I glanced at the wrist-top. No wonder it was so sophisticated. Too sophisticated for a simple administrator. Carson Sobol had given it to her, and through it, had notified her of his death. Had it broken her heart? I couldn't tell, not from three years distance.

She caught me staring at it, and brought her arm down. I turned away, taking a deep breath as the reality of my situation hit me. Anetka Sobol had out-maneuvered me. She had put me in precisely the kind of case I never wanted.

I was working for the Tracker. I was leading a Disappeared to her death and probably the death of her son. "I don't get it," I said. "If something happens to your son, Anetka still won't inherit."

Sylvy's smile was small. "She inherits by default. My son will disappear, and stop voting the proxy program. She'll set up a new proxy program and continue to vote the shares. I'm sure the Board thinks she's the person behind the votes anyway. No one knows about our son."

"Except for you, and me, and the Wygnin." I closed my eyes. "Anetka had no idea you'd had a son."

"No one did," Sylvy said. "Until now."

I rubbed my nose with my thumb and forefinger. Anetka was good. She had discovered that I was the best and the quickest Retrieval Artist in the business. She had studied me and had known how to reach me. She had also known how to play at being an innocent, how to use my past history to her advantage. She hired me to find her Original, and once I did, she planned to get rid of him. It would have been easy for her too; no hit man, no attempt at killing. She wouldn't have had to do anything except somehow—surreptitiously—let the Wygnin know how to find the Original. They would have taken him in payment for the Third Dynasty's crimes, he would have stopped voting his shares, and she would have controlled the corporation.

Stopping Anetka wasn't going to be easy. Even if I refused to report, even if Sylvy and her son returned to hiding, Anetka would continue looking for them.

I had doomed them. If I left this case now, I ensured that one of my colleagues would take it. They would find Sylvy and her son. My colleagues weren't as good as I was, but they were good. And they were smart enough to follow the bits of my trail that I couldn't erase.

The only solution was to get rid of Anetka. I couldn't kill her. But I could think of one other way to stop her.

I opened my eyes. "If I could get Anetka out of the business, and allow you and your son to return home, would you do so?"

Sylvy shook her head. "This is my home," she said. She glanced at the fake adobe walls, the southwestern decor. Her fingers touched a blanket hanging on the wall beside her. "But I can't answer for my son."

"If he doesn't do anything, he'll be running for the rest of his life."

She nodded. "I still can't answer for him. He's an adult now. He makes his own choices."

As we all did.

"Think about it," I said, handing her a card with my chip on it. "I'll be here for two days."

11

THEY HIRED ME, of course. What thinking person wouldn't? I had to guarantee that I wouldn't kill Anetka when I got her out of the business—and I did that, by assuring Sylvy that I wasn't now nor would I ever be an assassin—and I had to guarantee that I would get the Wygnin off her son's trail.

I agreed to both conditions, and for the first time in years, I did something other than tracking a Disappeared.

Through channels, I let it drop that I was searching for the real heir to Carson Sobol's considerable fortune. Then I showed some of my actual research—into the daughter's history, the falsified birth date, the inaccurate records. I managed to dump information about Anetka's cloning and her sex change, and I tampered with the records to show that her clone mark had been faked just as her sex had. Alterations, done at birth, made her look like a clone when she really wasn't.

I made sure that my own work on-line looked like sloppy detecting, but I hid the changes I made in other files. I did all of this quickly and thoroughly, and by the time I was done, it appeared as though Carson Sobol had hidden his own heir—originally a son—by making him into a daughter and passing him off as a clone.

At that point, I could have sat back and let events move forward by themselves. But I didn't. This had become personal.

I had to see Anetka one last time.

I set an appointment to hand deliver my final bill.

12

HIS TIME she was wearing emeralds, an entire sheath covered with them. I had heard that there would be a gala event honoring one of the galaxy's leaders, but I had forgotten that the event would be held in Armstrong, at one of the poshest restaurants on the Moon.

She was sweeping up her long hair, letting it fall just below the mark on the back of her head, when I entered. As she turned, she stabbed an emerald hair comb into the bun at the base of her neck.

"I don't have much time," she said.

"I know." I closed the door. "I wanted give you my final bill."

"You found my sister?" There was a barely concealed excitement in her voice.

"No." The room smelled of an illegal perfume. I was surprised no one had confiscated it when she got off the shuttle and then I realized she probably hadn't taken a shuttle. Even the personal items bag she wore that first day had been part of her act. "I'm resigning."

She shook her head slightly. "I might have known you would. You have enough money now, so you're going to quit."

"I have enough information now to know you're not the kind of person I relish working for."

She raised her eyebrows. The movement dislodged the tiny emerald attached to her left cheek. She caught it just before it fell to the floor. "I thought you were done investigating me."

"Your father's dead," I said. "He has been for three years, although the Third Dynasty has managed to keep that information secret, knowing the effect his death would have had on galactic confidence in the business."

She stared at me for a moment, clearly surprised. "Only five of us knew that."

"Six," I said.

"You found my mother." She stuck the emerald in its spot.

"You found the alarm. You knew she'd been notified of your father's death."

The emerald wasn't staying on her cheek. Anetka let out a puff of air, then set the entire kit down. "I really didn't appreciate the proxy program," she said. "It notified me of my insignificance an hour after my father breathed his last. It told me to go about my life with my own fortune and abandon my place in the Third Dynasty to my Original."

"Which you didn't do."

"Why should I? I knew more about the business than she ever would."

"Including the Wygnin."

She leaned against the dressing table. "You're much better than I thought."

"And you're a lot more devious than I gave you credit for."

She smiled and tapped her left cheek. "It's the face. Youth still fools."

Perhaps it did. I usually didn't fall for it, though. I couldn't believe I had this time. I had simply thought I was being as cautious as usual. What Anetka Sobol had taught me was that being as cautious as usual wasn't cautious enough.

"Pay me, and I'll get out of here," I said.

"You've found my mother. You may as well tell me where she is."

"So you can turn your Original over to the Wygnin?"

That flat look came back into her eyes. "I wouldn't do that."

"How would you prevent it? The Wygnin have a valid debt."

"It's twenty-seven years old."

"The Wygnin hold onto markers for generations." I paused, then added, "As you well know."

"You can't prove what I do and do not know."

I nodded. "True enough. Information is always tricky. It's so easy to tamper with."

Her eyes narrowed. She was smart, probably one of the smartest people I'd ever come up against. She knew I was referring to something besides our discussion.

"So I'm getting out." I handed her a paper copy of the bill—rare, unnecessary, and expensive. She knew that as well as I did. Then, as soon as she took the paper from my hand, I pressed my wrist-top to send the electronic version. "You owe me money. I expect payment within the hour."

She crumpled the bill. "You'll get it."

"Good." I pulled open the door.

"You know," she said, just loud enough for me to hear, "if you can find my mother, anyone can."

"I've already thought of that," I said, and left.

13

THE WYGNIN CAME for her later that night, toward the end of the gala. Security tried to stop them until they showed a valid warrant for the heir of Carson Sobol. The entire transaction caused an interstellar incident, and the vidnets were filled with it for days. The Third Dynasty used its attorneys to try to prove that Anetka was the eighth clone, just as everyone thought she was, but the Wygnin didn't believe it.

The beautiful thing about a clone is that it is a human being. It's simply one whose heritage matches another person's exactly, and whose facts of birth are odder than most. These are facts, yes, but they are facts that can be explained in other ways. The Wygnin simply chose to believe my explanations, not Anetka's. It was the sex change that did it. The Wygnin believed that anyone who would change a child's sex to protect it would also brand it with a clone mark, even if the mark wasn't accurate.

Over time, the lawyers lost all of their appeals, and Anetka disappeared into the Wygnin culture, never to be heard from again.

Oh, of course, the Third Dynasty still believes it's being run by Anetka Sobol voting her shares, as she always has, through a proxy program. Her Original apparently decided not to return to claim his prize. He acts as he always planned to, secretly. Only Sylvy Sobol, her son, and I know the person voting those shares isn't Anetka.

After Anetka's future was sealed, I stopped paying attention to the business of the Third Dynasty. I still don't look. I don't want to know if I have traded one monster for another. Some cold-heartedness is trained—and I can make myself think that Carson Sobol never once treated young Anetka with love, affection, or anything bordering civility—but I am smart enough to know that most cold-heartedness is bred into the genes. Just because Anetka is gone, doesn't mean the Original won't act the same way in similar circumstances.

And what is my excuse for my cold-heartedness? I'd like to say I've never done anything like this before, but I have—always in the name of my client, or a Disappeared. This time, though, this time, I did it for me.

Anetka Sobol had out-thought me, had compromised me, and had made me do the kind of work I'd vowed I'd never do. I let a front use me to open a door that would allow other Trackers to find a Disappeared.

People disappear because they want to. They disappear to escape a bad life, or a mistake they've made, or they disappear to save themselves from a horrible death. A person who has disappeared never wants to be found.

I always ignored that simple fact, thinking I knew better. But one man is never a good judge of another, even if he thinks he is.

I tell myself Anetka Sobol would have destroyed her Original if she had had the chance. I tell myself Anetka Sobol was greedy and self-centered. I tell myself Anetka Sobol deserved her fate.

But I can't ignore the fact that when I learned that Anetka Sobol had used me, this case became personal, in a way I would never have expected. Maybe, just maybe, I might have found a different solution, if she hadn't angered me so.

And now she haunts me in the middle of the night. She wakes me out of many a sound sleep. She keeps me restless and questioning. Because I didn't go after her for who she was or what she was planning. I had worked with people far worse than she was. I had met others who had done horrible things, things that made me wonder if they were even human. Anetka Sobol wasn't in their league.

No. I had gone after her for what she had done to me. For what she had made me see about myself. And because I hadn't liked my reflection in the mirror she held up, I destroyed her.

I can't get her back. No one comes back intact from the Wygnin. She will spend the rest of her days there. And I will spend the rest of mine thinking about her.

Some would say that is justice. But I have come to realize, in a universe as complex as this one, justice no longer exists.

ABOUT THE STORIES

WHEN I FINISHED putting together my short story collection, *Recovering Apollo 8 and Other Stories*, in 2009, I wrote about the genesis of the stories in the afterword. I didn't want to spoil the surprises for my readers, yet I wanted to talk about the stories themselves as honestly as I could.

Many readers told me that the afterword added a lot of fun to the collection. So I decided to follow the same format here.

In mystery fiction, it's even more important to keep the twists to yourself until the reader is done with the story. So for your own sake, don't skip ahead to this section until you've read the story in question.

Warning: Spoilers Ahead.

***

Cowboy Grace: My best friend in high school was named Janine Plunkett. Janine was a tall girl with a soft voice that would have made Jennifer Tilly proud. Janine was Catholic, from a big family, and she dreamed of having a big family of her own.

We were so different that my mother—always one with a sharp but insightful comment—called us Mutt and Jeff. Certainly, we looked odd. I was tiny in those years. Janine towered over me. We were also different in our attitudes toward life. Janine's was softer than mine, more insightful, and more forgiving.

She was the maid of honor at my wedding even though she tried to talk me out of marrying my first husband. After he and I got engaged, she never again said a disloyal word about him. She married the following year, and I was not the best matron of honor a woman could have had. Partly because I lived 500 miles away and was poor, but partly because I wasn't a girly girl. Janine was.

She gave birth to her first child on the same day that I finished the first draft of my first novel. She had her second child the week I finished my second novel. And then her calls and letters stopped. My life got complicated, and so did hers. We saw each other a few times, but we didn't have a lot to say.

I marveled that her life had gone exactly as she wanted it to—at least from the outside. She was perplexed that I hadn't yet started a family and didn't plan to. We exchanged letters and Christmas cards until we were in our early thirties. That Christmas, I didn't get a card from her.

I didn't think much about it. People get busy. They miss the cards. So I sent her one of my novels, dedicated to her, when it came out, and got the most heartbreaking letter in return that I've ever received.

The letter was from her husband. My friend Janine Plunkett McCusker, beloved wife and mother of two darling little girls, had died the previous June of breast cancer. Her husband, a man of few words, wrote simply, "No one should die like that."

I was heartbroken. No one had even told me she was ill. I would have sent flowers and cards and letters and books. I would have gone to see her, even though we were now half a continent apart. Instead, I was silent because I didn't know, writing a book I was dedicating to her, a book she never saw.

Shortly after I got that news, I wrote "Cowboy Grace." I know who I am in that story. I'm not Grace. I'm her friends in that seedy bar. The story veered away from Janine fairly early—Grace and Janine have little in common. But at least, with Grace, I got to make the breast cancer go away. No one had to "die like that." You'll note it's one of the few stories in this volume in which no one dies at all.

To my surprise, the mystery magazines didn't want to publish this story. So it was included in a collection put out by Golden Gryphon, known for its science fiction publishing. Still, the story became an Edgar finalist—one of the highest honors in the world, in my opinion. Had it won, I would have dedicated the award to Janine.

I do every time I mention the story. Because she was such an influence, and such an amazing person, who left the world much too young. When she was 18, she was middle-aged. She died at 36. Maybe it was right that she knew what she wanted out of life; she had so little time to achieve it—and yet she managed.

She managed very well.

***

Spinning: Yes, spinning came out of a spinning class I took in the late 1990s. And no, I never imagined what my instructor sounded like in bed. Although there were times—especially in the middle of that class—when I wanted to kill her.

It was that impulse which inspired the story. I came home from class one evening, barely able to walk, and wrote the opening paragraph.

Like "Cowboy Grace," "Spinning" was a finalist for the Edgar Award. It also placed eighth in *Ellery Queen Mystery Magazine*'s Readers Choice awards and was picked up for a best-of-the-year collection (*The Year's Finest Mystery and Crime Stories: Second Annual Edition*).

***

Jury Duty: "Jury Duty" is another story that the digest mystery magazines wouldn't take. Both editors complained that the protagonist was not very sympathetic, which is, for me, part of the point. I often find unsympathetic people interesting in short bursts. I could use Pamela as the protagonist of a short story, but not the protagonist of a novel. I think in large doses, she'd be annoying. At this length, she's intriguing. Or at least, I think so.

So did the folks at *Crimewave*, a British mystery magazine. Readers liked the story. It made many best-of-the-year lists, and ended up in a year's best volume (*The Deadly Bride and 21 of the Year's Finest Crime and Mystery Stories*).

The inspiration for this story came from my own weird jury duty experience. I didn't expect to be on a jury; I know way too much about forensics, police procedures, and the legal system. But I live in a small town, and everyone ends up on a jury at one point or another.

My jury proved that old adage that every witness perceives events differently. What I thought was an open-and-shut case was, to half of the jurors, the complete opposite. We discussed, voted, and fought, just like jurors did in *Twelve Angry Men*. Except for the born-again Christian in our midst, who insisted on opening our session with a prolonged prayer. No one else wanted to pray, but she wasn't taking no for an answer. So rather than fight with her, we all waited until the prayer was over to begin.

The prayer session, the incompetent attorney (who fell asleep while presenting his own argument [not kidding]), the juror who added information about the defendant she shouldn't have shared (nor should she have been on the jury in the first place), all were too incredible to slide into a bit of fiction. It took me years to distill that experience into a story.

What remains of my experience is simply the description of the courtroom, the claustrophobic atmosphere of that jury room, and nothing else. Still, everything is fodder for fiction in one way or another.

***

The Perfect Man: I have also written a novel under this name. It's a similar story, but the novelist in question is a male romance writer. I published the book under the name Kristine Dexter.

I've often thought about what would happen if a romance writer met her perfect man. Most of the alpha males in romance novels would be utter creeps in real life. Please understand that I love romance fiction and I am a romance writer under three different pen names (Kristine Grayson, Kristine Dexter, and Kris DeLake) as well as my own. But I'm not sure I'd want to meet any of my heroes from my romance novels (except maybe Blackstone from *Utterly Charming*, just to see if a man can be that handsome), and I certainly wouldn't want to be in a relationship with them.

This story, "The Perfect Man," was written before the novel. I didn't have a complete idea until Denise Little asked me into her anthology *Murder Most Romantic*. It was the word "murder" that caught my eye and made the entire idea work. Even though the murders in this story are very far off-stage.

"The Perfect Man" also made it into a year's best collection (*The World's Finest Mystery And Crime Stories: Third Annual Collection*).

***

The Secret Lives of Cats: Writers probably shouldn't admit to having favorites among their own work. It's probably like admitting you have a favorite child among your own children. But "The Secret Lives of Cats" is one of my favorite stories.

The idea came from something I had seen online: a German man developed a tiny camera that he attached to his cat's collar so he could see what the cat did all day. Then the man posted the pictures on the Internet. (Later, some Americans used his diagram to build their own cameras, and they published their pictures in newspapers all over the country.)

The cat's pictures were of mundane things, like car tires, that seemed new because of the perspective. And I got to thinking: what happened if that cat took a picture of a crime?

The story wrote itself, and became one of my most popular mystery stories ever. It won *The Ellery Queen Readers Choice Award* as the best piece of fiction the magazine published *all year*. It was also a finalist for the prestigious Anthony Award.

***

Discovery: In May of 2001, the acclaimed science fiction writer Jack Williamson invited me and my husband, writer Dean Wesley Smith, to speak at a symposium at Eastern New Mexico University. The symposium, on the future of science and science fiction, was marvelous. So was Portales, the town where Jack had lived most of his very long life.

On our way out of town, however, we witnessed a horrific train accident. The train hit a cattle truck, sending cows and metal flying. The driver wasn't killed—not by the accident, not by the train, not by the engineers. But Dean nearly was—by a badly injured bull—as Dean ran from our van to rescue that driver.

Much of what happened that day—from the accident itself, to the horrors on the ground—were a bit too much for a straight fictional account. But I had to write about the accident somehow. I finally got the chance a few years later when I was reading about legal thrillers. I knew then that I had a way of talking about this unusual accident without making it seem too impossible for fiction.

Honestly, I didn't give Pita Cardenas much thought. She was just the perfect person to tell the story—and of course, she was her own woman. But she—and the story—got nominated for a Shamus award for the best private eye story of the year. And at Bouchercon that year, a lot of people asked if I was going to write more stories about Pita.

I hope to. I simply haven't gotten to them yet.

***

Patriotic Gestures: I am fascinated by the way that time changes opinions and points of view. I'm also fascinated by the way that our definition of crime changes.

When Dana Stabenow asked me into her anthology, *At the Scene of the Crime*, I accepted quickly. She wanted forensic analysis stories. I write a lot of stories about crime scene technicians, and I didn't want to repeat myself.

Then some local teenagers got arrested for knocking down mailboxes with a baseball bat, and the 2008 election season started heating up, with discussions of flag pins, and somehow all of that combined into this story. (I can't always explain the alchemy of combination. That part just seems to happen.)

"Patriotic Gestures," which came out during the last week of the year, still managed to make a year's best collection (*Between the Dark and the Daylight and 27 More of the Best Crime and Mystery Stories of the Year*), which pleases me a great deal.

***

Details: In 1997, I retired from my editing post at *The Magazine of Fantasy & Science Fiction*. I never wanted to edit again (and I didn't change my mind until *Fiction River* started up in 2012). I wanted to write stories that interested me, and I needed time to do that.

One of the stories I wanted to write was "Details." It came out pretty much as it is here: I "listened" to the narration just like George's granddaughter Sarah did. The story itself surprised me; I thought it was going in one direction when it went in another entirely.

"Details" won *The Ellery Queen Readers Choice Award* for best story of the year, pleasing me, surprising me, and convincing me that my retirement from editing at the age of 37 had been one of the best decisions of my life.

***

G-Men: A few years ago, Lou Anders, the editor of Pyr Books, asked me to contribute a story to an alternate history mystery anthology. I agreed, not realizing I had just agreed to walk an incredible tight rope.

Alternate history stories are extremely difficult. It's hard to keep your storytelling balance when you're thinking "What if Germany had won World War II?" because you might get too caught up in the alternate history part and forget the story part.

Mystery stories are also difficult. You have to come up with a crime and *solve* it in twenty to fifty pages, something a lot of writers can't do over the space of a novel. Keeping a mystery short requires a lot of dancing on the head of a pin. Again, if you use too much information, you kill the story.

Suddenly, I had two forms that required a lot of juggling while telling a story. And I was under extreme novel deadlines. So I decided to pass on the anthology.

Fortunately, I discussed this with my husband first. Dean is a tremendous plotter. He also knows my writing better than anyone else. He asked me what would have happened if J. Edgar Hoover died in 1968.

Now, I write mystery novels under the name Kris Nelscott. Those novels are set in the late 1960s. Dean's question was brilliant because I wouldn't have to research 1968. I immediately had an answer.

Unfortunately, my answer was that 1968 was too late: Hoover had to die in the early 1960s to make a significant difference to history.

And there was my alternate history part of the story. Hoover's death became a murder, which gave me the mystery part of the story. I'd like to say this one wrote itself, but it didn't. Instead, I had to research 1964, do a lot of thinking, and a lot of brainstorming with Dean to get any words on the page at all.

The words paid off. "G-Men" is the first story (that we can find) to appear in both a mystery best-of-the-year collection (*The Best American Mysteries 2009*) and a science fiction best-of-the-year collection (*The Year's Best Science Fiction 26*). It also inspired me to write a full novel based on this story. *The Enemy Within*, published by WMG Publishing, will appear on bookshelves in April 2014.

***

The Retrieval Artist: I got a severe case of bronchitis in the late 1990s and the doctor ordered me to stay in bed. I don't stay in bed. I can't. I have to be doing something. So I sat on the couch and read a series of novels about the Witness Protection Program.

Because I'm also a science fiction writer, I found myself asking what kind of witness protection program would exist in a science fiction universe. I came up with the whole Disappeared system. As I healed from the bronchitis, I wrote this story.

It appeared in *Analog*, a science fiction magazine. But it is, at heart, a detective story. It made several recommended reading lists as one of the best science fiction novellas of the year. And it got nominated for science fiction's most prestigious award, the Hugo.

By then, I had already finished *The Disappeared*, which is the first novel in my Retrieval Artist series. While "The Retrieval Artist" short story happens late in Miles Flint's career, *The Disappeared* is the origin story, telling how he became a Retrieval Artist in the first place.

So far, I have published nine Retrieval Artist novels, several Retrieval Artist novellas (this is one of them), and one short story. I'm currently writing more novels to round out the Anniversary Day saga that includes the novels *Anniversary Day* and *Blowback*. Another novella, *A Murder of Clones,* will be published in *Fiction River: Moonscapes* in February 2014. It inspired one of the Anniversary Day saga novels, as well.

The novels are set on the moon. Otherwise, they're a standard mystery series. Each novel stands alone, but is better when read in tandem with the others. I call this series my 87th Precinct (for you Ed McBain fans). I expect to write these stories until I die.

"The Retrieval Artist" is the very first one, however, and all it did was whet my appetite for the rest. I hope it does the same for you.

***

I am startled and pleased by the acclaim I've received in the mystery genre. Because I got my start in science fiction, I still see myself as an interloper in the mystery field. I learned at Bouchercon a few years back that readers don't look at me that way at all. They see me as a mystery writer who happens to write the occasional science fiction story.

I guess it all depends on what you like to read. Fortunately, I like to read in every genre. So I write in all genres. And sometimes I blend them. I can't help myself. My mind never goes down the straight and narrow path.

As you can probably tell.

ABOUT THE AUTHOR

USA Today bestselling author Kristine Kathryn Rusch writes in almost every genre. Generally, she uses her real name (Rusch) for most of her writing. Under that name, she publishes bestselling science fiction and fantasy, award-winning mysteries, acclaimed mainstream fiction, controversial nonfiction, and the occasional romance. Her novels have made bestseller lists around the world and her short fiction has appeared in eighteen best of the year collections. She has won more than twenty-five awards for her fiction, including the Hugo, *Le Prix Imaginales,* the *Asimov's* Readers Choice award, and the *Ellery Queen Mystery Magazine* Readers Choice Award.

To keep up with everything she does, go to kriswrites.com. To track her many pen names and series, see their individual websites (krisnelscott.com, kristinegrayson.com, krisdelake. com, retrievalartist.com, divingintothewreck.com, fictionriver. com). She lives and occasionally sleeps in Oregon.

Also by
Kristine Kathryn Rusch

The Retrieval Artist Series:

The Disappeared

Extremes

Consequences

Buried Deep

Paloma

Recovery Man

Duplicate Effort

Anniversary Day

Blowback

The Smokey Dalton Series (as Kris Nelscott):

A Dangerous Road

Smoke-Filled Rooms

Thin Walls

Stone Cribs

War at Home

Days of Rage

Street Justice (March 2014)